*There is no telling where
a scandal might lead...*

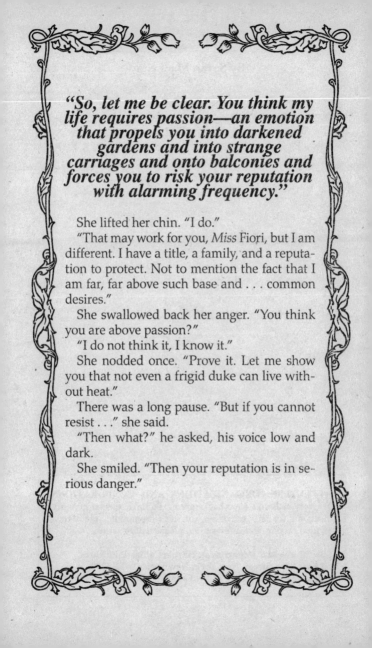

"So, let me be clear. You think my life requires passion—an emotion that propels you into darkened gardens and into strange carriages and onto balconies and forces you to risk your reputation with alarming frequency."

She lifted her chin. "I do."

"That may work for you, *Miss* Fiori, but I am different. I have a title, a family, and a reputation to protect. Not to mention the fact that I am far, far above such base and . . . common desires."

She swallowed back her anger. "You think you are above passion?"

"I do not think it, I know it."

She nodded once. "Prove it. Let me show you that not even a frigid duke can live without heat."

There was a long pause. "But if you cannot resist . . ." she said.

"Then what?" he asked, his voice low and dark.

She smiled. "Then your reputation is in serious danger."

By Sarah MacLean

ELEVEN SCANDALS TO START TO WIN A DUKE'S HEART
TEN WAYS TO BE ADORED WHEN LANDING A LORD
NINE RULES TO BREAK WHEN ROMANCING A RAKE
THE SEASON

Eleven Scandals to Start to Win a Duke's Heart

SARAH MacLEAN

AVON

An Imprint of HarperCollinsPublishers

This is a work of fiction. Names, characters, places, and incidents are products of the author's imagination or are used fictitiously and are not to be construed as real. Any resemblance to actual events, locales, organizations, or persons, living or dead, is entirely coincidental.

AVON BOOKS
An Imprint of HarperCollins*Publishers*
10 East 53rd Street
New York, New York 10022-5299

Copyright © 2011 by Sarah Trabucchi
ISBN 978-0-06-185207-7
www.avonromance.com

First Avon Books mass market printing: May 2011

Avon Trademark Reg. U.S. Pat. Off. and in Other Countries, Marca Registrada, Hecho en U.S.A.
HarperCollins® is a registered trademark of HarperCollins Publishers.

Printed in the U.S.A.

10 9 8 7 6 5 4 3 2 1

For Carrie,
with love and gratitude.
Thanks for getting me
back to Base Camp.

Un momento con una donna capricciosa
vale undici anni di vita noiosa.

A single moment with a fiery female
is worth eleven years of a boring life.
(Italian Proverb)

Eleven Scandals to Start to Win a Duke's Heart

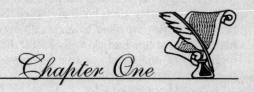

Chapter One

Trees are nothing but a canopy for scandal.
Elegant ladies remain indoors after dark.

—*A Treatise on the Most Exquisite of Ladies*

We hear that leaves are not the only things falling in gardens . . .

—*The Scandal Sheet, October 1823*

In retrospect, there were four actions Miss Juliana Fiori should have reconsidered that evening.

First, she likely should have ignored the impulse to leave her sister-in-law's autumn ball in favor of the less-cloying, better-smelling, and far more poorly lit gardens of Ralston House.

Second, she very likely should have hesitated when that same impulse propelled her deeper along the darkened paths that marked the exterior of her brother's home.

Third, she almost certainly should have returned to the house the moment she stumbled upon Lord Grabeham, deep in his cups, half–falling down, and spouting entirely ungentlemanly things.

But, she definitely should not have hit him.

It didn't matter that he had pulled her close and breathed his hot, whiskey-laden breath upon her, or that his cold, moist lips had clumsily found their way to the high arch of one cheek, or that he suggested that she might *like it just as her mother had.*

Ladies did not hit people.

At least, English ladies didn't.

She watched as the not-so-much a gentleman howled in pain and yanked a handkerchief from his pocket, covering his nose and flooding the pristine white linen with scarlet. She froze, absentmindedly shaking the sting from her hand, dread consuming her.

This was bound to get out. It was bound to become an "issue."

It didn't matter that he deserved it.

What was she to have done? Allowed him to maul her while she waited for a savior to come crashing through the trees? Any man out in the gardens at this hour was certain to be less of a savior and more of the same.

But she had just proven the gossips right.

She'd never be one of them.

Juliana looked up into the dark canopy of trees. The rustle of leaves far overhead had only moments ago promised her respite from the unpleasantness of the ball. Now the sound taunted her—an echo of the whispers inside ballrooms throughout London whenever she passed.

"You hit me!" The fat man's cry was all too loud, nasal, and outraged.

She lifted her throbbing hand and pushed a loose strand of hair back from her cheek. "Come near me again, and you'll get more of the same."

His eyes did not leave her as he mopped the blood

from his nose. The anger in his gaze was unmistakable.

She knew that anger. Knew what it meant.

Braced herself for what was coming.

It stung nonetheless.

"You shall regret this." He took a menacing step toward her. "I'll have everyone believing that you begged me for it. Here in your brother's gardens like the tart you are."

An ache began at her temple. She took one step back, shaking her head. "No," she said, flinching at the thickness of her Italian accent—the one she had been working so hard to tame. "They will not believe you."

The words sounded hollow even to her.

Of course they would believe him.

He read the thought and gave a bark of angry laughter. "You can't imagine they'd believe *you*. Barely legitimate. Tolerated only because your brother is a marquess. You can't believe *he'd* believe you. You are, after all, your mother's daughter."

Your mother's daughter. The words were a blow she could never escape. No matter how hard she tried.

She lifted her chin, squaring her shoulders. "They will not believe you," she repeated, willing her voice to remain steady, "because they will not believe I could possibly have wanted *you, porco.*"

It took a moment for him to translate the Italian into English, to hear the insult. But when he did, the word *pig* hanging between them in both languages, Grabeham reached for her, his fleshy hand grasping, fingers like sausages.

He was shorter than she was, but he made up for it in brute strength. He grabbed one wrist, fingers digging deep, promising to bruise, and Juliana attempted to wrench herself from his grip, her skin twisting and burning. She hissed her pain and acted on instinct, thanking her maker that she'd learned to fight from the boys on the Veronese riverfront.

Her knee came up. Made precise, vicious contact.

Grabeham howled, his grip loosening just enough for escape.

And Juliana did the only thing she could think of.

She ran.

Lifting the skirts of her shimmering green gown, she tore through the gardens, steering clear of the light pouring out of the enormous ballroom, knowing that being seen running from the darkness would have been just as damaging as being caught by the odious Grabeham . . . who had recovered with alarming speed. She could hear him lumbering behind her through a particularly prickly hedge, panting in great, heaving breaths.

The sound spurred her on, and she burst through the side gate of the garden into the mews that abutted Ralston House, where a collection of carriages waited in a long line for their lords and ladies to call for transport home. She stepped on something sharp and stumbled, catching herself on the cobblestones, scoring the palms of her bare hands as she struggled to right herself. She cursed her decision to remove the gloves that she had been wearing inside the ballroom—cloying or not, kidskin would have saved her a few drops of blood that evening. The iron gate swung shut behind her, and she hesitated for a fraction of a second, sure the noise would attract attention. A quick glance found a collection of coachmen engrossed in a game of dice at the far end of the alleyway, unaware of or uninterested in her. Looking back, she saw the great bulk of Grabeham making for the gate.

He was a bull charging a red cape; she had mere seconds before she was gored.

The carriages were her only hope.

With a low, soothing whisper of Italian, she slipped beneath the massive heads of two great black horses and crept quickly along the line of carriages. She heard the gate screech open and bang shut, and she froze, listening for the telltale sound of predator approaching prey.

It was impossible to hear anything over the pounding of her heart.

Quietly, she opened the door to one of the great hulking vehicles and levered herself up and into the carriage without the aid of a stepping block. She heard a tear as the fabric of her dress caught on a sharp edge and ignored the pang of disappointment as she yanked her skirts into the coach and reached for the door, closing it behind her as quietly as she could.

The willow green satin had been a gift from her brother—a nod to her hatred of the pale, prim frocks worn by the rest of the unmarried ladies of the *ton.* And now it was ruined.

She sat stiffly on the floor just inside the carriage, knees pulled up to her chest, and let the blackness embrace her. Willing her panicked breath to calm, she strained to hear something, *anything* through the muffled silence. She resisted the urge to move, afraid to draw attention to her hiding place.

"*Tego, tegis, tegit,*" she barely whispered, the soothing cadence of the Latin focusing her thoughts. "*Tegimus, tegitis, tegunt.*"

A faint shadow passed above, hiding the dim light that mottled the wall of the lushly upholstered carriage. Juliana froze briefly before pressing back into the corner of the coach, making herself as small as possible—a challenge considering her uncommon height. She waited, desperate, and when the barely there light returned, she swallowed and closed her eyes tightly, letting out a long, slow breath.

In English, now.

"I hide. You hide. She hides—"

She held her breath as several masculine shouts broke

through the silence, praying for them to move past her hiding place and leave her, for once, in peace. When the vehicle rocked under the movement of a coachman scrambling into his seat, she knew her prayers would go unanswered.

So much for hiding.

She swore once, the epithet one of the more colorful of her native tongue, and considered her options. Grabeham could be just outside, but even the daughter of an Italian merchant who had been in London for only a few months knew that she could not arrive at the main entrance of her brother's home in a carriage belonging to God knew whom without causing a scandal of epic proportions.

Her decision made, she reached for the handle on the door and shifted her weight, building up the courage to escape—to launch herself out of the vehicle, onto the cobblestones and into the nearest patch of darkness.

And then the carriage began to move.

And escape was no longer an option.

For a brief moment, she considered opening the door and leaping from the carriage anyway. But even she was not so reckless. She did not want to die. She just wanted the ground to open up and swallow her, and the carriage, whole. Was that so much to ask?

Taking in the interior of the vehicle, she realized that her best bet was to return to the floor and wait for the carriage to stop. Once it did, she would exit via the door farthest from the house and hope, desperately, that no one was there to see her.

Surely *something* had to go right for her tonight. Surely she had a few moments to escape before the aristocrats beyond descended.

She took a deep breath as the coach came to a stop. Levering herself up . . . reaching for the handle . . . ready to spring.

Before she could exit, however, the door on the opposite side of the carriage burst open, taking the air inside with it in a violent rush. Her eyes flew to the enormous man standing just beyond the coach door.

Oh, no.

The lights at the front of Ralston House blazed behind him, casting his face into shadow, but it was impossible to miss the way the warm, yellow light illuminated his mass of golden curls, turning him into a dark angel—cast from Paradise, refusing to return his halo.

She felt a subtle shift in him, a quiet, almost imperceptible tensing of his broad shoulders and knew that she had been discovered. Juliana knew that she should be thankful for his discretion when he pulled the door to him, eliminating any space through which others might see her, but when he ascended into the carriage easily, with the aid of neither servant nor step, gratitude was far from what she was feeling.

Panic was a more accurate emotion.

She swallowed, a single thought screaming though her mind.

She should have taken her chances with Grabeham.

For there was certainly no one in the world she would like to face less at this particular moment than the unbearable, immovable Duke of Leighton.

Surely, the universe was conspiring against her.

The door closed behind him with a soft click, and they were alone.

Desperation surged, propelling her into movement, and she scrambled for the near door, eager for escape. Her fingers fumbled for the handle.

"I would not if I were you."

The calm, cool words rankled as they cut through the darkness.

There had been a time when he had not been at all aloof with her.

Before she had vowed never to speak to him again.

She took a quick, stabilizing breath, refusing to allow him the upper hand. "While I thank you for the suggestion, Your Grace. You will forgive me if I do not follow it."

She clasped the handle, ignoring the sting in her hand at the pressure of the wood, and shifted her weight to release the latch. He moved like lightning, leaning across the coach and holding the door shut with little effort.

"It was not advice."

He rapped the ceiling of the carriage twice, firmly and without hesitation. The vehicle moved instantly, as though his will alone steered its course, and Juliana cursed all well-trained coachmen as she fell backward, her foot catching in the skirt of her gown, further tearing the satin. She winced at the sound, all too loud in the heavy quiet, and ran one dirty palm wistfully down the lovely fabric.

"My dress is ruined." She took pleasure in implying that he'd had something to do with it. He need not know the gown had been ruined long before she'd landed herself in his carriage.

"Yes. Well, I can think of any number of ways you could have avoided such a tragedy this evening." The words were void of contrition.

"I had little choice, you know." She immediately hated herself for saying it aloud.

Especially to him.

He snapped his head toward her just as a lamppost in the street beyond cast a shaft of silver light through the carriage window, throwing him into stark relief. She tried not to notice him. Tried not to notice how every inch of him bore the mark of his excellent breeding, of his aristocratic history—the long, straight patrician nose, the perfect square of his jaw, the high cheekbones that should have made him look feminine but seemed only to make him more handsome.

She gave a little huff of indignation.

The man had ridiculous cheekbones.

She'd never known anyone so handsome.

"Yes," he fairly drawled, "I can imagine it is difficult attempting to live up to a reputation such as yours."

The light disappeared, replaced by the sting of his words.

She'd also never known anyone who was such a proper ass.

Juliana was thankful for her shadowy corner of the coach as she recoiled from his insinuation. She was used to the insults, to the ignorant speculation that came with her being the daughter of an Italian merchant and a fallen English marchioness who had deserted her husband and sons . . . and dismissed London's elite.

The last was the only one of her mother's actions for which Juliana had even a hint of admiration.

She'd like to tell the entire lot of them where they could put their aristocratic rules.

Beginning with the Duke of Leighton. Who was the worst of the lot.

But he hadn't been at the start.

She pushed the thought aside. "I should like you to stop this carriage and let me out."

"I suppose this is not going the way that you had planned?"

She paused. "The way I had . . . planned?"

"Come now, Miss Fiori. You think I do not know how your little game was to have been played out? You, discovered in my empty carriage—the perfect location for a clandestine assignation—on the steps of your brother's ancestral home, during one of the best attended events in recent weeks?"

Her eyes went wide. "You think I am—"

"No. I *know* that you are attempting to trap me in marriage. And your little scheme, about which I assume your brother has no knowledge considering how asinine it is, might have worked on a lesser man with a lesser title. But I assure you it will not work on me. I am a *duke*. In a battle of reputation with you, I would most certainly win. In fact, I would have let you ruin yourself quite handily back at Ralston House if I were not unfortunately indebted to your brother at the moment. You would have deserved it for this little farce."

His voice was calm and unwavering, as though he'd had this particular conversation countless times before, and she was nothing but a minor inconvenience—a fly in his tepid, poorly seasoned bisque, or whatever it was that aristocratic British snobs consumed with soup spoons.

Of all the arrogant, pompous . . .

Fury flared, and Juliana gritted her teeth. "Had I known this was *your* vehicle, I would have avoided it at all costs."

"Amazing, then, that you somehow missed the large ducal seal on the outside of the door."

The man was infuriating. "It is amazing, indeed, because I'm sure the seal on the outside of your carriage rivals your conceit in size! I assure you, *Your Grace*"— she spit the honorific as if it were an epithet—"if I were after a husband, I would look for one who had more to recommend him than a fancy title and a false sense of importance." She heard the tremor in her voice but could not stop the flood of words pouring from her. "You are so impressed with your title and station, it is a miracle you do not have the word 'Duke' embroidered in silver thread on all of your topcoats. The way you behave, one would think you'd actually done something to earn the respect these English fools afford you instead of having been sired, entirely by chance, at the right time and by the right man, who I imagine performed the deed in exactly the same manner of all other men. Without finesse."

She stopped, the pounding of her heart loud in her ears as the words hung between them, their echo heavy in the darkness. *Senza finezza.* It was only then that she realized that, at some point during her tirade, she had switched to Italian.

She could only hope that he had not understood.

There was a long stretch of silence, a great, yawning void that threatened her sanity. And then the carriage stopped. They sat there for an interminable moment, he still as stone, she wondering if they might remain there in the vehicle for the rest of time, before she heard the shifting of fabric. He opened the door, swinging it wide.

She started at the sound of his voice, low and dark and much much closer than she was expecting.

"Get out of the carriage."

He spoke Italian.

Perfectly.

She swallowed. Well. She was not about to apologize. Not after all the terrible things that he'd said. If he was going to throw her from the carriage, so be it. She would walk home. Proudly.

Perhaps someone would be able to point her in the proper direction.

She scooted across the floor of the coach and outside, turning back and fully expecting to see the door swing shut behind her. Instead, he followed her out, ignoring her presence as he moved up the steps of the nearest town house. The door opened before he reached the top step.

As though doors, like everything else, bent to his will.

She watched as he entered the brightly lit foyer beyond, a large brown dog lumbering to greet him with cheerful exuberance.

Well. So much for the theory that animals could sense evil.

She smirked at the thought, and he turned halfway back almost instantly, as though she had spoken aloud.

His golden curls were once more cast into angelic relief, as he said, "In or out, Miss Fiori. You are trying my patience."

She opened her mouth to speak, but he had already disappeared from view. And so she chose the path of least resistance.

Or, at least, the path that was least likely to end in her ruin on a London sidewalk in the middle of the night.

She followed him in.

As the door closed behind her and the footman hurried to follow his master to wherever masters and footmen went, Juliana paused in the brightly lit entryway, taking in the wide marble foyer and the gilded mirrors on the walls that only served to make the large space seem more enormous. There were half a dozen doors leading this way and that, and a long, dark corridor that stretched deeper into the town house.

The dog sat at the bottom of the wide stairway leading to the upper floors of the home, and under his silent canine scrutiny, Juliana was suddenly, embarrassingly aware of the fact that she was in a man's home.

Unescorted.

With the exception of a dog.

Who had already been revealed to be a poor judge of character.

Callie would not approve. Her sister-in-law had specifically cautioned her to avoid situations of this kind. She feared that men would take advantage of a young Italian female with little understanding of British stricture.

"I've sent word to Ralston to come and fetch you. You may wait in the—"

She looked up when he stopped short, and met his gaze, which was clouded with something that, if she did not know better, might be called concern.

She did, however, know better.

"In the—?" she prompted, wondering why he was moving toward her at an alarming pace.

"Dear God. What happened to you?"

"Someone attacked you."

Juliana watched as Leighton poured two fingers of scotch into a crystal tumbler and walked the drink to where she sat in one of the oversized leather chairs in his study. He thrust the glass toward her, and she shook her head. "No, thank you."

"You should take it. You'll find it calming."

She looked up at him. "I am not in need of calming, Your Grace."

His gaze narrowed, and she refused to look away from the portrait of English nobility he made, tall and towering, with nearly unbearable good looks and an expression of complete and utter confidence—as though he had never in his life been challenged.

Never, that was, until now.

"You deny that someone attacked you?"

She shrugged one shoulder idly, remaining quiet. What could she say? What could she tell him that he would not turn against her? He would claim, in that imperious, arrogant tone, that had she been more of a lady . . . had she had more of a care for her reputation . . . had she behaved more like an Englishwoman and less like an Italian . . . then all of this would not have happened.

He would treat her like all the rest.

Just as he had done since the moment he had discovered her identity.

"Does it matter? I'm sure you will decide that I staged the entire evening in order to ensnare a husband. Or something equally ridiculous."

She had intended the words to set him down. They did not.

Instead, he raked her with one long, cool look, taking

in her face and arms, covered in scratches, her ruined dress, torn in two places, streaked with dirt and blood from her scored palms.

One side of his mouth twitched in what she imagined was something akin to disgust, and she could not resist saying, "Once more, I prove myself less than worthy of your presence, do I not?"

She bit her tongue, wishing she had not spoken.

He met her gaze. "I did not say that."

"You did not have to."

He threw back the whiskey as a soft knock sounded on the half-open door to the room. Without looking away from her, the duke barked, "What is it?"

"I've brought the things you requested, Your Grace." A servant shuffled into the room with a tray laden with a basin, bandages, and several small containers. He set the burden on a nearby low table.

"That is all."

The servant bowed once, neatly, and took his leave as Leighton stalked toward the tray. She watched as he lifted a linen towel, dipping one edge into the basin. "You did not thank him."

He cut a surprised glance toward her. "The evening has not exactly put me in a grateful frame of mind."

She stiffened at his tone, hearing the accusation there.

Well. She could be difficult as well.

"Nevertheless, he did you a service." She paused for effect. "Not to thank him makes you piggish."

There was a beat before her meaning became clear. "Boorish."

She waved one hand. "Whatever. A different man would have thanked him."

He moved toward her. "Don't you mean a better man?"

Her eyes widened in mock innocence. "Never. You

are a duke, after all. Surely there are none better than you."

The words were a direct hit. And, after the terrible things he'd said to her in the carriage, a deserved one.

"A different woman would realize that she is squarely in my debt and take more care with her words."

"Don't you mean a better woman?"

He did not reply, instead taking the seat across from her and extending his hand, palm up. "Give me your hands."

She clutched them close to her chest instead, wary. "Why?"

"They're bruised and bloody. They need cleaning."

She did not want him touching her. Did not trust herself.

"They are fine."

He gave a low, frustrated growl, the sound sending a shiver through her. "It is true what they say about Italians."

She stiffened at the words, dry with the promise of an insult. "That we are superior in all ways?"

"That it is impossible for you to admit defeat."

"A trait that served Caesar quite well."

"And how is the Roman Empire faring these days?"

The casual, superior tone made her want to scream. Epithets. In her native tongue.

Impossible man.

They stared at each other for a long minute, neither willing to back down until he finally spoke. "Your brother will be here at any moment, Miss Fiori. And he is going to be livid enough as it is without seeing your bloody palms."

She narrowed her gaze on his hand, wide and long and oozing strength. He was right, of course. She had no choice but to relinquish.

"This is going to hurt." The words were her only warning before he ran his thumb over her palm softly, investigating the wounded skin there, now crusted in dried blood. She sucked in a breath at the touch.

He glanced up at the sound. "Apologies."

She did not reply, instead making a show of investigating her other hand.

She would not let him see that it was not pain that had her gasping for breath.

She had expected it, of course, the undeniable, unwelcome reaction that threatened whenever she saw him. That surged whenever he neared.

It was loathing. She was sure of it.

She would not even countenance the alternate possibility.

Attempting a clinical assessment of the situation, Juliana looked down at their hands, nearly entwined. The room grew instantly warmer. His hands were enormous, and she was transfixed by his fingers, long and manicured, dusted with fine golden hairs.

He ran one finger gently across the wicked bruise that had appeared on her wrist, and she looked up to find him staring at the purpling skin. "You will tell me who did this to you."

There was a cool certainty in the words, as though she would do his bidding, and he would, in turn, handle the situation. But Juliana knew better. This man was no knight. He was a dragon. The leader of them. "Tell me, Your Grace. What is it like to believe that your will exists only to be done?"

His gaze flew to hers, darkening with irritation. "You will tell me, Miss Fiori."

"No, I will not."

She returned her attention to their hands. It was not often that Juliana was made to feel dainty—she towered over nearly all of the women and many of the men in London—but this man made her feel small. Her thumb was barely larger than the smallest of his fingers, the one that bore the gold-and-onyx signet ring—proof of his title.

A reminder of his stature.

And of how far beneath him he believed her to be.

She lifted her chin at the thought, anger and pride and hurt flaring in a hot rush of feeling, and at that precise moment, he touched the raw skin of her palm with the wet linen cloth. She embraced the distraction of the stinging pain, hissing a wicked Italian curse.

He did not pause in his ministrations as he said, "I did not know that those two animals could do such a thing together."

"It is rude of you to listen."

One golden brow rose at the words. "It is rather difficult not to listen if you are mere inches from me, shouting your discomfort."

"Ladies do not shout."

"It appears that Italian ladies do. Particularly when they are undergoing medical treatment."

She resisted the urge to smile.

He was not amusing.

He dipped his head and focused on his task, rinsing the linen cloth in the basin of clean water. She flinched as the cool fabric returned to her scoured hand, and he hesitated briefly before continuing.

The momentary pause intrigued her. The Duke of Leighton was not known for his compassion. He was known for his arrogant indifference, and she was surprised he would stoop so low as to perform such a menial task as cleaning the gravel from her hands.

"Why are you doing this?" she blurted at the next stinging brush of linen.

He did not stay his movements. "I told you. Your brother is going to be difficult enough to deal with without you bleeding all over yourself. And my furniture."

"No." She shook her head. "I mean why are *you* doing this? Don't you have a battalion of servants just waiting to perform such an unpleasant task?"

"I do."

"And so?"

"Servants talk, Miss Fiori. I would prefer that as few people as possible know that you are here, alone, at this hour."

She was trouble for him. Nothing more.

After a long silence, he met her gaze. "You disagree?"

She recovered quickly. "Not at all. I am merely astounded that a man of your wealth and prominence would have servants who gossip. One would think you'd have divined a way to strip them of all desire to socialize."

One side of his mouth tightened, and he shook his head. "Even as I am helping you, you are seeking out ways to wound me."

When she replied, her tone was serious, her words true. "Forgive me if I am wary of your goodwill, Your Grace."

His lips pressed into a thin, straight line, and he reached for her other hand, repeating his actions. They both watched as he cleaned the dried blood and gravel from the heel of her palm, revealing tender pink flesh that would take several days to heal.

His movements were gentle but firm, and the stroke of the linen on the abraded skin grew more tolerable as he cleaned the wounds. Juliana watched as one golden curl fell over his brow. His countenance was, as always, stern and unmoving, like one of her brother's treasured marble statues.

She was flooded with a familiar desire, one that came over her whenever he was near.

The desire to crack the façade.

She had glimpsed him without it twice.

And then he had discovered who she was—the Italian half sister of one of London's most notorious rakes, the barely legitimate daughter of a fallen marchioness and her merchant husband, raised far from London and its manners and traditions and rules.

The opposite of everything he represented.

The antithesis of everything he cared to have in his world.

"My only motive is to get you home in one piece, with none but your brother the wiser about your little adventure this evening."

He tossed the linen into the basin of now-pink water and lifted one of the small pots from the tray. He opened it, releasing the scent of rosemary and lemon, and reached for her hands once more.

She gave them up easily this time. "You don't really expect me to believe that you are concerned for my reputation?"

Leighton dipped the tip of one broad finger into the pot, concentrating on her wounds as he smoothed the salve across her skin. The medicine combated the burning sting, leaving a welcome, cool path where his fingers stroked. The result was the irresistible illusion that his touch was the harbinger of the soothing pleasure flooding her skin.

Which it wasn't.

Not at all.

She caught her sigh before it embarrassed her. He heard it nonetheless. That golden eyebrow rose again, leaving her wishing that she could shave it off.

She snatched her hand away. He did not try to stop her.

"No, Miss Fiori. I am not concerned for your reputation."

Of course he wasn't.

"I am concerned for my own."

The implication that being found with her—being linked to her—could damage his reputation stung, perhaps worse than her hands had earlier in the evening.

She took a deep breath, readying herself for their next verbal battle, when a furious voice sounded from the doorway.

"If you don't take your hands off of my sister this instant, Leighton, your precious reputation will be the least of your problems."

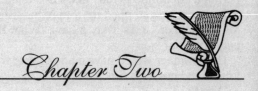

Chapter Two

There is a reason why skirts are long and bootlaces complex.
The refined lady does not expose her feet. Ever.

—A Treatise on the Most Exquisite of Ladies

It appears that reformed rakes find brotherly duty something of a challenge . . .

—The Scandal Sheet, October 1823

It was quite possible that the Marquess of Ralston was going to kill him.

Not that Simon had anything to do with the girl's current state.

It was not his fault that she'd landed herself in his carriage after doing battle with, from what he could divine, a holly bush, the cobblestones of the Ralston mews, and the edge of his coach.

And a man.

Simon Pearson, eleventh Duke of Leighton, ignored the vicious anger that flared at the thought of the purple bruise encircling the girl's wrist and returned his attention to her irate brother, who was currently stalking the perimeter of Simon's study like a caged animal.

The marquess stopped in front of his sister and found his voice. "For God's sake, Juliana. What the hell happened to you?"

The language would have made a lesser woman blush. Juliana did not even flinch. "I fell."

"You fell."

"Yes." She paused. "Among other things."

Ralston looked to the ceiling as though asking for patience. Simon recognized the emotion. He had a sister himself, one who had given him more than his share of frustration.

And Ralston's sister was more infuriating than any female should be.

More beautiful, as well.

He stiffened at the thought.

Of course she was beautiful. It was an empirical fact. Even in her sullied, torn gown, she put most other women in London to shame. She was a stunning blend of delicate English—porcelain skin, liquid blue eyes, perfect nose, and pert chin—and exotic Italian, all wild raven curls and full lips and lush curves that a man would have to be dead not to notice.

He was not dead, after all.

He was simply not interested.

A memory flashed.

Juliana in his arms, coming up on her toes, pressing her lips to his.

He resisted the image.

She was also bold, brash, impulsive, a magnet for trouble, and precisely the kind of woman he wanted far away from him.

So, of course, she'd landed in his carriage.

He sighed, straightening the sleeve of his topcoat and returning his attention to the tableau before him.

"And how did your arms and face get scratched?" Ralston continued to hound her. "You look like you ran through a rosebush!"

She tilted her head. "I may have done so."

"*May* have?" Ralston took a step toward her, and Juliana stood to face her brother head-on. Here was no simpering miss.

She was tall, uncommonly so for a female. It was not every day that Simon met a woman with whom he did not have to stoop to converse.

The top of her head came to his nose.

"Well, I was rather busy, Gabriel."

There was something about the words, so utterly matter-of-fact, that had Simon exhaling his amusement, calling attention to himself.

Ralston rounded on him. "Oh, I would not laugh too hard if I were you, Leighton. I've half a mind to call you out for your part in tonight's farce."

Disbelief surged. "Call *me* out? I did nothing but keep the girl from ruining herself."

"Then perhaps you'd like to explain how it is that the two of you were alone in your study, her hands lovingly clasped in your own, when I arrived?"

Simon was instantly aware of what Ralston was doing. And he did not like it. "Just what are you trying to say, Ralston?"

"Only that special licenses have been procured for less."

His eyes narrowed on the marquess, a man he barely tolerated on a good day. This was not turning out to be a good day. "I'm not marrying the girl."

"There's no way I'm marrying him!" she cried at the same moment.

Well. At least they agreed on something.

Wait.

She didn't want to marry *him*? She could do a damned sight worse. He was a duke, for God's sake! And she was a walking scandal.

Ralston's attention had returned to his sister. "You'll marry whomever I tell you to marry if you keep up with this ridiculous behavior, sister."

"You promised—" she began.

"Yes, well, you weren't making a habit of being accosted in gardens when I made that vow." Impatience infused Ralston's tone. "Who did this to you?"

"No one."

The too-quick response rankled. Why wouldn't she reveal who had hurt her? Perhaps she had not wanted to discuss the private matter with Simon, but why not with her brother?

Why not allow retribution to be delivered?

"I'm not a fool, Juliana." Ralston resumed pacing. "Why not tell me?"

"All you need know is that I handled him."

Both men froze. Simon could not resist. "Handled him how?"

She paused, cradling her bruised wrist in her hand in a way that made him wonder if she might have sprained it. "I hit him."

"Where?" Ralston blurted.

"In the gardens."

The marquess looked to the ceiling, and Simon took pity on him. "I believe your brother was asking where on his person did you strike your attacker?"

"Oh. In the nose." She paused in the stunned silence that followed, then said defensively, "He deserved it!"

"He damn well did," Ralston agreed. "Now give me his name, and I'll finish him off."

"No."

"Juliana. The strike of a woman is not nearly enough punishment for his attacking you."

She narrowed her gaze on her brother, "Oh, really? Well, there was a great deal of blood considering it was the mere strike of a woman, Gabriel."

Simon blinked. "You bloodied his nose."

A smug smile crossed her face. "That's not all I did."

Of course it wasn't.

"I hesitate to ask . . ." Simon prodded.

She looked to him, then to her brother. *Was she blushing?*

"What did you do?"

"I . . . hit him . . . elsewhere."

"Where?"

"In his . . ." She hesitated, her mouth twisting as she searched for the word, then gave up. "In his *inguine*."

Had he not understood the Italian perfectly, the circular movement of her hand in an area generally believed to be entirely inappropriate for discussion with a young woman of good breeding would have been unmistakable.

"Oh, dear God." It was unclear whether Ralston's words were meant as prayer or blasphemy.

What was clear was that the woman a gladiator.

"He called me a pie!" she announced, defensively. There was a pause. "Wait. That's not right."

"A tart?"

"Yes! That's it!" She registered her brother's fists and looked to Simon. "I see that it is not a compliment."

It was hard for him to hear over the roaring in his ears. He'd like to take a fist to the man himself. "No. It is not."

She thought for a moment. "Well, then he deserved what he received, did he not?"

"Leighton," Ralston found his voice. "Is there somewhere my sister can wait while you and I speak?"

Warning bells sounded, loud and raucous.

Simon stood, willing himself calm. "Of course."

"You're going to discuss me," Juliana blurted.

Did the woman *ever* keep a thought to herself?

"Yes. I am," Ralston announced.

"I should like to stay."

"I am sure you would."

"Gabriel . . ." she began, in a soothing tone Simon had only ever heard used with unbroken horses and asylum inmates.

"Do not push your luck, sister."

She paused, and Simon watched in disbelief as she considered her next course of action. Finally, she met his gaze, her brilliant blue eyes flashing with irritation. "Your Grace? Where will you store me while you and my brother do the business of men?"

Amazing. She resisted at every turn.

He moved to the door, ushering her into the hallway. Following her out, he pointed to the room directly across from them. "The library. You may make yourself comfortable there."

"Mmm." The sound was dry and disgruntled.

Simon held back a smile, unable to resist taunting her one final time. "And may I say that I am happy to see that you are willing to admit defeat?"

She turned to him and took a step closer, her breasts nearly touching his chest. The air grew heavy between them, and he was inundated with her scent—red currants and basil. It was the same scent he had noticed months ago, before he had discovered her true identity. *Before everything had changed.*

He resisted the impulse to look at the expanse of skin above the rich green edge of her gown instead taking a step back.

The girl was entirely lacking a sense of propriety.

"I may admit defeat in the battle, Your Grace. But never in the war."

He watched her cross the foyer and enter the library, closing the door behind her, and he shook his head.

Juliana Fiori was a disaster waiting to happen.

It was a miracle that she had survived half a year with the *ton*.

It was a miracle they had survived half a year with her.

"She took him out with a knee to the . . ." Ralston said, when Simon returned to the study.

"It would seem so," he replied, closing the door firmly, as though he could block out the troublesome female beyond.

"What the hell am I going to do with her?"

Simon blinked once. Ralston and he barely tolerated one another. If it were not for the marquess's twin being a friend, neither of them would choose to speak to the other. Ralston had always been an ass. He was not actually asking for Simon's opinion, was he?

"Oh, for Chrissakes, Leighton, it was rhetorical. I know better than to ask you for advice. Particularly about sisters."

The barb struck true, and Simon suggested precisely where Ralston might go to get some advice.

The marquess laughed. "Much better. I was growing concerned by how gracious a host you had become." He stalked to the sideboard and poured three fingers of amber liquid into a glass. Turning back he said, "Scotch?"

Simon resumed his seat, realizing that he might be in for a long evening. "What a generous offer," he said dryly.

Ralston walked the tumbler over and sat. "Now. Let's talk about how you happen to have my sister in your house in the middle of the night."

Simon took a long drink, enjoying the burn of the liquor down his throat. "I told you. She was in my carriage when I left your ball."

"And why didn't you apprise me of the situation immediately?"

As questions went, it was a fairly good one. Simon swirled the tumbler of whiskey in his hand, thinking. Why hadn't he closed the carriage door and fetched Ralston?

The girl was common and impossible and everything he could not stomach in a female.

But she was fascinating.

She had been since the first moment he'd met her, in the damned bookshop, buying a book for her brother. And then they'd met again at the Royal Art Exhibition. And she'd let him believe . . .

"Perhaps you would tell me your name?" he had asked, eager not to lose her again. The weeks since the bookshop had been interminable. She had pursed her lips, a perfect moue, and he had sensed victory. "I shall go first. My name is Simon."

"Simon." He had loved the sound of it on her tongue, that name he had not used publicly in decades.

"And yours, my lady?"

"Oh, I think that would ruin the fun," she had paused, her brilliant smile lighting the room. "Don't you agree, Your Grace?"

She had known he was a duke. He should have recognized then that something was wrong. But instead, he had been transfixed. Shaking his head, he had advanced upon her slowly, sending her scurrying backward to keep her distance, and the chase had enthralled him. "Now, that is unfair."

"It seems more than fair. I am merely a better detective than you."

He paused, considering her words. "It does appear that way. Perhaps I should simply guess your identity?"

She grinned. "You may feel free."

"You are an Italian princess, here with your brother on some diplomatic visit to the King."

She had cocked her head at the same angle as she had this evening while conversing with her brother. "Perhaps."

"*Or, the daughter of a Veronese count, whiling away your spring here, eager to experience the legendary London Season.*"

She had laughed then, the sound like sunshine. "How disheartening that you make my father a mere count. Why not a duke? Like you?"

He had smiled. "A duke, then," *adding softly,* "that would make things much easier."

She'd let him believe she was more than a vexing commoner.

Which, of course, she wasn't.

Yes, he should have fetched Ralston the moment he saw the little fool on the floor of his carriage, squeezed into the corner as though she were a smaller woman, as though she could have hidden from him.

"If I'd come to fetch you, how do you think that would have worked?"

"She'd be asleep in her bed right now. That's how it would have worked."

He ignored the vision of her sleeping, her wild raven hair spread across crisp, white linen, her creamy skin rising from the low scoop of her nightgown. *If she wore a nightgown.*

He cleared his throat. "And if she'd leapt from my carriage in full view of all the Ralston House revelers? What then?"

Ralston paused, considering. "Well, then, I suppose she would have been ruined. And you would be preparing for a life of wedded bliss."

Simon drank again. "So it is likely better for all of us that I behaved as I did."

Ralston's eyes darkened. "That's not the first time you have so baldly resisted the idea of marrying my sister, Leighton. I find I'm beginning to take it personally."

"Your sister and I would not suit, Ralston. And you know it."

"You could not handle her."

Simon's lips twisted. There wasn't a man in London who could handle the chit.

Ralston knew it. "No one will have her. She's too bold. Too brash. The opposite of good English girls." He paused, and Simon wondered if the marquess was waiting for him to disagree. He had no intention of doing so. "She says whatever enters her head whenever it happens to arrive, with no consideration of how those around her might respond. She bloodies the noses of unsuspecting men!" The last was said on a disbelieving laugh.

"Well, to be fair, it did sound like this evening's man had it coming."

"It did, didn't it?" Ralston stopped, thinking for a long moment. "It shouldn't be so hard to find him. There can't be too many aristocrats with a fat lip going around."

"Even fewer limping off the other injury," Simon said wryly.

Ralston shook his head. "Where do you think she learned that tactic?"

From the wolves by whom she had clearly been raised.

"I would not deign to guess."

Silence fell between them, and after a long moment, Ralston sighed and stood. "I do not like to be indebted to you."

Simon smirked at the confession. "Consider us even."

The marquess nodded once and headed for the door. Once there, he turned back. "Lucky, isn't it, that there is a special session this autumn? To keep us all from our country seats?"

Simon met Ralston's knowing gaze. The marquess did not speak what they both knew—that Leighton had thrown his considerable power behind an emergency

bill that could have waited easily for the spring session
of Parliament to begin.

"Military preparedness is a serious issue," Simon said
with deliberate calm.

"Indeed it is." Ralston crossed his arms and leaned
back against the door. "And Parliament is a welcome
distraction from sisters, is it not?"

Simon's gaze narrowed. "You have never pulled
punches with me before, Ralston. There is no need to
begin now."

"I do not suppose I could request your assistance with
Juliana?"

Simon froze, the request hanging between them.

Simply tell him no.

"What kind of assistance?"

Not precisely "No," Leighton.

Ralston raised a brow. "I am not asking you to wed the
girl, Leighton. Relax. I could use the extra set of eyes on
her. I mean, she can't go into the gardens of our own home
without getting herself attacked by unidentified men."

Simon leveled Ralston with a cool look. "It appears
that the universe is punishing you with a sibling who
makes as much trouble as you did."

"I am afraid you might be right." A heavy silence fell.
"You know what could happen to her, Leighton."

You've lived it.

The words remained unspoken, but Simon heard
them, nonetheless.

Still, the answer is no.

"Forgive me if I am not entirely interested in doing
you a favor, Ralston."

Much closer.

"It would be a favor for St. John, as well," Ralston
added, invoking the name of his twin brother—the good
twin. "I might remind you that my family has spent quite
a bit of energy caring for *your* sister, Leighton."

There it was.

The heavy weight of scandal, powerful enough to move mountains.

He did not like having such an obvious weakness.

And it would only get worse.

For a long moment, Simon could not bring himself to speak. Finally, he nodded his agreement. "Fair enough."

"You can imagine how much I loathe the very idea of asking you for assistance, Duke, but think of how much you will enjoy rubbing it in my face for the rest of our days."

"I confess, I was hoping not to have to suffer you for so very long."

Ralston laughed then. "You are a cold-hearted bastard." He came forward to stand behind the chair he had vacated. "Are you ready, then? For when the news gets out?"

Simon did not pretend to misunderstand. Ralston and St. John were the only two men who knew the darkest of Simon's secrets. The one that would destroy his family and his reputation if it were revealed.

The one that was bound to be revealed sooner or later.

Would he ever be ready?

"Not yet. But soon."

Ralston watched him with a cool blue gaze that reminded Simon of Juliana. "You know we will stand beside you."

Simon laughed once, the sound humorless. "Forgive me if I do not place much weight in the support of the House of Ralston."

One side of Ralston's mouth lifted in a smile. "We are a motley bunch. But we more than make up for it with tenacity."

Simon considered the woman in his library. "That I do not doubt."

"I take it you plan to marry."

Simon paused in the act of lifting his glass to his lips. "How did you know that?"

The smile turned into a knowing grin then. "Nearly every problem can be solved by a trip to the vicar. Particularly yours. Who is the lucky girl?"

Simon considered lying. Considered pretending that he hadn't selected her. Everyone would know soon enough, however. "Lady Penelope Marbury."

Ralston whistled long and low. "Daughter of a double marquess. Impeccable reputation. Generations of pedigree. The Holy Trinity of a desirable match. And a fortune as well. Excellent choice."

It was nothing that Simon had not thought himself, of course, but it smarted nonetheless for him to hear it spoken aloud. "I do not like to hear you discuss my future duchess's merits as though she were prize cattle."

Ralston leaned back. "My apologies. I was under the impression that you had selected your future duchess as though she were prize cattle."

The whole conversation was making him uncomfortable. It was true. He was not marrying Lady Penelope for anything other than her unimpeachable background.

"After all, it isn't as if anyone will believe the great Duke of Leighton would marry for love."

He did not like the tremor of sarcasm in Ralston's tone. Of course, the marquess had always known how to irritate him. Ever since they were children. Simon rose, eager to move. "I think I shall fetch your sister, Ralston. It's time for you to take her home. And I would appreciate it if you could keep your family dramatics from my doorstep in the future."

The words sounded imperious even to his ears.

Ralston straightened, making slow work of coming to his full height, almost as tall as Leighton. "I shall certainly try. After all, you have plenty of your own family dramatics threatening to come crashing down on the doorstep, do you not?"

There was nothing about Ralston that Simon liked.

He would do well to remember that.

He exited the study and headed for the library, opening the door with more force than necessary and coming up short just inside the room.

She was asleep in his chair.

With his dog.

The chair she had selected was one that he had worked long and hard to get to the perfect level of comfort. His butler had suggested it for reupholstering countless times, due in part, Simon imagined, to the fraying, soft fabric that he considered one of the seat's finest attributes. He took in Juliana's sleeping form, her scratched cheek against the soft golden threads of the worn fabric.

She had taken off her shoes and curled her feet beneath her, and Simon shook his head at the behavior. Ladies across London would not dare go barefoot in the privacy of their own homes, and yet here she was, making herself comfortable and taking a nap in a duke's library.

He stole a moment to watch her, to appreciate how she perfectly fit his chair. It was larger than the average seat, built specifically for him fifteen years prior, when, tired of folding himself into minuscule chairs that his mother had declared "the height of fashion," he had decided that, as duke, he was well within his birthright to spend a fortune on a chair that fit his body. It was wide enough for him to sit comfortably, with just enough extra room for a stack of papers requiring his attention, or, as was the case right now, for a dog in search of a warm body.

The dog, a brown mutt that had found his way into his sister's country bedchamber one winter's day, now traveled with Simon and made his home wherever the duke was. The canine was particularly fond of the library in the town house, with its three fireplaces and comfortable furniture, and he had obviously made a friend. Leopold was now curled into a small, tight ball, head on one of Juliana's long thighs.

Thighs Simon should not be noticing.

That his dog was a traitor was a concern Simon would address later.

Now, however, he had to deal with the lady.

"Leopold." Simon called the hound, slapping one hand against his thigh in a practiced maneuver that had the dog coming to heel in seconds.

If only the same action would bring the girl to heel.

No, if he had his way, he would not wake her so easily. Instead, he would rouse her slowly, with long, soft strokes along those glorious legs ... he would crouch beside her and bury his face in that mass of ebony hair, drinking in the smell of her, then run his lips along the lovely angle of her jaw until he reached the curve of one soft ear. He would whisper her name, waking her with breath instead of sound.

And then he would finish what she had started all those months ago.

And he would bring her to heel in an entirely different way.

He fisted his hands at his sides to keep his body from acting on the promise of his imagination. There was nothing he could do that would be more damaging than feeding the unwelcome desire he felt for this impossible female.

He simply had to remember that he was in the market for the perfect duchess.

And Miss Juliana Fiori was never going to be that.

No matter how well she filled out his favorite chair.

It was time to wake the girl up.

And send her home.

Chapter Three

Ladies' salons are hotbeds of imperfection.
Exquisite ladies need not linger within.

—*A Treatise on the Most Exquisite of Ladies*

Surely there is no place more interesting in all of
London than the balcony beyond a ballroom . . .

—*The Scandal Sheet, October 1823*

"I thought that your season was over and we were
through with balls!"

Juliana collapsed onto a settee in a small antechamber off the ladies' salon of Weston House and let out a
long sigh, reaching down to massage the ball of her foot
through her thin slipper.

"We should be," her closest friend Mariana, the newly
minted Duchess of Rivington, lifted the edge of her
elaborate blue gown and inspected the place where her
hem had fallen. "But as long as Parliament remains in
session, seasonal balls will be all the rage. Every hostess wants her autumnal festivity to be more impressive

than the last. You only have yourself to blame," Mariana said wryly.

"How was I to know that Callie would start a revolution in entertaining on my behalf?" Calpurnia, Mariana's sister and Juliana's sister-in-law, had been charged with smoothing Juliana's introduction to London society upon her arrival that spring. Once summer had arrived, the marchioness had recommitted herself to her goal. A wave of summer balls and activities had kept Juliana in the public eye and kept the other hostesses of the *ton* in town after the season was long finished.

Callie's goal was a smart marriage.

Which made Juliana's goal survival.

Waving a young maid over, Mariana pulled a thimble of thread from her reticule and handed it to the girl, who was already crouching down to repair the damage. Meeting Juliana's gaze in the mirror, she said, "You are very lucky that you could cry off Lady Davis's Orange Extravaganza last week."

"She did not really call it that."

"She did! You should have seen the place, Juliana . . . it was an explosion of color, and not in a good way. Everything was orange—the clothes . . . the floral arrangements . . . the servants had new livery, for heaven's sake . . . the food—"

"The food?" Juliana wrinkled her nose.

Mariana nodded. "It was awful. Everything was carrot-colored. A feast fit for rabbits. Be grateful you were not feeling well."

Juliana wondered what Lady Davis—a particularly opinionated doyenne of the *ton*—would have thought if she had attended, covered in scratches from her adventure with Grabeham the week prior.

She gave a little smile at the thought and moved to restore half a dozen loose curls to their rightful places. "I thought that now you are a duchess, you do not have to suffer these events?"

"I thought so, too. But Rivington tells me differently. Or, more appropriately, the Dowager Duchess tells me differently." She sighed. "If I never see another cornucopia, it will be too soon."

Juliana laughed. "Yes, it must be very difficult being one of the most-sought-after guests of the year, Mariana. What with being madly in love with your handsome young duke and having all of London spread before you."

Her friend's eyes twinkled. "Oh, it's a wicked trial. Just wait. Someday you'll discover it for yourself."

Juliana doubted it.

Nicknamed the Allendale Angel, Mariana had made quick work of meeting and marrying her husband, the Duke of Rivington, in her first season. It had been the talk of the year, an almost instant love match that had resulted in a lavish wedding and a whirlwind of social engagements for the young couple.

Mariana was the kind of woman whom people adored. Everyone wanted to be close to her, and she never lacked for companionship. She had been the first friend that Juliana had made in London; both she and her duke had made it a priority to show the *ton* that they accepted Juliana—no matter what her pedigree.

At Juliana's first ball, it had been Rivington who had claimed her first dance, instantly stamping her with the approval of his venerable dukedom.

So different from the other duke who had been in attendance that evening.

Leighton had shown no emotion that night, not when she'd met his cool honeyed gaze across the ballroom, not when she'd passed close to him on the way to the refreshment table, not when he'd stumbled upon her in a private room set apart from the ball.

That wasn't precisely true. He had shown emotion there. Just not the kind she had wished.

He'd been furious.

"Why didn't you tell me who you were?"

"Does it matter?"

"Yes."

"Which part? That my mother is the fallen Marchioness of Ralston? That my father was a hardworking merchant? That I haven't a title?"

"All of it matters."

She had been warned about him—the Duke of Disdain, keenly aware of his station in society, who held no interest for those whom he considered beneath him. He was known for his aloof presence, for his cool contempt. She had heard that he selected his servants for their discretion, his mistresses for their lack of emotion, and his friends—well, there was no indication that he would stoop to something so common as friendship.

But until that moment, when he discovered her identity, she had not believed the gossip. Not until she had felt the sting of his infamous disdain.

It had hurt. Far more than the judgment of all the others.

And then she had kissed him. Like a fool. And it had been remarkable. Until he had pulled away with a violence that embarrassed her still.

"You are a danger to yourself and others. You should return to Italy. If you stay, your instincts will find you utterly ruined. With extraordinary speed."

"You enjoyed it," Juliana said, accusation in her tone keeping the pain at bay.

He leveled her with a cool, calculated look. *"Of course I did. But unless you are angling for a position as my mistress— and you'd make a fine mistress—"* She gasped, and he drove his point home like a knife to her chest. *"You would do well to remember your station."*

That had been the moment that she decided to remain in London. To prove to him and all the others who judged her behind their fluttering lace fans and their cool English glances that she was more than what they saw.

She ran a fingertip over the barely noticeable pink mark at her temple—the last vestige of the night when she'd landed herself in Leighton's carriage, bringing back all the painful memories of those early weeks in London, when she was young and alone and still hoped that she could become one of them—these aristocrats.

She should have known better, of course.

They would never accept her.

The maid finished Mariana's hem, and Juliana watched as her friend shook out her skirts before twirling toward her. "Shall we?"

Juliana slouched dramatically. "Must we?"

The duchess laughed, and they moved to reenter the main room of the salon.

"I heard that she was spied in a torrid embrace in the gardens the night of the Ralston autumn ball."

Juliana froze, immediately recognizing the high, nasal tone of Lady Sparrow, one of the *ton*'s worst gossips.

"In her brother's gardens?" The disbelieving gasp made it clear that Juliana was the object of their conversation.

Her gaze flew to a clearly furious Mariana, who appeared ready to storm the room—and its gossiping inhabitants. Which Juliana could not allow her to do. She placed one hand on her friend's arm, staying her movement, and waited, listening.

"She *is* only a *half* sibling."

"And we all know what *that* half was like." A chorus of laughter punctuated the barb, which struck with painful accuracy.

"It's amazing that so many invite her to events," one

nearly drawled. "Tonight, for example . . . I had thought Lady Weston a better judge of character."

So had Juliana.

"It is somewhat difficult to invite Lord and Lady Ralston without extending the invitation to Miss Fiori," a new voice pointed out.

A snort of derision followed. "Not that they are much better . . . with the marquess's scandalous past and the marchioness—so very uninteresting. I still wonder what she did to win him."

"And let's not even discuss Lord Nicholas, marrying a country bumpkin. Can you imagine!"

"Never doubt what poor stock can do to good English blood. It's clear that the mother has . . . left her mark."

The last came on a high-pitched cackle, and Juliana's fury began to rise. It was one thing for the vicious harridans to insult her, but it was an entirely different thing for them to go after her family. Those she loved.

"I do not understand why Ralston doesn't just give the sister a settlement and send her back to Italy."

Neither did Juliana.

She'd expected that to happen any number of times since she arrived, unbidden, on the steps of Ralston House. Her brother had never once even suggested it.

But she still had trouble believing that he didn't want her gone.

"Don't listen to them," Mariana whispered. "They're horrible, hateful women who live to loathe."

"All it will take is for one person of quality to find her doing something base, and she'll be exiled from society forever."

"That shouldn't take long. Everyone knows Italians have loose morals."

Juliana had had enough.

She pushed past Mariana and into the ladies' salon, where the threesome were retouching their maquillage at the large mirror on one wall of the room. Tossing a broad smile in the direction of the women, she took perverse pleasure in their stillness—a combination of shock and chagrin.

Still laughing at her own joke was the coolly beautiful and utterly malicious Lady Sparrow, who had married a viscount, rich as Croesus and twice as old, three months before the man had died, leaving her with a fortune to do with as she wished. The viscountess was joined by Lady Davis, who apparently had not had her fill of the legendary orange extravaganza, as she was wearing an atrocious gown that accentuated her waist in such a way as to turn the woman into a perfect, round gourd.

There was a young woman with them whom Juliana did not know. Petite and blond, with a plain round face and wide, surprised eyes, Juliana fleetingly wondered how this little thing had found herself in with the vipers. She would either be killed, or be transformed.

Not that it mattered to Juliana.

"My ladies," she said, keeping her voice light, "a wiser group might have made certain they were alone before indulging in a conversation that eviscerates so many."

Lady Davis's mouth opened and closed in an approximation of a trout before she looked away. The plain woman blushed, clasping her hands tightly in front of her in a gesture easily identified as regret.

Not so Lady Sparrow. "Perhaps we were perfectly aware of our company," she sneered. "We simply were not in fear of offending it."

With perfect timing, Mariana exited the antechamber, and there was a collective intake of breath as the other ladies registered the presence of the Duchess of Rivington. "Well, that is a pity," she said, her tone clear and imperious, entirely befitting of her title. "As I find myself much offended."

Mariana swept from the room, and Juliana swallowed

a smile at her friend's impeccable performance, rife with entitlement. Returning her attention to the group of women, she moved closer, enjoying the way they shifted their discomfort. When she was close enough to smell their cloying perfume, she said, "Do not fret, ladies. Unlike my sister-in-law, I take no offense."

She paused, turning her head to each side, making a show of inspecting herself before tucking an errant curl back into her coiffure. When she was certain that she held their collective attention, she said, "You have issued your challenge. I shall meet it with pleasure."

She did not breathe until she exited the ladies' salon, anger and frustration and hurt rushing through her to dizzying effect.

It should not have surprised her that they gossiped about her. They'd gossiped about her since the day she'd arrived in London.

She'd simply thought they would have stopped by now.

But they had not. They would not.

This was her life.

She bore the mark of her mother, who remained a scandal even now, twenty-five years after she had deserted her husband, the Marquess of Ralston, and her twin sons, fleeing this glittering, aristocratic life for the Continent. She'd landed in Italy, where she'd bewitched Juliana's father, a hardworking merchant who swore he had never wanted anything in his life more than he wanted her—the raven-haired Englishwoman with bright eyes and a brilliant smile.

She'd married him, in a decision that Juliana had come to identify as precisely the kind of reckless, impulsive behavior that her mother had been known for.

Behavior that threatened to surge in her.

Juliana grimaced at the thought.

When she behaved impulsively, it was to protect herself. Her mother had been an entitled aristocrat with a childish penchant for drama. Even as she'd aged, she had not matured.

Juliana supposed she should have been grateful that the marchioness deserted them when she had, or think of the scars they would all have borne.

Juliana's father had done his best to raise a daughter. He had taught her to tie an excellent knot, to spot a bad shipment of goods, and to haggle with the best and worst of merchants . . . but he'd never shared his most important bit of knowledge.

He'd never told her that she had a family.

She'd only learned about her half brothers, born of the mother she'd barely known, after her father had died—when she'd discovered that her funds had been placed in a trust, and that an unknown British marquess was to be her guardian.

Within weeks, everything had changed.

She had been dropped, summarily, on the doorstep of Ralston House, with three trunks of possessions and her maid.

All thanks to a mother without a thimbleful of maternal instinct.

Was it any surprise that people questioned the character of her daughter?

That the daughter questioned it, as well?

No.

She was nothing like her mother.

She'd never given them a reason to think she was.

Not on purpose, at least.

But it didn't seem to matter. These aristocrats drew strength from insulting her, from looking down their long, straight noses at her and seeing nothing but her mother's face, her mother's scandal, her mother's reputation.

They did not care who she was.

They cared only that she was not like them.

And how tempted she was to show them how very unlike them she really was . . . these unmoving, uninteresting, passionless creatures.

She took a deep, stabilizing breath, looking over the ballroom to the faraway doors leading to the gardens beyond. Even as she began to move, she knew that she should not head for them.

But in all the emotions flooding her, she could not find the room to care about what she should not do.

Mariana came from nowhere, placing a delicate gloved hand on Juliana's elbow. "Are you all right?"

"I am fine." She did not look at her friend. Could not face her.

"They're horrid."

"They're also right."

Mariana pulled up short at the words, but Juliana kept moving, focused singularly on the open French doors . . . on the salvation they promised. The young duchess caught up quickly. "They are not right."

"No?" Juliana sliced a look at her friend, registering the wide blue eyes that made her such a perfect specimen of English femininity. "Of course they are. I am not one of you. I never will be."

"And thank God for that," Mariana said. "There are more than enough of us to go around. I, for one, am very happy to have someone unique in my life. Finally."

Juliana paused at the edge of the dance floor, turning to face her friend. "Thank you." *Even though it isn't true.*

Mariana smiled as though everything had been repaired. "You're very welcome."

"Now, why don't you go find your handsome husband and dance with him. You would not like tongues to begin wagging about the state of your marriage."

"Let them wag."

Juliana's lips twisted in a wry smile. "Spoken like a duchess."

"The position does have a few perks."

Juliana forced a laugh. "Go."

Mariana's brow furrowed with worry. "Are you sure you are all right?"

"Indeed. I am just heading for some fresh air. You know how I cannot bear the heat in these rooms."

"Be careful," Mariana said with a nervous look toward the doors. "Don't get yourself lost."

"Shall I leave a trail of *petits fours*?"

"It might not be a bad idea."

"Good-bye, Mari."

Mariana was off then, her shimmering blue gown swallowed up by the crowd almost instantly, as though they could not wait for her to join their masses.

They would not absorb Juliana in the same way. She imagined the crowd sending her back, like an olive pit spit from the Ponte Pietra.

Except, this was not as simple as falling from a bridge.

Not as safe, either.

Juliana took a few moments to watch the dancers, dozens of couples swirling and dipping in a quick country dance. She could not resist comparing herself to the women twirling before her, all in their pretty pastel frocks, with their perfectly positioned bodies and their tepid personalities. They were the result of perfect English breeding—raised and cultivated like grapevines to ensure identical fruit and inoffensive, uninteresting wine.

She noticed the girl from the salon taking her place on one side of the long line of dancers, the flush on her cheeks making her more alive than she had first seemed. Her lips were tilted up in what Juliana could only assume was a long-practiced smile—not too bright as to seem forward, not too dim as to indicate disinterest. She appeared a plump grape, ready for picking. Ripe for inclusion in this simple, English vintage.

The grape reached the end of the line, and she and her partner came together.

Her partner was the Duke of Leighton.

The two were weaving and spinning straight toward her, down the long line of revelers, and there was only one thought in Juliana's head.

They were mismatched.

It was not merely the way they looked, everything but their similarly too-golden hair ill suited. She was somewhat plain—her face just a touch too round, her blue eyes a touch too pale, her lips something less than a perfect pink bow—and he was . . . well . . . he was *Leighton*. The difference in their statures was immense—he towered well over six feet, and she was small and slight, barely reaching his chest.

Juliana rolled her eyes at the look of them. He probably liked the idea of such a small female, something he could set in motion with the flick of a finger.

But they were mismatched in other ways, too. The grape enjoyed the dance, it was obvious from the twinkle in her eyes as she met the gazes of the other women in line. He did not smile as he danced, despite the fact that he clearly knew the steps to the reel. He did not enjoy himself. Of course, this was not a man who would take pleasure in country dances. This was not a man who took pleasure anywhere.

It was surprising that he had been willing to stoop to such a common activity as dancing in the first place.

The two had reached the end of the revelers and were mere feet from Juliana when Leighton met her gaze. It was fleeting, a second or two at the most, but as she met his honey brown eyes, awareness twisted deep in her stomach. It was a feeling she should have been used to by then, but it never failed to surprise her.

She always hoped that he would not affect her. That

someday, those few, fleeting moments of the past would be just that—the past.

Instead of a reminder of how out of place she was in this world.

She spun away from the dance, heading for the wide glass doors and the dark night with newfound urgency. Without hesitation, she stepped through to the stone balcony beyond. Even as she exited the room, she knew she should not. She knew that her brother and the rest of London would judge her for the action. Balconies were hothouses of sin in their eyes.

Which would be ridiculous, of course. Surely, nothing bad could come of a stolen moment on the balcony. It was *gardens* that she must avoid.

It was cold outside, the air biting and welcome. She looked up into the clear October sky, taking in the stars above.

At least something was the same.

"You should not be out here."

She did not turn at the words. The duke had joined her. She was not entirely surprised.

"Why not?"

"Anything could happen to you."

She lifted one shoulder. "My father used to say that women have a dozen lives. Like your cats."

"Cats only have nine lives here."

She smiled over her shoulder at him. "And women?"

"Far fewer. It is not wise for you to be here alone."

"It was perfectly wise until you arrived."

"This is why you are . . ." He trailed off.

"This is why I am always in trouble."

"Yes."

"Then why are you here, Your Grace? Don't you risk your own reputation by being so near to me?" She turned to find him several yards away and gave a short laugh.

"Well. I don't suppose you could possibly be ruined from such a distance. You are safe."

"I promised your brother that I would shield you from scandal."

She was so very tired of everyone thinking she was one step from scandal.

She narrowed her gaze on him. "There is an irony in that, don't you find? There was a time when you were the biggest threat to my reputation. Or do you not remember?"

The words were out before she could stop them, and his countenance grew stony in the shadows. "This is neither the time nor the place to discuss such things."

"It never is, is it?"

He changed the subject. "You are fortunate that it was I who found you."

"Good fortune? Is that what this is?" Juliana met his eyes, searching for the warmth she had once seen there. She found nothing but his strong patrician gaze, unwavering.

How could he be so different now?

She turned back to the sky, anger flaring. "I think it best for you to leave."

"I think it best for you to return to the ball."

"Why? You think that if I dance a reel, they will open their arms and accept me into the fold?"

"I think they will never accept you if you do not try."

She turned her head to meet his eyes. "You think I want them to accept me."

He watched her for a long moment. "I think you should want us to accept you."

Us.

She squared her shoulders. "Why should I? You are a rigid, passionless group, more concerned with the proper distance between dance partners than in the world in which you live. You think your traditions and your manners and your silly rules make your life desirable. They don't. They make you snobs."

"You are a child who knows not the game that she plays."

The words stung. Not that she would show him that.

She stepped closer, testing his willingness to stand his ground. He did not move. "You think I consider this a game?"

"I think it is impossible for you to consider it otherwise. Look at you. The entire *ton* is mere feet away, and here you are, a hairsbreadth from ruin." His words were steel, the strong planes of his face shadowed and beautiful in the moonlight.

"I told you. I don't care what they think."

"Of course you do. Or you wouldn't still be here. You would have returned to Italy and been done with us."

There was a long pause.

He was wrong.

She did not care what they thought.

She cared what he thought.

And that only served to frustrate her more.

She turned back to face the gardens, gripping the wide stone railing on the balcony and wondering what would happen if she ran for the darkness.

She would be found.

"I trust your hands have healed."

They were back to being polite. Unmoved.

"Yes. Thank you." She took a deep breath. "You seemed to enjoy the dancing."

There was a beat as he considered the statement. "It was tolerable."

She laughed a little. "What a compliment, Your Grace." She paused. "Your partner appeared to enjoy your company."

"Lady Penelope is an excellent dancer."

The grape had a name.

"Yes, well, I had the good fortune of meeting her earlier this evening. I can tell you she does not have excellent choice in friends."

"I will not have you insulting her."

"You will not *have* me? How are you in a position to make demands of me?"

"I am quite serious. Lady Penelope is to be my bride. You will treat her with the respect she is due."

He was going to marry the ordinary creature.

Her mouth dropped in surprise. "You are engaged?"

"Not yet. But it is a mere matter of formality at this point."

She supposed it was right that he be matched with such a perfect English bride.

Except it seemed so *wrong.*

"I confess, I have never heard anyone speak so blandly about marriage."

He crossed his arms against the cold, the wool of his black formal coat pulling taut across his shoulders, emphasizing his broadness. "What is there to say? We suit well enough."

She blinked. "Well enough."

He nodded once. "Quite."

"How very impassioned."

He did not rise to her sarcasm. "It's a matter of business. There is no room for passion in a good English marriage."

It was a joke. It must be.

"How do you expect to live your life without passion?"

He sniffed, and she wondered if he could smell his pompousness. "The emotion is overrated."

She gave a little laugh. "Well, that might possibly be the most British thing I have ever heard anyone say."

"It is a bad thing to be British?"

She smiled slowly. "Your words, not mine." She continued, knowing she was irritating him. "We all need passion. You could do with a heavy dose of it in all areas of your life."

He raised a brow. "I am to take this advice from you?" When she nodded, he pressed on. "So, let me be clear. You think my life requires passion—an emotion that propels you into darkened gardens and into strange carriages and onto balconies and forces you to risk your reputation with alarming frequency."

She lifted her chin. "I do."

"That may work for you, *Miss* Fiori, but I am different. I have a title, a family, and a reputation to protect. Not to mention the fact that I am far above such base and . . . common desires."

The arrogance that poured off of him was suffocating.

"You are a duke," she said, sarcasm in her tone.

He ignored it. "Precisely. And you are . . ."

"I am far less than that."

He raised one golden eyebrow. "Your words, not mine."

Her breath whooshed out of her as though she had been struck.

He deserved a powerful, wicked set down. The kind that would ruin a man for good. The kind only a woman could give.

The kind she desperately wanted to give him.

"You . . . *asino*." His lips pressed into a thin line at the insult, and she dropped into a deep, mocking curtsy. "I apologize, *Your Grace*, for the use of such base language." She looked up at him through dark lashes. "You will permit me to repeat it in your superior English. You are an *ass.*"

He spoke to her through his teeth. "Rise."

She did, swallowing back her anger as he reached for her, his strong fingers digging into her elbow, turning her back to the ballroom. When he continued, his voice was low and graveled at her ear. "You think your precious passion shows that you are better than us, when all it shows is your selfishness. You have a family who is endeavoring to garner society's acceptance for you, and still nothing matters to you but your own excitement."

She hated him then. "It is not true. I care deeply for them. I would never do anything to—" She stopped. *I would never do anything to damage them.*

The words were not precisely true. Here she was, after all, on a darkened terrace with *him*.

He seemed to understand her thoughts. "Your recklessness will ruin you . . . and likely them. If you cared even a little, you would attempt to behave in the manner of a lady and not a common—"

He stopped before the insult was spoken.

She heard it anyway.

A calm settled deep within her.

She wanted this perfect, arrogant man brought to his knees.

If he imagined her reckless, that's what she would be.

Slowly, she removed her arm from his grasp. "You think you are above passion? You think your perfect world needs nothing more than rigid rules and emotionless experience?"

He stepped back at the challenge in her soft words. "I do not think it. I know it."

She nodded once. "Prove it." His brows drew together, but he did not speak. "Let me show you that not even a frigid duke can live without heat."

He did not move. "No."

"Are you afraid?"

"Disinterested."

"I doubt that."

"You really give no thought to reputations, do you?"

"If you are concerned for your reputation, Your Grace, by all means, bring a chaperone."

"And if I resist your tempestuous life?"

"Then you marry the grape and all is well."

He blinked. "The grape?"

"Lady Penelope." There was a long pause. "But . . . if you cannot resist . . ." She stepped close, his warmth a temptation in the crisp October air.

"Then what?" he asked, his voice low and dark.

She had him now. She would bring him down.

And his perfect world with him.

She smiled. "Then your reputation is in serious danger."

He was silent, the only movement the slow twitch of a muscle in his jaw. After several moments, she thought he might leave her there, her threat hovering in the cold air.

And then he spoke.

"I shall give you two weeks." She did not have time to revel in her victory. "But it shall be you who learns the lesson, Miss Fiori."

Suspicion flared. "What lesson?"

"Reputation always triumphs."

Chapter Four

The walk or trot will do.
Delicate ladies never gallop.

—*A Treatise on the Most Exquisite of Ladies*

The Fashionable Hour comes earlier and earlier . . .

—*The Scandal Sheet, October 1823*

The next morning, the Duke of Leighton rose with the sun.

He washed, dressed in crisp linen and smooth buckskin, pulled on his riding boots, tied his cravat, and called for his mount.

In less than a quarter of an hour, he crossed the great foyer of his town house, accepting a pair of riding gloves and a crop from Boggs, his ever-prepared butler, and exited the house.

Breathing in the morning air, crisp with the scent of autumn, the duke lifted himself into the saddle, just as he had every morning since the day he assumed the dukedom, fifteen years earlier.

In town or in the country, rain or shine, cold or heat, the ritual was sacrosanct.

Hyde Park was virtually empty in the hour just after dawn—few were interested in riding without the chance of being seen, and even fewer interested in leaving their homes at such an early hour. This was precisely why Leighton so enjoyed his morning rides—the quiet punctuated only by hoofbeats, by the sound of his horse's breath mingled with his own as they cantered through the long, deserted paths that only hours later would be packed with those still in town, eager to feed on the latest gossip.

The *ton* traded on information, and Hyde Park on a beautiful day was the ideal place for the exchange of such a commodity.

It was only a matter of time until his family was made the commodity of the day.

Leighton leaned into his horse, driving the animal forward, faster, as though he could outrun the tattle.

When they heard about his sister, the gossips would swarm, and his family would be left with little to protect their name and reputation. The Dukes of Leighton went back eleven generations. They had fought alongside William the Conqueror. And those who held the title and the venerable position so far above the rest of society were raised with one unimpeachable rule: *Let nothing besmirch the name.*

For eleven generations, that rule had gone unchallenged.

Until now.

Over the last several months, Leighton had done all he could to ensure that his character was untainted. He had dismissed his mistress, thrown himself into his work in Parliament, and attended scores of functions hosted by those who held sway over the *ton*'s perception of character. He had danced reels. Taken tea. Shown himself at

Almack's. Called on the most respected families of the aristocracy.

Spread a reasonable and accepted rumor that his sister was in the country, for the summer. And then for autumn. And, soon enough, for the winter.

But it was not enough. Nothing would be.

And that knowledge—the keen understanding that he could never entirely protect his family from the natural course of events—threatened his serenity.

There was only one thing left.

An unimpeachable, proper wife. A future darling of the *ton*.

He was scheduled to meet with Lady Penelope's father that day. The Marquess of Needham and Dolby had approached Leighton the prior evening and suggested they meet "to discuss the future." Leighton had seen no reason to wait, as the faster he had the marquess's agreement that a match would be suitable, the faster he would be prepared to face the tongues that could begin wagging at any moment.

A half smile played across his lips. The meeting was mere formality. The marquess had come barely short of proposing to Leighton himself.

It would not have been the first proposal he received that evening.

Nor the most tempting.

He sat up straight in his saddle, reining in the horse, regaining control once more. A vision flashed, Juliana facing him like a warrior on the balcony of Weston House—tossing out her challenge as though it was nothing more than a game. *Let me show you that not even a frigid duke can live without heat.*

The words echoed around him in her lilting Italian accent, as though she were there, whispering in his ear once more. *Heat.*

He closed his eyes against the thought, giving the

horse rein again, as though the biting wind at his cheeks would combat the word and its effect upon him.

She'd baited him. And he'd been so irate at the arrogance in her tone—at her certainty that every tenet upon which his life was built was laughable—that he'd wanted nothing more in that moment than to prove her wrong. He'd wanted to prove her insistence that his world contained nothing of value was as ridiculous as her silly dare.

So he'd given her two weeks.

It had not been an arbitrary length of time. He would give her two weeks to try her best with him, and he would show her at the end of the time, that reputation ruled the day. He would send the announcement of his impending nuptials to the *Times*, and Juliana would learn that passion was a tempting . . . and ultimately unfulfilling path.

If he hadn't accepted her ridiculous challenge, she would have no doubt found someone else to needle into her plans—someone with less of a debt to Ralston and less of an interest in keeping her from ruin.

He'd done her a favor, really.

Let her do her worst.

Please.

The wicked word flashed, and with it a vision of Juliana as temptress. Her long, naked limbs tangled in his linen sheets, her hair spread like satin across his pillow, her eyes, the color of Ceylon sapphires, promising him the world as her full lips curved, and she whispered his name, reaching for him.

For a moment, he allowed himself the fantasy—all it would ever be—imagining what it would be like to ease her down, to lie across her long, lush body and bury himself in her hair, in her skin, in the hot, welcome core of her and give himself up to the passion she held so dear.

It would be paradise.

He'd wanted her from the first moment he'd seen her, young and fresh and so very different than the porcelain dolls who were paraded before him by mothers who reeked of desperation.

And for a fleeting moment, he'd thought he might be able to have her. He'd thought she was an exotic, foreign jewel, precisely the kind of wife that would so well match the Duke of Leighton.

Until he'd realized her true identity and the fact that she was entirely lacking in the pedigree required of his duchess.

Even then, he'd considered making her his. But he did not think that Ralston would take well to his sister's becoming mistress to any duke, much less a duke he took particular pleasure in disliking.

The path of his thoughts was interrupted—blessedly—by the thunder of another set of hoofbeats. Leighton eased back in his saddle, slowing once more and looking across the meadow to see a horse and rider in full gallop, coming toward him at a reckless pace, even for a rider with such obvious skill. He paused, impressed by the synchronized movement of master and beast. His eyes tracked the long, graceful legs and pistoning muscles of the black, then turned to the form of the rider, at one with his horse, leaning low over the creature's neck, whispering his encouragement.

Simon made to meet the rider's gaze, to nod his appreciation, one master horseman to another. And froze.

The eyes he met were a brilliant blue, sparkling with a mix of defiance and satisfaction.

Surely he had conjured her up.

For there was absolutely no possible way that Juliana Fiori was here, in Hyde Park, at dawn, dressed in men's clothing, riding a horse at breakneck speed, as though she were on the track at Ascot.

Without thinking, he brought his mount to a stop, unable to do anything but watch as she charged toward him, either unaware of or uninterested in the disbelief and fury surging within him, the emotions waging powerful, unsettling war for primary position in his mind.

She was upon him then, stopping so quickly that he knew immediately that this was not the first time she had ridden her mount so hard or so fast or so well. He watched, speechless, as she peeled off one black glove and stroked the long column of the horse's neck, whispering words of encouragement in soft, breathless Italian to the massive animal as it leaned into her touch. She curved her long fingers into the beast's pelt, rewarding it with a deep scratch.

Only then, once the horse had been properly praised, did she turn to him, as though this was a perfectly normal, entirely appropriate meeting. "Your Grace. Good morning."

"Are you a madwoman?" The words were harsh and graveled, their sound foreign to his own ears.

"I've decided that if London . . . and you . . . are so convinced of my questionable character, there is no reason to worry so much about it, is there?" She waved a hand in the air as though she were discussing the possibility of being caught in the rain. "Lucrezia has not had such a run since we arrived. And she adored it . . . did you not, *carina*?" She leaned low again, murmuring to the horse, which preened at the loving words of her mistress and snorted her pleasure at being so well praised.

Not that he could blame the beast.

He shook off the thought. "What are you doing here? Do you have any idea what might happen if you were caught? What are you wearing? What would possess you to . . ."

"Which of those questions would you like me to answer first?"

"Do not test me."

She was not intimidated. "I already told you. We are out for a ride. You know as well as I that there is little risk of our being seen at this hour. The sun is barely awake itself. And as for how I am dressed . . . don't you think it better that I dress as a gentleman? That way, if someone *were* to see me, they would think nothing of it. Far less than they would if I were out in a riding habit. That, and it's much less fun to ride sidesaddle, as I'm sure you can imagine."

She slid the hand she had bared down the long length of her thigh, underscoring her attire, and he could not help but track the movement, taking in the shapely curve of her leg, tucked tightly against the flank of the horse. Tempting him.

"Can't you, Your Grace?"

He snapped his gaze up to meet hers, recognizing the smug amusement there. He did not like it. "Can't I what?"

"Can't you imagine that it's less fun to ride sidesaddle? So proper. So . . . *traditional.*"

Familiar irritation flared and with it, sanity. He took a long look around them, checking the wide-open expanse of meadow for other riders. It was empty. Thank God. "What would possess you to take such a risk?"

She smiled then, slowly, with the triumph of a cat whiskers-first in a bowl of cream. "Because it feels wonderful. Why else?"

The words were a blow to the head, soft and sensual and utterly confident.

And entirely unexpected.

"You should not say such things."

Her brows knitted together. "Why not?"

"It is inappropriate." He knew the words were asinine even as he spoke them.

She gave a long-suffering sigh. "We're rather past that, are we not?" When he did not reply, she pressed on, "Come now, Your Grace, you are not here on your horse, the sky still streaked with night, because you find riding merely agreeable. You are here because you agree that it feels wonderful." He pressed his lips together in a thin line, and she gave a knowing little laugh that sent a shiver of awareness through him. She pulled on her glove, and he watched the movement—transfixed by the precise way she fitted the leather to the delicate web of her fingers. "You may deny it, but I saw it."

He could not resist. "Saw what?"

"Envy." She pointed a long finger at him in a gesture he should have found insolent. "Before you knew it was me on this horse . . . you wanted to *be* me. You wanted to give your horse full rein and ride . . . with passion." With a flick of the reins, she pointed her horse toward the wide expanse of meadow, empty and waiting.

He watched her closely, unable to look away from her, from the way she fairly shimmered with energy and power.

He knew what was coming.

He was ready for it.

"I'll race you to the Serpentine." The words were a soft lilt of Italian, left hanging in the air behind her as she was already moving. Within seconds, she was at a full gallop.

Without thinking, he was after her.

His mount was faster, stronger, but Simon kept the creature in check, watching Juliana. She rode like a master, moving with her horse, leaning low over the mare's neck. He could not hear, but he knew she was talking to the beast, giving her soft words of encouragement, of praise ... gifting her with freedom to run as fast as she wished.

From his position two lengths behind, his eyes traced Juliana's long, straight spine, the full curve of her backside, the way her thighs clenched and released, giving silent, irresistible commands to the horse beneath her.

Desire hit him hard and intense.

He rejected it almost instantly.

It was not her. It was the situation.

And then she looked back over her shoulder, her blue eyes glittering when she confirmed that he had followed her. That he was behind her. She laughed, the sound traveling on the biting wind and the early-morning sunshine, wrapping around him as she returned her attention to the race.

He gave his horse full rein, relinquishing control to the beast.

He passed her in seconds, beginning the wide arc that followed along a densely wooded area of the Park, leading down through the meadow to the curve of the Serpentine Lake. He gave himself up to the movement—to the way that the world tipped and slid away, leaving nothing but man and steed.

She was right.

It felt wonderful.

He looked back, unable to stop himself from looking for her, several lengths behind, and watched as she peeled off, guiding her mount off the path he had chosen, barely slowing down as she disappeared into the wooded thicket beyond.

Where in damnation was she headed?

He hauled up on the reins, his horse lifting off its front legs to follow the command, turning nearly in midair. And then he was after her, charging into the woods seconds behind her.

The morning sun had not reached beyond the trees,

but the lack of light did not stop Simon from riding hard down the dimly lit path that had been barely visible from the meadow. Emotion rose in his throat, part fury, part fear, as the path twisted and turned, teasing him with glimpses of Juliana ahead.

He followed a particularly sharp turn and paused at the top of a long, shadowed straightaway, where she was urging her mount on, toward an enormous felled tree that blocked the path.

With terrifying clarity, he saw her purpose. She was going to jump it.

He called her name in a harsh shout, but she did not slow, did not turn back.

Of course she didn't.

His heart stopped as horse and rider took to the air in perfect form, clearing the barrier with feet to spare. They landed and tore around a corner on the far side of the tree, and Simon swore, vivid and angry, and leaned into his mount, desperate to get to her.

Someone needed to take the girl in hand.

He cleared the tree trunk without concern, wondering how long she would keep him on this chase, each long stride of the horse beneath him making him more and more irate.

Coming around the turn, he pulled up hard on the reins.

There, in the middle of the path, was Juliana's mare, calm and collected.

And riderless.

He leapt down from his horse before the animal had come to a full stop, calling her name once into the still morning air before he saw her, leaning against a tree to one side of the path, hands on her knees as she caught her breath, cheeks red with exertion and cold, eyes bright with excitement and something he did not have the patience to identify.

He stormed toward her. "You reckless female!" he thundered. "You could have killed yourself!"

She did not flinch in the face of his anger; instead, she smiled. "Nonsense. Lucrezia has leapt much higher, much more treacherous obstacles."

He stopped mere feet from her, fists clenched. "I don't care if she's the devil's own steed. You were asking to be hurt."

She uncrossed her arms, spreading them wide. "But I am unharmed."

The words did nothing to settle him. Instead, they made him more irritated. "I can see that."

One side of her mouth tilted up in an expression many would have found endearing. He found it annoying. "I am more than unharmed. I am quite exhilarated. Did I not tell you we had twelve lives?"

"You cannot survive twelve scandals, though, and you are well on your way. Anyone could have found you." He could hear the peevishness in his tone. He hated himself for it.

She laughed, the sound bright in the shadowed grove. "It's been two minutes."

"If I hadn't followed you, you might have been set upon by thieves."

"This early?"

"It might be late for them."

She shook her head slowly, taking a step toward him. "But you did follow me."

"But you did not *know* I would." He did not know why it mattered. But it did.

She stepped closer, cautiously, as though he were a wild animal.

He felt like an animal. Out of control.

Simon took a deep breath and was inundated with her scent.

"Of course you were going to follow me."

"Why would you think that?"

She lifted one shoulder in an elegant shrug. "Because you wanted to."

She was close enough to touch, and his fingers flexed at his side, itching to reach for her, to pull her to him and prove her right. "You're wrong. I followed you to keep you from getting into more trouble." She was looking up at him with her bright eyes and her full lips, curved in a small smile that promised endless secrets. "I followed you because your impulsiveness is a danger to yourself and others."

"You are sure?"

The entire conversation was getting away from him. "Of course I am," he said, casting about for proof. "I haven't time for your little games, Miss Fiori. I'm to meet with Lady Penelope's father today."

Her gaze flickered away for the briefest of instants before returning to his. "You'd best be off, then. You would not want to miss such an important appointment."

He read the dare in her eyes.

Go.

He wanted to.

He was going to.

One strand of long black hair had come loose from her cap, and he reached for it instinctively. He should have pushed it back from her face—should not have touched it to begin with—but once he had it in his grasp, he could not stop himself from wrapping it once, twice around his fist, watching it cut a swath across the soft leather of his riding glove, wishing he could feel the silken strand against his skin.

Her breath quickened, and his gaze fell to the rise and fall of her chest beneath her coat. The men's clothing should have renewed his fury, but instead it sent a powerful rush of desire through him. A mere handful of buttons kept her from him—buttons that could easily be dispatched, leaving her in nothing but the linen of her shirt, which could be freed from breeches, providing access to soft female skin beyond.

His gaze returned to hers, and that's when he saw it. Gone were the bold challenge and the smug satisfaction, replaced with something raw and powerful, immediately identifiable.

Desire.

Suddenly, he saw how he could regain control of the moment. Of himself.

"I think you wanted me to follow you."

"I—" Her voice caught, and she stopped. He felt the heady triumph of a hunter who had spied his first prey. "I did not care."

"Liar." The word was whispered, low and dark in the heavy morning air. He tugged on the lock of hair, pulling her toward him, until mere inches separated them.

Her mouth opened on a quick intake of breath, stealing his attention.

And when he saw those wide lush lips barely parted, begging for him, he did not resist. He did not even try.

She tasted like spring.

The thought exploded through him as he settled his lips on hers, lifting his hands to cup her cheeks, tilting her toward him, affording him better access to her. He could have sworn she gasped his name . . . the sound soft and breathy and intoxicating as hell. He pulled her more tightly against him, pressing her to him. She came willingly, moving against him as though she knew what he wanted before he did.

And perhaps she did.

He ran his tongue along her full, bottom lip, and when she gasped at the sensation, he did not wait, taking her mouth again, stroking deep, thinking of nothing but her. And then she was kissing him back, matching his movements, and he was lost in the feel of her—her hands moving with torturous slowness along his arms until they finally, finally reached his neck, her fingers threading into his hair, the softness of her lips, and the maddening, magnificent little sounds she made at the back of her throat as he claimed her.

And it was a claiming—primitive and wicked.

She pressed closer to him, the swell of her breasts pressing high on his chest, and pleasure flared. He deepened the kiss, running his hands down her back to pull her against him where he wanted her most. The breeches afforded her a freedom of movement that no skirts ever could have, and he palmed one long lovely thigh, hitching her leg up until she cradled the throbbing length of him at her warm core.

He broke the kiss on a soft groan as she rocked against him in a rhythm that set him aflame. "You are a sorceress." In that moment, he was an innocent lad chasing after his first bit of skirt, desire and excitement and something far more base colliding deep within in a tumult of sensation.

He wanted her laid bare right here, on the dirt path at the center of Hyde Park, and he did not care who saw them.

He took the soft lobe of her ear between his teeth, worrying the flesh there until she called out high and clear, "Simon!"

The sound of his given name punctuating the quiet dawn brought him back to reality. He pulled back, dropping her leg as though it burned. He stepped away, breathing heavily, watching as confusion chased desire from her countenance.

She stumbled at the instant loss of him, unable to bear her own weight with so little warning. He reached out to catch her, to steady her.

The moment she regained her footing, she pulled her

arm from his and took a long step backward. Her gaze shuttered, the emotion there cooling, and he wanted to kiss her again, to bring the desire back.

She turned away from him before he could act on the desire, heading for her mount, still at the center of the pathway. He watched, unmoving, as she lifted herself up into the saddle with practiced ease. She looked down at him from above with all the grace of a queen.

He should apologize.

He had mauled her in the middle of Hyde Park. If someone had come upon them—

She stopped the thought with her words. "It seems you are not so immune to passion as you think, Your Grace."

And with a cool flick of her wrist she was off like a shot, her horse thundering up the path from which they had come.

He watched as she disappeared, listening for the break in the hoofbeats as she took the felled tree once more . . .

Hoping the fleeting silence would drown out the echo of his title on her lips.

Chapter Five

One never knows where ruffians might lurk.
Elegant ladies do not leave the house alone.

—*A Treatise on the Most Exquisite of Ladies*

Remarkable, is it not, the decisions that can be made
over a still-smoking rifle?

—*The Scandal Sheet, October 1823*

The Marquess of Needham and Dolby took careful
aim at a red grouse and pulled the trigger on his
rifle. The report sounded loud and angry in the afternoon air.

"Damn. Missed it."

Simon refrained from pointing out that the marquess had missed all five of the creatures at which he'd
aimed since suggesting that they converse outside,
"like men."

The portly aristocrat took aim and fired once more, the
sound sending a shiver of irritation through Simon. No
one hunted in the afternoon. Certainly no one who was

such a poor shot should be so interested in hunting in the afternoon.

"Blast it!"

Another miss. Simon had begun to fear for his own well-being. If the older man wanted to shoot up the gardens of his massive estate on the banks of the Thames, far be it from Simon to dissuade him of the activity, but he could not help but regret his proximity to such ineptitude.

Apparently, even the marquess had his limits. With a muttered curse, he passed the rifle off to a nearby footman and, hands clasped stoutly behind his back, started down a long, winding path away from the house. "All right, Leighton, we might as well get down to it. You want to marry my eldest."

Bad shot or no, the marquess was no fool.

"I believe that such a match would benefit both our families," he said, matching the older man's stride.

"No doubt, no doubt." They walked in silence for several moments before the marquess continued, "Penelope will make a fine duchess. She's not horse-faced, and she knows her place. Won't make unreasonable demands."

They were the words that Simon wanted to hear. They underscored his selection of the lady for the role of his future wife.

So why did they so unsettle him?

The marquess continued. "A fine, sensible girl—ready to do her duty. Good English stock. Shouldn't have any trouble breeding. Doesn't have any illusions about marriage or the other fanciful things some girls think they deserve."

Like passion.

A vision flashed, unheeded, unwelcome—Juliana Fiori, smirking around her words. *Not even a frigid duke can live without heat.*

Nonsense.

He stood by his statement from the night before—passion had no place in a good English marriage. And it seemed that Lady Penelope would agree.

Which made her the ideal candidate for his wife to be.

She was entirely suitable.

Precisely what he needed.

We all need passion.

The words were a whisper at the back of his mind, the mocking tone, lilting with an Italian accent.

He gritted his teeth. She had no idea what he needed.

With a curt nod, Simon said, "I am happy to hear that you approve a match."

"Of course I do. It's a fine marriage. Two superior British lines of aristocracy. Equals in reputation and in stock," the marquess said, removing the glove from his right hand and extending it to Simon.

As Simon shook the hand of his future father-in-law, he wondered if the marquess would feel differently once the secrets of Leighton House were aired.

The Leighton stock would not carry such a pristine reputation, then.

Simon only hoped that the marriage would lend enough weight for them all to survive the scandal.

They turned back toward Dolby House, and Simon released a long, slow breath.

One step closer. All he had to do was propose to the lady, and he would be as prepared as he could be.

The marquess cut him a glance. "Penelope is at home—you are welcome to speak with her now."

Simon understood the meaning behind the words. The marquess wanted the match announced and completed. It was not every day that a duke went looking for a wife.

He considered the possibility. There was, after all, no reason to postpone the inevitable.

Two weeks.

He'd given her two weeks.

It had been a ridiculous thing for him to do—he could use those weeks—could have been planning a wedding during their course. Could have been married before the end of them if he'd insisted upon it.

And instead, he'd offered them up to Juliana's silly game.

As though he had time for her games and reckless behavior and improper attire and—

Irresistible embraces.

No. This morning had been a mistake. One that would not be repeated.

No matter how much it wanted repeating.

He shook his head.

"You disagree?"

The marquess's words pulled Simon from his reverie. He cleared his throat. "I should like to court her properly, if you'll allow it."

"No need for it, you know. It's not as if it's a love match." Vastly entertained by the idea, the marquess laughed big and brash from the depths of his overhanging midsection. Simon did his best to keep his irritation from showing. When the laughter died down, his future father-in-law said, "I'm just saying that everyone knows you're not one for silly emotions. Penelope won't expect courting."

Simon tilted his head. "Nevertheless."

"It makes no difference to me how you do it, Leighton," said the older man, running his wide hands over his wider girth. "My only advice is that you begin as you mean to go on with her. Wives are much easier to manage if they know what to expect from a marriage."

The Marchioness of Needham and Dolby was a lucky woman indeed, Simon thought wryly. "I shall take that under advisement."

The marquess nodded once. "Shall we have a brandy? Drink to an excellent match?"

There was little Simon wanted to do less than spend more time with his future father-in-law. But he knew better than to dismiss the request. He could no longer afford to live above this particular fray.

He would never be able to again.

After a pause, he said, "I would enjoy that very much."

Two hours later, Simon was back at his town house, in his favorite chair, hound at his feet, feeling far less triumphant than he would have expected to be. The meeting could not have gone better. He was to be aligned with a family of high regard and impeccable reputation. He had not seen Lady Penelope—had not wanted to see her, frankly—but all was well, and he imagined it was only a matter of securing the lady's agreement before they were officially affianced.

"I assume that the outcome of your visit was satisfactory."

He stiffened at the words, turning to meet his mother's cold gray eyes. He had not heard her enter. He rose to his feet. "It was."

She did not move. "The marquess has given his consent."

He moved to the sideboard. "He has."

"It is early for drink, Leighton."

He turned back, a tumbler of scotch in his hand. "Consider it celebratory."

She did not speak, nor did her gaze leave him. He wondered what she was thinking. Not that he had ever understood what lurked beneath the icy exterior of this woman who had given him life.

"Soon, you will be a mother-in-law," he paused. "And a dowager."

She did not rise to his bait. She never had.

Instead, she gave a single curt nod, as though everything were settled. As though everything were *simple.* "When do you plan on procuring a special license?"

Two weeks.

He closed his eyes against the thought, taking a drink to cover his hesitation. "Don't you think that I should speak to Lady Penelope first?"

The duchess sniffed once, as though the question insulted several of her senses. "It's not as though dukes of marriageable age are a common occurrence, Leighton. She's about to make the best match in years. Just get it done."

And there it was, in the cool, unmoving tenor of his mother's words. *Get it done.* The demand . . . the expectation that a man like Simon would do whatever it took to ensure the safety and honor of his name.

He returned to his chair and deliberately relaxed into it—a feat of strength considering his frustration—taking a minuscule amount of pleasure in his mother's stiffening at his outward calm. "I needn't behave like an animal, Mother. I shall court the girl. She deserves some emotion, don't you think?"

She did not move, her cool gaze showing nothing of her thoughts, and Simon realized that he'd never once been the recipient of his mother's praise. He wondered, fleetingly, if she had the capacity for praise. Likely not. There was little need for emotion in the aristocracy. Lesser still where their offspring were concerned.

Emotion was for the masses.

He'd never seen her in a state of feeling. Never happy, never sad, never angry, never entertained. He'd once heard her say that amusements were for those with less pedigree than theirs. When Georgiana had been a child, all laughter and good nature, and the duchess had barely been able to suffer her. "Try not to sound so common, child," she would say, lip just barely curled in the closest approximation to distaste he'd ever seen her display. "Your sire is the Duke of Leighton."

Georgiana would grow serious then, a sliver of her exuberance gone forever.

He stiffened at the memory, long buried. No wonder his sister had fled when she'd discovered her situation. Their mother showed no sign of maternal love on the best of days.

He had not been much better.

"You are the sister to the Duke of Leighton!"

"Simon . . . it was a mistake."

He'd barely registered her whisper. "Pearsons do not make mistakes!"

And he had left her there, in the backwoods of Yorkshire.

Alone.

When he had told their mother about the scandal that loomed, she had not moved; her breathing had not changed. Instead, she'd watched him with those cool, all-knowing eyes, and said, "You must marry."

And they had never spoken of Georgiana again.

Regret flashed.

He ignored it.

"Sooner than later, Leighton," the duchess said. "Before."

Someone with less understanding of the duchess would think she had failed to complete the thought. Simon knew better. His mother did not use extraneous words. And he understood perfectly what she meant.

She did not wait for his response, knowing intuitively that her demand would be heeded. Instead, she turned on her heel and left the room, its contents gone from her mind before the door to the library closed behind her.

Trusting that Leighton would do what was needed to be done.

Before.

Before their secrets were discovered.

Before their name was dragged through the mud.

Before their reputation was ruined.

If he'd been told four months ago that he would be rushing toward marriage to shore up the reputation of the family, he would have laughed, long and imperious, and sent the informant packing.

Of course, four months ago, things had been different.

Four months ago, Simon had been the most sought after bachelor in Britain, with no expectations of a change in that stature.

Four months ago, nothing could have touched him.

He swore, low and dark, and rested his head back against his chair as the door to the library opened once more. He kept his eyes closed.

He did not want to face her again. Not her; not what she represented.

There was a delicate throat-clearing. "Your Grace?"

Simon straightened instantly. "Yes, Boggs?"

The butler crossed the room, extending the silver platter in his hand toward Simon. "I apologize for the intrusion. But an urgent message has arrived for you."

Simon reached for the heavy ecru envelope. Turned it in his hand. Saw Ralston's seal.

A ripple of tension shot through him.

There was only one reason for Ralston to send him an urgent note.

Georgiana.

Perhaps there was no more time for before.

"Leave me."

He waited for Boggs to exit the room, until he heard the soft, ominous sound of door against jamb.

Only then did he slide one long finger beneath the seal, feeling the thick weight of the moment deep in his gut. He removed the single sheet of paper, unfolded it with resignation.

Read the two lines of text there.

And released the breath he had not known he had been holding in a short, angry burst, crushing the single page in his wicked grip.

The Serpentine at five o'clock.
I shall dress properly this time.

"Exspecto, Exspectas, Exspectat . . ."

She whispered the Latin words as she skipped stones across the surface of the Serpentine Lake, trying to ignore the sun, sinking toward the horizon.

She should not have sent the note.

"Exspectamus, Exspectatis, Exspectant . . ."

It was well past five. If he had planned to come, he would have already come.

Her companion and maid, Carla, made an indelicate sound of discomfort from her position on a wool blanket several feet away.

"I wait, you wait, she waits . . ."

If he took it to Ralston . . . she'd never be able to leave the house again. Not without a battalion of servants and chaperones and, very likely, Ralston himself.

"We wait, you wait, they wait."

She tossed another stone and missed her target, wincing at the hollow sound the pebble made as it sank to the bottom of the lake.

"He is not coming."

She turned at the Italian words, flat and full of truth, and met Carla's deep brown gaze. The other woman was clutching a woolen shawl to her chest, bracing herself against the autumn wind. "You only say that because you want to return to the house."

Carla lifted one shoulder and pulled a disinterested frown. "It does not make the words any less true."

Juliana scowled. "You are not required to stay."

"I am required to do just that, actually." She sat down beneath a stout tree. "And I would not mind it if this country weren't so unbearably cold. No wonder your duke is in such dire need of thaw."

As if to punctuate the words, the wind picked up again, threatening to take the bonnet from Juliana's head. She held it down, wincing as its ribbons and lace adornments lashed at her face. It was a wonder that a piece of headwear could be so troublesome and so useless all at once.

The wind lessened, and Juliana felt safe releasing the hat.

"He is not my duke."

"Oh? Then why are we standing here in the frigid wind, waiting for him?"

Juliana's gaze narrowed on the young woman. "You know, I'm told English lady's maids are far more biddable. I'm considering making a switch."

"I recommend it. I can then return to civilization. *Warm* civilization."

Juliana leaned down and picked up another stone. "Ten more minutes."

Carla sighed, long and dramatic, and Juliana felt a smile tug at her lips. As contrary and immovable as she was, Juliana was comforted by her presence. She was a piece of home in this strange new world.

This bizarre world that was filled with brothers and sisters and rules and regulations and balls and bonnets and incredible, infuriating men.

Men to whom one did not send flirtatious, inviting notes in the middle of the day, on one's brother's stationery.

She closed her eyes as a wave of embarrassment coursed through her.

It had been the worst kind of idea, the kind that arrived on a wave of triumph so acute that it turned every thought into a stroke of brilliance. She'd returned to her bedchamber that morning before the rest of Ralston House had risen, drunk on excitement and power from her encounter with Leighton, thrilled that she had shaken that enormous, immovable man to his core.

He'd kissed her.

And it had been nothing like the meek, simpering kisses of the boys she'd known in Italy, stolen as they teasingly lifted her from her father's merchant ship onto the cobblestone wharf. No . . . this kiss had been the kiss of a man.

The kiss of a man who knew what he wanted.

A man who had never had to ask for what he wanted.

He had tasted just as he had done all those months ago, of strength and power and something both unbearable and irresistible.

Passion.

She'd dared him to discover the emotion but had been unprepared to discover it herself.

It had taken all her energy to mount her horse and leave him there, alone, in the early-morning light.

She had wanted more.

Just as she always did where he was concerned.

And when she returned home, heady with the success of their first interaction and full with the knowledge that she had shaken him to his core, just as she'd promised, she had not been able to resist flaunting her success. Before Ralston had risen, she had crept into his study and written a message for Leighton, more dare than invitation.

A harsh gust of wind blew through the meadow, sending white-edged ripples across the surface of the lake. Carla protested colorfully as Juliana turned her back to the blunt force of the wind, clutching her cloak tightly together.

She should not have sent the note.

She skipped a stone across the water.

It had been a terrible idea.

And another.

What had made her think he would come? He was no fool.

And another.

Why didn't he come?

"Enough, *idiota*. He doesn't come because he has a brain in his head. Unlike you." She muttered the words aloud to the lake.

She'd had enough of waiting for him. It was freezing and the light was waning and she was going home. Immediately.

Tomorrow, she would consider her next course of action—she was by no means giving up. And she had one week and five days to do everything she could to bring the arrogant man down.

The fact that he'd ignored her summons would only serve to urge her on.

Her commitment renewed, Juliana turned and made her way toward the tree where her companion sat. "*Andiamo.* Let's go home."

"Ah, *finalmente*," said the maid in a happy little burst as she leapt to her feet. "I thought you would never give up."

Give up.

The words rankled. She was not giving up. She was simply ensuring that she had all her fingers and toes for the next battle.

As though the elements had sensed her conviction, the wind blew again, harsh and angry, and Juliana reached to secure her bonnet just as the silly thing flew off her head. With a little squeak, she turned to watch it fly toward the lake, tumbling across the water like one of the stones that Juliana had skipped earlier. It landed, unbelievably, on the far end of a wide fallen log, the long ribbons floating in the dark cold lake, taunting her.

Carla snickered, and Juliana turned to meet the maid's twinkling brown eyes. "You are lucky I do not send you to fetch it."

One of Carla's dark eyebrows raised. "I am amused at the suggestion that I would do such a thing."

Juliana ignored the impertinent remark and returned her attention to the bonnet, taunting her from its resting place. She would not allow a piece of millinery to get the better of her. *Something* would go right this afternoon.

Even if she had to march into the middle of the Serpentine Lake to make it so.

Removing her cloak, Juliana headed for the log, stepping up and throwing her arms wide for balance to make her way to the ill-behaved headwear mocking her from several yards away.

"*State attenta,*" Carla called out, and Juliana ignored the urging for care, singularly focused on the bonnet. The wind began to pick up, teasing at the blue frills on the hat, and Juliana stilled, waiting to see if the hat would blow away.

The wind slowed.

The hat remained.

Well. As her sister-in-law, Isabel, would say, now it was the principle of the thing.

Juliana continued her journey before the hat was sacrificed to the gods of the Serpentine.

Just a few more feet.

And then she'd have the bonnet in hand and she could go home.

Nearly there.

She crouched slowly, shifting her balance and reaching out. The tips of her fingers touched a curl of blue satin.

And then the hat was gone, blown off the log, and in a moment of frustration Juliana forgot her precarious position and lunged.

The waters of the Serpentine were as cold as they appeared. Colder.

And deeper.

She came up sputtering and swearing like a Veronese dockworker to Carla's raucous laughter. Instinctively, she rolled her body to face shore, only to find her skirts entangled in her legs, pulling her under.

Confusion flared and she kicked out, breaking the surface again briefly, gasping for air and not entirely understanding what was happening.

Something was wrong.

She was an expert swimmer, why couldn't she stay afloat?

She kicked once more, her legs caught in a mass of muslin and twill, and she realized that the heavy skirts were weighing her down. She could not reach the surface.

Panic flared.

She extended her arms again, kicking wildly in one last desperate attempt at air.

To no avail.

Her lungs were on fire, straining under the burden of holding in the last of her precious air . . . air she knew she was about to—

She exhaled, the sound of the air bubbles rising to the surface of the lake punctuating her fate.

I am going to drown.

The words drifted through her mind, eerily calm.

And then something strong and warm grasped one of her outstretched hands, jerking her up . . . until she could—

Thank God.

She could breathe.

Juliana took a great, gasping breath, coughing and sputtering and heaving, focusing on nothing but breathing as she was pulled from the deeper water until her feet touched firm, blessed ground.

Not that her legs could hold her upright.

She collapsed into her savior, wrapping her arms around a warm, sturdy neck—a rock in a sea of uncertainty.

It took a few moments for her to come back to place and time—to hear Carla keening like a Sicilian grandmother from the lakeshore, to feel the cold bite of wind on her face and shoulders, to register the movement of her rescuer as he held her, chest deep in the water, as she trembled—either from the cold or the fear or both.

His hands stroked along her back, and he whispered soft, calm words into her hairline. In Italian.

"Just breathe . . . I've got you . . . You are safe now . . . Everything is all right." And somehow, the words convinced her. He *did* have her. She *was* safe. Everything *would* be all right.

She felt his chest rise and fall against her as he took a deep, calming breath. "You're safe," he repeated. "You little fool . . ." he whispered, the tone just as soothing as ever, ". . . I have you now." His hands stroked rhythmically down her arms and up her spine. "What in hell were you doing in the lake? What if I hadn't been here? Shh . . . I've got you now. *Sei al sicura.* You're safe."

It took her a moment to recognize the tenor, and when she did, she snapped her attention to him, looking at him with clear eyes for the first time.

Her breath caught in her throat.

Simon.

Disheveled and soaked to the skin, his blond hair turned dark with the water that dripped down his face, he looked the opposite of the poised, perfect duke she had come to expect him to be. He looked sodden and unkempt and winded . . .

And wonderful.

She said the first thing that came to her mind. "You came."

And he'd saved her.

"Just in time, it seems," he replied in Italian, understanding that she was not ready for English.

A fit of coughing overtook her, and she could do nothing but hold on to him for several minutes. When she was once more able to breathe, she met his steady gaze, his eyes the color of fine brandy.

He'd saved her.

A shiver rippled through her at the thought, and the tremor spurred him to action. "You are cold."

He lifted her into his arms and carried her out of the water to the lake's edge, where Carla was near hysteria.

The maid released a torrent of Italian. *"Madonna!* I thought you were gone! Drowned! I screamed and screamed! I was desperate for help!" To Simon, still in Italian, "I curse the fact I cannot swim! If only I could return to my youth and learn!" Then back to Juliana, clutching her to her chest. *"Mi Julianina!* Had I known . . . I would never have let you out onto that log! Why, the thing is obviously the devil's own oak left behind!" Then, back to Simon, "Oh! Thank the heavens that you were here!" The flow of words stopped abruptly. *"Late."*

If Juliana had not been so cold, she would have laughed at the disdain that coated the last of the maid's words. True, he had been late. But he had come. And if he hadn't—

But he had.

She stole a glance at him. He had not missed Carla's insinuation that if he had arrived on time, all of this might have been avoided. He stilled, his face firm and unmoving, like that of a Roman statue.

His clothes were plastered to him—he had not removed his coat before entering the lake, and the layers he wore seemed to blend together. Somehow, the sodden clothing made him seem larger, more dangerous, immovable. She watched a droplet of water slither down his forehead, and itched to brush it away.

To kiss it away.

She ignored the thought, certain that it was the product of her close encounter with death and nothing else, and redirected her gaze to his mouth, set in a firm, straight line.

And she instantly wanted to kiss that instead.

A muscle twitched at the corner of his lips, the only sign of his irritation.

More than irritation.

Anger.

Possibly fury.

Juliana shivered and told herself it was from the wind and the water and not the man who towered over her. She wrapped her arms about herself to ward off the cold and thanked Carla softly when the maid rushed to collect the cloak she had cast off prior to her adventure and place it over her shoulders. The garment did nothing to combat the cold air or the cold look with which Leighton had fixed her, and she shivered again, huddling into the thin twill.

Of all the men in all of London, why did *he* have to be the one to save her?

Turning her attention to a nearby rise, she saw a handful of people clustered together, watching. She could not make out their faces, but she was certain that they knew precisely who she was.

The story would be all over London by tomorrow.

She was flooded with emotion . . . exhaustion and fear

and gratitude and embarrassment and something more base that twisted inside her and made her feel like she might be sick all over his once-perfect, now-destroyed boots.

All she wanted was to be alone.

Willing her shivering to subside, she met his gaze once more, and said, "Th-thank you, Your G-grace." She was rather impressed that this close to having died by drowning, she was able to achieve cool politeness. In English no less. She stood with the help of Carla, and said the words that she desperately wanted not to say. "I am in your debt."

She turned on one heel and, thinking only of a warm bath and warmer bed, set off for the entrance to the Park.

His words, spoken in perfect Italian, stopped her in her tracks.

"Do not thank me yet. I've never in my life been so livid."

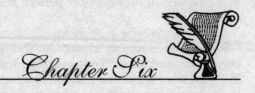

Chapter Six

Water is for boiling and cleansing—never for amusement.
Refined ladies take care not to splash in their bath.

—*A Treatise on the Most Exquisite of Ladies*

We're told of exciting discoveries in our very own
Serpentine . . .

—*The Scandal Sheet, October 1823*

$\mathcal{S}$imon ignored the thickness in his tone, the anger
that he could barely contain.

The girl had nearly killed herself, and she thought this
was *over*?

She was very likely cold and exhausted and in some
kind of shock, but she was more addlepated than he
imagined if she thought he would allow her to trot home
without a single explanation for her unreasonable, irrational, life-threatening behavior. He saw the combination of fear and desperation in her gaze. *Good.* Perhaps
she would think twice before repeating today's actions.

"You are not going to tell Ralston, are you?"

"Of course I am going to tell Ralston."

She took a step toward him, switching to English. She was skilled at pleading in her second language. "But why? It shall only upset him. Needlessly."

Disbelief took his breath. "*Needlessly?* On the contrary, Miss Fiori. Your brother most definitely *needs* to know that you require a chaperone who will prevent you from behaving with reckless abandon."

She threw up her hands. "I was not behaving recklessly!"

She was mad. "Oh, no? How would you describe it?"

Silence fell, and Juliana considered the question. She nibbled the corner of her lower lip as she thought and, against his will, he was drawn to the movement. He watched the way her lips pursed, the crisp white edge of her teeth as she worried the soft pink flesh. Desire slammed through him hard and fast, and he stiffened at the blinding emotion. He did not want her. She was a madwoman.

A stunning, goddess of a madwoman.

He cleared his throat.

Nevertheless.

"It was entirely reasonable behavior."

He blinked. "You climbed out onto a tree trunk," he paused, irritation flaring again with the words.

She was unable to keep her gaze from the tree trunk in question. "It seemed perfectly sturdy."

"You fell into a *lake*." He heard the fury in his voice.

"I didn't expect it to be so deep!"

"No, I don't imagine you did."

She clung to her defense. "I mean, it did not seem to be like any lake I've ever encountered."

"That's because it's not like any lake you've ever encountered."

She looked back at him. "It's not?"

"No." He said, barely able to contain his irritation. "It isn't a real lake. It is man-made."

Her eyes widened. "Why?"

Did it matter?

"As I was not alive for the event, I could not hazard a guess."

"Leave it to the *English* to fabricate a lake," she tossed over her shoulder to Carla, who snickered.

"And leave it to the *Italians* to fall into it!"

"I was retrieving my hat!"

"Ah . . . that makes it all much more logical. Do you even know how to swim?"

"Do I know how to *swim*?" she asked, and he took more than a little pleasure in her offense. "I was raised on the banks of the Adige! Which happens to be a *real* river."

"Impressive," he said, not at all impressed. "And tell me, did you ever *swim* in said river?"

"Of course! But I wasn't wearing"—she waved a hand to indicate her dress—"sixteen layers of fabric!"

"Why not?"

"Because you don't *swim* in sixteen layers of fabric!"

"No?"

"No!"

"Why not?" *He had her now.*

"Because you will drown!"

"Ah," he said, rocking back on his heels. "Well, at least we've learned something today."

Her eyes narrowed, and he had the distinct impression that she wanted to kick him. *Good.* Knowing that she was furious made him feel slightly more stable.

Dear God. She'd nearly drowned.

He'd never been so terrified in all his life as when he'd come over the ridge—berating himself for allowing this fiery, emotional Italian to direct his afternoon, knowing that he should be at home, living his orderly life—and seen the horrifying tableau below: the maid, shrieking for help; the unmistakable ripples on the surface of the lake; and the billows of sapphire fabric marking the spot where Juliana was sinking.

He'd been certain that he was too late.

"I told you." Her words stopped the direction of his thoughts. "I had every good reason to go out there. If not for the wind and these heavy clothes, I would have been just fine."

As if to underscore her point, the wind picked up then, and her teeth began to chatter. She wrapped her arms around herself and suddenly she looked so . . . *small*. And fragile. The utter opposite of how he thought of her, bright and bold and indestructible. And in that moment, his anger was thoroughly overpowered by a basic, primal urge to wrap himself around her and hold her until she was warm again.

Which of course, he could not do.

They had an audience—and the chatter would be loud enough without his adding fuel to its fire.

He cursed softly, and the sound was lost on the wind as he moved toward her, unable to stop himself from closing the gap between them. He turned her to ensure that he caught the full force of the gale—protecting her from the cold gust.

If only he could protect himself from her.

When he spoke, he knew the words were too rough. Knew they would sting. "Why must you constantly test me?"

"I do care, you know. I do care what you think."

"Then why?"

"Because you expect me to fail. You expect me to do wrong. To be reckless. To ruin myself."

"Why not work to prove me wrong?"

"But don't you see? I *am* proving you wrong. If I *choose* recklessness, where is the failure? If I choose it for myself, you cannot force it upon me."

There was a long pause. "Perversely, that makes sense."

She smiled, small and sad. "If only I actually wanted it this way."

The words settled, and a hundred questions ran through his mind before she shivered in his arms. "You're freezing."

She looked up at him, and he caught his breath at her brilliant blue eyes. "H-how are you n-not?"

He was not even close to cold. He was on fire. Her clothes were soaking wet and ruined, her hair had come loose from its fastenings, and she should have looked like a bedraggled child. Instead, she looked stunning. The clothes molded to her shape, revealing her lush curves, the water only emphasizing her stunning features—high cheekbones, long, spiked lashes framing enormous blue eyes, porcelain skin. He tracked one drop of water down the curve of her neck to the hollow of her collarbone, and he had an intense desire to taste the droplet on his tongue.

She was alive.

And he wanted her.

Thankfully, she shivered again before he could act on the unacceptable desire.

He had to get her home before she caught pneumonia.

Or before he went entirely mad.

He turned to her maid. "Did you come by carriage?" he asked in quick Italian.

"No, Your Grace."

"It will be faster if I take your mistress home in my curricle. Meet us at Ralston House." He clasped Juliana's elbow and began to steer her toward a nearby rise.

"You j-just assume that she will follow your orders?" Juliana asked, her tone suggesting the very idea was ridiculous. He ignored her, instead meeting the maid's gaze.

"Yes, Your Grace." She dropped into a quick curtsy and hurried away.

He returned his attention to Juliana, who scowled.

Her irritation returned some of his sense. And some of his anger. Last night and this morning, her impulsive behavior had risked her reputation. This afternoon, it had risked her life.

And he would not have it.

They walked several yards in silence before he spoke, "You could have died."

She gave the briefest of hesitations, and he thought perhaps she would apologize again. *It would not be entirely unwarranted.*

He sensed the tensing of her shoulders, the straightening of her spine. "But I did not." She tried for a smirk. Failed. "Twelve lives, remember?"

The words were rife with defiance—of him, of nature, of fate itself. And if they had not made him so irate, he might have found room to admire her tenacity of spirit.

Instead, he wanted to shake her.

He resisted the impulse. Barely.

They reached his curricle, and he lifted her, shivering, into the vehicle, then climbed in beside her.

"I shall ruin your seat."

Her words, so ridiculous in light of everything that had happened in the past few minutes, set him off. He paused in the act of lifting the reins and turned an incredulous gaze toward her. "It is a wonder that you are able to find concern for my upholstery when you seem to care so little for things of much more import."

Her dark brows arched perfectly. "Such as?"

"Such as your person."

She sneezed, and he cursed, "And now you're going to fall ill if you don't keep warm, you daft female."

He reached behind them for a traveling rug, and thrust it at her.

She took it and covered herself. "Thank you," she said firmly, before looking away and staring straight ahead.

He set the curricle in motion after a long moment, wishing he'd been less forceful. More courteous.

He did not feel at all courteous. Did not think he could muster courtesy.

They exited Hyde Park before she spoke, and he barely heard her over the sound of hoofbeats against the cobblestones. "You needn't speak to me as though I am half-witty."

He could not resist. "I believe you mean half-*witted*."

She turned away, and he heard an irritated Italian curse over the wind. After a long moment, she said, "I did not *plan* to drown myself."

There was sulking in her tone, and he felt a slight twinge of sympathy for her. Perhaps he should not be so hard on her. But, damned if he could stop. "Plan or no, if I hadn't come along, you would have drowned."

"You came," she said simply, and he recalled that as she had coughed up water and trembled with relief in the moments after he'd rescued her, she'd whispered the same words. *You came.*

He'd tried not to.

He'd thrown away her reckless note—the cleverly disguised missive that had fooled everyone into thinking that the Marquess of Ralston had sent the correspondence—tossed it into a wastepaper basket in his study.

He'd pretended it wasn't there as he read the rest of his correspondence.

And still as he discussed a handful of outstanding issues with his man of business.

And even as he had opened the package that arrived from his mother less than an hour after she had left him—the package that had contained the Leighton sapphire, the betrothal ring that had been worn by generations of Duchesses of Leighton.

Even then, as he'd placed the ring on his desk, in full view, that crumpled piece of paper taunted him, spreading Juliana throughout his orderly, disciplined house. Everywhere he looked, he saw her missive, and he'd wondered what she would do if he did not respond.

He'd imagined that she would not think twice about assuming a more scandalous course of action—and then her bold, black scrawl had been replaced with her bold, black curls and her flashing blue eyes. And they'd been in his bedchamber . . .

He had called for his curricle and driven entirely too fast for a man who was determined to avoid her.

And he'd almost been too late.

His hands tightened on the reins, and the horses shifted uneasily under the tension. He forced himself to relax.

"And aren't you lucky that I came? I nearly didn't. Sending me such a message was both immodest and infantile." He did not give her an opportunity to reply, his next words exploding on a wave of irritation. "What would possess you to dive into a frigid lake?"

"I didn't *dive*," she pointed out. "I fell. It was a mistake. Although I suppose you never make those."

"Not life-threatening ones, usually, no."

"Well. We cannot all be as perfect as you are."

She was changing the topic, and he was in no mood to allow it. "You did not answer my question."

"Was there an inquiry hidden in all of that judgment? I did not notice."

He found himself comforted by the fire in her. He cut her a glance. "The lake. Why were you in there in the first place?"

"I told you. I followed my hat."

"Your hat."

"I like the hat. I did not want to lose it."

"Your brother would have bought you a new hat. I would have bought you a *dozen* if it would have kept me from having to . . ."

He stopped.

From having to watch you nearly die.

"I wanted that one," she said, quietly. "And I am sorry you had to rescue me . . . or that you shall have to replace this upholstery . . . or buy new boots . . . or whatever other trouble my situation has caused you."

"I didn't say—"

"No, because you are too proper to finish the sentence, but that's what you were *going* to say, isn't it? That you would buy me a dozen bonnets if it would keep you from having to keep me out of trouble? Again?"

She sneezed again.

And the sound nearly did him in.

He nearly stopped the carriage and yanked her to him and gave her the thrashing she deserved for taunting him . . . and then terrifying him.

But he didn't.

Instead, he pulled the carriage to a stop in front of Ralston House with all decorum, despite the anger and frustration roiling within.

"And now we have arrived," she said, peevishly, "and your tiresome position as savior may be passed off to another."

He threw down the reins and descended from the carriage, biting his tongue, refusing to correct her view of the situation—refusing to allow himself to be pulled further into the maelstrom of emotion that this woman seemed to call into being every time she came near.

Last night, she'd labeled him emotionless.

The idea seemed utterly laughable today.

By the time he reached her side of the carriage, she had already helped herself down and was heading toward the door. *Obstinate female.*

He gritted his teeth as she turned back from the top step, looking down at him with all the self-confidence of a queen despite her sodden, bedraggled clothes and her hair, collapsed around her. "I am sorry that I have so *inconvenienced* you on what I can only imagine was a perfectly planned day. I shall do my best to avoid doing so in the future."

She thought him inconvenienced?

He had been many things that afternoon, but *inconvenienced* was not one of them. The tepid word didn't come close to how he felt.

Irate, terrified, and completely unbalanced, yes. But not even close to inconvenienced.

The entire afternoon made him want to hit something. Hard.

And he imagined that the conversation he was about to have with her brother would do little to combat that impulse.

But he would be damned if she would see that.

"See that you do," he said in his most masterful tone as he started up the steps after her, rejecting the impulse to leave her there, summarily, on her doorstep, and get as far from her as he possibly could. He would see her inside. And only then he would get as far from her as he possibly could. "As I told you yesterday, I haven't time for your games."

Simon was there. In the house. With her brother.

He had been for nearly three-quarters of an hour.

And they had not called for her.

Juliana stalked the perimeter of the Ralston House library, the petticoats of her amethyst skirts whipping about her legs.

She couldn't believe that neither of them had even thought that perhaps she would like to be a part of the discussion of her afternoon adventure. With a little huff of displeasure, she headed for the window of the library, which looked out on Park Lane and the blackness of Hyde Park beyond.

Of course they hadn't called for her. They were imperious, infuriating men, two more annoying of whom could not be found in all of Europe.

An enormous carriage sat outside the house, lanterns blazing, waiting for its owner. Leighton's crest was emblazoned on the door to the massive black conveyance, boasting a wicked-looking hawk complete with feather in its talon—spoils of battle, no doubt.

Juliana traced the shield on the glass. How fitting that Leighton was represented by a hawk. A cold, solitary, brilliant animal.

All calculation and no passion.

He had barely cared that she'd nearly died, instead saving her with cool calculation and bringing her home without a moment's pause for what could have been a most tragic occurrence.

That wasn't exactly true.

There had been a moment in the Park during which he'd seemed to be concerned for her welfare.

Just for a moment.

And then he'd simply seemed to want to be rid of her.

And the trouble she caused.

Depositing her unceremoniously in the foyer of Ralston House and leaving her to face her brother alone, he'd said with all calm, "Tell Ralston I shall return this evening. Dry."

He had returned, of course—Leighton was nothing if not true to his word—and she would wager that the two men were laughing at her expense even now in Ralston's study, drinking brandy or scotch or whatever infuriating, aristocratic males drank. She'd like to pour a vat of that liquor over their combined heads.

She looked down at the dress with disgust. She'd chosen it for *him,* knowing she looked lovely in purple. She'd wanted him to see that. Wanted him to notice her.

And not because of their wager.

This time, she had wanted him to regret the things he had said to her.

I haven't time for your games.

It had been a game at the start—the letter, the blatant invitation—but once she'd fallen into the lake, once he'd rescued her, any playfulness had disappeared along with her bonnet, lost to the bottom of the Serpentine.

And when he'd held her in his warm, strong arms and whispered soft words of Italian to her—that had felt more serious than anything she'd ever felt before.

But he'd scolded her, then, all cool and unwavering, as though the whole episode had been a colossal waste of his time and energy.

As though she were nothing but trouble.

And she hadn't felt much like playing games any longer.

Of course, she'd never tell him that. What purpose would it serve except to place a self-satisfied smirk on his face and give him the upper hand—as usual. And she couldn't bear to do that, either.

Instead, she was waiting patiently in the library, resisting the urge to rush down to her brother's study and discover just how much of her reckless behavior Leighton had recounted—and just how much trouble she was in.

Below, the coachman moved, leaping down from his seat, and hurrying to open the carriage door wide for his master. She knew she should turn away from the window, but then Leighton appeared, his golden curls gleaming briefly in the lanternlight before disappearing beneath his hat.

He stopped before the open door and she could not look away; spying was an irresistible temptation. He turned to speak to the coachman, squaring his shoulders against the wind that swirled leaves from the Park about his feet and lashed at his greatcoat. A lesser man would have shown some kind of response to such a violent gust—a wince, a grimace—but not the great Duke of Leighton. Not even nature could distract him from his course.

She watched the movement of his lips as he spoke and wondered what he was saying, where he was going. She leaned forward, her forehead nearly touching the mottled glass pane, as though she might be able to hear him if she were an inch closer.

The coachman nodded once and dipped his head, stepping back to hold the door.

He was leaving.

The duke did not need a step to climb into his great black carriage, he was large and strong enough to manage without one, and she watched as he reached for the handle to pull himself up, wishing that, just once, he would miss his mark, or stumble, or look anything less than he always did—perfect.

He paused, and she held her breath. Perhaps the action was not so easy after all. He turned his head. And looked straight at her.

She gasped and stepped back from the window immediately, hot embarrassment washing through her at having been caught, followed instantly by irritation at having been embarrassed.

It was *he* who should be embarrassed, not her.

It was *he* who had insulted her that afternoon, it was *he* who had come to speak with her brother that evening and not asked to see or speak with her.

She could have taken ill. Did he not care for her well-being?

Apparently not.

She would not let him scare her away. It was her house, after all. She had every right to look *out* the window. It was looking *in* windows that was rude.

And, besides, she had a wager to win.

She took a deep breath and returned to her place.

He was still looking up at her.

When she met his warm, amber gaze, gleaming in the light of the house, he raised one imperious, golden brow, as if to claim victory in their silent battle.

Resistance flared, hot and powerful. *She would not allow him to win.*

She crossed her arms firmly over her chest in a manner utterly improper for a lady and raised a brow of her own, hoping to surprise him, prepared to stand there all night, until he backed down.

It was not surprise she found as she looked down at him, however. Something lightened in the firm, angled lines of his face as he watched her—something vaguely like humor—before he turned and, with perfect precision, lifted himself into his carriage.

She did not waver as the coachman closed the door, hiding the duke from her view. She secretly hoped that he was watching her from behind the darkened windows of the conveyance as she released a long peal of laughter.

Whether he had allowed it or not, she had won.

And it felt wonderful.

"Juliana? May I come in?"

Her laughter was cut short as her sister-in-law entered, her head peeking around the edge before the door opened wide. Juliana spun toward her visitor, dropping her arms and dropping quickly to sit on the wide bench beneath the window. "Of course. I was . . ." She waved one hand in the air. "It is not important. What is it?"

Callie approached, a half smile on her face, to join Juliana. "I came to confirm that you are feeling well, and it sounds as though you are quite recovered from your adventure. I am so very happy that you are safe," she added, taking Juliana's hand. "I never thought I would say it, but thank goodness for the Duke of Leighton."

Juliana did not miss the dryness in her sister-in-law's tone. "You do not like him."

"The duke?" Callie sat next to Juliana, her eyes shuttering. "I do not know him. Not really."

Juliana recognized the evasion. "But . . . ?"

Callie considered her words for a long moment before speaking. "I will say that he—and his mother, for that matter—has always seemed arrogant, imperious, and unmoving in a way that makes him appear uncaring. To my knowledge, he has an interest in only one thing—his reputation. I've never cared for people with such rigid opinions." She paused, then confessed, "No. I did not like him, until today. Now that he has rescued you, I think I shall have to reevaluate my opinion of the duke."

Juliana's heart pounded as she considered her sister-in-law's words.

He has an interest in only one thing—his reputation.

"I think I shall host a dinner party," Silence met the pronouncement, until Callie prodded, "Would you like to know *why* I am hosting a dinner party?"

Juliana was pulled from her thoughts. "Must you have a reason other than this is London, and we have a dining room?"

"You shall pay for that." Callie smiled. "I think we should thank the duke for his rescuing you. And, if we expand the guest list to include a handful of eligible gentlemen—"

Juliana groaned, seeing her sister-in-law's plans. "Oh, Callie, please . . . how embarrassing."

Callie waved one hand. "Nonsense. The story is likely tearing through London as we speak; if we are to mitigate any exaggeration, we must take ownership of the truth. Additionally, I think it important for us to extend a modicum of gratitude for your life, don't you?"

"Must we do so in front of half of London?"

Callie laughed. " 'Half of London,' really, Juliana. No more than a dozen others."

Juliana knew Callie well enough to understand that there was no point in arguing.

"As an added benefit, it will not hurt to have the Duke of Leighton on our side, you know. His friendship can only make you more attractive to other men of the *ton*."

"And if I do not want to attract other men of the *ton*?"

Callie smiled. "Are you saying you want to attract the duke?"

It was a deliberate misunderstanding, Juliana knew. But she felt the wash of color on her cheeks nonetheless. Hoping to escape notice, she gave her sister-in-law a long-suffering look. "No."

Callie took a deep breath. "Juliana, it is not as though we are planning to force you into marriage, but it would not hurt for you to meet a man or two. Whom you like. Company you enjoy."

"You've been attempting this for months. To no avail."

"At some point, you will meet someone to whom you are drawn."

"Perhaps. But he will likely not be drawn to me."

He will likely find me troublesome.

"Of course he will be drawn to you. You're beautiful and entertaining and wonderful. I am inviting Benedick as well."

The Earl of Allendale was Callie's older brother. Juliana allowed her surprise to show. "Why do you say that in such a manner?"

Callie's smile was too bright. "No reason. Don't you like him?"

"I do . . ." Juliana's gaze narrowed. "Callie, please do not play matchmaker. I am not right for men like Benedick. Or any of the others either."

"I am not matchmaking!" The protest was loud. And

false. "I simply thought you would like a familiar face. Or two."

"I suppose that would not be so bad."

Callie turned worried. "Juliana, has someone been rude?"

She shook her head. "No. They're all extraordinarily polite. Very gracious. Impeccably British. But they also make it more than clear that I am not . . . what they seek. In a companion."

"In a *wife*," Callie corrected quickly. "A companion is a different thing altogether."

Companion was likely the precise role that all of London—save her family—was expecting her to assume. They considered her too much of a scandal to be a wife. And Juliana did not like the word, anyway. She shook her head. "Callie, I've said from the beginning . . . from the day I arrived here in England . . . marriage is not for me."

And it was not.

"Nonsense," Callie said, dismissing the idea. "Why would you think such a thing?"

Because the daughter of the Marchioness of Ralston is not exactly the wife of whom every man dreams.

Of course, she could not say that.

She was saved from having to reply by the opening of the library door.

Ralston entered, his eyes finding them on the window seat, and Juliana watched as he drank in his wife, his features softening, his love clear.

She did not deny that it would be wonderful to have such a thing.

She simply did not waste her time wishing for it.

Ralston approached, taking Callie's hand in his, lifting the fingers to his lips for a brief kiss. "I've been looking for you." He turned to Juliana. "Both of you."

Callie looked to Ralston. "Tell your sister she's beautiful."

He looked surprised. "Of course she's beautiful. If only she were a touch taller, she'd be perfect."

She laughed at the feeble joke. She was taller than half the men in London. "A common complaint."

"Gabriel, I'm serious," Callie was not going to let either sibling off the hook. "She thinks that she cannot land a husband."

Her brother's brows knitted together. "Why not?" he asked his wife.

"I don't know! Because obstinacy runs in your blood?"

He pretended to consider the frustrated statement. "It's possible. I am not certain that I could land a husband either."

Juliana grinned. "It is because you are too tall."

One side of his mouth kicked up. "Very likely."

Callie gave a little aggravated sound. "You are both impossible! I have dinner to oversee. You"—she pointed a finger at her husband, then indicated Juliana—"talk some sense into her."

When the door had closed behind Callie, Ralston turned to Juliana.

"Please do not make me discuss it."

He nodded once. "You realize that she's going to be relentless about this. You'll have to come up with an excellent reason why you don't want to marry, or you'll be having this conversation for the rest of your life."

"I have a good reason."

"No doubt you think you do."

She scowled at the insinuation that she did not *actually* have a good reason not to marry.

"You shall be happy to learn that I have decided against locking you in the attic for the rest of your days to keep you from more adventures," he said, changing the subject. "But you are not far from such a fate. Do have a care, Juliana." His dimple flashed. "I find I quite like having a sister."

His words warmed her. She quite liked having a brother. "I do not mean to make trouble."

He raised a brow.

"Not *all* the time. Not this afternoon." *Except she had meant to make trouble. Just not the kind he need know about.* "Not the kind that ends at the bottom of a lake," she qualified.

He moved to a sideboard and poured himself a scotch, then sat by the fireplace, indicating that she should join him.

When she took the chair opposite his, he said, "No, you mean to make the kind of trouble that ends in setting down half of London society."

She opened her mouth to refute the point, and he continued. "There's no use in telling me otherwise, Juliana. You think it is only our dark hair and blue eyes that make us siblings? You think I do not know what it is like to have them watch your every move? To have them wait for you to prove that you are every inch what they expect you to be?"

There was a long pause. "It's different."

"It's not."

"They didn't think you were going to be like her."

He did not pretend to misunderstand. "You're nothing like her."

How could he know that?

He leaned forward, elbows on his knees, his blue eyes unwavering. "I know it. I know what she was like. She was indifferent. Uncaring. She made a cuckold of her husband. She left her children . . . twice. That is not you."

She wanted to believe him.

"She was also a scandal."

He gave a little huff of laughter. "It's not the same thing at all. You are unexpected and exciting and charming. Yes. You're willful and irritating as hell when you want to be, but you're not a scandal."

She had been in Hyde Park that morning. She had been on the balcony the night before. If Ralston knew that she had wagered two weeks of passion with the duke, he'd have a fit.

Yes, she was a scandal.

Her brother simply didn't know it.

"I fell in the Serpentine today."

"Yes, well, that doesn't usually happen to women in London. But it's not so much of a scandal as it is a challenge. And if you'd stop nearly getting yourself killed . . ." He trailed off, and silence stretched between them. "She was real scandal. The kind from which families do not recover. You are not like her. Not at all."

"Leighton thinks I am."

Ralston's eyes darkened. "Leighton compared you to our mother?"

She shook her head. "Not in so many words. But he thinks I'm a danger to the reputations around me."

Ralston waved a dismissive hand. "First, Leighton is an ass, and has been since he was in short pants." Juliana could not help her giggle, and Ralston smiled at the sound. "Second, he is too conservative. He always has been. And third"—he gave a wry smile—"I have suffered more than my fair share of blows to my reputation, and we are still invited to parties, are we not?"

"Perhaps everyone is just waiting for us to cause a scene."

He settled back in his chair. "It's possible."

"Why is he so cautious?"

The question was out before she could stop it, and she immediately regretted it. She did not want Ralston to sense her interest in the duke.

Not that it was anything more than a passing interest. *Not at all.*

Ralston seemed not to notice. "He has always been so. Since we were boys. At school, he couldn't speak a sentence without mentioning that he was heir to a dukedom. Always stiff and proper and all about the title. I've always thought his behavior ridiculous. Why assume the responsibilities of a title if you're not willing to enjoy the benefits?"

He met her eyes, honestly confounded by the idea of feeling responsible to a title, and Juliana could not help but grin. Her brother had a rake inside him. A tame one, now that he was married, but a rake nonetheless.

Silence fell, and Juliana had to bite her tongue to keep from pressing her brother for more.

"Callie wants to have him to dinner. To thank him. Publicly."

He thought for a moment. "That seems to be sound logic."

"Along with a half a dozen other eligible bachelors."

He offered her a sympathetic look. "You do not actually believe that I can alter her from this course?"

"No, I suppose I do not." She paused. "She thinks proximity to the duke will help my reputation."

"She's probably right. I can't say I like the man, but he does hold a certain sway over society." One side of his mouth lifted in a half smile. "A trait I've never been able to claim." Silence fell, and they were both lost to their thoughts. Finally, Ralston said, "I won't pretend their opinions don't matter, Juliana. I wish to hell they didn't; of course they do. But I promise you. You are nothing like her."

She closed her eyes against his words. "I want to believe you."

"But you find yourself believing them."

Her gaze widened. How did he know that?

A wry smile crossed his face. "You forget, sister. I have been in your position. I have wanted to show them all that I was above them, all the while fearing that I was precisely what they thought."

That was it. That was how she felt.

"It is different for you," Juliana said, and she hated the pout in her voice.

He took a drink. "It is. Now."

Because he was the marquess.

Because he was English.

Because he was male.

"Because you are one of them."

"Bite your tongue!" he said. "What an insult!"

She did not find it amusing. She found it infuriating.

"Ah, Juliana. It's different for me because I now know what it is to have someone expect me to be more than what I am. Now I know what it is to *want* to be more."

The meaning of his words sank in. "Callie."

He nodded. "I no longer focus on meeting their expectations because I am too focused on outdoing hers."

She could not help but smile. "The wicked Marquess of Ralston, inveterate libertine, laid low by love."

He met her gaze, all seriousness. "I am not saying that you must marry, Juliana. On the contrary, if you prefer a life free of marriage, God knows you have enough money to live it. But you must ask yourself what you think your life should be."

She opened her mouth to answer him, only to realize that she had no answer. She'd never given it much thought—not since her father had died and everything had changed. In Italy, marriage and family had not been out of the question, she supposed . . . but they had been so far off that she'd never really given them much thought. But here, in England . . .

Who would want her?

Unaware of her thoughts, Ralston stood, ending the conversation with one final thought. "I never thought I would say it, but love is not as bad as I thought it would be. Should it come for you, I hope you will not turn it away out of hand."

She shook her head. "I hope it will not come for me."

A smile flashed. "I have heard that before, you know. I've said it . . . Nick has said it . . . but, be warned. St. Johns do not seem to be able to avoid it."

But I am not a St. John. Not really.

She did not speak the words.

She liked the illusion.

Chapter Seven

Amusement is expressed in delicate smiles.
Laughter is too coarse for the elegant lady.

—*A Treatise on the Most Exquisite of Ladies*

The age-old question is answered: In battle, marble trumps gold.

—*The Scandal Sheet, October 1823*

Juliana looked over the edge of the Duke of Rivington's box at the Theatre Royale, considering the mass of silk and satin below. Half of the *ton* appeared to be in attendance at this special presentation of *The Lady of Livorno*, and the other half was surely put out that they could not secure a ticket.

"My word," Mariana said, joining her to watch the tableau spread out before them, "I thought autumn was for country houses and hunting trips!"

"Yes, well, whoever decreed such apparently neglected to tell London society this year."

"This is what happens when Parliament convenes

special sessions. We all go mad from the autumn air. Is that *wheat* in Lady Davis's hair?" Mariana lifted her opera glasses, inspecting the unfortunate coiffure with a shake of her head before surveying the rest of the boxes in the theatre before the performance began and she would be forced to pretend she did not care for the audience as much as for the company of actors. "Ah. Densmore is here with a woman I've never seen before. One can assume she's a lightskirt."

"Mari!" She might not have been in London for long, but even Juliana knew that discussion of courtesans was not appropriate conversation for the theatre.

Mariana looked up, eyes twinkling. "Well, it's true!"

"What is true?" The Duke of Rivington had made his way through the throngs of visitors in search of a moment of his time and ran the back of one finger down his wife's arm.

Juliana felt a pang of envy at the absentminded affection, barely noticed by husband or wife, and ignored it. Mariana turned to her duke with a brilliant, happy smile. "I was just saying that Densmore must be here with a lady of the evening. I've never seen her before."

Rivington was used to his wife's boldness, and instead of chastising her he sought the Densmore box, taking a long look at the viscount's companion. "I think you may be right, sweeting."

"You see?" Mariana nearly preened with satisfaction. "I'm an excellent judge of character."

"Either that, or you're becoming an excellent gossip," Juliana said wryly.

Rivington laughed loudly. "Much more likely. Miss Fiori, I am afraid I must steal her away for a moment." He turned back to Mari. "Come and say hello to Lady Allen, would you? I need you to entertain her for a bit while I discuss a matter with her husband."

Mariana looked over Rivington's shoulder at the couple

in question, a somewhat staid pair, each with pursed lips and unfortunate jowls. Rolling her eyes, she handed her opera glasses to Juliana. "See what else you can discover while I'm gone. I expect a full report when I return."

She was gone then, through a crowd of people, to do her duty as wife of one of the most revered men in the realm. Juliana watched in wonder as her friend approached the baroness and engaged the woman in conversation. Within moments, Lady Allen was smiling up at Mariana, obviously satisfied with her company.

As much as people talked about Mariana's marriage as that most rare of things—the love match—it was undeniable that the relationship was as much a brilliant political partnership as it was a romance. Mariana was the very best of ducal wives; that her duke happened to be mad about her was a happy coincidence.

Lasting love was not something with which Juliana was familiar. She was the product of a match devised from fleeting infatuation. Her mother had bewitched her father, from what Juliana could tell, and had deserted them both when she became tired of domesticity. Juliana's father had never remarried, though he'd had several opportunities to do so—she had always thought that he'd made the most sensible choice. After all, why risk loving again when history suggested that such behavior would end in pain and anger and loss?

In the last several months, she had come to see that love was not a myth—she'd stood happily by as her half brothers had found it. Gabriel and Callie's love blossomed just as Juliana arrived in England, and she had watched as they resisted it—futilely. When they had succumbed to the emotion, all of London had been surprised, and Juliana had hoped only that *their* love would not end in sadness. Within months, Nick had found his Isabel, and it was impossible to deny their devotion to each other.

But all love began this way—fiery and passionate and devoted. What happened when fire waned and devotion became tiresome?

She watched as Callie stretched to whisper into Ralston's ear on the opposite side of the box. Her brother smiled broadly—something he had rarely done when Juliana had arrived in the spring—placing his hand on the small of his wife's back and leaning down to reply.

From the pink wash that spread over Callie's cheeks, Juliana imagined her brother's words were not entirely fit for the theatre.

Something coiled deep within Juliana . . . something that she might have identified as envy if she spent too much time considering it.

But she knew better than to be envious of their love. It was a vague, ephemeral emotion that, within months—years, if one were lucky—would ultimately fade.

And then what?

No, Juliana did not want love.

But passion . . . the kind that made her brother say wicked things to his wife at the theatre . . . that was another thing entirely.

She wouldn't mind that.

She thought back to the morning two days earlier, to the moment in Hyde Park when the Duke of Leighton had leapt from his horse, eyes flashing with anger and frustration, and kissed her. Thoroughly.

With passion.

And he'd made her want, damn him.

She wanted that of which he'd given her a taste.

Desire. Lust. Sensuality. Even the conflict was compelling.

But not him.

She refused to want him.

She lifted the binoculars and scanned the theatre, searching for something that would serve to redirect her attention. Several boxes away, Viscount Densmore appeared to be leering down the amply filled, alarmingly low-cut bodice of his companion—it appeared Mari had been right about her. A few yards farther, Lady Davis and Lady Sparrow were at risk of falling out of their box as they craned their necks toward some distant point before huddling behind fluttering fans held in the universal position for scandalous conversation. While Juliana had no love for either of the horrible women, she had to admit that they were expert gossips. Tracking their line of sight, she hoped for a welcome distraction.

When she arrived at the reason for their frenzied whispers, she vowed never to gossip again.

There, in the box directly opposite, stood the Duke of Leighton and the grape, in quiet, private conversation. In full view of half of London.

Several feet away from the perfect, poised couple, rounding out the portrait of aristocratic bliss—and very likely sending the rest of the theatre into convulsions of excitement over what was most definitely a sign of impeding marriage—were the Duchess of Leighton and a plump lady and portly gentleman who Juliana could only imagine were the grape's parents.

Lady Penelope.

She had better start thinking of her as Lady Penelope.

Why? Soon enough she'll be the Duchess of Leighton.

She ignored the wave of distaste that flooded her at the thought.

What did she care whom he married?

She didn't.

Why did she care that he had selected someone who was everything Juliana was not? Poised perfection, absolutely no trouble, not even a bit scandalous?

She *didn't.*

No? Then why not put down the opera glasses?

She could put down the opera glasses anytime she wanted.

She *meant* to put down the opera glasses.

He looked up and stared directly at her.

If they had burst into flame, she could not have lowered the opera glasses more quickly.

Or with more carelessness.

The binoculars hit the marble balustrade with a wicked crack, and the gold eyepiece fell to the carpeted floor.

It was dreadfully quiet in the box all of a sudden, as the collected visitors and family turned at the sound, finding Juliana openmouthed, staring at the long enamel handle that remained in her hand.

An enormous wave of embarrassment coursed through her, and Juliana took the first avenue of escape, falling to her knees on the floor of the at once too-dark and utterly not-dark-enough box to retrieve the glasses which . . . devil take them . . . must have bounced under a chair, because they were nowhere to be seen.

Searching blindly under the chairs, it took her a moment to realize that by crawling on the floor of the Duke of Rivington's theatre box, she'd just made a bad situation much, *much* worse. Ladies Sparrow and Davis were very likely watching *her* now, waiting to see how she would extricate herself from this mortifying situation.

And she would not even think about *him*.

Certainly he had seen it all. And she imagined him lifting one imperious, golden brow in her direction as if to say, *Thank goodness it is Ralston who must deal with you and not I.*

She cursed under her breath, deciding that this particular situation could not be made worse by a few choice words in Italian.

Her fingers brushed against something cool and smooth, and she grasped the fallen glasses. She lifted her head, to find herself staring at the shins of Callie's brother, the Earl of Allendale. A gentleman of the highest caliber, Benedick was almost certainly there to help her to her feet.

She was not ready.

He seemed to sense that, instead crouching down beside her. "Shall I pretend to help with the search until you are ready to face them?" he whispered, and the lighthearted amusement in his tone helped to steady her pulse.

She met his clear brown gaze, so like Callie's, and matched his whisper with her own. "Do you think I might stay here, my lord?"

"For how long?"

"Forever is too long, is it?"

He pretended to consider the question. "Well, as a gentleman, I would be required to remain by your side . . . and I *was* hoping to see the performance," he teased. When she smiled, he offered her a hand and some quiet advice. "Keep smiling. If they see that you are embarrassed, you'll hate yourself for it."

With a deep breath, she allowed him to lift her to her feet. She could feel hundreds of eyes on her, but she refused to look.

Refused to check to see if one set of those eyes belonged to the arrogant duke opposite them. Through her forced smile, she said, "I've caused a scene, haven't I?"

One side of Lord Allendale's mouth rose in amusement. "Yes. But it's a theatre. So take comfort in the fact that you are not the first to do so here."

"The first to do so from so far above the stage, however."

He leaned in close, as if to share a secret. "Nonsense. I once saw a viscountess lose her wig because she was leaning too far over the edge." He gave a mock shudder. "Horrifying."

She laughed, the sound equal parts amusement and relief. Benedick was handsome and charming and so much kinder than—

Than no one.

"First the Serpentine and now this."

"You are an adventuress, it would seem," he teased. "At least in this case, you are in no danger."

"Really? Why does it feel so much more terrifying?"

Benedick smiled down at her. "Would you like to take a bow?"

Her eyes widened. "I couldn't!"

"No?"

"It would be—"

"It would make for a far more interesting evening, that is certain."

And Leighton would hate it.

The thought brought a grin to her face. A real one.

She shook her head. "I think I have caused enough trouble for one evening," she said to the earl, turning to face the rest of the box. She held up the glasses triumphantly, announcing, "I found them!"

Mariana laughed, clapping her hands twice in a sign that she was thoroughly entertained. Ralston's smirk indicated that his irritation at her scene was overpowered by his pride that she would not cower in fear of the rest of the *ton*. Her brother had never cared much for society, and Juliana had that for which to be thankful.

As for the visitors to the box, they seemed to be attempting to recall the proper etiquette for the moment when the sister of a marquess reappeared after spending entirely too long on the floor of a theatre box—not that Juliana believed there was an appropriate amount of time to spend on the floor of a theatre box—the lights in the theatre began to dim, and it was time for the *real* performance to begin.

Thank God.

Juliana was soon seated at the end of the first row of seats, next to Mariana, who had no doubt returned to Juliana's side to protect her from further embarrassment. The lights came up on stage, and the play began.

It was impossible for Juliana to focus on the play. It was a farce, and a good one if the audience's laughter was any indication, but she was struggling with residual nerves, a lingering impulse to flee the theatre, and an unbearable desire to look at the Duke of Leighton's box.

An unbearable desire that, by the end of the first scene, proved irresistible.

She stole a glance from the corner of her eye and saw him.

Watching the play with avid interest.

Her fingers tightened around the delicate gold binoculars in her hands, reminding her of their existence. *Of the ease with which she could see him clearly.*

It was entirely reasonable for her to check the state of the most important component of the opera glasses, she reasoned. While the handle was broken, it would certainly be a tragedy if the glasses themselves were ruined as well. Any halfway-decent friend would replace them if they were broken.

Of course she would test the glasses.

She *should* test the glasses.

It was altogether expected.

She lifted the eyepiece and peered at the stage. No cracked lenses—Juliana could see the brilliant scarlet satin of the lead actress, she could almost make out the individual strands of the thick black moustache worn by the lead actor.

Perfect working order.

But there was no assurance that the glasses had not been broken in some other way.

Perhaps they were now affected by light?

Altogether possible. She would do well to find out.

In the name of friendship.

She swung the glasses as casually as possible in a wide arc from the stage, stopping only when she found his gleaming golden curls. Something on the stage made the audience laugh. He did not laugh . . . did not even smile, until the grape turned to him, as if to check to see that he was enjoying himself. Juliana watched as he forced a smile, leaning close to speak softly in her ear. Her smile grew broader, more natural, and she all of a sudden did not seem so very grapelike.

She seemed quite lovely.

Juliana felt ill.

"Do you see anything of interest?"

She inhaled sharply, nearly dropping the glasses at the whispered question.

She turned to meet Mariana's gaze. "I—I was merely testing the opera glasses. I wanted to be certain that they were in working condition."

"Ah." A small smile played across her friend's lips. "Because I could have sworn you were looking at the Duke of Leighton."

"Why would I be doing that?" Juliana said, and the question came out at a near-inhuman pitch. She thrust the broken glasses into Mariana's lap. "Here. They work."

Mariana lifted the glasses, making absolutely no attempt to hide that she *was* looking at the Duke of Leighton. "I wonder why he is with Penelope Marbury?"

"He's going to marry her," Juliana grumbled.

Mariana gave Juliana a quick look of surprise. "Really. Well. She's made the catch of a lifetime."

The cod served at luncheon must have been off. It was the only reason why she would feel so very . . . queasy.

Mariana returned to her inspection. "Callie tells me that you've had several run-ins with him."

Juliana shook her head, and whispered, "I don't know

what she is talking about. We haven't run at all. There was a riding incident, but I didn't think Callie knew about it . . ." She stopped talking as she noted that Mariana had lowered the glasses and was staring at her in shock. "I think I have misunderstood."

Mariana recovered and said with a triumphant grin. "Indeed you have. How I adore that you still have not mastered English turns of phrase!"

Juliana clasped her friend's hand. "Mari! You must not repeat it!"

"Oh, I won't. On one condition."

Juliana looked to the ceiling for salvation. "What?"

"You must tell me everything! A 'riding incident' sounds so very scandalous!"

Juliana did not reply, instead turning resolutely to the stage. She tried to pay attention to the action on the stage but the story—of two lovers avoiding discovery of their clandestine affair—was rather too familiar. She was in the midst of her own farce . . . broken opera glasses and scandalous meetings and all, and she'd just been discovered.

And she was not amused.

"He's looking at you," Mariana whispered.

"He is not looking at me," she replied out of the corner of her mouth.

But she could not help but turn her head.

He was not looking at her.

"He *was* looking at you."

"Well, I am not looking at *him*."

And she did not look at him.

She did not look during the whole of the first act, as the lovers slammed in and out of doors and the audience howled with laughter, not as the curtain fell on them locked in a passionate embrace, in full view of her husband and his sister . . . who for some reason cared a bit too much about the skirts her brother was chasing.

She did not look as the candles were lit around the theatre, throwing London society back into view, and not as the stream of visitors to the Rivington box began once more and she had the opportunity to look without scrutiny.

She did not look while the Earl of Allendale entertained her during intermission, nor when Mariana suggested they go to the ladies' salon to repair themselves—a thinly veiled ruse to get Juliana talking—nor after she declared that no, she did not have reason to attend the salon, and Mariana was forced to go alone.

She did not look until the lights had dimmed once more and the audience was settling in for the second act.

And then she wished she hadn't.

Because he was guiding the grape into her seat, his large hand lingering at her elbow, sliding down her arm as he took his seat beside her.

And she found she could not look away.

The caress was over quickly—although it seemed to Juliana that it stretched out interminably—and Lady Penelope, unmoved, turned to the stage, immediately absorbed in the next act.

The duke, however, looked at Juliana, fully meeting her gaze. Distance and dim lights should have made her somewhat uncertain but, no . . . he was looking at her.

There was no other explanation for the shiver of awareness that shot down her spine.

He knew she had seen the caress.

Had wanted her to see it.

And suddenly there was not enough air in the box.

She stood abruptly, drawing Ralston's attention as she headed for the exit. She leaned down to speak quietly in his ear, "I find I have something of a headache. I am going into the hallway for some air."

His gaze narrowed. "Shall I take you home?"

"No no . . . I shall be fine. I will be just outside the

box." She smiled feebly. "Back before you realize that I am gone."

Ralston hesitated, debating whether he should allow her to leave. "Do not go far. I don't want you wandering through the theatre."

She shook her head. "Of course not."

He stayed her movement with one firm hand on her wrist. "I mean it, sister. I am well aware of the trouble you can find in a theatre during a performance."

She raised a dark brow in a gesture they shared. "I look forward to hearing more about that soon."

His teeth flashed white in the darkness. "You'll have to ask Callie."

She smiled. "You can be sure that I will."

And then she was in the hallway, which was empty save a handful of footmen, and she could breathe once more.

There was a cool breeze blowing through the corridor, and she headed instinctively for its source, a large window on the back end of the theatre where the hallway ended abruptly above what must have been the stage. The window had been left open to the October evening, a chair beneath it, as though waiting for her arrival. It was likely too far from the box for Ralston's taste, but it was a perfectly public place nonetheless.

She sat, leaning on the sill and looking out over the rooftops of London. Candlelight flickered in the windows of the buildings below, and she could just make out a young woman sewing several floors down. Juliana wondered, fleetingly, whether the girl had ever been to the theatre . . . whether she'd ever even *dreamed* of the theatre.

Juliana certainly hadn't . . . not like this, with a family of aristocrats that she'd never known existed. Not with jewels and silks and satins and marquesses and earls and . . . dukes.

Dukes who infuriated her and consumed her thoughts and kissed her like she was the last woman on earth.

She sighed, watching as the light from the waxing moon reflected on the tile roofs, still wet from a brief rain that afternoon.

She had started something that she could not finish.

She'd wanted to tempt him with passion—to punish his arrogance by bringing him to his knees—but after the embarrassing episode at the lake, when he'd all but told her that she was the very last thing he would ever find tempting . . .

There were ten days left in their agreement, and he was courting Lady Penelope, planning a lifetime of proper, perfect marriage with a woman who had been reared to be a duchess.

The wager was supposed to end in Leighton's triumphant set down; so why did it feel like it was Juliana who would be the losing party?

"Why aren't you in your seat?"

She gave a little start at the words, laced with irritation.

He had followed her.

She should not care that he had sought her out.

Of course, she did.

She turned, attempting to appear calm. "Why aren't *you* in *your* seat?"

He scowled at that. "I saw you leave the box without escort."

"My brother knows where I am."

"Your brother has never in his life accepted an ounce of responsibility." He came closer. "Anything could happen to you out here."

Juliana made a show of looking down the long, quiet hallway. "Yes. It's very threatening."

"Someone should be looking out for your reputation. You could be accosted."

"By whom?"

He paused at that. "By anyone! By an actor! Or a footman!"

"Or a duke?"

His brows knitted together, and there was a pause. "I suppose I deserve that."

He did not deserve it. Not really. She turned back to the window. "I did not ask you to come after me."

There was a long moment of silence, and she was expecting him to leave when he said, softly, "No. You didn't."

She snapped her head around at the admission. "Then why are you here?"

He ran a hand through his golden curls and Juliana's eyes widened at the movement, so uncontrolled and unlike him, a mark of his disquiet.

"It was a mistake."

Disappointment flared, and she did her best to hide it, instead making a wide sweep of the corridor with one hand. "One easily corrected, Your Grace. I believe your box is on the opposite side of the theatre. Shall I ask a footman to escort you back? Or are you afraid of being accosted?"

His lips pressed into a straight line, the only indication that he had registered the sarcasm in her words. "I don't mean coming after you, although Lord knows that was likely a mistake as well, albeit an unavoidable one." He stopped, considering his next words. "I mean all of it. The wager, the two weeks, the morning in Hyde Park . . ."

"The afternoon in Hyde Park," she added softly, and his gaze flew to hers.

"I would have preferred not to have given the gossip-mongers something to discuss, but of course I do not regret saving you." There was something in the words, irritation mixed with an emotion that Juliana could not quite identify, but it was gone when he continued, coolly, "The rest, though, it cannot continue. I should never have agreed to it to begin with. That was the mistake. I'm beginning to see that you are virtually incapable of behaving with decorum. I should never have humored you."

Humored her.

The meaning of the words echoed even as he danced around what he was really trying to say.

She was not good enough for him.

She never had been.

And she would never be good enough for the world in which he lived.

As much as she had sworn that she would change his view of her, that she would prove him wrong and make him beg for her forgiveness . . . for her attention . . . the resolve in his tone gave her pause.

She refused to be hurt by him; it would give him too much power over her. Would give them *all* too much power over her. There were others who did not think her somehow less because she had been born in Italy, because she had been born common, because she struggled with the rules and restrictions of this new world.

She would not be hurt.

She would be angry.

Anger, at least, was an emotion she could master.

And as long as she was angry, he would not win.

"Humored me?" she asked, standing and turning so that they were face-to-face. "You may be accustomed to others simply accepting your view of a situation, Your Grace, but I am not one of your adoring minions."

His jaw steeled at the words, and she pressed on. "You did not appear to be merely humoring me when you agreed to two weeks; and you most definitely were not merely humoring me in Hyde Park several mornings ago." Her chin lifted, light and firm with a mix of anger and conviction. "You gave me two weeks. By my count, I still have ten days."

She stepped closer to him, until they were nearly touching, and heard the shift in his breathing—the tension that would have been imperceptible were she not so close.

Were she not so angry.

Were she not so drawn to him.

"I mean to use them," she whispered, knowing that she tempted fate and that, with a word of refusal, he could end it all.

The moment stretched into an eternity, until she could no longer meet his unreadable gaze. She lowered her attention to his lips—to their firm, strong lines.

A mistake.

Suddenly, the open window did nothing for the stifling air in the theatre. The memory of his kisses was cloying in the dim hallway . . . the desire for more of them overwhelmed all else.

Her eyes skidded back to his, their amber darkened to a rich oak.

He wants me, too.

The thought sent a shiver of fire through her.

He stepped closer. They were touching now, just barely, the swell of her breasts brushing his wide chest. Her breath caught.

"You don't need me for your scandals. You've got an earl in the palm of your hand."

Confusion flared at the words and his nearness. "An earl?"

"I saw you with Allendale, laughing and . . . cozy." The last came out like gravel.

"Allendale?" She repeated like an imbecile, willing her mind clear. *What was he talking about?* Understanding dawned. "Oh. Benedick."

Something not altogether safe flashed in his eyes. "You should not refer to him with such familiarity."

A thread of excitement weaved its way through her. He looked angry. No . . . he looked livid. *He looked jealous.*

The look was gone before she could savor it, shuttered behind his careful gaze, but courage surged nonetheless, and she gave him a small, teasing smile. "You mean I should not refer to him by his name?"

"Not by *that* name."

"You did not ascribe to such rules when we met . . . Simon." She said his name on a whisper, and the breath of it curled between them like temptation.

He inhaled sharply. "I should have."

"But you wanted me to think you something you were not."

"I think we were both guilty of hiding our true identities."

Sadness flared, mixed with anger. "I did not hide."

"No? Then why did I believe you were—"

More. She heard the word. Loathed it.

"You seemed to think me enough then." She lifted her chin, her lips a hairsbreadth from his.

Desire was coming off him in waves. He might not *want* to want her—but he did. She could feel it.

He leaned in, and she held her breath, waiting for the feel of those unforgiving lips—wanting them with a desperation to which she would never admit.

The world faded away, and there was nothing but this moment, the two of them in a quiet darkness, his golden gaze on hers, his warmth consuming her. His mouth hovered above hers; she could feel his soft breath on her skin and she wanted to scream with the anticipation . . .

"You are a scandal waiting to happen."

The words were a kiss of breath, their feel running

counter to their message. And then he was gone, stepping back, away from her—leaving her alone and unsatisfied and utterly wanting.

"One I cannot afford," he added.

"You want me." She winced at the desperation in the accusation; wished, instantly, that she could take it back.

He was stone. "Of course I want you. I would have to be dead not to want you. You're bright and beautiful, and you respond to me in a way that makes me want to throw you down and bend you to my will." He stopped, meeting her wide eyes. "But actions have consequences, Miss Fiori. A fact you would do well to remember before running headlong into your childish games."

She narrowed her gaze. "I am not a child."

"No? You haven't any idea what you're doing. What if you were to teach me about your precious passion, Juliana? What then? What next?"

The question whipped through her. She had no answer.

"You've never in your life considered the future, have you? You've never imagined what came next, after whatever you are experiencing in the here and now." He paused, then cut deeper. "If that does not speak to your childishness, nothing does."

She hated him then. Hated the way he stripped her bare. The way he knew her failings before she knew them herself.

He continued. "I am removing myself from our wager. I should never have agreed to it in the first place. You are a danger to yourself. And to me. And I haven't the luxury to teach you the lesson you so richly deserve."

She knew she should acquiesce. Knew she should release him—release them both—from the stupid, damaging agreement that threatened their reputations, their feelings, their reason.

But he made her so irate, she could not let him win.

"You say removing, I say *reneging*." The word was a taunt.

A muscle in his jaw twitched. "I should tell Ralston everything."

She raised a brow. "And you think that will *help* your cause?" They faced off in the dimly lit hallway, and Juliana could feel the fury pouring out of him. Reveled in it—it was so rare to see his emotion. She could not resist poking the lion. "Take heart. I should not need so very long to bring you to your knees."

His eyes grew instantly dark, and she knew that she had gone too far. She thought for a moment that he might shake her, recognized the barely controlled anger in his corded muscles.

"I have bested far worse threats to my reputation than you, Miss Fiori. Do not think for a moment that you will prevail. Temptation is no match for reputation." He paused. "You want your ten days? Keep them. Do your best."

"I intend to."

"Do not expect me to make it easy for you."

She should have taken pleasure in the way he turned on one heel and left—in the way she had damaged his cool façade.

But as she watched him return to his box—and to the perfect English bride he had selected—it was not triumph that flared.

It was something suspiciously like longing.

Chapter Eight

Rudeness is the ultimate test of perfection.
The delicate lady holds her tongue.

—*A Treatise on the Most Exquisite of Ladies*

The most exciting finds at the *modiste* are not wisps of
silk, but whispers of scandal . . .

—*The Scandal Sheet, October 1823*

Englishwomen spend more time buying clothes
than anyone in all of Europe."

Juliana leaned back on the divan in the dressmaker's
fitting room. She had spent more hours than she would
care to admit on that particular piece of furniture, upholstered in a fine, scarlet brocade that was just expensive
enough and just bold enough to echo the proprietress of
the shop.

"You must never have seen the French shop," Madame
Hebert said drily as she artfully pinned the waist of the
lovely cranberry twill she was fitting to Callie.

Mariana laughed as she inspected an evergreen velvet.

"Well, we cannot allow the French to best us at such an important activity, can we?" Hebert replied with a pointed grunt, and Mariana hastened to reassure her. "After all, we have already won their very best seamstress to our side of the Channel."

Juliana grinned as her friend narrowly avoided a diplomatic disaster.

"And besides," Mariana continued, "Callie spent far too long in horrible clothing. She has much to make up for. We just come along for the excitement . . ." She paused. "And perhaps a winter cloak in this green?"

"Your Grace would look beautiful in the velvet." Hebert did not look up from her work. "May I suggest a new gown in the dupioni to match? It will make you the belle of a winter ball."

Mariana's eyes lit up as Valerie spread out the stunning green silk—heavier than most with a dozen different greens shimmering through it. "Oh, yes . . ." she whispered. "You may certainly make such a suggestion."

Juliana laughed at the reverence in her friend's tone. "And with that, we are here for another hour," she announced, as Mariana headed behind a nearby screen to be measured, poked, and pinned.

"Not too tight," Callie said quietly to the dressmaker before smiling at Juliana. "If autumn remains as social as it has been, I cannot imagine what will come of winter. You're going to need new dresses as well, you know. In fact, we have not discussed what you shall wear to your dinner."

"Not my dinner." Juliana laughed. "And I am sure I have something suitable."

"Callie's selected an excellent crop of London's lords, Juliana," Mariana sang from behind the screen. "Each one more eligible than the last."

"So I have heard."

Callie inspected the waist of her gown in the mirror.

"And all but Leighton have accepted." She met Juliana's eyes in the mirror. "Including Benedick."

Juliana ignored the reference to the Earl of Allendale, knowing she should not press Callie further on the event. Nevertheless, "Leighton is not coming?"

Callie shook her head. "It is unclear. He simply has not responded." Juliana held her tongue, knowing that she should not press the issue any more. If he did not wish to attend the dinner, what business was it of hers? "I am trying to find the good in him . . . but it is not easy. Ah, well. We shall have a lovely time without him."

"Would you like me to have Valerie show you some fabrics, Mademoiselle Fiori?" Hebert interjected, as excellent a businesswoman as she was a dressmaker.

"No." Juliana shook her head. "I have plenty of dresses. My brother need not be bankrupted today."

Callie met Juliana's gaze in a large looking glass. "Don't think I don't know about your little secret gifts with Gabriel. You know he loves to buy you clothes and whatever else you want. And I know where all his new books and pieces of music come from."

Juliana smiled. When she had first come to England, feeling entirely disconnected from this new world and her new family, she had been convinced that her daunting half brothers would hate her because of who she represented—the mother who had deserted them without looking back when they were boys. It did not matter that that same mother deserted Juliana, as well.

Except it had mattered. Gabriel and Nick had accepted her. Without question. And while their relationship as siblings continued to evolve, Juliana was learning—later than most—what it was to be a sister. And as part of that immensely pleasurable lesson, she and her eldest brother had begun a game of sorts, exchanging gifts often.

She smiled at her sister-in-law, who had been so instrumental in building the relationship between her brother and her, and said, "No gifts today. I am still reserving hope that the season will come to an end before I require a formal winter wardrobe."

"Don't say such things!" called Mariana from behind her screen. "I want a reason to wear this gown!"

They all laughed, and Juliana watched as Madame Hebert artfully draped the fabric of Callie's gown over her midsection. Callie considered the folds of fabric in the mirror before saying, "It's perfect."

And it was. Callie looked lovely. _Gabriel would not be able to keep his eyes off her,_ Juliana thought wryly.

"Not too tight," Callie said.

It was the second time she had whispered the words.

Their meaning dawned.

"Callie?" Juliana said, meeting her sister-in-law's guilty gaze in the mirror. Juliana tilted her head in a silent question, and Callie's wide, lovely grin was all the answer that she needed.

Callie was with child.

Juliana leapt from her seat, joy bursting through her. "_Maraviglioso!_" She approached the other woman and pulled her into an enormous embrace. "No wonder we are shopping for more gowns!"

Their shared laughter attracted Mariana's attention from behind the dressing screen. "What is _maraviglioso_?" She poked her blond head around the edge of the divider. "Why are you laughing?" She narrowed her gaze on Juliana. "Why are you _crying_?" She disappeared for a heartbeat, then hobbled out, clutching a length of half-pinned green satin to her, poor Valerie following behind. "What did I miss?" She pouted. "I always miss everything!"

Callie and Juliana laughed again at Mariana's pique, then Juliana said, "Well, you'll have to tell her."

"Tell me what?"

Callie's cheeks were on fire, and she was certainly wishing that they weren't all in the middle of a fitting room with one of London's best dressmakers standing a foot away.

Juliana could not stop herself. "It appears my brother has done his duty."

"Juliana!" Callie whispered, scandalized.

"What? It is true!" Juliana said simply, with a little shrug.

Callie grinned. "You are just like him, you know."

There were worse insults coming from a woman who madly loved the *him* in question.

Mariana was still catching up. "Done his—Oh! Oh, my! Oh, Callie!" She began to hop with excitement, and the long-suffering Valerie had to run for a handkerchief to protect the silk from Mariana's tears.

Hebert quit the room—either to escape smothering in a wayward embrace or being caught in the emotional fray as the two sisters clutched each other and laughed and cried and laughed and chattered and cried and laughed.

Juliana smiled at the picture the Hartwell sisters made—now each so happily married and still so deeply connected to each other—even as she realized that there was no place for her in this moment of celebration. She did not begrudge them their happiness or their connection.

She simply wished that she, too, had such an unbridled, uncontested sense of belonging.

She slipped from the fitting room to the front room of the shop, where Madame Hebert had escaped moments earlier. The Frenchwoman was standing at the entrance to a small antechamber, blocking the view to another customer. Juliana headed for a wall of accents—buttons and ribbons, frills and laces. She ran her fingers along the haberdashery, brushing a smooth gold button here, a scalloped lace there, consumed with Callie's news.

There would be two new additions to the family in the spring—Nick's wife, Isabel, was also with child.

Her brothers had overcome their pasts and their fears of repeating the sins of their father, and they had taken that unfathomable leap—marrying for love. And now they had families. Mothers and fathers and children who would grow old in a happy, caring fold.

You've never in your life considered the future, have you? You've never imagined what came next?

Leighton's words from the theatre echoed through her mind.

Juliana swallowed around a strange lump in her throat. She no longer had the luxury of thinking of her future. Her father had died, and she had been upended, shipped to England and delivered into a strange family and a stranger culture that would never accept her. There was no future for her in England. And it was easier—less painful—not to fool herself into imagining one.

But when she saw Callie and Mariana looking happily toward their idyllic futures, filled with love and children and family and friends, it was impossible not to envy them.

They had what she could never have. What she would never be offered.

Because they belonged here, in this aristocratic world where money and title and history and breeding all mattered more than anything else.

She lifted a long feather from a bowl, one that must have been dyed; she'd never seen such inky blackness in a plume so large. She could not imagine the bird that would produce such a thing. But as she ran her fingers through its softness, the feather caught the sunlight streaming into the shop, and she knew immediately that it was natural. It was *stunning*. In the bright afternoon light, the feather was not black at all. It was a shimmering mass of blues and purples and reds so dark that it merely gave the illusion of blackness. It was alive with color.

"*Aigrette.*"

The dressmaker's word brought Juliana out of her reverie. "I beg your pardon?"

Madame Hebert raised a black brow. "So polite and British," she said, continuing when Juliana gave her a half smile. "The feather you hold. It is from the egret."

Juliana shook her head. "Egrets are white, I thought."

"Not the black ones."

Juliana looked down at the feather. "The colors are stunning."

"The rarest of things are usually that way," the dressmaker replied, lifting a large wooden frame filled with lace. "Excuse me. I have a duchess who requires an inspection of my lace." The distaste in her tone surprised Juliana. Surely the Frenchwoman would not speak ill of Mariana in front of her . . .

"Perhaps if the French had moved more quickly, Napoleon would have won the war." Disdain oozed across the shop, and Juliana turned quickly toward the voice.

The Duchess of Leighton stood not ten feet from her.

It was hard to believe that this woman, petite and pale, had spawned the enormous, golden Leighton. Juliana struggled to find something of him in his mother. It was neither in her pallid coloring nor in her parchment skin, so thin as to be nearly translucent, nor was it in the eyes, the color of a winter sea.

But those eyes, they seemed to see everything. Juliana held her breath as the duchess's cool gaze tracked her from head to toe. She resisted the urge to fidget under the silent examination, refused to allow the woman's obvious judgment to rattle her.

Of course, it did rattle her.

And suddenly, she saw the similarities in crystal clarity. The stiff chin, the haughty posture, the cold perusal, the ability to shake a person to her core.

She was his mother—him in all the very worst of ways. *But she did not have his heat.*

There was nothing in her but an unwavering stoicism that spoke of a lifetime of entitlement and lack of emotion.

What turned a woman to stone?

No wonder he did not believe in passion.

The duchess was waiting for Juliana to look away. Just like her son, she wanted to prove that her ancient name and her straight nose made her better than all others. Certainly, her unwavering gaze seemed to say, it made her better than Juliana.

Ignoring her rioting nerves, Juliana remained steadfast.

"Your Grace," Madame Hebert said, unaware of the battle of wills taking place in her front parlor, "my apologies for the delay. Would you care to look at the lace now?"

The duchess did not look away from Juliana. "We have not been introduced," she said, the words sharp and designed to startle. They were a cut direct, aimed to remind Juliana of her impertinence. *Of her place.*

Juliana did not respond. Did not move. Refused to look away.

"Your Grace?" Madame Hebert looked from Juliana to the duchess and back again. When she continued, there was uncertainty in her tone. "May I introduce Miss Fiori?"

There was a long pause, which might have been seconds or hours, then the duchess spoke. "You may not." The air seemed to go out of the room with the imperious statement. She continued, without releasing Juliana's gaze. "I admit to a modicum of surprise, Hebert. There was a time when you serviced a far less . . . common . . . clientele."

Common.

If the rushing in her ears had not been so loud, Juliana would have admired the older woman's calculation. She had chosen the perfect word—the one that would provide the quickest and most violent set down.

Common.

The very worst of insults from someone who lived life up on high.

The word echoed in her head, but in the repetition, Juliana did not hear the Duchess of Leighton.

She heard her son.

And she could not help but reply.

"And I had always thought she serviced a far more civilized one." The words were out before she could stop them, and she resisted the impulse to clap one hand over her mouth to keep from saying anything more.

If it were possible, the duchess's spine grew even straighter, her nose tipped even higher. When she spoke, the words dripped with boredom, as though Juliana were too far below her notice to merit a response. "So, it is true what they say. Blood will out."

The Duchess of Leighton exited the shop, taking the air with her as the door closed, its little bell sounding happily in ironic punctuation.

"That woman is a shrew."

Juliana looked up to see Mariana heading toward her, concern and anger on her face. She shook her head. "It seems that duchesses can behave as they please."

"I don't care if she's the Queen. She has no right to speak to you in such a way."

"If she were queen, then she really *could* speak to me however she liked," Juliana said, ignoring the shaking in her voice.

What had she been thinking, goading the duchess on?

That was the problem, of course. She hadn't been thinking of the duchess at all.

She'd been thinking of flashing amber eyes and a halo of golden locks and a square jaw and an immovable countenance that she desperately wanted to move.

And she'd said the first thing that came to her mind.

"I should not have spoken to her in such a manner. If it gets out . . . it will be a scandal." Mariana shook her head and opened her mouth to reply, almost certainly with reassuring words, but Juliana continued with a small smile. "Is it wrong that I cannot help but feel that she deserved it?"

Mariana grinned. "Not at all! She did deserve it! And much more! I loathe that woman. No wonder Leighton is so stiff. Imagine being raised by *her.*"

It would have been horrible.

Instead of feeling set down, Juliana was reinvigorated. The Duchess of Leighton might think herself above Juliana and the rest of the known world, but she was not. And while Juliana had little interest in proving such to the hateful woman, she found herself recommitted to showing the duke precisely what he was missing in his life of cold disdain.

"Juliana?" Mariana interrupted her thoughts. "Are you all right?"

She would be.

Juliana pushed the thought away, turning to the normally unflappable *modiste,* who had watched the scene unfold with shock and likely horror, and offered an apology. "I am sorry, Madame Hebert. I seem to have lost you an important customer."

It was honest. Juliana knew that Hebert would have no choice but to attempt to win back the favor of the Duchess of Leighton. One did not simply stand aside as one of the most powerful women in London took her business elsewhere. The repercussions of such an altercation could end the dressmaker if not handled properly.

"Perhaps Her Grace," she indicated Mariana, "and the marchioness," she waved one hand in the direction of the fitting room and Callie, "can help to repair the damage I have done."

"Ha!" Mariana was still irate. "As though I would stoop to conversing with that—" She paused, rediscovering her manners. "But, of course, Madame, I will happily help."

The dressmaker spoke. "There is nothing in need of repair. I've plenty of work, and I do not require the Duchess of Leighton to *suffer* my clientele." Juliana blinked, and the *modiste* continued. "I've got the Duchess of Rivington in my shop, as well as the wife *and sister* of the Marquess of Ralston. I can do without the old lady." She lowered her voice to a conspiratorial whisper. "She shall die soon enough. What are a handful of years without her business?"

The pronouncement was so brash, so matter-of-fact, that it took a moment for the meaning to settle. Mariana smiled broadly, and Juliana gave a bark of disbelieving laughter. "Have I mentioned how very much I love the French?"

The modiste winked. "We foreigners must stay together, *non*?"

Juliana smiled. "*Oui.*"

"*Bon.*" Hebert nodded once. "And what of the duke?"

Juliana pretended not to understand. "The duke?"

Mariana gave her a long-suffering look. "Oh, please. You are terrible at playing coy."

"The one who saved your life, *mademoiselle*," the dressmaker said, a teasing lilt in her voice. "He is a challenge, *non*?"

Juliana turned the egret feather in her hand, watching as the brilliant, hidden colors revealed themselves before meeting the dressmaker's gaze. "*Oui.* But not in the way you think. I am not after him. I simply want to . . ."

To shake him to his core.

Well, she certainly couldn't say that.

Madame Hebert removed the plume from Juliana's hand. She moved to the wall of fabric on one side of the shop and leaned down to remove a bolt of fabric. Turning out several yards of the extravagant cloth, she looked up at Juliana. "I think you should allow your brother to buy you a new gown."

The *modiste* set the feather down on the glorious satin. It was scandalous and passionate and . . .

Mariana laughed at her shoulder, low and wicked. "Oh, it's *perfect.*"

Juliana met the dressmaker's gaze.

It would bring him to his knees.

"How quickly can I have it?"

The modiste looked to her, intrigued. "How quickly do you need it?"

"He is coming to dinner two evenings from now."

Mariana snapped to attention, shaking her head. "But Callie said he has not accepted the invitation."

Juliana met her sister-in-law's eyes, more certain of her path than ever before. "He shall."

"It is not that I do not wish our military to be well funded, Leighton, I'm simply saying that this debate could have waited for the next session. I've a harvest to oversee."

Simon threw a card down and turned a lazy glance on his opponent, who was worrying a cheroot between his teeth in the telling gesture of a soon-to-be loser. "I imagine it's less the harvesting and more the foxhunting that you are so loath to miss, Fallon."

"That, as well, I won't deny. I've better things to do than spend all of autumn in London." The Earl of Fallon discarded in irritated punctuation. "You can't want to stay, either."

"What I want is not at issue," Simon said. It was a lie. What he wanted was entirely at issue. He would endorse a special session of Parliament to discuss the laws governing cartography if it kept visitors from turning up on the doorstep of his country manor and discovering his secrets.

He set his cards down, faceup. "It seems you should spend more time on your cards than on searching for ways to shirk your duties as a peer."

Simon collected his winnings, stood from the table, and ignored the earl's curse as he left the small room into the corridor beyond.

The evening stretched before him, along with invitations to the theatre and half a dozen balls, and he knew that he should return to his town house, bathe and dress and head out—every night he was seen as the portrait of propriety and gentility was a night that would help to secure the Leighton name.

It did not matter that he was coming to find the rituals of society tiresome.

This was how it was done.

"Leighton."

The Marquess of Needham and Dolby was huffing up the wide staircase from the ground floor of the club, barely able to catch his breath as he reached the top step. He stopped, one hand on the rich oak banister, and leaned his head back, pushing out his ample torso to heave a great breath. The buttons on the marquess's yellow waistcoat strained under the burden of his girth, and Simon wondered if the older man would require a physician.

"Just the man I was hoping to see!" the marquess announced once he had recovered. "Tell me, when are you going to speak to my daughter?"

Simon stilled, considering their surroundings. It was an entirely inappropriate location for a conversation that he would like to keep private. "Perhaps you'd like to join me in a sitting room, Needham?"

The marquess did not take the hint. "Nonsense. There's no need to keep the match quiet!"

"I am afraid I disagree," Simon said, willing the muscles in his jaw to relax. "Until the lady agrees—"

"Nonsense!" the marquess fairly bellowed again.

"I assure you, Needham, there are not many who consider my thoughts nonsense. I should like the match kept quiet until I have had a chance to speak directly to Lady Penelope."

Needham's already beady gaze narrowed. "Then you'd best get it done, Leighton." Simon's teeth clenched at the words. He did not like being ordered about. Particularly by an idiotic marquess who was a poor shot.

And yet, it seemed he had little choice. He gave a curt nod. "Presently."

"Good man. Good man. Fallon!" the marquess called as the door to the card room opened and Simon's opponent stepped into the hallway. "You're not going anywhere, boy! I plan to lighten your pockets!"

The door closed behind the portly marquess, and Simon gave a silent prayer that he was as bad at cards as he was at shooting. There was no reason for Needham to have a good afternoon after so thoroughly ruining Simon's.

The enormous bay window that marked the center staircase of White's overlooked the street, and Simon paused in the afternoon light to watch the carriages pass on the cobblestones below and consider his next move.

He should head straight to Dolby House and speak to Lady Penelope.

Each day that passed simply prolonged the inevitable.

It was not as though he had not eventually planned to marry; it was the natural course of events. A means to an end. He needed heirs. And a hostess.

But he resented having to marry now.

He resented the reason.

A flash of color caught his eye on the opposite side of the street, a bright scarlet peeking through the mass of muted colors that cloaked the other pedestrians on St. James's Street. It was so out of place, Simon moved closer to the window to confirm that he had seen it—a bright scarlet cloak and matching bonnet, a lady in a man's world. On a man's street.

On his street. Across from his club.

What woman would wear scarlet in broad daylight on St. James's?

The answer flashed the instant before the crowd cleared, and he saw her face.

And when she looked up toward the window—she couldn't see him, couldn't know he was there—he was unbalanced by the wave of disbelief that coursed through him.

Had he not—the evening before, for God's sake— warned her off such bold, reckless behavior? Had he not given her a lesson in childishness? In consequences?

He had. *Just before he had told her to do her best to win their wager.*

This was her next move.

He could not believe it.

The woman deserved to be turned over someone's knee and given a sound thrashing. And he was just the man to do it.

He was instantly in motion, hurrying down the stairs and ignoring the greetings of the other members of the club, barely forcing himself to wait for his cloak, hat, and gloves before heading out the door to catch her as she left the scene of her assault on his reputation.

Except she was not on the run.

She was waiting, quite patiently, across the street, in conversation with her little Italian maid—whom Simon vowed to see on the next ship back to Italy—as though the whole situation were perfectly normal. As though she were not breaking eleven different rules of etiquette by doing so.

He headed straight for her, not at all certain what he would do when he reached her.

She turned just as he reached them. "You really should be more careful crossing the street, Your Grace. Carriage accidents are not unheard of."

The words were calm and genial, spoken as though they were in a drawing room rather than on the London street that boasted all the best men's clubs. "What are you doing here?"

He expected her to lie. To say she had been shopping and taken a wrong turn, or that she had wanted to see St. James's Palace and was simply passing by, or to say that she was searching for a hackney.

"Waiting for you, of course."

The truth set him back on his heels. "For me."

She smiled, and he wondered if someone in the club had drugged him. Surely this was not happening. "Precisely."

"Do you have any idea how improper it is for you to be here? Waiting for me? On the street?" He could not keep the incredulity from his tone. Hated that she had shaken emotion from him.

She tilted her head, and he saw the wicked gleam in her eye. "Would it be more or less improper for me to have knocked on the door of the club and requested an audience?"

She was teasing him. She had to be. And yet, he felt he should answer her question. In case. "More. Of course."

Her smile became a grin. "Ah, so then you prefer this."

"I prefer neither!" He exploded. Then realizing that they remained on the street across from his club, he took her elbow and turned her toward her brother's home. "Walk."

"Why?"

"Because we cannot remain standing here. It is not done."

She shook her head. "Leave it to the English to outlaw *standing*." She began to walk, her maid trailing behind.

He resisted the urge to throttle her, taking a deep breath. "How did you even know that I was here?"

She raised a brow. "It is not as though aristocrats have much to do, Your Grace. I have something to discuss with you."

"You cannot just decide to discuss something with me and seek me out." Perhaps if he spoke to her as though she were a simpleton, it would settle his ire.

"Whyever not?"

Perhaps not.

"Because it is not done!"

She gave him a small smile. "I thought we had decided that I care little for what is done." He did not respond. Did not trust himself to do so. "Besides, if you decide you want to speak to me, you are welcome to seek me out."

"Of course I am welcome to seek you out."

"Because you are a duke?"

"No. Because I am a man."

"Ah," she said, "a much better reason."

Was that sarcasm in her tone?

He did not care.

He just wanted to get her home.

"Well, you were not planning to come to me."

Damned right. "No. I was not."

"And so I had to take matters into my own hand."

He would not be amused by her charming failures in

language. She was a walking scandal. And somehow, he had come to be her escort. He did not need this. "Hands," he corrected.

"Precisely."

He helped her cross the street to Park Lane and Ralston House before asking, quick and irritated, "I have better things to do today than to play nanny to you, Juliana. What is it you want?"

She stopped, the sound of her given name hanging between them.

"Miss Fiori." He corrected himself too late.

She smiled then. Her blue eyes lit with more knowledge than a woman of twenty years should have. "No, Your Grace. You cannot take it back."

Her voice was low and lilting and barely there before it was whisked away on the wind, but he heard it, and the promise it carried—a promise she could not possibly know how to deliver. The words went straight to his core, and desire shot through him, quick and intense. He lowered the brim of his hat and turned away, heading into the wind, wishing that the autumn leaves whipping around them could blow away the moment.

"What do you want?"

"What things do you have to do?"

Nothing I want to do.

He swallowed back the thought.

"It is not your concern."

"No, but I am curious. What could an aristocrat possibly have to do that is so pressing that you cannot escort me home?"

He did not like the implication that he lived a life of idleness. "We have purpose, you know."

"Truly?"

He cut her a look. She was grinning at him. "You are goading me."

"Perhaps."

She was beautiful.

Infuriating, but beautiful.

"So? What is it that you have to do today?"

Something in him resisted telling her that he had planned to visit Lady Penelope. Planned to propose. Instead, he offered her a wry look. "Nothing important."

She laughed, the sound warm and welcome.

He was not going to see Lady Penelope today.

They walked in silence for a few long moments before they arrived at her brother's home, and he turned to face her finally, taking her in. She was vibrant and beautiful, all rose-cheeked and bright-eyed, her scarlet cloak and bonnet turning her into the very opposite of a good English lady. She'd been outside, boldly marching through the crisp autumn air instead of inside warming herself by a fire with needlepoint and tea.

As Penelope was likely doing at that very moment.

But Juliana was different from everything he had ever known. Everything he had ever wanted. Everything he had ever been.

She was a danger to herself . . . but most of all, she was a danger to him. A beautiful, tempting danger he was coming to find increasingly irresistible.

"What do you want?" he asked, the words coming out softer than he would have liked.

"I want to win our wager," she said, simply.

The one thing he would not give her. Could not afford to give her.

"It will not happen."

She lifted one shoulder in a little shrug. "Perhaps not. Especially not if we do not see each other."

"I told you I would not make it easy for you."

"Difficult is one thing, Your Grace. But I would not have expected you to hide from me."

His eyes widened at her bold words. "*Hide* from you?"

"You have been invited to dinner. And you are the only person who has not yet responded. Why not?"

"Certainly not because I am hiding from you."

"Then why not reply?"

Because I cannot risk it. "Do you have any idea how many invitations I receive? I cannot accept them all."

She smiled again, and he did not like the knowledge in the curve of her lips. "Then you decline?"

No.

"I have not decided."

"It is the day after tomorrow," she said, as though he were a small child. "I would not have thought you to be so callous with your correspondence, considering your obsession with reputation. Are you sure you are not hiding from me?"

He narrowed his gaze. "I am not hiding from you."

"You do not fear that I might win our wager after all?"

"Not in the least."

"Then you will come?"

"Of course."

No!

She grinned. "Excellent. I shall tell Lady Ralston to expect you." She started up the steps to the house, leaving him there, in the waning light.

He watched her go, standing on the street until the door closed firmly behind her, and he was consumed with the knowledge that he had been bested by an irritating Italian siren.

Chapter Nine

The hour on an invitation serves a purpose.
The refined lady is never late.

—*A Treatise on the Most Exquisite of Ladies*

Surely no meal is more sumptuous than one served
with marriage in mind . . .

—*The Scandal Sheet, October 1823*

*H*e was the last to arrive to dinner. Deliberately.
Simon leapt down from his carriage and made
his way up the steps of Ralston House, knowing that he
was committing a grave breach of etiquette. But he was
still feeling manipulated into attending the dinner at all,
so he took perverse pleasure in knowing that he was several minutes late. He would, of course, make his apologies, but Juliana would know immediately that he had no
interest in being managed by an impetuous female.

He was the Duke of Leighton. Let her try to forget it.

He could not help the wave of triumph that coursed
through him as the door swung open, revealing the

large, empty entryway of the Ralston home, proving what he had already known would be the case—they had begun dinner without him.

Entering the house, he handed his hat, cloak, and gloves to a nearby footman before heading for the wide center staircase that would lead to the second floor and the dining room. The quiet conversation coming from abovestairs grew louder as he drew closer, finally turning down the long, brightly lit hallway and entering the massive dining room, where guests were waiting for dinner to begin.

They had held the meal for him.

Which made him feel like an ass.

Of course, no one seemed particularly put out by waiting for him. Indeed, everyone appeared to be having a lovely time, especially the cluster of eligible gentlemen crowded so tightly around Juliana that all Simon could see of her were the gleaming ebony curls piled on top of her head.

Instantly, the reason for the dinner became clear.

Lady Ralston was playing matchmaker.

The thought was punctuated by a loud burst of laughter from the group, her high, lovely, feminine chuckle set apart from the others—low and altogether too masculine. The collection of sounds set Simon on immediate edge. He had not expected this.

And he found that he did not like it.

"So happy you decided to join us, Leighton."

Ralston's sarcastic words shook Simon from his reverie. He ignored the marquess, instead turning his attention to Lady Ralston. "I do apologize, my lady."

The marchioness was all graciousness. "No need, Your Grace. Indeed, the extra time afforded us all an opportunity to chat."

The gentle reminder of the collection of simpering men surrounding Juliana returned his attention there, and he watched, carefully hiding his thoughts as first one man, then the next peeled away from the group to be seated—ultimately leaving only the Earl of Allendale and, on his arm, Juliana.

Dressed in the most magnificent gown Simon had ever seen.

No wonder the others had been so entranced.

The dress was a scandal in itself, silk the color of midnight that shimmered around her in candlelight, giving her the illusion of being wrapped in the night sky. It was a combination of the darkest reds and blues and purples giving the appearance that she was wearing the richest of color and simultaneously no color at all. The bodice was cut entirely too low, showing a wide expanse of her creamy white skin, pale and pristine—tempting him to come closer. To touch her.

She wore the dress with a bold confidence that no other woman in the room—in London—would have been able to affect.

She knew that wearing black would cause a scene. Knew it would make her look like a goddess. Knew it would drive men—drive him—to want nothing more than to strip her out of that glorious gown and claim her.

Simon shook off the improper thought and was flooded with an intense urge to remove his coat and shield her from the greedy glances of the other men.

Surely Ralston knew this dress was entirely improper. Surely he knew that his sister was encouraging the worst kind of attention. Simon passed a cool gaze over the marquess, seated at the head of the table, appearing to know no such thing.

And then Juliana was passing him, a whisper of silk and red currants, escorted by the Earl of Allendale, to take her own seat at the center of the long, lavish banquet, smiling at the so-called gentlemen who immediately turned their attention to her.

He wanted to take each one of the mincing men out in turn for their improper glances. He should have refused this invitation. Every moment he was with this impetuous, impossible female, he felt his control slipping.

He did not care for the sensation.

He took his seat next to the Marchioness of Ralston, the place of honor that had been held for him as the duke in attendance who was not family. He spent the first three courses in polite conversation with Lady Ralston, Rivington, and his sister, Lady Margaret Talbott. As they ate, Simon attempted to ignore the activity at the center of the table, where a collection of gentlemen—who outnumbered the ladies at the dinner—attempted to gain Juliana's attention.

It was impossible for him to ignore Juliana, however, as she laughed and teased with the others around the table, gifting them with her wide, welcome smile and sparkling eyes. Instead, while half participating in the conversation near him, Simon silently tracked her movements. She leaned toward the men across the table—Longwood, Brearley, and West—each untitled and self-made, each lobbying harder than the last for her attention.

West, the publisher of the *Gazette*, was regaling her with some idiotic story about a journalist and a street carnival.

"—I will say this, at least he returned the hat!"

"The reporter's hat?" Longwood asked, as though the two of them were in a traveling show.

"The *bear's* hat!"

Juliana dissolved into laughter along with the rest of the foolish group.

Simon returned his attention to his plate.

Could they not even find aristocrats with whom to match her? It was not as though she need stoop so low as to marry *a commoner.*

During the fourth course, Juliana's attention was claimed almost entirely by Lord Stanhope, who would make a terrible match, notorious for his twin loves of gambling and women. To be fair, he always won at cards, but surely Ralston did not want his sister married to an inveterate rake.

Casting a sidelong glance at the marquess, who appeared to be equally entertained by Stanhope, Simon realized the problem with his logic. Rakes *enjoyed* the company of rakes.

He did his best to focus on the veal throughout the fifth course, pretending not to notice the long, graceful column of Juliana's neck and jaw. Summarily ignoring his desire to place his lips to the spot where her neck met her shoulder—that place that would smell like her, warm and soft and begging for his tongue.

He knew he should not look, but everything about her called to him. She was a siren.

If he was not careful, he would drown in her.

A burst of laughter brought him back to the moment, to the event. The conversation had shifted from the autumn season to politics to art and music, the gentlemen hanging on Juliana's every lilting word. The Earl of Allendale was holding court, regaling the entire table with tales of Lord and Lady Ralston's courtship.

Juliana listened with rapt attention, her sparkling gaze glued to Allendale, and a pang of discontent flared deep in Simon's gut. What would it be like to be the source of such pleasure? To be the man who elicited such a vibrant response? Such approval?

"Suffice it to say, I had never seen two people so destined for each other," Allendale said, his gaze lingering a touch too long on Juliana in a manner that Simon did not care for.

Juliana grinned. "It is a pity it took my brother so long to realize it."

The earl matched her smile as the rest of the company laughed. It was the second time Simon had seen Allendale give special attention to Juliana, and it did not escape him that the topic was appropriately romantic for any budding tendre between the two.

Simon sat back in his chair.

Allendale was entirely wrong for her. Too good-natured. Too genial. She'd run roughshod over him before he knew what had hit him.

He was not man enough for her.

Simon looked to Ralston, hoping that the marquess had seen the questionable exchange between his sister and brother-in-law, but Ralston only had eyes for his wife. He lifted his glass and toasted his wife. "I am endeavoring to make up for it."

Simon looked away, uncomfortable with the obvious affection between the marquess and the marchioness. His attention returned to Juliana, her blue eyes softening as she took in the intimate moment.

The *too*-intimate moment.

He did not belong here.

Not with her. Not with her family and the way they were all so comfortable—freely speaking, even at a formal dinner, somehow making all attendees so very comfortable.

So unlike his own family.

So compelling.

It was not for him.

A blush high on her cheeks, the marchioness raised her own glass. "As we are toasting, I think it only right that we toast His Grace for his role in rescuing our Juliana, don't you agree, my lord?"

The words, projected down the table at her husband, surprised Simon; prior to her marriage, Lady Calpurnia Hartwell had been a first-rate wallflower who would never have commanded such attention. She had found her voice.

Ralston raised his glass. "A capital idea, my darling. To Leighton. With thanks."

Around the table, the gentlemen raised their glasses and drank to Simon, and he was torn between a keen respect for the way this family manipulated society—by making their thanks entirely public and admitting Juliana's adventure, they had effectively removed the wind from the gossips' sails—and a hot irritation that he had been so well-and-truly used.

The Duchess of Rivington leaned in with a knowing smile, interrupting his thoughts. "Consider yourself fairly warned, Your Grace. Now that you have saved one of us, you shan't be able to escape!"

Everyone laughed. Everyone except Simon, who forced a polite smile and took a drink.

"I admit, I feel sorry for His Grace," Juliana chimed in, a lightness in her tone that he did not entirely believe. "I imagine he had hoped his heroism would gain him more than our constant companionship."

He loathed this conversation. Affecting a look of ducal boredom, he said, "There was nothing heroic about it."

"Your modesty is putting the rest of us to shame, Leighton," Stanhope called out, jovially. "The rest of us would happily accept the gratitude of such a beautiful lady."

A plate was set in front of him, and he made a project of cutting a piece of lamb, ignoring Stanhope.

"Tell us the story!" West said.

"I would prefer we didn't rehash it, Mr. West," he said, forcing a smile. "Particularly not to a newspaperman. I've had enough of the tale, myself."

The statement was met with a round of dissent from the rest of the dinner attendees, each calling for a recounting.

Simon remained silent.

"I agree with His Grace." The raucous chatter around

the table quieted at the soft statement, light with an Italian accent, and Simon, surprised, snapped his gaze to meet Juliana's. "There is not much more to it than that he saved my life. And without him—" She paused.

He did not want her to finish the sentence.

She demurred with a smile. "Well—It is enough to say that I am very grateful that you came to the park that afternoon"—she returned her attention to the rest of the group with a light—"and even more grateful that he can swim."

The table gave a collective chuckle at the words, but he barely heard it. In that moment, there was nothing he would not give to be alone with her—a fact that shook him to his core.

"Hear hear," said Allendale, raising his glass. "To the Duke of Leighton."

Around the table, glasses rose, and he avoided Juliana's eyes lest he betray too much of his thoughts.

"Even I shall have to rethink my opinion of you, Leighton," Ralston said wryly. "Thank you."

"And now, you have been forced to accept not only our dinner invitation, but also our gratitude," Juliana said from across the table.

Everyone assembled laughed to break the seriousness of the moment. Everyone that is, except Juliana, who broke their eye contact, looking down at her plate.

He considered their past, the things they had said—the ways they had lashed out, hoping to scratch if not to scar. He heard his words, the cutting way with which he had spoken to her, the way he had pushed her into a corner until she'd had no choice but to lie down or lash out.

She had fought back, proud and magnificent.

And suddenly, he wanted to tell her that.

He wanted her to know that he did not find her common, or childish, or troublesome.

He found her quite remarkable.

And he wanted to start over.

If for no other reason, than because she did not deserve his criticism.

But perhaps for more than that.

If only it were so easy.

The door to the dining room opened, and an older servant entered, discreetly moving to Ralston. He leaned low and whispered in his master's ear, and Ralston froze, setting his fork down audibly.

Conversation stopped.

Whatever the news the servant brought, it was not good.

The marquess was ashen.

Lady Ralston stood instantly, rounding the table toward her husband, caring nothing about her guests. About making a scene.

Juliana spoke, concern in her voice. "What is it? Is it Nick?"

"Gabriel?"

Heads turned as one to the doorway, to the woman who had spoken Ralston's given name.

"*Dio.*" Juliana's whisper was barely audible, but he heard it.

"Who is she?" Simon did not register who asked the question. He was too focused on Juliana's face, on the fear and anger and disbelief there.

Too focused on her answer, whispered in Italian.

"She is our mother."

She looked the same.

Tall and lithe and as untouchable as she had been the last time Juliana had seen her.

Instantly, Juliana was ten again, covered in chocolate from the cargo unloaded on the dock, chasing her cat through the old city and into the house, calling up to her father from the central courtyard, sunlight pouring down around her. A door opened, and her mother stepped out onto the upper balcony, the portrait of disinterest.

"Silenzio, *Juliana. Ladies do not screech.*"

"*I'm sorry,* Mama."

"*You should be.*" Louisa Fiori *leaned over the edge of the balcony. "You are filthy. It is as though I had a son instead of a daughter.*" *She waved one hand lazily toward the door.* "*Go back to the river and wash before you come into the house.*"

She turned away, the hem of her pale pink gown disappearing through the double doors to the house beyond.

It was the last Juliana had seen of her mother.

Until now.

"Gabriel?" their mother repeated, entering the room with utter poise, as though it had not been twenty-five years since she had hosted her own dinners at this very table. As though she were not being watched by a roomful of people.

Not that such a thing would have stopped her. She had always adored attention. The more scandalous, the better.

And this would be a scandal.

No one would remember the Serpentine tomorrow.

She lifted her hands. "Gabriel," there was satisfaction in her tone. "My, what a man you have become. The marquess!"

She was behind Juliana now, not having realized that her daughter, too, was in the room. There was a roaring in Juliana's ears, and she closed her eyes against it. Of course her mother had not noticed. Why would she expect such a thing?

If she had, she would have looked for Juliana. She would have said something.

She would have wanted to see her daughter.

Wouldn't she?

"Oh! It appears that I have interrupted something of a dinner party! I suppose I should have waited until morning, but I simply could not bear being away from home a moment longer."

Home.

Juliana winced at the words.

The men around the table stood, their manners arriving late but impeccable. "Oh, please, do not stand for me," the voice came again, unrelenting, dripping with English politesse and a hint of something else—the sound of feminine guile. "I shall simply put myself in a receiving room until Gabriel has time for me."

The statement ended on a lilt of amusement, and Juliana opened her eyes at the grating sound, turning her head just slightly to see her brother, jaw steeled, ice in his cold blue gaze. To his left stood Callie, fists clenched, furious.

If Juliana had not been at risk of becoming utterly unhinged, she would have been amused by her sister-in-law—ready to slay dragons for her husband.

Their mother was a dragon if ever there was one.

There was an enormous pause, silence screaming in the room until Callie spoke. "Bennett," she said, with unparalleled calm, "would you escort Signora Fiori to the green parlor? I'm sure the marquess will be along momentarily."

The aging butler, at least, seemed to understand that he had been the harbinger of what was sure to be the biggest scandal London had seen since . . . well, since the last time London had seen Louisa Hathbourne St. John Fiori. He nearly leapt to do his mistress's bidding.

"Signora Fiori!" their mother said with a bright laugh—the one Juliana remembered as punctuation to a lie. "No one has called me that since I left Italy. I am still the Marchioness of Ralston, am I not?"

"You are not." Ralston's voice was brittle with anger.

"You are married? How wonderful! I shall simply have to do with Dowager Marchioness, then!"

And with that simple sentence, Juliana was unable to breathe. Her mother had just renounced a decade of marriage, a husband, a life in Italy.

And her own daughter.

In front of a dozen others who would not hesitate to recount the tale.

Juliana closed her eyes, willing herself to remain calm.

Focusing on her breath, rather than the fact that her legitimacy had, with a few words from a long-forgotten woman, been thrown into question.

When she reopened her eyes, it was to meet the one gaze she did not wish to find.

The Duke of Leighton was not looking at her mother. He was watching Juliana. And she hated what she saw in his normally cold, unreadable amber eyes.

Pity.

Embarrassment and shame coursed through her, straightening her spine and reddening her cheeks.

She was going to be ill.

She could not remain in the room a moment longer.

She had to leave.

Before she did something thoroughly unacceptable.

She stood, pushing back her chair, not caring that ladies did not leave the dinner table midmeal, not caring that she was breaking every rule of this ridiculous country's ridiculous etiquette.

And she fled.

The dinner party disbanded almost immediately upon the arrival of the Dowager Marchioness or Signora Fiori or whoever she was, and the rest of the attendees had made hasty retreats, ostensibly to allow the family time and space with which to address her devastating arrival, but much more likely to have been in the foul hope of spreading their first-person accounts of tonight's dramatics.

Simon could think only of Juliana: of her face as she listened to her mother's high-pitched cackle; of her enormous, soulful eyes as the wicked woman had made her scandalous pronouncement that she was not a Fiori, but a St. John; of the way she'd left the room, all square shoulders and straight spine, with stunning, remarkable pride.

He watched the other guests' conveyances trundle down the street, listening with half an ear as the Duke and Duchess of Rivington discussed whether or not they should remain or leave their family in peace.

As they climbed into their coach, Simon heard the duchess ask quietly, "Should we at least look in on Juliana?"

"Leave her for tonight, love," was Rivington's idiotic reply before the door closed, and the carriage set off in the direction of their home.

Simon clenched his teeth. Of course they should have sought out Juliana. Someone had to make sure that the girl was not planning a midnight return to Italy.

Not him, of course.

He climbed up into his own coach—full with the memory of her on another scandalous evening.

She was not his concern.

He could not afford the scandal. He had his own family to worry about. Juliana was fine. Would be, at least. The woman had to be impervious to embarrassment by now.

And if she wasn't?

With a wicked curse, he rapped on the ceiling of the coach and instructed the coachman to turn around. He did not even question his destination.

She was in the stables.

There were several stableboys loitering outside, and they came immediately to their feet at the sight of the Duke of Leighton. He waved them back and entered the building, thinking of nothing but finding her.

He did not hide his footsteps as he made his way down the long row of stalls to where she was, following the soft whispers of Italian and the smooth rustle of her clothes.

He stopped just outside the stall door, transfixed by her.

Her back was to him, and she was brushing her horse with a hard-bristled brush, each short, firm stroke coming on a little puff of breath. Periodically, the mare would shuffle and lean toward her mistress, turning her head for extra attention. When Juliana stroked the animal's long, white muzzle, the horse was unable to contain its pleasure, nuzzling Juliana's shoulder with a snort.

Simon could not blame the animal for preening under the affection.

"She did not even know I was there," Juliana whispered in Italian as she worked her way down the mare's broad back. "And if I hadn't been, if I'd never come here, she would not have acknowledged her time with me at all."

There was a pause, the only sound the light rustle of her bold, silk gown, entirely counter to her soft, sad whisper, and his heart went out to her. It was one thing to be deserted by a mother, but what a crushing blow it must have been to have her mother reject the life they had shared?

The sound of the brush slowed. "Not that I care if she acknowledges it at all."

He heard the lie in the words, and something deep in his chest constricted, making it difficult to breathe.

"Perhaps now we can return to Italy, Lucrezia." She put her forehead to the high black shoulder of the horse. "Perhaps now Gabriel will see that my staying was a terrible idea."

The whispered words, so honest, so rife with sorrow and regret, were nearly his undoing. From the moment he'd met her, he'd thought she enjoyed the scandal that followed her everywhere. Thought she embraced it, invited it.

But as he stood in this darkened stable, watching her brush her enormous horse, dressed in a devastatingly beautiful gown and desperate for some way to escape the events of the evening, Simon was overcome with a single realization.

Scandal was not her choice.

It was her burden.

Her bold words and her brave face were not borne out of pleasure but out of self-preservation.

She was as much a victim of circumstance as he was.

The awareness hit him like a fist to the gut.

But it changed nothing.

"I would not place a wager on your brother allowing you to leave," he said in Italian.

Juliana spun toward him, and he registered the fear and nervousness in her wide blue eyes an instant before it was gone, replaced with irritation.

Her fire was not gone.

"How long have you been there?" she asked in English, taking a step back, pressing herself against the side of the horse, who sidestepped once and gave a little, distraught nicker.

He stilled, as though moving closer to her would scare her off. "Long enough."

Her gaze darted around the stall, as though she were looking for an escape route. As though she were terrified of him. And then she seemed to remember that she wasn't terrified of anything.

Her eyes narrowed on him, blue and beautiful. "Eavesdropping is a terrible habit."

He leaned against the doorjamb, giving her space. "You may add it to my list of unpleasant traits."

"There isn't enough paper in England to list them all."

He raised a brow. "You wound me."

She scowled, turning back to the horse. "If only it were so. Don't you have somewhere to be?"

So it was to be this way. She did not want to discuss the events of the evening. He watched as she resumed the long, firm strokes of the horse's flanks. "I was invited to a dinner party, but it ended early."

"It sounds like it was a terrible bore," she said, her voice dry as sand. "Shouldn't you be at your club? Recounting the devastating blow to our reputation to other arrogant aristocrats in a cloud of cheroot smoke as you drink scotch stolen from the North Country?"

"What do you know about cheroot smoke?"

She tossed him a look over her shoulder. "We do not have such restrictive rules in Italy."

It was his turn for dryness. "Really? I had not noticed."

"I am quite serious. Surely you have something better to do than stand in the stables and watch me groom my horse."

"In an evening gown."

The most incredible gown he'd ever seen.

She gave one of her little shrugs. "Don't tell me there's a rule about that, too."

"A rule about ladies wearing evening gowns to groom horses?"

"Yes."

"Not in so many words, no."

"Excellent." She did not stop her movements.

"That said, I must say I have never witnessed a lady so well attired grooming a horse."

"You still haven't."

He paused. "I beg your pardon?"

"You still haven't witnessed a lady doing so. I think tonight has made it quite clear that I am no lady, don't you?" She leaned down and tapped the mare's forelock, inspecting one hoof. "I don't have the kind of stock required for the honor."

And with that, the conversation turned, and the air in the room grew heavy.

She turned back to him, meeting his gaze with complete seriousness. "Why did you come looking for me?"

Damned if he knew.

"Did you think that now that our mother is back, you could come to me in the stables, and I would behave the way she always did?" The words hung between them, brash and unpleasant, and Simon wanted to shake her for saying them. For cheapening his concern. For suggesting that she was nothing better than her mother had been.

She pressed on. "Or perhaps you could not resist the opportunity to enumerate the additional ways that I am damaged goods after tonight? I assure you, there is nothing you could say that I have not already considered myself."

He deserved it, he supposed, but he could not help but defend himself. Did she really think that he would take this opportunity—this night—to set her down? "Juliana, I—" He took a step toward her, and she put up a hand to stay his movement.

"Don't tell me this has changed everything, Leighton."

She had never called him that. Your Grace, in that mocking tone that set him instantly on edge. Or Simon.

But now, in all seriousness, she used his title. The shift unsettled him.

She laughed, the sound cold and brittle and altogether unlike her. "Of course it hasn't. This has merely underscored all that you already know. All that you've known since the beginning. How is it you say it? I am a scandal waiting to happen?" She tilted her head, feigning deep thought. "Perhaps I have already happened. But, if there were any doubt, the woman standing in that dining room is more than enough, isn't she?" There was a long silence before she added, in Italian, so softly that he was almost unsure he heard it, "She's ruined everything. Again."

There was a devastating sadness in the words, a sadness that echoed around them until he could not bear it. "She's not you," he said in her language, as though speaking it in Italian could make her believe it.

She wouldn't believe it, of course.

But he did.

"*Sciocchezze!*" Her eyes glistened with angry tears as she resisted his words, calling them nonsense as she turned away, presenting him with her back. He almost didn't hear the rest of the statement, lost in the harsh hiss of the brush. "She is what I come from. She is what I shall become, isn't that how it goes?"

The words sliced through him, making him unreasonably furious with her for thinking them, and he reached for her, unable to stop himself. Turned her toward him, met her wide eyes. "Why would you say that?" He heard the roughness in his tone. Tried to clear it. Failed. "Why would you think that?"

She laughed, the sound harsh and without humor. "I'm not the only one. Isn't that what you believe? Aren't those the words by which aristocrats like you live? Come now, Your Grace. I've met your mother." Then, in English, "Blood will out, will it not?"

He stopped. They were words that he had heard

countless times—one of his mother's favorite sayings. "Did she say that to you?"

"Haven't you said it to me?" She lifted her chin, proud and defiant.

"No."

One side of her mouth kicked up. "Not in so many words. It bears true for you, doesn't it? Looking down at the lesser creatures from up on high. Blood will out—the very motto of the Duke of Disdain."

The Duke of Disdain.

He'd heard it before, of course, the epithet that was whispered as he passed. He'd simply never given it much thought. Never realized the aptness of the name. Never realized the truth of it.

Emotion was for the masses.

It had always been easier to be the Duke of Disdain than to let them see the rest of him. The part that was not so disdainful.

He hated that Juliana knew the nickname. Hated that she thought of him that way. He met her glittering blue gaze and read the anger and defensiveness there. He could deal with those responses from her. But not the sadness.

He could not bear her sadness.

She read his thoughts, and her eyes flashed fury. "Don't. Don't you dare pity me. I don't want it." She tried to shake off his grip. "I'd rather have your disinterest."

The words shocked him into letting her go. "My disinterest?"

"That's what it is, is it not? Boredom? Apathy?"

He'd had enough.

"You think my feelings toward you *apathetic*?" His voice shook, and he advanced on her. "You think you *bore* me?"

She blinked under the heat of his words, stepping back toward the side of the stall. "Don't I?"

He shook his head slowly, continuing toward her, stalking her in the small space. "No."

She opened her mouth then closed it, not knowing what to say.

"God knows you are infuriating . . ." Nervousness flared in her eyes. "And impulsive . . ." Her back came up against the wall, and she gave a little squeak, even as he advanced. "And altogether maddening . . ." He placed one hand to her jaw, carefully lifting her face to his, feeling the leap of her pulse under his fingertips. "And thoroughly intoxicating . . ." The last came out on a low growl, and her lips parted, soft and pink and perfect.

He leaned close, his lips a fraction from hers.

"No . . . you are not boring."

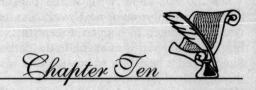

Chapter Ten

Hay and horses make for unpleasant *eau de toilette*.
The stables are no place for a exquisite lady.

—*A Treatise on the Most Exquisite of Ladies*

Across our great nation, vicars draft sermons on the
prodigal son . . .

—*The Scandal Sheet, October 1823*

Juliana had been enthralled by him as he'd crossed
the stall, stalking her until she could go no farther,
caging her with his long arms, and touching her—giving
her the contact that she had not known she yearned for
until that moment. And his voice, that low, dark rumble
of whiskey and velvet, had scrambled her thoughts,
making her forget why she was here in this dark stable
to begin with.

He had hovered there, a breath away, waiting for her.
Waiting as though he could have stood for hours, for
days, while she considered her options, while she decided what to do next.

But she did not need days or hours.

She barely needed seconds.

She did not know what would happen later that evening or tomorrow or next week. She did not know what she wanted to happen. Except this. She wanted him. She wanted this moment, in the darkened stables. She wanted a heartbeat of passion that would last her through whatever was to come.

He was enormous, his wide shoulders blocking out the dim light from the lantern on the wall of the stables, casting him into harsh, wicked shadow. She could not see his eyes but imagined their amber depths flashing with barely contained passion.

Perhaps it was not the case . . . but she preferred to believe that he could not get enough of her.

She placed her hands on him, feeling her way up his arms, reveling in the way that his muscles rippled beneath the wool of his coat, wishing that there were less fabric between them. Her fingers traced over broad, tense shoulders, to his neck, where she finally, finally connected with warm, soft skin. He bent his head as she tangled her hands in his soft, golden curls, either to afford her better access or because he no longer had the strength to resist.

She liked the idea of the latter.

His lips were at her ear now, his breath coming in ragged bursts, and she delighted in the sound, so contrary to his normal, cool countenance.

"You do not sound bored."

He gave a harsh laugh and tortured her with a whisper at her ear. "If I had a hundred years to describe how I feel right now, bored would not make an appearance."

She turned her head at the words, her gaze colliding with his. "Be careful, Simon. You shall make me like you. And then where will we be?"

He did not answer, and she waited for him to close the

distance between them. Marveled at his control when he did not. His endless, unwavering control.

She could not match it. Did not try.

She pressed her lips to his and gave herself up to his kiss.

The moment their lips touched, Simon moved. He inhaled deeply and wrapped his arms around her, enveloping her in the heat and strength and scent of him—fresh lemon and tobacco flower.

He pulled her closer, his grip strong and powerful, his hands setting her aflame. There was something different about this kiss from the one that morning in Hyde Park . . . that had been a kiss of frustration and fury, fear and anger.

This kiss was an exploration.

It sought and found, chased and captured. It was a kiss that suggested they had an eternity during which to learn each other, and when his tongue ran rough-smooth across her bottom lip, sending wave after wave of sensation rocketing through her, she hoped they *did* have an eternity. Surely, it would take that long for her to tire of this. *Of him.* She gasped at the feel of him, so powerful, so wicked.

He lifted his head at the sound, his shadowed eyes searching hers. "Is this . . ."

Her fingers stretched into his soft golden curls, pulling him back to her. "It is perfect."

He growled his satisfaction at her answer, moving his hands to cup her face in his palms, tilting her head to the perfect angle, and taking her mouth in a single stark claiming that stole her breath. As he tormented her with deep, luxurious kisses that made it impossible to think or speak or do anything but feel.

Her legs turned to water, and he caught her, lifting her off her feet as though she weighed nothing at all. She met his force with her own, desperate to wrap around him even as her legs became tangled in silk and cotton. She kicked out, nearly hitting him in the shin, and he lifted his mouth from hers, curious.

"There is too much fabric in these damned gowns," she said, frustrated.

He set her down and one strong, warm hand stroked down her neck to the wide bare expanse of skin there. "I find there is the right amount in certain places." He ran one finger along the edge of her dress, setting her skin on fire. "This gown is the most beautiful thing I've ever seen."

She pressed toward him, unable to stop herself. Knowing that it was utterly wanton behavior. "I had it made for you." She kissed him again, nipping his bottom lip before she added, "I thought you would like it. I thought you would not be able to resist it."

"You thought right. But, I am coming to see your point. Entirely too much fabric." And then he pulled the edge of the gown down, revealing the pebbled, aching tip of one breast. "So beautiful." The whisper was dark and velvet, and she watched as he traced a single finger in a circle there once, twice. Then the finger moved, tilting her chin up to meet his dark gaze. "Yes or no?"

It was an imperious question, spoken as though he was gifting her with one fleeting moment to decide what she wanted before he took the lead once more and she tumbled, headfirst, into the world of which he was master.

"Yes," she whispered, her fingers threading into his hair and pulling him to her. "Yes, Simon."

Something flashed, dark and unhinged in his eyes, and he lowered his head, taking her lips in a searing kiss before he tracked his lips down her throat and across the pale skin of her breast. Her fingers flexed in his curls.

Yes. Simon.

He was in control.

He was ruining her for all others.

And she did not care.

His tongue brushed against the devastatingly sensitive skin at the tip of her breast, and she bit her lip, arching. Acquiescing.

"Juliana?"

If the barn had gone up in flames, she could not have been more shocked than she was by the sound of her brother calling her name.

Simon went instantly rigid, straightening and immediately restoring the edge of her dress to its proper place as he did so, and she scrambled to push past him, fumbling with her skirts, spinning in a circle to get her bearings as she said, "In—in here, Gabriel." She finally picked up the hard-bristled brush again, and said, loudly, "And she particularly enjoys it when I brush her flanks firmly."

"I've been looking everywhere for you—what are you doing in the stables alone in the middle of the—" Ralston stepped into the stall and froze, taking in first Simon, then Juliana. It did not take him long to read the situation.

Correctly.

When he moved, he was like lightning.

Ignoring Juliana's gasp, he stormed past her and grasped the lapels of Simon's topcoat, pulling him away from the wall where he had leaned, attempting to appear casual. Ralston spun the duke around, throwing him out the stall door and into the wall opposite, sending the horses stabled along the corridor into a chorus of nervous whinnies.

"Gabriel!" she cried, following them into the hallway in time to see her brother grasp Simon's cravat in one hand and deliver a powerful blow to the jaw with the other.

"I've wanted to do that for twenty years, you arrogant bastard," Ralston growled.

Why wasn't Simon fighting back?

"Gabriel, stop!"

Her brother didn't listen. "On your feet."

Simon stood, rubbing his fast-bruising jaw with one hand. "You received the first one for free, Ralston."

Ralston's shoulders were tensed, his fists raised and ready for battle. If he was feeling anything like Juliana had been feeling when she left the house, he would not stop until one or both of them were unconscious; considering Leighton's flashing eyes and tensed muscles, Juliana imagined it would be both of them.

"I shall pay the fee for the rest with pleasure," Ralston stormed at the duke again, getting in a quick jab before Leighton blocked the next blow and sent Ralston's head snapping back with a wicked hook.

Juliana winced at the sound of flesh on flesh and, without thinking, intervened.

"No! No one is paying any fee! Not now, not ever!" Juliana pushed between them, both hands up—a referee in a perverse boxing match.

"Juliana, get out of the way." Leighton's words were soft and dark.

"Speak to her with such familiarity again, and I'll see you at dawn," Ralston said, furious. "In fact, give me one reason not to call you out right now."

"Because we've had enough scandal for one evening, Gabriel," Juliana answered. "Even I can see that."

And like that, the fight went out of him.

She did not lower her hands until he lowered his. But when he did, she said, "Nothing happened."

He gave a little humorless laugh, meeting Leighton's gaze over her head. She saw the murderous glint in his eyes. "You forget I have not always been an old married man, sister. I know when nothing has happened. Ladies do not look like you do when *nothing* has happened. Men like Leighton do not happily take punches when *nothing* has happened."

She felt a blush rising on her cheeks, but stood her ground. "You are wrong. *Nothing happened.*"

Except something did happen, a little voice whispered teasing in a dark corner of her mind. *Something wonderful.*

She ignored it. "Tell him, Your Grace."

Simon did not speak, and she looked over her shoulder at him. "Tell him," she repeated.

It was as though she were not there. He was looking directly over her head, right into Ralston's eyes.

"What if it were your sister, Leighton," Ralston said softly from behind her. "Would it be nothing then?"

Something flashed in Simon's gaze. Anger. *No.* Frustration. No, something else. Something more complicated.

And she saw what he was about to do a moment before he did it.

She had to stop him.

"No! Don't—"

She was too late.

"I'll marry her."

She saw the words more than heard them—watched as his perfect lips formed the syllables even as their sound was masked by the roar in her ears.

She turned immediately to her brother. "No. He won't marry me."

Silence stretched long and tense, filling the barn to the rafters. Uncertainty flared, and she looked to Simon again. His face was cold and unmoving, his eyes fixed on Ralston as though he were waiting for a pronouncement of death.

And he was.

He did not want to marry her. She was not his pretty

English bride, who was likely fast asleep and far from scandal. But he would, because that was what was done. Because he was the kind of man who did what was expected without argument. Without fight.

He would marry her not because he wanted her . . . but because he should.

Not that she wanted him to want her.

Liar.

She would be damned if she would suffer for his misplaced nobility.

Ralston did not meet her gaze, did not turn his attention from the duke.

She looked to Leighton, amber eyes guarded. He nodded once.

Oh for—

She turned back to Gabriel. "Hear me, brother. I won't marry him. *Nothing happened.*"

"No, you won't marry him."

Shock coursed through her. "I won't?"

"No. The duke appears to have forgotten that he is already affianced."

Her jaw dropped. *It couldn't be true.* "What?"

"Go on, Leighton. Tell her it's true," Ralston said, fury in his words. "Tell her that you are not so perfect after all."

Anger flared in Simon's eyes. "I have not asked the lady."

"Only her father," Ralston said, all smugness.

She wanted Simon to refute the point, but she saw the truth in his eyes.

He was engaged.

He was engaged, and he had been kissing her. In the stables. As though she were worth nothing more than a tumble.

As though she were her mother.

Even as he had told her she was nothing like her mother.

She turned to him, not hiding the accusation in her eyes, and to give him credit, he did try to speak. "Juliana—"

She simply did not want to hear him. "No. There is nothing to say."

She watched the long column of his throat work, thinking that perhaps he was looking for the right thing to say before she remembered that this was *Leighton,* who always had the right thing to say.

Except for when there clearly was no right thing.

Ralston stepped in, then, ending the moment. "If you come within three feet of my sister again, Leighton, you'd best have your seconds chosen."

There was a long, tense moment before Leighton said, "It will not be a problem to stay away from her. It would not have been if you kept a tighter leash on those under your care."

And with those cold, unfeeling words, the Duke of Disdain left the stables.

Her mother had returned.

"Redeo, Redis, Redit . . ."

Her mother had returned *for God knew what reason.*

"Redimus, Reditis, Redeunt . . ."

Her mother had returned for God knew what reason *and Juliana had nearly gotten herself ruined in the stables.*

"I return, you return, she returns . . ."

Her mother had returned for God knew what reason and Juliana had nearly gotten herself ruined in the stables *by the Duke of Leighton.*

And she'd enjoyed it.

Not the mother returning part, but the other.

That part had been quite . . . magnificent.

Until he'd been engaged. And had happily turned his back and exited her life.

Leaving her to deal with her mother.

Who had returned.

She sighed, slapping the palms of her hands against the cool brocade coverlet on her bed.

Was it any wonder that she could not sleep?

It was not exactly as though she had had the easiest of evenings.

He'd left.

Well, first he'd proposed marriage.

After making her feel *wonderful.*

After proposing marriage to another woman.

Something twisted deep inside her. Something easily identified.

Longing. She did not even understand it. He was an awful man, arrogant and proud, cold and unfeeling. Except for when he was not those things. Except for when he was teasing and charming and filled with fire. With passion.

She closed her eyes, trying to ignore the ache in her chest.

He'd made her want him. And then he'd left.

"I leave, you leave . . ."

Verb conjugations were not helping.

Frustrated, she leapt from the bed, yanking open the door and heading down the wide, dark hallway of Ralston House, running the tips of her fingers along the wall, counting doors until she reached the center staircase of the town house. Padding down the steps, she registered a dim light coming from her brother's study.

She did not knock.

Ralston stood at the enormous windows of his study, one hand playing idly with a glass orb she had bought him several months ago as he stared into the great black abyss beyond. His dark hair was mussed, and he'd removed his coat and waistcoat and cravat.

Juliana winced as she registered the bruise on his jaw from where Simon had hit him.

She had done very little but cause him trouble.

If their positions were reversed, she would have tossed her out on her ear months ago.

He looked over when Juliana entered, but did not scold her for her trespass. She took a seat by his desk and pulled her bare feet up beneath her dressing gown as he turned back to the window.

Neither sibling spoke for a long while, and the silence stretched wide and somehow comfortable between them. Juliana took a deep breath. "I would like to clean the air."

Ralston smirked. "*Clear* the air."

That did make more sense. She narrowed her gaze. "I am about to apologize, and you mock me?"

He half smiled. "Go on."

"Thank you." She paused. "I am sorry."

"For what?" He looked honestly confused.

She gave a little laugh. "There is a great deal, no?" She thought for a moment. "I suppose I am sorry that everything falls to you."

He did not reply.

"Where is she?"

The glass sphere rolled between his fingers. "Gone."

Juliana paused, a ripple of emotion shooting through her. She did not pause to inspect it. She was not certain that she wanted to. "Forever?"

He bowed his head, and she thought she heard him laugh. "No. If only it were that easy. I didn't want her in this house."

She watched him, her strong, sturdy brother, who seemed to carry the weight of the world on his shoulders. "Where did you send her?"

He turned to face her then, the orb spinning. "She did not know you were here, you know. She did not expect you. That is why she did not look for you in the room. At dinner."

She nodded. It did not make her mother's dismissal any easier. "Does she know I am here now?"

"I told her." The words were soft, laced with something that might have been an apology. She nodded, and silence fell again. He returned to the desk and took the seat across from her. "You are my sister. You take precedence."

Was he reminding her or himself?

She met his eyes. "What does she want?"

He leaned forward on his elbows. "She says she doesn't want anything."

"Except her position as dowager marchioness." Juliana could not keep the sarcasm from her tone.

"She'll never have that."

She couldn't. The *ton* would never accept her. The gossipmongers would feed on this scandal for years. When Juliana had arrived in London six months ago, they had swarmed, and the sordid tale of their mother's desertion had been dredged from the bottom of the great river of drama that nourished society. Even now, with connections to some of the most powerful families in London, Juliana existed on the fringes of polite society—accepted by association rather than on her own merit.

It would all start over again. Worse than before.

"You don't believe her, do you?" she asked. "That she wants nothing."

"No."

"Then what?"

He shook his head. "Money, family . . ."

"Forgiveness?"

He thought for a long moment, then lifted one shoulder in the shrug they all used when they did not have an answer. "It is a powerful motivator. Who knows?"

A rush of heat flared, and she leaned forward, shaking her head. "She can't have it. She can't . . . what she did to you . . . to Nick . . . to our fathers . . ."

One side of his mouth rose almost imperceptibly. "To you . . ."

To me.

He leaned back in his chair, shifting the glass weight from one hand to the other. "I never thought she would return."

She shook her head. "One would think the scandal alone would have kept her away."

He gave a little laugh at that. "You forget that she is our mother—a woman who has always lived as though scandal was for others. And, in fairness, it always has been."

Our mother.

Juliana was reminded of the conversation in the stables with Simon. How much of this woman was in Juliana? How much of her lack of caring and complete disregard for others lurked deep within her daughter?

Juliana stiffened.

"You are not like her." Her attention snapped to her brother, his fiery blue gaze firmly upon her.

Tears pricked at his honesty. "How do you know that?"

"I know. And someday, you will as well."

The words were so simple, their sentiment so certain, that Juliana wanted to scream. How could he know? How could he be so certain that she was not precisely the woman their mother was? That, along with her height and her hair and her blue eyes, she had not inherited a complete and utter disregard for those around her, whom she was supposed to love?

Blood will out.

Instead, she said, "The scandal . . . when they hear . . . that she's back . . ."

"It will be enormous." She met his serious blue gaze. "The way I see it, we have two options. We either pack up and head for the country—her in tow—and hope that the gossip fades."

If wishing would make it so . . .

She wrinkled her nose. "Or?"

"Or we square our shoulders and face it head-on."

It was not a choice. Not for her. Not for him either.

One side of her mouth lifted in a half smile. "Well, let it not be said that Ralston House does not keep London happily in gossip."

There was a pause, and he started to laugh, a rumbling sound that came from deep in his chest. And soon, she was laughing, too.

Because at that moment, it was either laugh or cry.

As the laughter died down, Ralston leaned back in his seat and looked to the ceiling. "Nick must be told."

Of course. Their brother and his new wife lived in Yorkshire, but this was news that he must hear as soon as possible. She nodded. "Will he come?"

His brows rose, as though he had not considered the possibility. "I don't know. Nick and she . . . they . . ." He trailed off and they sat in silence again, each lost in thought.

She was back.

And with her, decades of long-buried questions.

She met her brother's gaze. "Gabriel," she whispered, "what if she is here to stay?"

Something flared in his blue eyes, a combination of anger and concern. He took a deep breath, as though collecting his thoughts. "Don't for a minute imagine she's here for good, Juliana. If there is one thing I know about that woman, it is that she is unable to stomach constancy. She wants something. And when she's obtained it, she'll leave." He set the crystal sphere down on the table. "She will go. She will go, and everything will return to normal."

In the six months since she had arrived in London, Juliana had had many opportunities to see the man beneath the Marquess of Ralston's devil-may-care façade. Enough opportunities to know that he did not believe his words.

Couldn't believe them.

It was an understatement to say that their mother's return changed everything. It was not simply that she would unearth a scandal twenty-five years in the making. It was not simply that she seemed to have little concern for the impact she had on society and even less remorse for her actions. It was not simply that she had marched into Ralston House as though she had never left.

Even if all that could be erased—if Gabriel tossed her out and shipped her off to the Outer Hebrides, never to be heard from again—nothing would ever be the same.

For, before tonight, they could have pretended—had pretended—that she was gone for good. Certainly, Juliana had always wondered if her mother was still alive, where she was, what she was doing, whom she was with. But somewhere in a deep, quiet part of her, she'd always assumed that her mother was gone forever.

And she'd begun to come to terms with it when she arrived in London, met her brothers, been given a chance at a new life. A life in which her mother's specter continued to loom, but less heavy and foreboding than before.

No longer.

"You don't really believe that," she said.

There was a long pause, then, "She wants to speak with you."

She noticed the change in topic but made no move to correct it. She picked an invisible piece of lint from the sleeve of her dressing gown. "I'm sure she does."

"You may deal with her as you wish."

She watched him carefully. "What do you think I should do?"

"I think you should make the decision for yourself."

She pulled her knees up to her chin again, setting her heels on the smooth leather seat. "I don't think I want to speak to her. Not yet."

Someday, maybe. Yes. But not now.

He nodded once. "Fair." Silence fell, and he organized several piles of correspondence, the bruise on his jaw shimmering in the candlelight.

"Does it hurt?"

One hand went to the side of his face, exploring the lesion with tentative fingertips. "Leighton has always been able to throw a punch. It's a side benefit to his being enormous."

One side of Juliana's mouth kicked up. Her brother had not answered the question. She imagined it hurt very much.

"I'm sorry for that, as well."

He met her gaze, blue eyes glittering with anger. "I don't know how long the two of you—"

"We—"

He sliced a hand through the air, staying her words. "And, frankly, I don't want to know." He sighed, long and tired. "But stay away from him, Juliana. When we said we wanted to make you a good match, Leighton was not who we imagined."

Even her brother thought Simon too good for her.

"Because he is a duke?"

"What? No," Ralston said, truly perplexed by her instant defensive response. "Because he's an ass."

She smiled. She couldn't help it. He said it in such an obvious, matter-of-fact way. "Why do you think that?"

"Suffice it to say, the duke and I have had our fair share of altercations. He's arrogant and supercilious and utterly impossible. He takes his name far too seriously and his title even more seriously than that. I can't stand him, frankly, and I should have remembered that over the last few weeks, but he's seemed so concerned about your reputation that I was willing to ignore my prejudice." He gave her a wry look. "Now I see I should have known better."

"You were not the only one who was fooled," she said, more to herself than to him.

He stood. "On the bright side, I have been waiting to hit him for twenty years. So that was one thing that went right today." He flexed his hand. "Do you think he has a bruise to match mine?"

The masculine pride in his tone made her laugh, and she stood, as well. "I'm sure it's much larger. And uglier. And far more painful. I hope so, at least."

He came around the desk and chucked her on the chin. "Correct answer."

"I am a quick lesson."

He laughed this time. "A quick study."

She tilted her head. "Truly?"

"Truly. Now. A favor?"

"Yes?"

"Stay the hell away from him."

The ache in her chest returned at the words. She ignored it. "I want nothing to do with the difficult man."

"Excellent." He believed her.

Now, she simply had to believe herself.

Chapter Eleven

Even at balls, one must be wary of the vulgar.
Elegant ladies steer clear of dark corners.

—*A Treatise on the Most Exquisite of Ladies*

Fluttering sparrows and their companions recently received their due . . .

—*The Scandal Sheet, October 1823*

The steps leading up to Dolby House were covered in vegetables.

The Marchioness of Needham and Dolby had taken her harvest ball more than seriously, covering the front of the house with onions, potatoes, what looked like several different kinds of wheat, and gourds of every conceivable size and color. A path had been created for guests, not a straight shot up the steps and into the house, but a meandering, curving, walkway flanked with spoils of the harvest that made seven steps feel like seventy, and those following it feel utterly ridiculous.

Juliana alighted from the carriage and eyed the

squash- and wheat-strewn pathway skeptically. Callie followed her down and gave a little chuckle at the exhibition. "Oh, my."

Ralston took his wife's arm and led the way through the extravagant labyrinth. "This is all your doing, you know," he whispered at her ear, and Juliana could hear the humor in his tone. "I hope you're happy."

Callie laughed. "I have never had the opportunity to meander through a vegetable patch, my lord," she teased. "So yes, I am quite happy."

Ralston rolled his eyes heavenward. "There will be no meandering, Empress. Let's get this over with." He turned toward Juliana, indicating that she should precede him up the steps. "Sister?"

Juliana pasted a bright smile on her face and stepped up alongside him. He leaned down, and said quietly, "Keep the smile on your face, and they shan't know how to respond."

There was no question that by now, a full day since the return of their mother, the *ton* would be buzzing with the news. There had been a brief discussion that afternoon of not attending this particular ball, hosted at the home of Lady Penelope—the future Duchess of Leighton—but Callie had insisted that if they were to weather this storm, they had to attend any events to which they received invitations, whether Leighton was going to be in attendance or not. Soon, after all, there would be markedly fewer to accept.

And tonight, at least, the full narrative of the prior evening's events at Ralston House would be hazy at best.

She increased the brightness of her smile and trod along the path between turnips and marrows, squash and courgettes, into what was destined to be one of the longest nights of her life.

Once divested of her cloak, Juliana turned to face the pit of vipers that waited inside the ballroom of Dolby House.

The first thing she noticed were the stares. The entrance to the ballroom was from above, down a short flight of stairs almost certainly designed for the best—and least innocuous—entrance. As she hovered there at the top of the stairs, Juliana felt scores of eyes raking over her. Looking out across the room, she refused to allow her smile to fade even as she saw the telltale signs of gossip: bowed heads, fluttering fans, and brightly lit eyes, eager for a glimpse at whatever sordid drama might unfold.

Callie turned back to her, and she recognized a similarly-too-bright smile on her sister-in-law's face. "You're doing wonderfully. Once we're in the crush, everything will settle."

She wanted to believe that the words were true. She looked out over the crowd, desperate to appear as though something had captured her attention. And then something did.

Simon.

She caught her breath as hot memory flooded through her.

He stood at the far end of the ballroom, tall and handsome, in perfect formalwear and a linen cravat with lines so crisp it could have sliced butter. High on one cheek she noticed a red welt—it appeared that at least one of Ralston's blows from the evening prior had struck true—but the mark only made Simon more handsome. More devastating.

It only made her want him more.

He had not seen her, and still she resisted the simultaneous urges to smooth her skirts and turn and run for the exit. Instead, she focused on descending to the ballroom floor, where she could not see him.

Perhaps if she could not see him, she would stop thinking so much about him—about his kisses and his strong arms, and the way his lips had felt against her bare skin.

And the way he had proposed to Lady Penelope before he had come for Juliana in the stables.

Lady Penelope, in whose home Juliana stood.

She pushed the thoughts to the side as her brother came to her elbow and leaned low into her ear. "Remember what we discussed."

She nodded. "I shall be the belle of the ball."

He grinned. "As usual." She snorted her laughter, and he added, "Well, do attempt to do as little of *that* as possible."

"I live to do your bidding, my lord."

He gave a short bark of laughter. "If only that were true." His gaze grew serious. "Try to enjoy yourself. Dance as much as you can."

She nodded. *If anyone would ask her.*

"Miss Fiori?" The deep, warm request came from behind her, and she spun to face Callie's brother, the Earl of Allendale. He smiled, kindness in his brown eyes. He held out one hand. "Would you do me the honor?"

It had been planned, she knew it. Planned that she would have someone with whom to dance the moment she entered the ballroom. Planned that that someone would be an earl.

She accepted, and they danced a lively quadrille, and Benedick was the perfect gentleman, promenading her around the perimeter of the room after the dance, not leaving her side. "You do not have to be so careful with me, you know," she finally said, softly. "They cannot do much to me in a ballroom."

He gave a half smile. "They can do plenty to you in a ballroom. And besides, I have nowhere better to go."

They reached a quiet spot on the edge of the room and stood silently beside each other, watching other dancers trip across the floor in a country reel. "Don't you have other ladies to court?" she teased.

He shook his head in mock sadness. "Not a single one.

I am relieved of my duties as bachelor earl this evening."

"Ah," she said, "so something good has come of the trouble at Ralston House."

He flashed her a grin. "For me, at least." They fell back to watching the dancers for a while before Benedick said quietly, "It shall be all right, you know."

She did not look to him for fear of losing her mask of serenity. "I do not know that, but thank you very much for saying so."

"Ralston will do what needs to be done to make it all right. He shall have the full support of Rivington and me . . . and dozens of others."

But not the one man I hoped would stand with us.

She turned at the soft certainty in his warm tone, meeting his kind eyes and wondering, fleetingly, why it could not be this man who set her aflame. "I don't know why you would all risk so much."

He gave a little sound of refusal. "Risk," he said, as though it were a silly word. "It is not a risk for us. We are young, handsome aristocrats with plenty of land and plenty of money. What risk?"

She was surprised by his candor. "Not all of you seem to think so lightly of the damage to your reputation that an association with us might do."

"Well, Rivington and I haven't much choice, as we are related, if you would remember." She heard the teasing in his tone but did not find it very amusing. There was a beat of silence. "I assume you are referring to Leighton."

She stiffened. She couldn't help it. "Among others."

"I saw the way he watched you last night. I think Leighton will align himself with you faster than you would imagine."

The words—predicated on logic so faulty—stung. She shook her head. "You're wrong."

Benedick might think he had seen support in Leighton's manner last night, but he had misread the emotion.

He had seen frustration, irritation, desire perhaps. But not caring.

On the contrary, had Benedick seen the duke storm from the stables later that evening, after it was revealed that he was engaged, he would not think such things at all.

Simon was to be married.

The words had barely whispered through her mind when, as though she had conjured up his bride-to-be, Juliana caught a glimpse of the grape through the crowd, headed for the ladies' salon.

And she could not resist.

"I shall return," she whispered, already in motion.

She knew even as she headed for the salon that she should not follow Lady Penelope, that any conversation they might have would be more painful than no conversation at all, but she could not help herself. The grape had done what Juliana could not—she had caught Simon. And there was a perverse part of Juliana that simply had to know who this plain, perfect Englishwoman was.

What it was about her that had led the immovable Duke of Leighton to choose her for his duchess.

It was early enough that the salon was empty, save for a handful of servants, and Juliana crossed the main room of the salon to a small side chamber, where she found Penelope pouring water into a small washbasin, then setting her hands into the water, breathing deeply.

The grape appeared ill.

"You are not going to cash in your accounts, are you?"

Penelope spun toward her, the surprise in her eyes turning quickly to confusion. "Cash in my accounts?"

"It is possible I have it incorrect." Juliana moved her hand in a rolling motion. "To be ill. In Italian, we say *vomitare*." The grape's eyes went wide with understanding before a flush rose high on her cheeks. "Ah. I see you understand."

"Yes. I understand." Lady Penelope shook her head. "No. I am not going to cast up my accounts. At least, I don't think so."

Juliana nodded. *"Bene."* She indicated a chair near the basin. "May I join you?"

The grape's brow furrowed. Evidently it was not every day that she had a conversation such as this one.

But if she wanted to refuse, she was too polite to do so. "Please."

Juliana sat, waving one hand. "You need not stop what it is you were doing." She paused. "What is it that you were doing?"

Penelope eyed the washbasin before meeting Juliana's curious gaze. "It is just something that I do to calm myself."

"Wash your hands?"

One side of Penelope's mouth lifted in a self-deprecating smile. "It's silly."

Juliana shook her head. "I conjugate verbs."

"In Italian?"

"In Latin. And in English."

Penelope seemed to consider the idea. "And it works?"

With everything but Leighton. "Most of the time."

"I shall have to try it."

"Why are you in need of calming?"

Penelope lifted a long square of linen to dry her hands. "No reason."

Juliana laughed a little at the obvious lie. "I do not mean to offend, Lady Penelope, but you are not very good at hiding your feelings."

Penelope met Juliana's gaze. "You say whatever you are thinking, don't you?"

Juliana gave a little shrug. "When you have a reputation such as mine, there is little need to mince words. Is it the ball that makes you nervous?"

Penelope looked away, her eyes finding her reflection in a nearby mirror. "Among other things."

"Well, I can certainly understand that. They are horrible events, balls. I do not understand why anyone cares for them. All torturous whispers and silly dancing."

Penelope met Juliana's gaze in the mirror. "Tonight's ball shall be one for the ages."

"You refer to the gossip about my mother?"

"My engagement is to be announced tonight."

The words should not have been a surprise, and yet they slammed through Juliana.

He was announcing the engagement tonight.

"Your engagement to whom?" She knew she should not ask. Could not stop herself from doing so. In some perverse way, she had to hear the words from this woman—his future wife.

"The Duke of Leighton."

Juliana knew the words were coming, but they ripped through her, nonetheless.

"You are to marry the Duke of Leighton." *Stop talking.* "He has proposed to you."

Penelope nodded, lost in her own thoughts, her golden ringlets bobbing like the hair on one of Juliana's childhood dolls. "This morning."

Juliana swallowed around the knot in her throat. He'd obviously left Ralston House the prior evening with complete resolve—having narrowly escaped a bad match with Juliana . . . he'd happily secured a good one with . . .

Someone else.

And in a hideous twist of fate, Juliana was attending the betrothal ball.

All while her family's reputation was being ripped to shreds.

Belatedly, she remembered her manners. "How . . . happy . . . you must be!"

"Yes. I suppose I should be happy."

She did not seem happy.

In fact, Penelope's eyes had turned liquid, and she seemed very close to tears.

And, suddenly, Juliana felt sorry for the other woman. This woman, who was to marry Simon.

"You do not wish to marry him."

There was a long pause as Penelope appeared to collect herself. Juliana watched with amazement as the tears cleared from the other woman's eyes, returning them to their pale, porcelain blue, and a bright, white smile appeared on her face. She took a deep breath. "The Duke of Leighton is a good man. It is a fine match."

It did not escape Juliana's notice that Penelope had not answered the question. Juliana raised a brow. "You sound like one of them."

Penelope's brows knit together. "'Them'?"

Juliana waved a hand to the outer salon and the ballroom beyond. "The English."

Penelope blinked. "I *am* one of the English."

"I suppose you are." Juliana watched Penelope for a long while. "He *is* a good man."

"He will make me a fine husband."

Juliana rolled her eyes. "I would not go so far as to say that. He's arrogant and high-handed, and he'll want everything his cold, calculating way."

She should stop this now. Simon was to marry Lady Penelope. And it was not Juliana's place to become involved.

There was a long pause as Penelope considered the words, during which Juliana began to regret her bold speech. Just as she was about to apologize, Penelope said, "That is how marriage is."

The simple statement, spoken as though it was an irrefutable fact, was Juliana's undoing. She rose from her chair, having no choice but to move. "What is it with you English? You speak of marriage as though it is a business arrangement."

"It *is* a business arrangement," Penelope said, simply.

"And what of love?"

"I am sure that . . . in time . . . we shall develop a certain . . . fondness for each other."

Juliana could not stop her laugh. "I have developed a fondness for apple tarts, but I do not want to marry one." Penelope did not smile. "And passion?"

Penelope shook her head. "There is no room for passion in a good English marriage."

Juliana went still at the words, an echo from another ball. Another aristocrat. "Did he say that to you?"

"No, but it is . . . the way things are done."

The room grew instantly smaller, more cloying, and Juliana longed for air. Penelope was perfect for Simon. She would not challenge him, would breed him beautiful, golden-haired children, and host his dinner parties while he lived his quiet life, unfettered by scandal, uncomplicated by passion.

Juliana had never had a chance with him.

And only now, as the truth coiled through her, did she realize how much she had wanted one.

There is no room for passion in a good English marriage.

She turned for the door. "Well, at least in that, you are an excellent match."

Just as Juliana reached the entryway to the larger salon, the grape found her skin. "It is not easy, you know. You think English ladies do not grow up imagining love? Of course we do. But we are not bred for love. We are bred for reputation. For loyalty. We are bred to turn our backs on passion and take the hand of security. Is it the stuff of novels? No. Do we like it? It does not matter. It is our duty."

Juliana took in the words. Duty. Reputation. Security. She would never understand this world, this culture. She would never be one of them. And it was that which would always set her apart. Always make her worthy of their whispers.

Never make her worthy of *him*.

Not in the way this sturdy Englishwoman was.

The ache returned, and before she could make her excuses, Penelope offered a small, quiet smile. "We leave love to the Italians."

"I'm not sure we want it." The conversation was over. "My felicitations, Lady Penelope."

She left Penelope to her washbasin and her future and passed through the main room, ignoring both the cluster of women gathered there, heads bent in the rapt pleasure of the purest essence of balls—gossip and fashion.

"I heard she's back and swearing that she was never in Italy." The words rose above covert whispers, meant to be heard. Meant to wound and incite.

And Juliana could not help herself.

She turned to see Lady Sparrow holding court over her minions. She smirked, an asp about to strike, meeting Juliana's gaze, and saying, baldly, "Which means someone is not who she says she is."

There was a collective gasp at the suggestion. To suggest someone's illegitimacy was the highest form of insult. And to do it while the person in question was in the room . . .

No drama tonight. The family didn't need it.

Sparrow should have been called Vulture. She was circling as though she had spied carrion. "Because it would not surprise me if she'd simply heard that there was money and station to be had here. I mean, we don't know anything about her. She might not be Italian at all. She might be something else entirely?"

Juliana wanted to turn and prove just how Italian she was. In small, vicious words that would sear the skin from Sparrow's ears.

But would it change anything?

It would not garner their acceptance. It would not make this night, or any to come, easier. It would not remove the scandal from their name, nor would it make her worthy in their eyes.

In his eyes.

She resisted the thought. This was not about him.

Or was it?

Wasn't he one of them? Hadn't he judged her just as they had? Didn't he expect her to cause a scandal everywhere she went?

Hadn't she proven him right?

"Something else?"

"A gypsy?"

"A Spaniard?"

If she weren't so angry, Juliana would have laughed at the way the word had been said, as though it were synonymous with *witch.* What was wrong with Spaniards?

"We could ask her ourselves," Lady Sparrow said, and the group of women turned to face her. Each face smirking a more wicked smile than the last.

This was how it would be now.

This was what it was to have scandal surround you—real scandal, not some cheap approximation of a black mark on your reputation because you were Italian, or outspoken, or clumsy, or because you resisted their silly rules.

This was what he was afraid of.

And as she stared at their wicked smiles, reading the viciousness in their eyes, she could not blame him.

She would marry the grape as well.

A flood of hot anger and embarrassment coursed through her, and Juliana wanted to scream and rant and throw things at the horrible women. Her muscles tensed with an unbearable desire to lash out. But she had been in London for eight months, and she had learned that there were more painful things than physical blows.

And she'd had enough.

Instead, she turned and checked her reflection in the

mirror, making a show of tucking a curl back into her coiffure, before returning her attention to them, affecting as much boredom as she could.

"You know as well as I, Lady Sparrow, that I am whatever you and your"—she waved a lazy hand in the direction of the group—"harpies decide to make me. Italian, Spanish, gypsy, changeling. I welcome whichever mantle you choose . . . as long as you do not make me English."

She watched as understanding dawned in their shocked faces.

"For surely there is nothing worse than being one of you."

He had pretended not to see her arrive.

Just as he had pretended not to care when she'd laughed and danced in the arms of the Earl of Allendale.

Just as he'd pretended not to count the minutes she spent in the ladies' salon.

Instead, he had feigned vast interest in the conversation around him—in the opinions of the men who were eager to share his thoughts on the military-spending bill, and to garner the respect and support of the Duke of Leighton.

But when she quietly exited the ballroom, heading down a long, dark corridor toward the back of the house, where God only knew who or what might be waiting for her, he could not pretend any longer.

And so he crossed the ballroom, politely dismissing those who thought to stop him in conversation, and followed Juliana into the recesses of the ancestral home of the woman to whom he was betrothed.

The second woman to whom he had proposed marriage in the past twenty-four hours.

The only one who had accepted his suit.

Juliana had refused him.

He was still unable to wrap his head around the ridiculous truth.

She hadn't even *considered* the possibility of marrying him.

She'd simply turned to her brother and suggested in a tone that most people reserved for children and servants, that Simon Pearson, eleventh Duke of Leighton, knew not what he was saying.

As though he offered himself up in marriage to anyone who came along.

He should be thrilled with this turn of events . . . after all, everything was now going according to plan. He was marrying the impeccable Lady Penelope, and, within moments, would align their two families, officially shoring up his defenses in preparation for the attacks that would come when scandal hit.

He passed several closed, locked doors before the hallway curved to the right, and he stopped in complete darkness, waiting for his eyes to adjust to the light. Once he could make out the doors down the long stretch of hall, he continued.

He should think himself the luckiest of men that he had avoided a terrible match with Juliana Fiori.

He should be down on his knees, thanking his Maker for a narrow miss.

Instead, he was following her into the darkness.

He did not like the metaphor.

She was a sorceress.

She'd seemed so fragile there in that small stall, brushing her horse, talking to herself in soft, self-deprecating tones.

What man could resist such a tableau?

Ralston might have thought *Leighton* the perpetrator, the years-older gentleman taking advantage of a barely out twenty-year-old. Certainly, Simon had played into the role . . . and he'd accepted the fists and the accusations, and he'd *proposed*.

And as much as he tried to convince himself that he did it out of a sense of what was right, the truth was that in the moment, he'd done it because he'd wanted her. Wanted to brand her as his and finish what they had started.

The kiss had felt like nothing he had ever experienced. The softness of her skin, the feel of her fingers in his hair, the way she turned him inside out with a little sigh, the way he grew hard and aching with the mere memory of the way she whispered his name, the way she begged him to taste her on those soft, pink . . .

He opened a door, looking into a dark room. Pausing, listening. She was not there. He closed the door with a curse.

He'd never felt this way. Never been so consumed with frustration or desire or . . .

Passion.

He froze at the word, shaking his head.

What was he doing?

This was the final moment before his engagement to Lady Penelope was made public . . . before the gates closed and locked on all other paths save this one—down which lay his future duchess and their life together. And he was following another woman down a dark hallway.

It was time for him to remember who he was.

Penelope would make a sound wife. And an excellent duchess.

A vision flashed—not Penelope. Nothing like Penelope. Ebony curls and eyes the color of the Aegean Sea. Full, ripe lips that whispered his name like a prayer. A laugh that carried on the wind as Juliana rode away from him in Hyde Park, teased him at dinner, on the streets of London, in her stables.

She lived with passion. And she would love with it as well.

He ignored the thought.

She was not for him.

He turned around. Resolute. Saw the light in the darkness, marking the corridor returning to the ballroom. Headed for it.

Just as she spoke from the shadows.

"Simon?"

His given name, in her lilting Italian, breathy with surprise, was a siren's call.

He turned to her.

"What are you—"

He grabbed her by the shoulders, pulled her into the first room he found, and closed the door behind them, quickly, sealing them inside a conservatory.

She backed up, toward the large bay window and a pool of silver moonlight, managing only a few steps before she kicked a cello. She cursed in a whisper of Italian that was too loud to even be called a whisper, as she lunged to keep it from crashing to the ground.

If he weren't so furious with her for intruding on his space and his thoughts and his *life*, he might have laughed.

But he was too busy worrying that her brother might happily disembowel him if they were discovered in what would never be believed to be a coincidentally compromising position.

The woman was impossible.

And he was thrilled that she was there.

A problem, that.

"What are you doing following me down a darkened hallway?" she hissed.

"What are you doing *heading* down a darkened hallway?"

"I was attempting to find some peace!" She turned away, headed for the window, muttering in Italian. "In this entire city, is there a single place where I am not *plagued* with company?"

Simon did not move, taking perverse pleasure in her agitation. He should not be the only one to be rattled. "It is you who should not be here, not I."

"Why, does the house come with the bride?" she snapped before switching to English. "And how is it that you speak Italian so well?"

"I find it is not worth doing anything if one does not do it well."

She offered him a long-suffering look. "Of course you would say that."

There was a long silence. "Dante."

"What about him?"

One side of his mouth lifted at her peevishness. "I have a fondness for him. And so, I learned Italian."

She turned to him, her black hair gleaming silver, the long column of her throat porcelain in the moonlight. "You learned Italian for Dante."

"Yes."

She returned her attention to the gardens beyond the window. "I suppose I should not be surprised. Sometimes I think the *ton* is a layer of hell."

He laughed. He could not help it. She was magnificent sometimes. When she was not infuriating.

"Shouldn't you be out there instead of here, sulking about in the darkness?"

"I think you mean skulking." She need not know how close she was to the truth in her error.

She set the sheet music on the stand with a huff of irritation. "Fine. Skulking. It is a silly word, anyway."

It was a silly word, but he found he liked the way she said it.

He liked the way she said many things.

Not that he had any right to.

"What are you doing in here?" he asked.

She sat on the piano bench, squinting into the darkness, trying to see him. "I wanted to be alone."

He was taken aback by her honesty. "Why?"

She shook her head. "It's not important."

Suddenly, nothing in the world seemed so important. He stood, knowing he should not move closer to her.

Moved closer to her anyway.

"The gossip," he said. Of course it was the gossip. She would certainly bear the brunt of it.

She gave a little half laugh, making room for him on the piano bench. The movement was so natural—as though she hadn't thought for a moment.

As though he belonged there.

He sat, knowing it was a terrible idea.

Knowing nothing good could come of his being this close to her.

"Apparently, I am not her daughter, but rather a cunning gypsy who has pulled the linen over your eyes." She smiled at the words, finally meeting his gaze.

She might have been a gypsy then, with streaks of silver moonlight in her hair, and a soft, sad smile in her beautiful blue eyes turned black with the night. She was bewitching.

He swallowed. "Wool."

She was confused. "Wool?"

"Pulled the wool over our eyes," he corrected, his fingers itching to touch her, to smooth back a curl that had come loose at her temple. "You said linen."

She tilted her head, the column of her throat lengthening as she considered the words. "In Italian, it is *lana.* I was confused."

"I know." He was feeling confused himself.

She sighed. "I shall never be one of you."

"Because you cannot tell the difference between linen and wool?" he teased. He did not want her to be sad. Not now. Not in this quiet moment before everything changed.

She smiled. "Among other things." Their gazes met for

a long moment and he steeled himself against the desire to touch her. To run his fingers across her smooth skin and pull her close and finish what they had started the night before. She must have sensed it, because she broke the connection, turning away. "So you are betrothed."

He didn't want to discuss it. Didn't want it to be real. Not here.

"I am."

"And the announcement shall be made tonight."

"It shall."

She met his gaze. "You will have your perfect English marriage after all."

He leaned back, stretching his long legs out in front of him. "You are surprised?"

One shoulder lifted in an elegant shrug. He was coming to like those shrugs that spoke volumes. "The game was never one I could win."

He was surprised. "Are you admitting defeat?"

"I suppose so. I release you from the wager."

It was precisely what he had expected her to do. What he'd wanted her to do. "That does not sound like the warrior I have come to know."

She gave him a small wry smile. "Not so much a warrior any longer."

His brows snapped together. "Why not?"

"I—" She stopped.

He would have given his entire fortune to hear the rest of the sentence. "You—?" he prompted.

"I came to care too much about the outcome."

He froze, watching her, taking in the way her throat worked as she swallowed, the way she fiddled with a piece of trim on her rose-colored gown. "What does that mean?"

"Nothing." She did not meet his gaze. Instead, shaking her head once more. "I am sorry that you felt that you had to watch over me. I am sorry that Gabriel hit you. I am sorry that I came to be something you . . . regret."

Regret.

The word was a blow more painful than anything Ralston had delivered.

He had felt many things for her in the past week . . . in the past months. But regret had never been one of them.

"Juliana—" Her name came out like gravel as he reached for her, knowing that when he had her in hand, he might not let her go.

She stood before he could touch her. "It would be a problem if we were discovered. I must go."

He stood, too. "Juliana. Stop."

She turned, taking a step back, into the darkness, placing herself just out of reach. "We are not to speak. Not to see each other," she rattled, as though the words could build a wall between them.

"It is too late for that." He stepped toward her. She stepped back. "Ralston will be looking for me."

He advanced. "Ralston can wait."

She hurried backward. "And you have a fiancée to claim."

"She can wait as well."

She stopped, finding her strength. "No she can't."

He did not want to talk about Penelope.

He met her, toe-to-toe. "Explain yourself." The whisper was low and dark.

"I—" She looked down, giving him the top of her head. He wanted to bury his face in those curls, in the smell and feel of her.

But first, she would explain herself.

She did not speak for an eternity—so long that he thought she might not. And then she took a deep breath, and said, "I told you not to make me like you." The words were full of defeat.

"You like me?" She looked up, her blue eyes reflecting

the light from the window behind him, and he caught his breath at her beauty. He lifted a hand, ran the backs of his fingers across her cheek. She closed her eyes at the caress.

"Yes." The whisper was plaintive and soft, barely audible. "I don't know why. You're a horrible man." She leaned into him. "You're arrogant and irritating, and you have a temper."

"I do not have a temper," he said, lifting her face toward him, so he could look his fill. She opened her eyes and gave him a look of complete disbelief, and he amended, "Only when I am around you."

"You think you are the most important man in all of England," she continued, her voice a thread of sound in the darkness, punctuated by little catches in her words as his fingers trailed along the line of her jaw. "You think you're right all the time. You think you know everything . . ."

Her skin was so soft.

He should leave the room. It was wrong for him to be here with her. If they were caught, she would be ruined, and he would have no choice but to leave her in ruin. He had been engaged mere hours.

This was all wrong.

He should go.

A gentleman would go.

"You covered all that with 'arrogant.'" He traced the column of her neck.

"I—" She gasped as he pressed a soft kiss to the base of her throat. "I thought you might need further explanation."

"Mmm," he spoke against the skin of her shoulder. "An excellent point. Go on."

She took a deep breath as his lips and tongue played up the side of her neck. "What were we discussing?"

He smiled at her ear before he took the soft, velvety lobe between his teeth. "You were telling me all the reasons that you should not like me."

"Oh . . ." The word turned into a little moan as he tongued the sensitive skin of her ear. She clutched his forearms at the sensation. "Yes. Well. Those are the major reasons."

"And yet, you like me anyway." He moved, pressing soft kisses along the edge of her gown, easing down the smooth expanse of skin there, her chest rising and falling as she gasped for breath. She did not reply for a long while, and he slid a finger beneath the silk, stroking, seeking, until he found what he was looking for, hard and ready for him. "Juliana?"

"Yes, damn you, I like you."

He rewarded her by pulling the gown down and baring the rose-tipped breast to the moonlight. "There's something you should know," he whispered, the words coming from far away.

"Yes?"

He blew a long stream of cool air across her puckered nipple, loving the way it tightened more, begging for his mouth.

He would taste her tonight.

Once, before he went back to his staid, respectable existence.

Just once.

A rush of pleasure coursed through him, and he grew hard and heavy at the thought.

"Simon"—she sighed—"you torture me."

He palmed one of her perfect breasts, rolling his thumb across its tip, reveling in the way she gave herself up to sensation.

"What is it?" she asked, the words broken around her pleasure.

"What is it?" he repeated.

"What should I know?"

He smiled at the question, dragging his gaze up to meet hers—heavy-lidded and gorgeous.

One more taste of her. One *last* taste.

"I like you, too."

Chapter Twelve

Music is the sound of the gods.
The delicate lady plays the pianoforte to perfection.

—*A Treatise on the Most Exquisite of Ladies*

We are assured that there is still time for the wedding
of the season . . .

—*The Scandal Sheet, October 1823*

He lifted her in his arms, turned, and carried her
back to the piano bench. Setting her down on
the hard wooden seat, he came to his knees before her,
cupping her face and tilting her to receive his kiss.

His hands came to her breasts, lifted them, bared them,
stroked across their peaks, pinching lightly until she
gasped, and he rewarded the sound, giving her everything she had not known she wanted. She whispered his
name as he suckled the pebbled tip of one breast, sending
excitement coursing through her. She plunged her fingers
into his lush golden curls, holding him to the spot where
he wreaked havoc on her flesh and her emotions.

He groaned at the feel of her hands in his hair, and the sound rippled through her like pleasure.

She knew she should not allow it.

Knew she risked everything.

Did not care.

As long as he did not stop.

He clasped her to him, worshipping her with lips and tongue and the wicked hint of teeth as his hands stroked down the length of her, pressing her closer and closer to him, until she thought they might become one.

"Simon . . ." she whispered his name and he stopped, lifting his head, his eyes flashing with heat.

"God, Juliana," he reached out one hand, stroking down one side of her cheek, and she turned her head impulsively, placing a warm, soft kiss on the pad of his thumb, tracing a circle there with her tongue before biting the flesh softly.

He growled at the sensation, pulling her to him for a kiss that was more claiming than caress. When he ended it, they were both breathing heavily, and her hands had found their way inside his topcoat to stroke his broad, firm chest.

"I want . . ." she started, the words breaking off as he returned his attention to her breasts, taking a nipple between his lips, rolling the tight peak between tongue and teeth until she could not think.

When he released her, he flashed a wolfish grin, and she could not help but reach out for him, letting her fingers play across his lips—as though touching the elusive smile could burn it into her memory. He took the tip of one finger into his mouth, sucking on it until she gasped. "What do you want, love?"

The endearment curled between them, and she was struck by a pang of longing . . . she wanted him. For more than a stolen moment in this dark, private place . . . for more than two weeks . . .

I want you to want me.

To choose me.

"Come closer." She spread her legs, knowing that she was being wanton. Knowing that if they were caught, she would be ruined, and he would walk away to be with his future bride. But she did not care. She wanted to feel him against her. She did not care that there were layers of fabric between them. Did not care that they would never be as close as she wanted.

His eyes closed briefly as though he were steeling himself against her, and she thought for a moment that he might refuse. But when he opened them, she saw desire flare there in the stunning amber depths, then he groaned his pleasure and gave her what she wanted, pressing closer.

"You are my siren," he said, running his hands along her thighs and down her calves, feeling the shape of her even as the silk of her gown kept them both from what they wanted. "My temptress . . . my sorceress . . . I cannot resist you, no matter how I try. You threaten to send me over the edge."

His hands came to her ankles, and she flinched at the instant, intense pleasure of his touch. Her eyes widened. "Simon, I don't—"

"Shh," he said, as his hands smoothed slowly up the inside of her legs, setting her stockings aflame. "I'm showing you what I mean."

His fingertips reached the lacy, scalloped edge of the stockings high on her thigh, and they both groaned at the feel of skin on skin. She snapped her legs closed, trapping his hands between her warm thighs.

She couldn't.

He shouldn't.

He leaned forward and placed his forehead on hers. "Juliana, let me touch you."

How could she resist such temptation?

She relaxed, opening her thighs, knowing that she was a wanton.

Not caring.

He smiled, his hands climbing higher and higher. "You are not wearing drawers."

She shook her head, barely able to speak through the anticipation. "I don't like them. We don't—in Italy."

He took her mouth in a wicked kiss. "Have I mentioned how I adore the Italians?"

The sentiment, so counter to every argument they'd ever had, made her laugh. Then his fingers reached her core, feathering over the soft hair there, parting, seeking, and sending a shock of sensation through her. And the laugh turned to a moan.

His mouth was at her ear now, and he whispered wicked things as his fingers sought. *Found.* She did not know what she wanted. Only that—

"Simon . . ." she whispered.

He slid one finger deep into her core, and she closed her eyes at the caress, leaning back at the sensation, the piano keys sighing beneath her movement.

"Yes," she whispered, embarrassed and bold all at once.

"Yes," he repeated, as a second finger joined the first, and his thumb did wicked, wonderful things, circling the secret folds of her.

She bit her lip. "Stop . . . don't stop."

His grin was wide and wicked. "Which one?"

He stroked deep, and she grasped his arm tightly, whispering. "Don't. Don't stop."

He shook his head, watching her. "I couldn't if I tried." Holding her gaze, he worked her in time with the movement of her hips, with the soft discordant tinkling of the piano keys beneath her. Everything faded except the feel of him, the strong, corded muscles of his arms, the magnificent way he touched her, driving her harder and faster toward something she did not understand and did not entirely trust.

She sat straight up, and he was there, one hand capturing her face, holding her to his lips. "I am here," he whispered against her.

Was he, really?

She stiffened, shaking her head, rocketing toward pleasure. "No. Simon . . ."

"Take it, Juliana." The demand crashed through her, so imperious that she could not follow it. She gasped at the pleasure, and he took her lips again, feeding her unbearable desire for more, for *him* where she ached and needed more than she would ever imagine, his beautiful amber gaze her anchor in the storm.

When he had wrung the last of her pleasure from her, he placed a soft kiss on the high arch of one cheek and righted her skirts, pulling her to him as she regained her strength. He held her there, quiet and unmoving for long minutes. Five. Maybe more.

Before she remembered where they were.

And why.

She pushed him back, away from her. "I must return." She stood, wondering how long she would be able to suffer this interminable evening.

The worst was yet to come.

"Juliana," he said, and she heard the plea in his voice, for what, she did not know. She waited, eager for him to say something that would make it better. That would make it right.

When he did not, she spoke. "You are to be married."

He lifted his hands. Paused. Dropped them in frustration. "I am sorry. I should not have—I should have—"

She flinched at the words—she couldn't help it. "Don't," she whispered. "Don't apologize." She moved to the door, had one hand on the handle when he spoke again.

"Juliana. I cannot—" He halted. Rethought. "I am marrying Lady Penelope. I have no choice."

There it was again, his cool, masterful tone.

She let her forehead rest on the cool mahogany of the door, so close that she could smell the rich stain on the wood.

He spoke again. "There are things you cannot understand. I *must*."

She laid her palm flat against the door, resisting the horrible temptation to throw herself at his feet and beg him to have her. *No.* She had more pride than that. There was only one way to survive this. With dignity intact.

"Of course you must," she whispered.

"You don't understand."

"You're right. I don't. But it is not important. Thank you for the lesson."

"The lesson?"

This was her chance to have the last word.

To at least feel like she had won.

"Passion is not everything, is it?" She was proud of the lightness in her tone, the way she tossed the words at him as though they did not matter. As though he had not just thrown her world into upheaval.

Again.

But she did not trust herself to look at him. That would have been too challenging a part to play.

Instead, she opened the door and slipped into the hallway, not feeling at all like she'd won.

Feeling like she'd lost terribly.

She had, after all, broken the most important of her rules.

She had wanted more than she could have.

She had wanted him, and more . . . she had wanted him to want her.

In the name of something bigger than tradition, bolder than reputation, more important than a silly title.

She hovered at the entrance to the ballroom, watching the swirling silks, the way the men walked, danced, spoke with the undeniable sense of entitlement and purpose, the long, graceful lines of the women, who knew without question that they belonged.

Here, nothing trumped the holy trinity of tradition, reputation, and title.

And for someone like her—who laid claim to none of the three—someone like him—who held all three with a casual right—was utterly, undeniably, out of reach.

And she had been wrong to even pretend to reach for him.

She could not have him.

She took a deep, stabilizing breath.

She could not have him.

"Oh, good. I found you. We must talk," Mariana whispered from her elbow, where she had materialized. "Apparently ours is not the only gossip to be had today."

Juliana blinked. "*Our* gossip?"

Mariana cut her a quick, irritated look. "Really, Juliana. You shall have to get past the idea that you own all the trouble in our family. We're a family. It's our burden to bear as well." Juliana did not have time to appreciate the sentiment as Mariana was already pressing on. "Apparently, there is another major event taking place tonight. One you will not like. Leighton is to be—"

"I know." Juliana cut off her friend. She didn't think she could bear hearing it again. Not even from Mariana.

"How do you know?"

"He told me."

Mariana's brows snapped together. "When?"

She shrugged one shoulder, hoping it would be enough for her sister-in-law's sister.

Apparently not. "Juliana Fiori! When did he tell you?"

She should have told her that Ralston told her. Or that

she'd overheard it in the ladies' salon. Usually, she was quicker.

Usually, she hadn't just had her heart broken.

Her heart was not broken, was it?

It certainly felt that way.

"Earlier."

"Earlier, when?"

"Earlier tonight."

Mariana squeaked. Actually squeaked.

Juliana winced. *She should have said last night.*

Juliana turned to face her. "Please don't make this an issue."

"Why were you with Leighton earlier tonight?"

No reason, only that I was very nearly ruined in the conservatory belonging to his future bride.

She shrugged again.

"Juliana, you know that might very well be your most annoying habit."

"Really? But I have so many."

"Are you all right?"

"You mean the shoulder? Yes. Fine."

Mariana's eyes narrowed. "You are being deliberately difficult."

"Possibly."

Mariana looked at her then. Really looked at her. And Juliana got instantly nervous. The young duchess's gaze softened almost instantly. "Oh, Juliana," she whispered. "You are not all right at all, are you?"

The soft, kind words proved to be Juliana's undoing. It was suddenly difficult to breathe, difficult to swallow, all her energy instantly devoted to resisting the urge to throw herself into her friend's arms and cry.

Which, of course, she could not do. "I must go."

"I'll come with you."

"No!" She heard the panic in her voice. Took a breath,

tried to keep it from rising again. "No. I am . . . you must stay."

Mariana did not like being told what to do. Juliana saw her hesitate, watched her consider denying the request. *Please, Mari.* "Fine. But you will take our carriage."

Juliana paused for a moment, considering. "I—yes. All right. I shall take your carriage. Mari—" She heard the crack in her voice. Loathed it. "I have to leave. Now. Before."

Before she had to watch the announcement of the betrothal unfold in a horrible, perverse tableau.

Mariana nodded once. "Of course. I'll see you out. You're obviously not feeling well. You've got a headache, clearly."

Juliana would have laughed if it had seemed at all amusing.

Mariana began to push through the crowd at the edge of the ballroom, Juliana following close behind. They had barely gone a dozen steps when the orchestra stopped playing, and there was a commotion on the dais where they sat. Conversation stopped as the Marquess of Needham and Dolby, a portly man who obviously liked his drink, boomed, "Attention!"

Juliana made the mistake of looking toward the dais. Saw Simon there, tall and unbearably handsome—the perfect duke. The perfect husband.

Perfect.

Mariana turned back to her, eyes wide, and Juliana squeezed her hand. "Faster."

"We can't . . ." Mariana shook her head. "Everyone will see."

Panic rose, and the ballroom tilted horribly, sending a wave of nausea through her. Of course they couldn't leave. Escape would only make them the subject of more talk. Not now. Not when the betrothal was taking some of the attention from their scandal. She hated her mother in that moment, more than ever before. Juliana closed her eyes, knowing what was to come. Not knowing how she would survive it.

She turned to the dais, and Mariana took her hand, squeezing tightly, a rock in a maelstrom of dread.

And Juliana listened quietly as the only man she'd ever wanted pledged himself to another.

It was over blessedly quickly, footmen passing champagne among the revelers, who raised their glasses and voices in toast to the happy couple. No one noticed that Mariana and Juliana politely refused the drink, nor did they realize that the moment the Duke of Leighton raised the hand of his future duchess to his lips, the two were headed for the exit.

It was an eternity until they dashed up the steps from the dance floor; once there, Juliana made the mistake of looking back—of taking one final glance at Simon and his bride.

He was watching her.

And she was unable to resist drinking him in—his golden curls, strong jaw, and full lips, and that serious amber gaze that made her feel like she was the only woman in the world.

Of course she wasn't.

Because his future bride stood next to him.

She turned and fled into the foyer, afraid that she would be sick if she stayed in the wretched house any longer. Thankfully, the servants at Dolby House were the best of the best, and a footman was already opening the door as she rushed for it, tears blurring her vision, Mariana on her heels.

She felt the cool air of the October night beyond and gave a little prayer of thanks. She was safe.

Or, she would have been . . .

If she had only remembered the vegetables.

Too late, she realized that the staircase remained smothered in fruits of the harvest, and by that time it was too late to stop. She'd already set one slippered foot on a large, round pompion, and sent the entire pyramid into collapse.

She heard Mariana call her name in alarm as she tumbled, riding a wave of gourds and onions and marrow down the dozen or so steps to the base of the staircase, landing in a heap. When she opened her eyes to ensure that she had survived the fall, she was surrounded by vegetables—many smashed open, their innards splattered across the cobblestone street.

Juliana watched as a turnip, barely the size of her fist, rolled past and came to a rest beneath a waiting carriage—one final, fallen soldier in her massacre.

"Oh, my . . ."

She looked up to find Mariana at the top of the steps, looking down at her, eyes wide, one hand to her open mouth. Two footmen stood just behind her, looking utterly uncertain of the protocol in this particular situation.

Juliana could not stop herself.

She began to laugh.

Not soft, quiet chuckles, either. Loud, raucous laughter that she could not hold in. Laughter that threatened her ability to breathe. Laughter that held all her sadness and frustration and anger and irritation.

Wiping a tear from her cheek, she looked up at Mariana and found that her friend's shoulders were shaking with laughter as well. And the footmen, too—they couldn't help it.

Their laughter sent another wave of emotion through her.

She cleared a space for her to stand, and her movements shook the others free. They all picked their way down the stairs, one footman bending to assist Juliana to her feet as she realized the full extent of the damage.

She had laid waste to Lady Needham's centerpiece.

The steps would have to be cleared before anyone could leave the ball.

And Juliana's lovely rose silk was covered in seeds and great gobs of pulp, entirely ruined.

She stood, thanking the footman and facing Mariana, who was still laughing—the response certainly as much horror as amusement.

"You've got . . ." She shook her head and waved one hand to indicate Juliana's entire body. "Everywhere."

Juliana pulled a long piece of wheat from her hair. "I suppose it is too much to ask that one of these carriages is yours?"

Mariana inspected the waiting vehicles. "Actually, it isn't at all. That one is ours."

Juliana headed for it. "Finally, something goes right."

Mariana opened her reticule and extracted a ransom in gold coins for the footmen. "If you could forget who, precisely, destroyed your mistress's décor . . ." She pressed the coins into their palms before dashing for the carriage and following Juliana inside.

"Do you think they will stay quiet?" Juliana asked as the coach lurched into motion.

"One can hope that they'll take pity on you."

Juliana sighed, leaning her head back on the smooth black upholstery. She let the motion of the carriage calm her for long minutes before she said, "Well, you must give me some credit."

Mariana snickered. "For?"

"I cannot be accused of going quietly into the night."

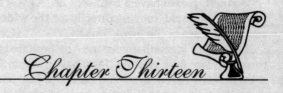

Chapter Thirteen

Unhappiness is for those who lack culture.
The exquisite lady faces all obstacles with grace.

—*A Treatise on the Most Exquisite of Ladies*

The harvest bounty is shockingly lacking this year . . .

—*The Scandal Sheet, October 1823*

*H*er horrendous evening was not over.

Bennett, the ancient butler who had served the Marquesses of Ralston for what Juliana suspected was forever, was awake when she arrived home—a rare occurrence as he was somewhat weathered, and there were plenty of younger servants who were more than capable of waiting for the master of the house to return.

Years of experience kept Bennett from responding to Juliana's state, without her cloak, which she'd left in her hurry to escape the ball—she would have to work out a way to recover it at some point, she supposed—and covered in marrow innards, among other things.

In fact, he gave her a little bow when she entered the

house—one she would have teased him for if she weren't exhausted and desperate for a bath and a bed.

"Bennett, please have a bath sent up. As you can see, I need it," she said, moving directly for the wide marble center staircase of the town house.

"Miss Fiori, you will excuse me," he hesitated and she turned to face him, waiting. "You have a visitor."

Excitement flared, brief and breathtaking, as her instant thought was that Simon had called. But, no . . . there was no way he had beaten her to Ralston House— not unless he'd fled the scene of his engagement upon the announcement. As lovely as that would have been, she knew better than even to think it. Simon would never do anything so scandalous.

She ignored the fact that earlier in the evening, they'd engaged in a rather shockingly scandalous interlude.

"A visitor? For me?"

The butler's face grew dark, betraying an emotion that Juliana did not like. "Yes, milady. Your mother."

Dread settled, heavy and cold. Juliana shook her head. "No. I am too tired to deal with her tonight. She can wait for Gabriel."

"She says she is here for you."

"Well, I am not receiving. She will have to try again."

"I am impressed. You have grown into quite the strong-willed young lady."

Juliana froze at the words, spoken in perfect, calm Italian behind her. She met Bennett's gaze, filled with regret, and waved him off with what she hoped was a reassuring smile before she turned to face her mother.

Whom she had not spoken to for a decade.

Her mother's gaze scanned over her, taking in her destroyed coiffure, ruined gown, and the clumps of unidentifiable muck sticking to her, and Juliana was instantly reminded of what it was like to be Louisa

Hathbourne's daughter—when not the recipient of cool disinterest, one was showered with distaste. She'd never been good enough for her mother. All those times she'd tried to prove herself worthy of Louisa's love . . . of her pride . . . she'd never received it.

"Do not for a moment think that you had anything to do with my character."

"I would not dream of it, Juli."

The diminutive—a favorite of her father's—sent a shock of sorrow and anger through Juliana. "Don't call me that."

Her mother moved from the doorway to the receiving room, extending one arm to Juliana. "Will you join me? I would like to speak with you. I have been waiting for quite a long while."

"And how does it feel to be the one waiting for someone to return? I imagine it is quite a novelty."

Louisa's smile was small and secret. "I deserved that."

"And much more, I assure you."

She considered ignoring her mother's request. Considered finding her bedchamber and letting the older woman stew in the receiving room until she got bored and went away.

But somewhere, deep inside, Juliana was still that ten-year-old girl. The one who rushed to do her mother's bidding in the hope that, today, she would be worthy of her attention.

She hated herself as she followed her mother into the receiving room. Hated herself as she took a seat across from her. Hated herself as she waited for this woman who had taken so much from her took more.

Time she did not want to give.

"I am sorry about Sergio. I did not know that he had passed away."

Juliana wanted to scream at her father's name on this

viper's tongue. Instead she matched her mother's calm, and said, "How could you? You never looked back once you left."

Louisa dipped her head once, acknowledging the hit. "You are right, of course."

Apologize. Juliana thought, the words a scream in her mind. *Don't you regret it?*

They sat in silence for a long moment, until Juliana was ready to leave. If Louisa thought she would carry the conversation, she was horribly wrong. She was just about to stand when her mother spoke again.

"I am happy you found Gabriel and Nick."

"So am I."

"Ah, so you see, something good did come of having me as a mother." There was self-satisfaction in the words. Of course there was. Louisa had never shied away from pointing out the good things about herself.

Perhaps because there were so few of them.

"Is this the moment when I am to tell you how grateful I am that you left me? That you left them?"

At least she knew not to respond to that. "What would you like me to say, Juli?"

Her voice turned to steel. "First, I would like you to stop using that name."

"Why? I had a part in naming you. We both called you that."

"Only one of you deserved to."

A look of boredom crossed Louisa's face. "Nonsense. I gave you life. That gives me as much right as anyone to call you whatever I like. But, very well, *Juliana*, answer the question." She switched to English. "What would you like from me?"

I want you to explain it. I want you to tell me why you would leave me. Why you would leave us. Why you would return.

Juliana gave a little humorless laugh, then answered

in English. "The very idea that you would ask that of me is ridiculous."

"You want me to apologize?"

"It would be an excellent beginning."

Louisa's cool blue gaze, so like her own, seemed to look through her. "We will be here a very long time if that is what you want."

Juliana shrugged one shoulder. "Excellent. Then we are done." She stood.

"Your father used to do that, too. The shrug. I am surprised that England has not beaten it out of you. It is not the most polite of mannerisms."

"England does not have a hold on me."

Suddenly, the words did not seem so true.

"No? Your English is very good for someone who does not care for the culture. I will be honest; I was surprised when Gabriel told me you were here. I cannot imagine it is easy for you to survive." Juliana stayed silent, refusing to give Louisa the pleasure of knowing she was right. Her mother pressed on. "I imagine it is just the same as it was for me. Difficult. You see, daughter, we are not so different."

We are not so different. They were the words she dreaded. The words she prayed were not true. "We are nothing like each other."

"You can say it over and over. It will not change the truth." Louisa leaned back in her seat. "Look at you. Just back from a ball, perhaps, but covered in something that indicates that you have not had the most respectable of evenings. What have you been doing?"

Juliana looked down at herself. Resisted the urge to pick at the fast-drying pulp that clung to her. "It is not your business."

"It doesn't matter. The point is that you are unable to resist adventure. You are unwilling to close yourself off to whatever pleasure happens to tempt you at any given time. My taste for excitement has been in you since you took your first breath. Resist all you like, but I am your *mother*. I am in you. The sooner you stop fighting it, the happier you will be."

No.

It was not true. It had been a decade since Louisa had seen Juliana last . . . ten years during which Juliana had had the opportunity to grow and change and *resist* the parts of her mother that lay dormant within.

She did not seek out adventure or scandal or ruin.

Did she?

Memories flashed: chasing through a darkened garden; hiding in a strange carriage; riding through Hyde Park in men's clothing; climbing out onto a log to fetch a replaceable bonnet; toppling a pyramid of harvest vegetables; waiting for Simon outside his club; kissing Simon in the barn; kissing Simon in the conservatory of his betrothed's home.

Kissing Simon.

She had virtually gone out of her way to cause scandal in the last week—and before that, since she arrived in London, she might not have sought out adventure, but she certainly had not resisted it when it came calling.

Dear God.

She looked to her mother, meeting those blue eyes that were so much like her own, the eyes that gleamed with a knowledge that Juliana at once feared and loathed.

She was right.

"What do you want from us?" She heard the tremor in her voice. Wished it was not there.

Louisa was quiet for a long time, unmoving, her cool gaze taking Juliana in. After several minutes, Juliana had had enough. "I've spent too much of my life waiting for you." She stood. "I am going to bed."

"I want my life back."

There was no sorrow in the words, no regret, either.

There wouldn't be. This was the closest her mother would ever come to either of those emotions. Regret was for people with a capacity for feeling.

Unable to stop herself, Juliana sat once more, on the edge of her chair, and took a long look at the woman who had given her life. Her beauty—the gift she had given all three of her children—was showing her age. There were strands of silver in her sable hair, her blue eyes were clouded with her years. There were a handful of lines on her face and neck, a blemish on one temple. A beauty mark just above one dark-winged eyebrow that Juliana remembered being less faded, more perfect.

The years had been kind to Louisa Hathbourne, but in a weathered, aged way that made the most beautiful of women think that she had lost everything.

Not that she gave any impression of feeling that way.

"You must know . . ." Juliana said, ". . . you cannot erase the past."

Irritation flared on her mother's face. "Of course I know that. I did not come back for my title. Or for the house. Or for Gabriel and Nicholas."

And certainly not for me, Juliana thought.

"But there comes a point when it is no longer easy to live the life I have lived."

Understanding flared. "And you think Gabriel will help you live a different life."

"He was raised to be marquess. Raised to protect his family at all costs. Why do you think I told your father to send you here if anything happened to him?"

Juliana shook her head. "You deserted him."

"Yes." Again, she was struck by the lack of regret in the answer.

"He would never support you . . ."

"We shall see." There was something in her eyes—a keen awareness born of years of self-interest and manipulation.

And then it all became clear.

This was London society, where reputation trumped all—even for the Marquess of Ralston. Especially for the new Marquess of Ralston, who had a wife and sister and unborn child to protect.

Juliana narrowed her gaze. "You knew. You knew you would cause a scandal. You knew he would do whatever it took to mitigate its damage. Not the damage to you . . . the damage to us. You think he'll give you a settlement. Something to keep you in the manner in which you are accustomed."

One side of her mother's mouth lifted in a half smile, and she brushed a speck from her gown—a design from several years ago. "You divined my strategy quite quickly. As I said, we are not so different, you and I."

"I would not be so certain of that, Mother." Ralston spoke from the doorway, and Juliana turned her attention to him and Callie, who was hurrying toward her. "Which part of, 'You are not to come near Ralston House again,' did you have difficulty understanding?"

Louisa looked up with a smile. "Well, it has been nearly two decades since I have been in England, darling. Meanings are troublesome at times." She raised a hand to Callie. "You must be the marchioness. I am sorry, I was so quickly escorted from the room last night that we were not properly introduced."

"No. You weren't," Ralston drawled.

"Do you know why she is here?" Juliana interrupted, outrage pushing her to her feet. "Do you know she wants money from you?"

"Yes," Gabriel said matter-of-factly before noticing Juliana's gown. "What on earth happened to you?"

"I think now is not the time to discuss it, Gabriel," Callie interrupted.

"You're not going to give it to her, are you?" Juliana

asked on a squeak, ignoring everything but the most important matter at hand.

"I have not yet decided."

"Gabriel!" She resisted the urge to stomp her foot.

He ignored her. "I would like you to leave, Mother. If you have need of us, you may send word. Nick has an excellent staff. They know how to reach us."

"She is living at Nick's town house?" Juliana said. "He shall be furious when he finds out!"

"Nonsense. Nick was always the child who liked me best," Louisa said casually, rising and heading for the door. "I wonder if Bennett has set my cloak aflame. That man always loathed me."

"I suspected that he had excellent taste," Juliana said, unable to keep quiet.

"Tut-tut, Juliana, one would think no one had ever taught you any manners."

"I was lacking in a feminine influence in my youth."

"Mmm." Louisa gave Juliana's gown a long inspection. "Tell me . . . do you think that if I had remained in Italy, you would still be covered in seeds and wheat tonight?"

She turned and exited the room, Juliana staring after her, wishing that she'd had a final barb to sling at her mother.

When Louisa had left the room, Callie turned to them, and said, "It is incredible that the two of you turned out so very *normal* with a mother such as that."

"I am not so very normal, Empress. And I am not sure about Juliana, either."

Callie looked at her with a wry smile. "The evening's great mystery has been solved—you toppled Lady Needham's harvest centerpiece?"

He turned to Juliana and raised one brow. "Dear God. And you ran off like an errant child?"

Juliana chewed on her lower lip. "Perhaps."

He scowled.

"What was I to do? It would have ruined the evening for everyone."

He sighed, then crossed to the sideboard and poured himself a scotch. "Just once, Juliana, I'd like you to attempt to refrain from causing a scandal. Not every time. Just once."

"Gabriel," Callie said quietly. "Have a care."

"Well, it is true. What did we discuss this evening before we left for the ball? We all needed to be on our very best behavior to even attempt to ride out the tornado that is our mother."

Juliana winced at the frustration in his words. "I didn't mean for it to happen, Gabriel . . ."

"Of course you didn't. You didn't mean to fall in the Serpentine or be accosted in our gardens or be nearly compromised by Leighton either, I'm guessing."

"Gabriel!" Callie was not so quiet this time.

Color washed over Juliana's cheeks. "No, I did not. But I see that you don't believe that."

"You have to admit that you make it rather difficult, sister."

She knew he was angry. Knew he felt trapped by their mother's arrival and her requests and the threat she was to their family reputation, as strong as spun sugar. She knew she should not take his criticism to heart. Knew that he was lashing out at her because he could.

But she was tired of everyone pointing out her flaws.

Especially when they were right.

"I have not exactly had the easiest of evenings. Aside from tumbling down a flight of stairs and having my first conversation in a decade with my mother, I've argued with you, ruined my gown, fled a ball, and watched . . ."

Watched Simon pledge himself to someone else.

"Watched?" he prompted.

Suddenly, she felt very tired. Tired from the day, from the last week, from the last seven months. Tired of London.

She shook her head. "Nothing."

There was a long pause as he watched her, and she deliberately evaded his gaze until he finally sighed. "Yes, well, I've had enough of this disaster of a day, myself."

He exited the room.

Callie watched him go before heaving a sigh herself. "He did not mean it, you know. He's just . . . she's not easy for him, either."

Juliana met her sister-in-law's kind eyes. Callie had always been a calm to Gabriel's storm. "I know. But he is not entirely wrong." They sat for long minutes in companionable silence before Juliana could no longer stay quiet.

"Leighton is marrying."

Callie nodded. "Lady Penelope has made a good match."

"She does not love him."

Callie tilted her head. "No, I don't imagine she does."

The silence stretched between them until Juliana could no longer bear it. Looking down at her hands, clasped tightly together, she said quietly, "When are they marrying? Was anything said?"

"I heard sometime in late November."

One month.

Juliana nodded, pressing her lips together.

It was done. He was gone.

She took a deep breath.

"I think I am through with London."

Callie's eyes widened. "Forever?"

"At least for now."

Simon needed a drink.

More than one.

He tossed his hat and gloves to the footman who had waited for his return home, relieved the man of his duties for the rest of the evening, and threw open the door to the library, taking perverse enjoyment in the way the great slab of oak crashed against the inside wall of the room.

He was the only one who was impressed, apparently. Leopold lifted his head and sniffed the air once, thoughtfully, before finding the entire event unworthy of excitement.

Simon moved to a sideboard and poured himself a tumbler of scotch, immediately throwing back the fiery liquid.

He was betrothed.

He poured another glass.

He was betrothed, and this evening, he'd nearly ruined a woman who was not his future bride.

He eyed the decanter for a brief moment before grabbing it and heading for his chair. Glowering at the dog, he offered his most masterful, "Off."

The damned animal yawned and eased from the chair with a long stretch, as though it had made the decision to move on its own.

This was what he had become—a duke unable to secure even the obedience of his own dog.

He took the chair, ignoring the way the dog stretched out in front of the warm fire burning in the hearth.

He let out a long breath that it seemed he had been holding since earlier in the evening . . . since the moment the Marquess of Needham and Dolby had thundered the announcement of his daughter's betrothal, and Simon had taken Lady Penelope's hand in his, raised it to his lips, and done his duty.

He'd felt it then, the burden. For now it was no longer his mother and his sister and the dukedom for which he was responsible. He was responsible for Lady Penelope as well. And even then it had not been his impending marriage or even his sister's impending ruin that consumed his thoughts.

It had been Juliana.

He had been keenly aware of her departure; he'd watched out of the corner of his eye as she and the Duchess of Rivington had made their way through the crowd, weaving in and out of the throngs of revelers until they reached the exit. Had she been moving any faster, she would have been running.

Not that he blamed her.

He wished he could have run from that ballroom as well. As it was, he had left as quickly as he could without drawing attention to himself.

And then she'd turned, and looked at him . . . into him.

And there had been something in her eyes that had terrified and taunted and tempted him.

Something that had stolen his breath and made him want to run after her.

He drank again, closing his eyes against the evening. But closing his eyes only served to heighten the memory of her. Her hair, her eyes, her skin, the way she had moved against him like a sorceress.

He had not meant to make things worse. Had not meant to touch her. Had not wanted to bring her any closer to ruin than he already had. He was not that man, for God's sake! He wasn't a rake. Yes, he'd kept a mistress now and then, and he'd had his fair share of dalliances, but he'd never ruined a girl. Never even come close.

He'd always prided himself on being a gentleman.

Until he'd met the one woman who made him want to throw gentlemanliness to the wind and drag her down to the floor and have his way with her.

Before announcing his engagement to someone else.

What had he become?

She'd been right to refuse his suit last night. Ralston, too.

But, God he wanted her.

And at another time, as another man, he would have had her. Without hesitation. As lover . . . as more.

As wife.

He cursed, loud and harsh in the silence, drawing the attention of the dog.

"Oh, I'm sorry, am I disturbing your rest?"

Leopold gave a long-suffering sigh and went back to sleep.

Simon poured himself another drink.

"You don't need that."

He laughed, the sound ragged in the silence of the room.

His mother had followed him home.

It appeared his horrendous evening had not ended.

"It is two o'clock in the morning."

She ignored him. "You left the ball early."

"It is not early. In fact, it is altogether too late for you to be making calls, don't you think?"

"I came to tell you that you did the right thing."

No, I did not. But I am happy you think so.

"It could not wait for a more reasonable hour?"

"No." She glided across the room to perch on the edge of the seat opposite him. She gave his chair a disapproving look. "That chair needs reupholstering."

"I shall take your opinion under advisement." He took a drink, ignoring her obvious distaste for the action.

He wondered how long he had to sit here before she would leave.

"Leighton——" she began, and he cut her off.

"You never use my name."

Her brow furrowed just barely, and he took perverse pleasure in his ability to throw her off track. "I beg your pardon?"

"Simon. You've never called me that."

"Why would I call you that?"

"It is my name."

She shook her head. "You have a title. Responsibilities. You are due the respect they demand."

"You didn't call me Simon as a child."

"You had a title then, too. Marquess of Hastings," she added, as though he were an imbecile. "What is this about, Leighton?"

He heard the irritation in her voice. "Nothing."

"Good." She nodded once before changing the subject. "The marchioness and I plan to begin arrangements for the wedding tomorrow. You, of course, must be certain to escort Lady Penelope in public as much as possible over the next month. And no more invitations to Ralston House. I really don't know what has happened to you; you've never associated with such . . . questionable stock before, and now that our name must remain unimpeachable, you're gallivanting about with Ralston and his . . . cheap family."

His gaze snapped to her. "Ralston is married to the sister of the Earl of Allendale and the Duchess of Rivington."

His mother waved a hand dismissively. "None of that matters now that the mother is back. And the sister." Her upper lip curled as though she had inhaled something offensive. "She is a disgrace."

He went still under the wave of anger that coursed through him at the sneering, disdainful words. There was nothing disgraceful about Juliana. She was beautiful and brilliant and, yes, perhaps too bold at times, but she was marvelous. And he wanted to toss his mother out for saying otherwise.

His knuckles whitened around the crystal tumbler. "I will not hear you speak so about the lady."

The duchess's eyes narrowed on him. "I had not

known that you held *Miss* Fiori in such high regard."
He did not miss the correction to Juliana's title. When
he remained quiet, she added, a wealth of cool understanding in her tone, "Do not tell me you want the
girl."

He did not speak. Did not look to his mother. "I see
you do." There was a long pause, then, "She is nothing, Leighton. No name, no breeding, nothing to recommend her except a thread of a relation to Ralston, who
is barely respectable himself now that their scandalous
mother has returned. My goodness, we're not even certain that she is who she says! The rumors have begun
again that she is illegitimate. Not even a connection to
Allendale and Rivington will save that family's reputation now . . ." The duchess leaned forward and steeled
her tone. "She is so far beneath you, she's barely good
enough to take to mistress."

Rage coursed through him. Yes, there had been a time
when he had suggested Juliana would make a good mistress himself, but it was long ago, long before he had
come to see . . .

How remarkable she was.

The duchess continued, boredom in her tone. "Look
elsewhere to warm your bed, Leighton. You can find
someone with increased . . . worth."

He took in the hateful words, let them wash over him.

And realized that he would never find anyone with
such worth as Juliana.

He would never have her. But, by God, he would not
allow her be maligned.

"Get out." The words were reserved, and he was impressed with his control.

Her eyes widened. "I beg your pardon?" There was a
thread of outrage in her tone.

"You heard me."

She did not move. "Leighton. Really. There's no need

for such dramatics. Since when have you become so pedestrian?"

"There's nothing pedestrian about it. I've had enough of you tonight, Mother. You have received what you want. I am marrying Lady Penelope—she of impeccable reputation and immense worth. I've had enough of doing your bidding for the time being."

The duchess stood, pulling herself up to her full, stoic height. "You will remember that I am your mother, Leighton, and due the respect of the station."

"And you will remember that I am *duke*, Mother, and the time is long past during which I took my marching orders from you. Go home, before I say something I will regret."

They stared at each other for a long moment, neither backing down until there was a soft knock on the door to the library.

Was this night never to end?

Simon spun away from his mother. "Damnation! What?"

Boggs entered, trepidation on his face. "Your Graces, my apologies. There is an urgent message for the duke. From Yorkshire."

Simon went cold, taking the note and dismissing the butler.

He broke the wax seal, and unfolded the paper, knowing that this was the note he had been dreading—the one that would change everything.

He read it quickly, then refolded it, placing it in his pocket. All this time, he'd been waiting . . . preparing for the message and, with it, any number of emotions—anger, fear, nervousness, irritation.

But what he felt was calm.

He stood, heading for the door.

"Leighton—" his mother called out, and he paused, back to her. Had that been a tremor in her voice? He looked over his shoulder, noticing her skin like parchment, her gray eyes set deep in her face, the hollow of her cheeks.

She looked weary.

And resigned.

"Is there news?"

The news they had been waiting for.

"You are a grandmother."

Chapter Fourteen

The country is where rumors go to hide.
Elegant ladies do not rusticate.

—*A Treatise on the Most Exquisite of Ladies*

Tragedy! Our favorite item from the Continent has
gone missing . . .

—*The Scandal Sheet, November 1823*

*A*fter traveling for five days on the hard, unforgiving roads of the English countryside, Juliana
had never been so happy as she was to see Townsend
Park.

If only she could get there.

The carriage had been stopped as soon as it had
turned off the post road and down the long drive leading to the great stone house that loomed, stately and
beautiful from the vast Yorkshire moors. When she had
explained to the two enormous guards that her brother
was the master of the house, and she was simply here for
a visit, one of the men had leapt on a horse and was off

like a shot to the great house—presumably to announce her arrival.

After a quarter of an hour, Juliana had descended from the carriage to stretch her legs by the side of the road while she waited to be approved for entry into the Park.

Security was serious business in this little corner of England.

On the surface, Townsend Park was the primary residence the Earl of Reddich, overseen by Juliana's half brother and Ralston's twin, Lord Nicholas St. John, and his wife Isabel, the earl's sister. But the manor was also known as Minerva House, a safe place for young women from across England who needed sanctuary from difficult circumstances. Until Nick had discovered Isabel and the house several months ago, the safety of its residents had been under constant threat.

No longer, thought Juliana as she looked up at the massive guard with whom she had been left. *These gentlemen seem ready to take on anything that comes their way.*

She could not deny that there was something comforting in knowing that once inside the confines of the Park, she would be protected from the world beyond its borders.

She kicked a stone, watching it disappear into the rushes that grew along the side of the drive, golden with the glow of the afternoon sun.

Perhaps she'd never leave.

She wondered if anyone would even notice.

Wondered if Simon would notice.

She knew better than to think about him—about the last time she had seen him, just over a week ago, looking every inch the happy bridegroom. But she couldn't help it. She'd spent five long days in the carriage from London, with little to do but play *Briscola* with Carla and think about him . . . and the way he touched her . . . the way he spoke her name . . . the way his gaze heated when he looked at her, until his eyes turned the color of honey straight from the comb.

She took a deep breath.

He was not for her.

And it was time she realized it and put him out of her mind.

By the time she returned to London, he would be married. And she would have no choice but to pretend their clandestine meetings had never happened. No choice but to play as though she and the Duke of Leighton had nothing more than a passing acquaintance.

That she did not know the way his voice deepened to velvet just before he kissed her.

She sighed and turned back to the house, to see her brother, high upon a horse, wide grin on his face, galloping toward her.

Meeting his smile with one of her own, she waved and called out to him. "My most handsome brother!"

He was off his horse before it stopped, scooping her into an exuberant hug, laughter in his voice. "I shall tell Gabriel you said so, you know."

She waved one hand as he set her on her feet. "As though it would be a surprise! He pales dreadfully in comparison. I am still not certain that you are twins at all."

Gabriel and Nick were identical in every way save one—a dreadful scar that curved down the side of Nick's face, narrowly missing his eye. The scar did nothing to mar his handsomeness, however; instead giving his open, friendly countenance a hint of mystery that drew women like moths to flame.

He nodded his thanks to the guard at the gate, then indicated the carriage. "Shall we get you to the house?"

She wrinkled her nose. "Must I return to my prison? Can't we walk instead?"

Waving the carriage past, he took up the reins of his

horse and they began the half-mile walk to the manor house. Nick asked a handful of polite questions about her journey before Juliana stopped him with, "I assume you have heard the news."

He nodded, lips set in a firm line. "Gabriel sent a messenger the evening she arrived." He paused. "How is she?"

"The same."

They walked for a moment in silence before he asked, "And how are you?"

She looked down at her feet, watching the tips of her boots peep out from beneath the hem of her wine-colored traveling cloak. "I am . . ." She turned to him, taking in his clear blue gaze, filled with interest and not a little concern, and then past him to the wide-open heath that stretched for miles in every direction. "I am happy to be here," she said. And it was the truth.

He smiled, offering her an arm, which she took with pleasure. Nick had always been the easier of her brothers—where Gabriel's temper ran hot, Nick was patient and understanding. He would not press her to discuss their mother, or anything else. But he would listen when she was ready to talk.

She was not ready.

Not yet.

"And how are things here?" she said, changing the subject. "You so rarely write, I sometimes think I do not have a middle brother."

He gave a little laugh. "Wild and well, as usual. We've had three new girls in the past month . . . four if you count the baby that arrived ten days ago."

Her eyes widened. "Baby?"

"One of the girls . . ." He trailed off.

He did not have to finish the sentence. The tale was an old one. One of the girls had made a mistake and found herself unmarried and with child. Perhaps a month ago,

Juliana would not have considered such a circumstance to be the product of ignorance or irresponsibility. But now . . .

Now, she knew too well how tempting men could be.

"At any rate, Isabel is working too hard." Nick interrupted her thoughts.

She smiled. "Isabel always works too hard."

"Yes, but now that she carries my child, I prefer to see her in bed eating biscuits. Perhaps you could nudge her in that direction."

Juliana laughed. Isabel was nearly as susceptible to nudging as one of the marble statues she loved so much. His smile turned soft at the laughter, and Juliana felt a pang of envy at the emotion she saw there.

"I see you think that an unreasonable request."

"Not unreasonable. Merely doomed to remain unfulfilled."

He barked his laughter as the object of their conversation came into view on the top steps of the manor house. Juliana waved to her sister-in-law, who returned the greeting and started down the steps toward them.

Juliana ran to meet Isabel, and the two embraced warmly before holding each other at arm's length for inspection.

"How is it that you have been traveling for five days and still look beautiful?" Isabel teased. "I can barely get down the stairs in the morning without ruining a gown!"

Juliana grinned at her sister-in-law, now five months pregnant and happily glowing. "Nonsense. You are gorgeous!" Juliana said, holding Isabel at arm's length and taking in the gentle swell of her abdomen. "And how lucky am I that I shall soon have two lovely nieces to indulge!"

"Nieces, are they?" Nick teased from behind.

Juliana grinned. "In this house? You think you will have a son?"

"A man can dream."

Isabel took Juliana's arm, leading her toward the house. "I am so happy you are here, and just in time for Bonfire Night!"

"There is a night for fire?"

Isabel waved a hand. "You will see."

Juliana looked over her shoulder at Nick. "Should I be concerned?"

"Possibly. It involves burning Catholics in effigy."

Juliana's eyes grew wide, and Isabel laughed. "Nick. Stop it. She still does not trust the English."

"And apparently, I should not!" Juliana said. "I should have known better than to come to the country. It is apparently a risk."

"Only a risk to your daily excitement," Isabel replied. "It's dreadfully boring compared to London."

"I thought you hated London," Nick said.

"I remain worried about fire," Juliana interjected.

"I don't hate London. Anymore," Isabel said to Nick, then turned immediately to Juliana. "Don't worry about the fire. You'll be fine. You'll see tomorrow. Now. Tell me everything that is happening in London—all I get is the news, weeks old, from *Pearls and Pelisses*!"

Nick groaned at the reference to the ladies' magazine that had once set all of London's unmatched females after him. "I do not know why we still take the damned magazine."

"The girls like it," Isabel said, referring to the rest of the population of Minerva House.

"Ahh," teased Juliana. "The *girls*. Well, they shall very much enjoy the next issue, I would imagine. Our mother has once again made us the talk of the town." She paused, then, unable to resist, continued. "At least, she had done before the Duke of Leighton chose his bride."

Nick and Isabel shared a shocked look. "Leighton is to marry?"

"He announced his betrothal to Lady Penelope Marbury last week." She was very proud of herself for keeping her tone even and unmoved. "Are you surprised? Dukes are required to marry, Nick."

Nick paused, thinking on the question. "Of course they are. I'm merely surprised that he hasn't said anything to us."

She blinked. "I was not aware that your relationship with the duke was close enough for him to write to you of his pending nuptials."

"Oh, it's not," Isabel chimed in. "But you would think that it might have come up in conversation at some point."

Warning bells sounded, and Juliana stopped walking. "Conversation?" Perhaps she had misunderstood. Her English was far from perfect.

"Yes. Leighton is here."

"Here?" She looked to Nick. Perhaps it was Isabel she was misunderstanding. "Why would he be here?"

He couldn't be here. Not now. Not when the only thing she needed was to be as far from him as possible.

"I suppose you'll find out soon enough . . ." Nick said. "He came as soon as the child was born."

A wave of panic passed through her.

The child.

He had a child.

She was overcome with emotion—a combination of sadness and shock and not a little bit of jealousy. Another woman had had his child. A woman to whom he had belonged for some length of time.

In a way that he would never belong to Juliana.

The knowledge was devastating.

"Juliana?" Isabel's voice sounded from far away. "You've gone pale. Are you ill?"

"Leighton . . . he is here now?"

"Yes. Juliana . . . is there something wrong? Has the

duke been rude to you?" She looked to Nick. "It's a wonder the man hasn't had a decent thrashing in twenty years."

Apparently Isabel did not care for Simon either. No one in her family seemed to like him, this man who had shipped one woman off to Yorkshire to birth his illegitimate child while he proposed marriage to another.

And while he did marvelous, unspeakable things to a third in darkened conservatories.

Her family suddenly seemed to have excellent judgment of character.

"Gabriel gave him a thrashing already."

"Did he? Good!" Isabel said.

"Did he? When?" This, from Nick.

"Last week," Juliana said, wishing they had not started down this path.

"Why?"

"No reason."

None Nick need know, at least.

Nick's brows rose. "I somehow doubt that." He paused. "So. You know Leighton."

She felt ill. "Vaguely."

Isabel and Nick shared a look before he said, "It does not seem at all vague, actually. It seems that you know him well enough to be unsettled by the idea that he is here."

"Not at all."

Why would she be unsettled by the fact that she'd escaped to Yorkshire only to find that the person from whom she'd escaped was already there?

With his secret child.

It was not the first secret he had kept from her.

Merely the most important.

"So," she said, walking once more, hoping to sound casual. "The child. Will he acknowledge it?"

That had not sounded at all casual. It had sounded as

though she were being strangled. Juliana was beginning to wish that her carriage had been set upon by highwaymen on the way there. Yes. Abduction at the hands of criminals would have been a better fate than this.

"It is not clear," Nick said.

She stopped again, turning back to Nick. "I beg your pardon. Did you say it is not clear?"

"There are a number of things that he must consider . . ."

Her anger began to rise. "What kind of things? You mean his future bride?"

Nick looked confused. "Among other things."

"Don't you think she deserves to know? Isabel? Wouldn't you have wanted to know before you married Nick?"

Isabel thought for a moment. "Perhaps . . ."

Juliana's eyes went wide. *Had everyone in the family lost their minds?* "Perhaps?" she squeaked.

Isabel looked surprised, then hurried to correct herself. "All right, yes. I suppose I would have."

"Precisely!" Juliana looked to Nick. "You see?"

She couldn't believe that Nick would even consider accepting less than acknowledgment from Leighton. This was his *child*. Legitimate or no, she deserved to know from whence she came.

She deserved to know that she had a family beyond her little world.

It was hard for Juliana to comprehend the idea that Simon might not acknowledge his child. Perhaps this was the way it was done here, in the British aristocracy—this perverse universe where people were less inclined to accept an illegitimate child than they were to accept a father who admitted his mistakes.

Mistakes.

She winced at the word.

The perfect duke, who surveyed with undeniable arrogance the failures of everyone around him, had made the worst kind of mistake.

She would never have dreamed he would be the kind of man to consider walking away from his own child.

It shouldn't matter.

As it was, she had no claim to him. He was pledged to Lady Penelope. What would change if he'd had an illegitimate child in the country?

Everything.

She knew it was true even before the word floated through her mind.

He would have been less than the Simon she knew. The kind of man who sent a woman away to bear his child was not the kind of man she believed him to be. Was not the kind of man she wanted him to be.

The kind of man she wanted for herself.

Juliana wanted to find him and shake him.

"Where is he? I want to speak with him."

Nick hesitated. "Juliana. There is more to it than that. It's not so simple. He's a duke . . . and a highly respected one at that. He has options to consider. A family to think on."

Her eyes narrowed. Perhaps she would begin the shaking with her brother.

"Well, he should have thought of that before he shipped the child and its mother off to Yorkshire!"

Isabel's jaw dropped, and Juliana realized that she had near-bellowed the words. She gave a little huff of indignation. If they thought she was going to apologize for being outraged at his typical, horrible arrogance, they were absolutely wrong.

"Juliana." Nick's voice was low and calm.

"Don't try to change my mind, Nick. Illegitimacy is a sore topic for me at the moment, as our mother has just thrown my own into public question. I won't let that . . . impossible man simply wave his hand and send his own flesh and blood away without recognition. It's unacceptable. And if you haven't the courage to tell him, I will."

She stopped, breathing heavily after her tirade, and met Nick's gaze, seeing the frustration there. Perhaps she should not have suggested he was a coward.

"Obviously, I did not mean—"

"Oh, I think you absolutely meant, sister, and you are lucky I am the good twin," he said. "If you feel so strongly about it, speak to Leighton. I've no interest in soliciting your ire. You will see him at dinner."

Something about the words did not sit right with Juliana, but she was still too angry and eager to face down Simon to even think twice about her brother. They had reached the foot of the wide stone steps leading up to the manor house, and Juliana looked up at the enormous door at the top, which stood open, beckoning her inside.

She was not willing to wait for him.

She'd had enough.

When Juliana found him, Simon was standing at the end of a long room, staring out a window, back to the doorway. She'd almost missed him, silhouetted by a brilliant blue sky that belied the storm building in her heart.

She stepped inside the room—taking note of his sheer size, tall and broad and devastatingly handsome—and hating that even now, in her anger, she was so very drawn to him. She wanted to run to him and wrap herself around him and beg him to be the man she thought him to be.

He was not for her.

She must remember that.

She headed across what appeared to be a sitting room; she cared little for her surroundings, as she was too eager to speak to Simon—to tell him precisely what she thought of his latest ducal decision.

She approached him from behind and offered no preamble. "I thought you were different."

He turned only his head toward her, his features vague in the afternoon shadows, making it easier for her to speak her mind. She waited for a moment, but he did not speak, did not refute her point, and so she continued, letting her ire rise. "I thought you a gentleman—the kind of man who made good on his promises and cared deeply for what was right in the world." She paused. "My mistake. I forgot that you only truly care for one thing—not honor or justice, but reputation."

She laughed, hearing the self-deprecation in the sound, the shaking in her voice as she continued. "I suppose I thought that even as you laughed at me and criticized me for having too much passion or being too reckless or not having enough care for my own reputation—I suppose I thought that maybe I—That maybe you—"

I suppose I thought that maybe you were different.

That maybe you had changed.

That maybe I had changed you.

She could not say any of those things to him.

She had no right to say them.

He turned to fully face her, and she realized that he was holding an infant in his arms.

The room came into stark relief. Not a sitting room. A nursery.

And he was here, holding a sleeping child so small that she fit easily in his hands.

She swallowed, stepping closer, peering into the little round, red face and the bluster went out of her. She no longer wanted to scream or shake him. She did not feel vindicated. She felt . . . lost.

In a different world—another time—they might have been in a similar nursery. Might have had a similar moment. A happier one.

Her voice caught as she spoke, looking at the baby and not the man. "I know what it is like to grow up knowing that a parent doesn't want you, Simon," she whispered. "I know what it's like to have the world know it, too. It is devastating. Devastating when you are four, when you are ten, when you are . . . twenty.

"I know what it is to be ridiculed and rejected by everyone."

What it is to be rejected by you.

Suddenly, his acceptance of this child meant everything to her. She did not know why—only that it was true.

"You must acknowledge her, Simon." There was a long silence. "You must. So there is scandal. You can weather it. You can. I—" *No. There was no I.* She was nothing to him. "We . . . we will stand beside you."

There were tears on her cheeks, and she knew she should be sorry for them. "You're here for her, Simon. You came to meet her. Surely that means something. You can want her. You can love her."

She heard the plea in her words, knew that she was talking about more than this child.

She should be embarrassed but could not find the energy to care.

All she cared about was him.

This man who had ruined her for all others.

From the beginning.

"Simon." she whispered, and in the name was an ocean of emotion.

He was everything she'd always sworn to hate . . . an arrogant aristocrat who had ruined an unsuspecting female and had a daughter whom he might not acknowledge.

She hated herself for noticing the strength and perfection of him.

For wanting him even as she should despise him.

He took a step toward her, and she stepped back, afraid to be closer to him. Afraid of what she might do. What she might allow him to do.

"Juliana, would you like to meet my niece?"

His niece.

"Your niece?"

"Caroline." The word was soft, filled with something she instantly envied.

"Caroline," she repeated, taking a step toward him, toward the cherub in his arms, with her little round face and her little rosebud of a mouth, and swirls of golden hair just like her uncle's.

Her uncle.

She let out a long breath. "You are her uncle."

One side of his mouth lifted in a barely there smile. "You thought I was her father."

"I did."

"And you did not think to confirm it before making such accusations?"

Warmth flooded her cheeks. "Perhaps I should have."

He looked down at the baby in his arms, and something tightened in Juliana's chest at the incongruous portrait they made—this enormous man, the portrait of propriety and arrogance, and his infant niece, barely the length of his hands.

"Caroline," he whispered once more, and she heard the awe in his voice. "She looks just like Georgiana. Just like she looked when she was born."

"Your sister."

He met her eyes. "Georgiana."

Understanding dawned. "She is the secret. The one you have been working to protect."

He nodded. "I had no choice. I had to protect the family. I had to protect her."

Juliana nodded. "How old is she?"

"Seventeen."

Not even out.

"Unmarried?" She did not have to ask the question.

He nodded once, stroking one finger along Caroline's tiny hand.

The baby was the reason for everything . . . for his anger at Juliana's recklessness . . . for his insistence that her reputation was paramount . . . for his impending marriage.

A knot formed in Juliana's throat, making it difficult to swallow.

"I thought I would get here and the answer would be clear. I thought it would be easy to send her away. To send them away."

She was transfixed by his soft, liquid voice, by the way he held the infant, so carefully.

"Then I met Caroline." In her sleep, the child grasped the tip of his finger tightly, and he smiled, wonder and sadness breaking across his beautiful features— features that so rarely betrayed his emotion. He exhaled, and Juliana heard the weight of his responsibility in the sound.

Tears pricked, and Juliana blinked them away.

When society heard, the scandal would be unbearable. Did he really think he could hide from them forever?

She knew she must tread lightly. "You sent your sister here to keep her . . . situation . . . a secret?"

He shook his head. "No. She ran. From the family . . . from me. She did not think I would support her. Support them. And she was right."

She heard the bitterness in his voice, saw how one side of his mouth curled in a grimace before he turned to cross the room and return the baby to her cradle.

From where he had lifted her.

Suddenly, Juliana realized the enormity of this moment upon which she had intruded; aristocratic males did not linger in nurseries. They did not hold children. But Simon had been here. Had been holding that baby with all the care she deserved.

There was such uncertainty in him—in this man who never doubted himself. Whom no one ever doubted. She ached for him. "She will forgive you."

"You don't know that."

"I do . . ." She paused. *How could she not forgive him?* "I know it. You came after her. After them both."

To take care of them.

"Do not make me into a hero, Juliana. I found her . . . discovered her situation . . . she would not tell me who the father was . . . and I was furious. I left her here. I wanted nothing to do with her."

She couldn't believe it. Wouldn't believe it.

"No . . ." She shook her head. "It's not true. You are here now."

He turned away from her and returned to the window to look out over the heath. He was quiet for a long moment. "But for how long?"

She moved toward him.

He spoke before she could. "I only came to decide what to do next. To make her tell me who the man is. To make arrangements to hide the child. To hide my sister. Do you still think me a hero?"

Her brow furrowed. "Do you still plan to do those things?"

He turned back to her. "I don't know. Perhaps. That was certainly an option when I was on my way here . . . but now . . ."

He trailed off.

She could not remain quiet. "Now?"

"I don't know!" The words echoed around the room, frustration and anger surprising them both. He thrust both hands through his hair. "Now, my well-laid plans seem completely unreasonable. Now, my sister won't speak to me. Now . . . now, I've held the damned child."

They were inches from each other and when he looked at her, she could see the anguish in his eyes. He reached toward her, the backs of his fingers trailing along her cheek, the movement so soft and lovely that she closed her eyes against the feeling. "You have made everything more complicated."

Her eyes flew open at the accusation. "What does that mean?"

"Only that when you are near, I forget everything that I am meant to remember—everything I am meant to be. And all I want is this."

He settled his lips to hers, the softness of the kiss enhancing the ache that had settled deep in her heart during their conversation. She let him guide the way, his lips moving against hers, desperate and gentle all at once. His tongue brushed against her and she opened for him, allowing him entrance, giving herself up to the slide of the caress.

This was not a kiss of celebration, but of devastation. It was a kiss that laid them both bare, and it tasted of regret as much as it did of desire. And even as she hated the emotion in it, she could not resist it.

Did not want to.

Her arms came up, fingers slid into the soft curls at the nape of his neck, and she kissed him back with everything in her, passion and emotion and longing. She met him stroke for stroke in the hopes that she could somehow convince him, with movement instead of words, that things could be different. That things could change.

And then they did.

He broke away with a curse, and she grew cold even before he stepped back from her, putting several feet between them—feet that felt like miles. They stood there for a long moment in the dimly lit space, breath coming in twin, harsh bursts.

He wiped the back of one hand across his mouth as if to erase the memory of her, and she winced at the movement. "I have to protect my family, Juliana. I have to do what I can to protect our name. To protect my sister. From them."

"I understand."

"No. You don't." His beautiful eyes betrayed his emotion. She could not look away from the emotion there, so rare, so tempting. "You can't. This cannot happen. I am the duke. It is my duty."

"You say it like I have asked you to deny that duty."

He closed his eyes. Took a deep breath. "You haven't."

"No," she protested. "I haven't."

"I know. But you make me want to deny it. You make me want to throw it all away. You make me think that it could all be different. But . . ." He trailed off.

This is how things are done.

She heard the words even though he did not speak them.

She wanted to rail at him. Wanted to scream that it could be different. That he could change the way things were done. That he was a duke, and the rest of his silly world would forgive him most anything—and who cared what the horrible lot of them thought anyway?

But she knew better. She had said as much to him before, countless times. And they meant nothing. They were mist on cold marble.

He pressed on. "I am not free to do as I please. I cannot simply turn my back on the world in which we live."

"The world in which *you* live, Simon," she corrected. "And yes, I think you are free to do as you please. You are not a god, not even a king, but just a man, just flesh and blood like the rest of us." She knew she should stop, but she was down this road now, unable to turn back. "This isn't about your sister, or your niece, or about what is right for them. This is about you. And your fears. You are not trapped by society. Your prison is of your own making."

He stiffened, and the emotion was instantly gone from his eyes—the cool, aloof Duke of Leighton returned. "You do not understand that of which you speak."

She had expected it; nonetheless, the words stung, and she moved away from him, to the cradle. She ran one finger down the soft, mottled skin of the sleeping baby's cheek. "Some things are more powerful than scandal, Simon."

He did not speak as she crossed the room, brushing past him to the door, where she turned back, and said, "I only hope you see that before it is too late for her."

She left the room, back straight, head high, determined not to show him how much she ached for him. The moment the door closed behind her, she sagged against it, the truth hitting her, hard and fast and cruel.

She loved him.

It changed nothing. He was still engaged to another, still obsessed with propriety and reputation. Still the Duke of Disdain. She would do well to remember it.

Perhaps, if she remembered it, she would love him less.

Because she did not think she could love him more.

She took a deep breath, a tiny sound catching in her throat.

They had lied, those who had extolled the virtues of love—its pleasures, its sublimity—those who had told her that it was beautiful and worthwhile.

There was nothing beautiful about it.

It was awful.

A battle raged in him, propriety and passion. Reputation and reward. And Juliana knew now, with sickening clarity, that it was this battle that she loved the most about him.

But now he was hurting her.

And she could not bear it.

Could not bear another moment of not being good enough for him.

And so she stood straight, coming away from the wall, and she did the only thing she could do.

She walked away.

Chapter Fifteen

Too-familiar servants are the worst kind of offense.
Refined ladies do not abide gossip in the kitchens.

—*A Treatise on the Most Exquisite of Ladies*

At long last, the appeal of the country has returned . . .

—*The Scandal Sheet, November 1823*

Simon wanted to put a fist through the wall of the nursery.

He'd left for Yorkshire the moment he'd received word that Georgiana's baby had come; he'd told himself he was coming for his sister and his niece and to ensure that the family's secrets remained just that—secret. And he had come for those things.

But he had also come to escape Juliana.

He should have known that once he arrived here, in this house filled with women, that he would be reminded of her. Should have known that when he drank scotch with Nick, he would see Juliana in Nick's eyes, in the way he laughed. Should have known that near her family, he would think of her constantly.

But what he had not expected was how much he thought of her when he was near his own family: when his mother had left the house, with barely a word of farewell; when his sister had refused to see him upon his arrival to Townsend Park; when he held his niece in his arms, consumed with how her slight weight could seem so heavy. He'd thought of Juliana at all those moments.

He'd wanted her by his side. Her strength. Her willingness to face down any foe. Her commitment to those for whom she cared.

For those she loved.

When she'd burst into the nursery to take him on, to champion the infant Caroline at all costs, it had been as though he had conjured her up. And somehow, in her railing, he had found comfort for the first time since arriving in Yorkshire.

She had faced him with a fierce commitment to what she believed was right. No one had ever fought him the way she had. The way she did. No one had ever held his feet to the flame the way she did.

She was everything he had never been—emotion and passion and excitement and desire. She cared nothing for his name or his title or his reputation.

She cared only for the man he might be.

She made him want to be that man.

But it was impossible.

He had proposed to Penelope, thinking she could save them all, and only now did he realize that, with that final act, he had ruined everything.

Simon stared at the door through which Juliana had fled, knowing that the best he could do for her—for both of them—was to keep away from her.

He owed her at least that.

She deserved better than ruin at his hands.

A flood of remorse coursed through him—for what he had done and what he would never do. He tried not to think on it as noise came, loud and welcome, from the cradle; Caroline was waking. He moved instinctively toward her, wanting to hold the little creature who did not know enough to see his flaws.

He was beside her in seconds, thankful for the odd lack of servants at the Park. In any other house, the niece of a duke would be surrounded by nurses and nannies, but here, she was alone at times, giving her uncle a chance to be near her without an audience.

He lifted her once more into his arms, hoping that the contact was enough for her to settle and return to sleep. Caroline had other plans, her little cries getting louder.

"Don't cry, sweeting," he said in what he hoped was a soothing voice. "Don't make me have to find a servant . . . or your mother—I've made a hash of things with her, as well."

The infant took no pity on him, squirming in his hands. He moved her against his chest, her head on his shoulder, one large hand spread over her back. "I am not enough to make you happy, am I? Of course, there's no reason to believe I should begin making the ladies in my life happy now."

"You could try a touch harder."

He turned at the words. His sister was crossing the nursery toward him, arms outstretched. He relinquished the baby and watched as Georgiana cradled her daughter. The child instantly settled into the arms of her mother, her cries becoming little whimpers. "She knows you."

Georgiana gave a little smile, not looking away from the infant. "We've had several months to get acquainted."

Several months during which he had been absent.

He was an ass.

"I hear you are to be married."

"News travels fast in this house," Simon said.

"It is a house populated entirely with women. What did you think would happen to the information?" She paused. "Are congratulations in order?"

"Lady Penelope will make a fine wife. Her family is ancient, her reputation, impeccable."

"As ours used to be?"

"As it still is."

She lifted her gaze to his, amber eyes—so like his own—seeing more than he would like. "Not for long, though."

He did not want to discuss his marriage to Penelope. He did not want to discuss their family name, their reputation. He wanted to discuss his sister. He wanted to start fresh.

Not that it would ever be possible.

"Georgiana . . ." he began, stopping when she turned away, ignoring him and crossing the room to a high table where she set Caroline down and began fussing about with her.

"You shan't want to stay for this bit, I don't imagine."

His brow furrowed at the words, and he moved closer, curious. "For what bit?" He peeked over his sister's shoulder, took note of her actions and instantly turned his back to the scene. "Oh! Yes. Ah—No." In all his ducal training, he had never been trained on the care and—cleaning—of infants. "Isn't there . . ." he cleared his throat. "Someone who can . . . do that . . . for you?"

He could not be certain, but he thought he heard his sister chuckle. "Children do not arrive with nurse in tow, Simon."

He did not like the mocking in her tone. "I know that. Of course I do. But you are—" He stopped. There were a dozen ways to end that sentence.

A duke's daughter . . . my sister . . . barely out of diapers yourself in my mind. . .

"I am a mother." She came around to face him, Caroline now quiet in her arms. His sister, whom he'd always considered fragile, now calm and strong, with a voice like steel. "Whatever you were about to say. It is of no import. I am her mother. And she is first. There isn't anything you can say that will change my mind."

His sister was no longer a delicate girl, but Juno, fully grown and protecting her young.

From him.

He, who should be doing the protecting, dammit.

"I don't want to change your mind."

She blinked. "You don't."

"No."

It was true.

She let out a long breath. "You'll let me stay with Caroline. You won't make me fight you."

For the last six months, he had been certain that sending the child away would be for the best. Even on the journey up, he'd toyed with the possibility, played over potential destinations in his mind, unwilling to release the hope that all could return to normal.

He now understood how ridiculous such an idea had been.

He could not bear the idea of sending Caroline away.

I know what it is like to grow up knowing that a parent does not want you, Simon. He'd seen the sadness in Juliana's eyes as she'd spoken the words. He wanted to take his fists to the people who had made her feel such devastation. And he never wanted his niece to feel that pain.

"Of course you shall stay with Caroline."

Georgiana's relief was clear. "Thank you, Simon."

He turned away, less than deserving of his sister's words of gratitude after his poor treatment during the past few months. He deserved her anger and her fury and her loathing, not her thanks.

For, even as she held her daughter in a loving embrace, he thought of the damage that would be wrought upon the family name.

The scandal would come. And they would weather it. He was prepared. Or would be once he married Lady Penelope. "I shall be married in a month. It will help defray the interest in your situation."

She laughed at that, and the sound grated. "Simon, a royal wedding itself would not defray the interest in my situation."

He ignored the words, heading for the door, wanting nothing but to be free of this room that had seemed so welcoming and turned so cloying. Georgiana spoke before he could exit. "You don't have to do it, you know. Nowhere is it written that you must shoulder the burden of our reputation. You don't have to marry her."

Of course he did.

He was the Duke of Leighton—one of the most powerful men in England, born to bear the weight of one of the most venerable titles in the aristocracy. He had spent his whole life preparing for this moment, when honor and duty came before all else.

Where was the honor in what he had done to Juliana? In the stables? In the park? In this room?

Shame coursed through him, his skin growing hot.

"It is not a question. I will marry the lady."

He would do what needed to be done.

He found St. John in the Earl of Reddich's study.

The door stood open, and he knocked once, firmly on the jamb, waiting for St. John to wave him into the room before assuming the ample leather chair on the far side of the great mahogany desk.

"One might almost think you were titled for how well you look behind that desk," he said.

Nick finished annotating a long column of numbers in the estate ledger and looked up. "Considering that the earl is ten and at school, I don't think he will mind if I keep the chair warm until he is ready for it." He leaned back. "It is the mistress of the house that we have to be worried about. She gets irritated when I use her desk."

"Why not get your own, then?"

St. John grinned. "I rather enjoy her when she's irritated."

Simon pretended not to hear the inappropriate comment. "I should like to talk about my sister."

"Excellent. I should like to talk about mine." Simon froze at the words, and St. John's eyes narrowed instantly. "Isabel thinks there is something between the two of you. And she is always right. It's infuriating, really."

"There is nothing between us."

"No?"

Yes.

"No." He attempted to sound emphatic. Hoped he succeeded.

"Mmm." Nick removed his spectacles and tossed them on the desk. "Well then. By all means, let's discuss Lady Georgiana."

Simon's relief came out on a wave of irritation. "I am happy that someone in this house remembers my sister's station."

Nick's brows rose. "I would exercise more care if I were you, Leighton."

Simon swore quietly, his hands balling in fists.

"Try again," Nick said.

Nicholas St. John was, very possibly, Simon's oldest friend, if he were to lay claim to one. The two, along with Ralston, had been the same year at Eton, and Simon, young and entitled, had spent too much time reminding the brothers—and the rest of the class—that the sons of the House of Ralston had come from questionable stock indeed. One day, he had pushed the easygoing Nick too far and suffered the consequences. Nick had bloodied his nose, and their friendship had begun.

It had waned in the years following their departure from school—Simon had become the Duke of Leighton, the head of the family, one of the most powerful men in England—and Nick had left for the Continent, disappearing into the East as a war raged. Leighton money had funded Nick's activities, but that was as close as Simon had come to his friend during those years.

When Juliana had arrived in London, Simon had done nothing to support the house of St. John. And still, when Georgiana arrived on the doorstep of Townsend Park, with child and little else, Nick and Isabel had taken her in. Protected her as though she were their own. And as Simon had railed against them, threatening this house, their names, even their lives, Nick had stood firm, protecting Georgiana at all costs.

A friend.

Perhaps his only friend.

And Simon owed Nick more than he could ever repay.

And now he was going to ask for more.

"She wants to remain here. With the child."

Nick leaned back in his chair. "And what do you want?"

What did he want?

He wanted it all to go back to the way it was. He wanted Georgiana safe in her bed at his country estate, preparing for autumn harvests and winter holidays. He wanted to be free of the burden that had been his since he had ascended to the dukedom . . . since before that.

And he wanted Juliana.

He stopped at the last, her name whispering through his mind.

But instead of bringing clarity, it served only to bring frustration.

He could not have her.

Not now, not ever.

And so he asked for what he could have.

"I want Georgiana to be safe. And Caroline—the child—I want them both to be safe."

Nick nodded. "They are safe here."

"Tell me how much you need."

Nick slashed one hand through the air. "No, Leighton. You've given us enough over the past six months. More than necessary."

"More than you expected."

"Well, you must admit . . . with the way you stormed out of here after discovering your sister's situation, we hardly expected you to become a benefactor of Minerva House."

He'd done it out of guilt.

Georgiana had been terrified of telling him the truth about her situation—that she was with child—that the father's identity would remain her secret. She'd been in tears, had virtually begged him to forgive her. To protect her.

And he'd walked away, angry and unsettled.

He'd returned to London, desperate to shore up their reputation.

Pretending that she was an inconvenience rather than his sister, and the only member of his family who had ever felt like family.

And so he had done the only thing he could do.

He had sent money.

A great deal of it.

"They are my responsibility. I will continue to care for them."

Nick watched him for a long moment, and Simon held his friend's gaze. He would not be denied this—the only way he could even begin to rectify his mistakes.

Nick nodded once. "You do what you feel needs to be done."

"You will let me know if anything . . . if she needs anything."

"I will."

"You are a good friend." It was the first time he'd ever said the words. To Nick . . . to anyone. The first time he had acknowledged a friendship that was more than a drink at the club or a fencing match. He surprised himself with the sentiment.

Nick's eyes widened at the words. "You would do the same."

The simple truth shook Simon to the core. *He would. Now.* But until recently, he might not have.

What had changed?

The answer was clear.

But he could not admit it. Not to himself. Certainly not to Nick.

"Now that that's settled," Nick said, reaching for a bottle of brandy and pouring two snifters' worth of the rich liquid, "shall we return to the topic of Juliana?"

No. She is too much on my mind as it is.

Simon took the offered glass, trying to keep from betraying his thoughts. "There is not much to say."

Nick drank, savoring the liquid and drawing out the moment. "Come, Leighton. You forget to whom you speak. Why not tell me the truth this time? I know my brother hit you. I know my sister flew into a near rage when she thought you might be here with your own child. Do you really want me to draw my own conclusions?"

They could not be any worse than the truth.

Simon remained silent.

Nick sat back, hands clasped together over his navy blue waistcoat—a portrait of calm. Simon loathed him for it. And then his friend spoke. "Fair enough. I shall tell you what I think. I think that you are beside yourself with discomfort at the situation your sister is in. I think you've proposed to Lady Penelope in some mad belief that *your* marriage can offset *Georgiana's* scandal. I think you are marrying for all the wrong reasons. And I think that my sister is proving it to you."

Simon had an instant desire to put his fist through Nick, who noticed the flash of anger with a wry smile. "You're welcome to hit me, old friend, but I can tell you it will not make this any easier. Or my words any less true."

Simon supposed he should have been impressed by Nick's astuteness, but when he really considered it, how difficult was it to see the truth?

He was foolish around her. She made him a fool.

She made him more than that.

She made him ache. And want.

And more.

He did not follow the thought. Would not.

Nick need not know such things.

Instead, he faced his friend in silence, and they sat like that, unmoving, not speaking, for long moments before one side of Nick's mouth rose in a small smile. "You realize you won't be able to avoid it."

Simon made a show of brushing an invisible speck from his coat sleeve, pretending to be bored, pretending not to care even as his mind and heart raced.

"Avoid what?"

"Avoid the way she makes you feel."

"And who is to say she makes me feel anything but irritation?"

Nick laughed. "The fact that you know precisely of whom I am speaking is enough. And you will discover that, in this family, irritation is a precursor to far more dangerous sentiments."

"I have discovered far too much about this family as it is," he said, hoping that years of practiced haughtiness would cover the other emotions roiling within.

"You can play the part of the disdainful duke all you like, Leighton. It won't change anything." Nick set his snifter down and stood, heading for the door, turning back before he opened it. "I suppose it is too much to ask that you stay away from her?"

Yes.

The idea of staying away from Juliana was incomprehensible.

And yet, he must.

What an ass he was. What a fool.

"Not at all."

Liar.

Nick made a little sound that spoke volumes.

"You do not believe me?"

Not that he should. Lord Nicholas St. John should remove him bodily from the house—for his sister's protection.

For Simon's.

"No, Leighton. I don't believe you. Not in the slightest." Nick opened the door.

"If you think I am a risk to her—to her reputation—why let me stay here?"

Nick turned to face him then, and Simon saw something in the other man's blue eyes—eyes so like Juliana's.

Sympathy.

"You are not a risk to her."

Nick did not know the way desire raged through him when she was near.

Simon stayed silent as Nick continued. "You are too careful, Leighton. Too cautious. Juliana is not part of your perfect, pristine life. She is riddled with scandal—as is our entire family. Not that we mind it much," he added in an aside, "but that alone will prevent you from touching her."

Simon wanted to disagree. He wanted to scream at the irresponsibility inherent in the words. His own sister was abovestairs, living proof of what happened when men lost control. When they made mistakes.

But before he had a chance to speak, Nick added, "Do not keep her from happiness, Simon. Perhaps you do not want it for yourself, but you know she deserves it. And she can make a good match."

With someone else.

A visceral hatred coursed through Simon at the thought.

"You say that like there is someone ready to make the offer." He did not mean the disdain in his tone.

Nick heard it nonetheless, and Simon saw anger flash in his friend's eyes. "I should give you the fight you so desperately want for saying that. You think that just because you would never dare to sully your precious reputation with someone like Juliana, there are not others who would line up for a chance at her?"

Of course there would be. She was intelligent and quick-witted and charming and mesmerizingly beautiful.

But before he could admit it, Nick exited the room, closing the door quietly behind him with a soft click, leaving Simon to his thoughts.

She did not want to be alone with her thoughts, so Juliana took solace in the least solitary place at Townsend Park.

The kitchens.

The Minerva House kitchens were precisely the way Juliana thought kitchens should be—loud and messy and filled with laughter and smells and people. They were the heart of the home that the house had become to all the women who lived there. That is to say, the Minerva House kitchens were nothing like the kitchens of other fine English manor houses.

Which was excellent, because Juliana had had enough of fine English things that day—fine English propriety, fine English arrogance, fine English dukes.

She wanted something real and honest.

When she came through the door, the cluster of women gathered around the enormous table at the center of the room barely looked up, continuing their boisterous conversation as Gwen, the manor's cook, took one look at Juliana and put her to work.

"This is Juliana," she said, as the other women made space for her around the oak table—long and lovely and scarred with years of meals and secrets. "Lord Nicholas's sister."

And with that, she was accepted. Gwen floured the space in front of Juliana and upended a copper bowl there, depositing a lump of thick dough in need of attention.

"Knead," said the tiny woman, and Juliana did not think of disobeying.

There were a half dozen other women around the table, each with her own task—chopping, cutting, mixing, pounding—a perfectly organized battalion of cooks, chattering away.

Juliana took a deep breath, breathing in the comfort in the room. She pressed the dough out into a flat, round disk and listened. This was the distraction she needed. Here, she would not have to think about Simon.

". . . I will say that he is one of the handsomest visitors we've had in a very long time."

"Perhaps ever," Gwen added, and there was a murmur of agreement from around the table.

"He looks like an angel."

"A wicked one . . . fallen from heaven. Did you see the way he stormed in here and demanded to see Georgiana?"

Juliana froze. *They were talking about Simon.* It appeared she would not be able to escape him after all.

"The biggest, too," added a tall, thin woman whom Juliana had never met.

"I wonder if he is that big all over," someone said, and the girls dissolved into a fit of giggles at the innuendo.

"He's a guest!" Gwen snapped a towel in the direction of the woman who had made the suggestive comment before smiling wide. "Not that I haven't had that thought myself."

"Please, tell me you are not speaking of whom I think you are speaking."

Juliana's head snapped up as the entire tableful of women laughed and cleared a space for the newcomer— Lady Georgiana.

It had to be her. She looked just like him, all golden-haired and amber-eyed. She was nowhere near his size, however. She was petite and lovely, like a porcelain doll, with the soft, round beauty of a woman who had just given birth. She did not look seventeen. Indeed, she looked much older. Wiser.

"If you thought we were speaking of your handsome brother, you are right," Gwen teased. "Are you feeling up to peeling apples?"

Gwen did not wait for an answer, placing a basketful of bright red apples in front of Georgiana. The younger girl did not protest, instead lifting a small paring knife and setting to work. A shock of surprise went through Juliana at the scene—the sister of a duke happily peeling apples in the kitchens of Minerva House—but she did not comment. "My handsome brother, is he?" Georgiana said, lifting her gaze to Juliana's with a smile.

Juliana went instantly back to work.

Fold, punch, fold, punch.

"You must admit, he is good-looking."

Juliana pretended not to hear.

Turn, flour, fold, punch.

"He has enough women in London throwing themselves at him. Do not give him the pleasure of such a reception here."

Pretended not to think of other women in his arms. Of Penelope in his arms.

Flip, fold, press.

"Nah, men like the duke are too cold, anyway." The tall woman added, "Look at what he's done, sending you and Caroline away for the scandal."

"He didn't exactly send us away."

The larger woman waved a hand in dismissal. "I don't care what happened. You're here with us instead of there with him, and that's enough for me. I like my men with heart."

"He has heart." Juliana didn't know she had spoken aloud until the conversation around the table went silent.

"He does, does he?" She looked up, cheeks flaming, and met Georgiana's curious eyes before returning to the dough. "We have not been introduced."

"This is Lord Nicholas's sister," Gwen hurried to say.

"Miss Fiori, is it?"

Juliana looked up again, hands wrist deep in pastry. "Juliana."

Georgiana nodded. "And what do you know of my brother's heart, Juliana?"

"I—I simply mean he must have a heart, no?" When none of the women replied, returned to the dough. "I don't know."

Fold, turn, fold.

"It sounds like you know quite a bit."

"I don't." She meant for it to sound more emphatic than it was.

"Juliana," Georgiana asked in a pointed way that was all too familiar, "are you . . . fond of my brother?"

She shouldn't be. He was everything she didn't want. Everything she loathed about England and aristocrats and men.

Except the parts of him that were everything she loved about them.

But his bad far outweighed the good.

Hadn't he just proven it?

Juliana slapped her hand into the dough, her hand spreading the mass flat on the table. "Your brother is not fond of me."

There was a long silence before she looked up to find Georgiana smiling at her. "That is not what I asked, though."

"No!" she burst out. "There is nothing about that man to be fond of." Georgiana's mouth dropped open as she continued. "All he cares about is his precious dukedom"—she collected the dough violently into a ball—"and his precious reputation." She punched the ball, enjoying the sensation of dough pressing through her fingers. She flipped the disk over and repeated the action before she realized that she had just insulted the lady's brother. "And you, of course, my lady."

"But he *is* handsome," Gwen interjected, trying for levity.

Juliana was not amused. "I don't care how big he is or how handsome. No, I am *not* fond of him."

There was stunned silence around the table, and Juliana blew a strand of hair from where it had come loose. She rubbed one floury hand across her cheek.

"Of course you aren't," Georgiana said carefully.

There was a chorus of agreement from around the

table, and Juliana realized just how silly she must look. "I am sorry."

"Nonsense. He is a very difficult man to be fond of. You needn't tell me that," Georgiana said.

Gwen snatched the dough from Juliana's grip, returning it to the bowl. "I think this is kneaded very well. Thank you."

"You are welcome." She heard the pout in her tone. Did not care for it.

"He's not so handsome, either," said the tall woman.

"I've seen handsomer," chimed another.

"Indeed," Gwen said, handing Juliana a freshly baked biscuit, still warm from the oven.

She nibbled on one end, amazed that this group of women whom she did not know ignored her mad behavior, returning to their tasks one by one.

What a fool she had become.

She stood at the thought, pushing the stool back so quickly that it tipped and barely righted itself. "I should not have . . . I didn't mean . . ."

Only one of the two beginnings was true.

She swore softly in Italian, and the women looked to each other, seeking for a translator in their midst. They did not find one.

"I must go."

"Juliana," Georgiana said, and she heard the plea in the girl's voice. "Stay. Please."

Juliana froze at the door, back to the room, feeling instantly sorry for anyone who had or would feel the way she did at that precise moment—the combination of shame and sadness and frustration and nausea that made her want to crawl into her bed and never come out again.

"I am sorry," she said. "I cannot stay."

She opened the door and hurried toward the stairs. If she could just reach the house's center staircase—if she could just find her way upstairs—things would be better. *She* would be better.

She increased her pace, eager to escape the embarrassment that seemed to be chasing her from the kitchens.

"Juliana!"

Embarrassment followed nonetheless, in the form of Lady Georgiana.

She spun back around, facing the smaller woman, wishing she could eliminate the last few minutes, the last hour, the whole trip to Yorkshire. "Please."

Georgiana smiled, a dimple flashing in her cheek. "Would you like to take a walk with me? The gardens are quite nice."

"I—"

"Please. I am told I should take air after the baby. I should like the company."

She made it impossible to refuse. They exited through a sitting room set off to one side of the corridor, out an unassuming doorway and down a small set of stone stairs into the vegetable garden at the side of the house.

They walked among the perfectly organized rows of plants in silence for long moments before Juliana could not bear in any longer. "I am sorry for what I said in the kitchens."

"Which part?"

"All of it, I suppose. I did not mean to criticize your brother."

Georgiana smiled then, running her fingers along a sprig of rosemary and bringing the scent to her nose. "That is unfortunate. I rather liked that you were willing to criticize my brother. So few ever do."

Juliana opened her mouth to speak, then closed it, uncertain of what to say. "I suppose that he does little to deserve their criticism," she said, finally.

Georgiana gave her a look. "Do you?"

The truth was far easier than attempting to say the

right thing. She gave a little self-deprecating laugh. "Not entirely, no."

"Good. He's infuriating, isn't he?"

Juliana's eyes widened in surprise, and she nodded. "Exceedingly so."

Georgiana grinned. "I think I like you."

"I am happy to hear it." They walked a while longer. "I have not said congratulations. On the birth of your daughter."

"Caroline. Thank you." There was a long pause. "I suppose you know that I am a terrible scandal in the making."

Juliana offered her a smile. "Then we are destined to be friends, as I am considered by many to be a terrible scandal already made."

"Really?"

Juliana nodded, pulling a sprig of thyme from a nearby shrubbery and lifting it to her nose, inhaling deep. "Indeed. I have a mother, as I'm sure you know. She is a legend."

"I've heard of her."

"She returned to England last week."

Georgiana's eyes widened. "No."

"Yes. Your brother was there." Juliana tossed the herb aside. "Everyone thinks I am made from the same clothing." Georgiana tilted her head in the way people did when they did not entirely understand her. Juliana rephrased. "They think I am like her."

"Ah. Cut from the same cloth."

That was it. "Yes."

"And are you?"

"Your brother thinks so."

"That was not the question."

Juliana considered the words. No one had ever asked her if she was like her mother. No one had ever cared. The gossips of the *ton* had immediately condemned her for her parentage, and Gabriel and Nick and the rest of the family had simply rejected the idea of any similarities out of hand.

But Georgiana stood across from her on this winding garden path and asked the question no one had ever asked. So, Juliana told the truth. "I hope not."

And it was enough for Georgiana. The path forked ahead of them, and she threaded one hand through Juliana's arm, leading the way back to the house. "Never fear, Juliana. When my news gets out, they will forget everything they have ever thought of you and your mother. Fallen angels make for excellent gossip."

"But you are the daughter of a duke," Juliana protested. "Simon is marrying to protect you."

Georgiana shook her head. "I am well-and-truly ruined. Absolutely irredeemable. Perhaps he can protect our reputation, perhaps he can quiet the whispers, but they will never go away."

"I am sorry," Juliana said, because she could not think of anything else.

Georgiana squeezed her hand and smiled. "I was, too, for a while. But now I am here for as long as Nick and Isabel will have me, and Caroline is healthy, and I find it difficult to care."

I find it difficult to care. In all the time that she had been in England, for all the times that she had scoffed at the disdainful words and glances from the *ton,* Juliana had never not cared. Even when she had tried her best, she had cared.

She had cared what Simon had thought.

Cared that he would never think her enough.

Even as she had known it to be true.

And she envied this strong, spirited woman who faced her uncertain future with such confidence.

"It may not be proper for me to say it," Juliana said, "but they are idiots for casting you aside. The ballrooms of London could benefit from a woman with such spirit."

Georgiana's eyes gleamed with wry humor. "It is not at all proper for you to say it. But we both know that the ballrooms of London can hardly bear one woman with spirit. What would they do with two of us?"

Juliana laughed. "When you decide to return, my lady, we shall cut a wide, scandalous path together. My family has a particular fondness for children with questionable parentage, you see——" She trailed off, realizing that she had gone too far. "I am sorry. I did not mean to say that . . ."

"Nonsense," Georgiana said, waving one hand in the air to dismiss the apology. "Caroline is most definitely of questionable parentage." She grinned. "So I am quite happy to know that there is at least one drawing room where we will be received."

"May I ask . . ."

Georgiana met her gaze with admiration. "You do not worry about propriety, do you, Miss Fiori?" Juliana looked away with chagrin. "It is an old tale, tiresome and devastatingly trite. I thought he loved me, and maybe he did. But sometimes love is not enough—more often than not, I think." There was no sadness in the tone, no regret. Juliana met Georgiana's amber gaze and saw honesty there, a clarity that belied her age.

Sometimes love is not enough.

They walked in silence back to the house, those words echoing over and over in Juliana's mind.

Words she would do well to remember.

Chapter Sixteen

Lifelong companionship begins with softness and temerity.
Delicate ladies do not speak freely with gentlemen.

—A Treatise on the Most Exquisite of Ladies

The Guy is not the only one with a fiery temperament this autumn . . .

—The Scandal Sheet, November 1823

*M*ost days of the year, the village of Dunscroft was a quiet place—the idyllic country life interrupted by the occasional loose bull or runaway carriage, but in the grand scheme of small English towns, there was little in the village worthy of note.

Not so on Bonfire Night.

All of Dunscroft had come out for the festivities, it seemed. It was just after sundown, and the village green was filled with the trappings of the celebration—lanterns had been lit around the perimeter of the greensward, bathing the stalls that lined the outside of the space in a lovely golden glow.

Juliana stepped down from the carriage and was immediately accosted by the smells and sounds of the carnival atmosphere. There were hundreds of people on the greensward, all enjoying one part of the fair or another—children in paper masks chased through the legs of their elders before tripping upon impromptu puppet shows or smiling girls with trays of candy apples.

There was a pig roasting several yards away, and Juliana watched as a group of young men nearby attempted to shake a living statue from his impressively rigid pose with their jesting and dancing. She laughed at the picture they made in their buffoonery, enjoying the welcome sensation.

"You see?" Isabel said from her side. "I told you that you had nothing to worry about."

"I am still not certain," Juliana replied with a smile. "I do not see the bonfire you promised."

A pyre had been set up at the center of the town square, an enormous pile of wood topped with a sorry-looking straw man. The head of the effigy listed dangerously to one side, threatening that it would take a light breeze rather than a blazing fire to bring him down. Children were running in circles around the unlit bonfire, singing and chanting, and a fat baby sat off to one side, covered in sticky toffee.

Juliana turned to her sister-in-law with a smile. "This does not seem at all frightening."

"Just wait until the children have eaten their fill of sweets, and there is a great inferno from which to protect them. Then you shall see frightening." Isabel peered through the crowd of people, searching. "Most of the girls should be here already. The house was empty save for Nick and Leighton when we left."

The mention of Simon set Juliana on edge. She'd been

thinking of him all day—had spent much of the morning finding reasons to move in and out of rooms, to fetch things from near the nursery and visit her brother in his study, all to no avail.

He'd all but disappeared.

She knew she should be happy that he was keeping his distance. Knew she should not tempt fate. He had made his choice, after all—it was only a matter of time before he returned to London and married another.

Someone he thought highly of.

Someone who matched him in name and station.

And now, instead of doing her best to forget him, she was standing in the middle of a mass of strange Englishmen, wearing one of her most flattering frocks, and wishing that he was here.

Wondering why he *wasn't* here.

Even as she knew he was not for her.

It should be easier—here in the country, protected from the rest of the world, from the scandal of long-missing mothers and illegitimate children, far from marriages of convenience and betrothal balls and whispers and gossip.

And still, she thought of him. Of his future.

Of her own.

And of how they would differ.

She had to leave.

She could not stay. Not if he was here.

Isabel lifted her nose to the air. "Ooh . . . do you smell apple tarts?"

The question shook Juliana from her reverie. This was a carnival, and all of Yorkshire was in celebration, and she would not let the future change the now. There was enough time to worry about it tomorrow.

"Shall we have one?" she asked her sister-in-law with a smile.

They set off down the long line of stalls in search of

pastry, as Isabel said, "You are warned, once I start, it is possible I shan't stop until I have turned into an apple tart."

Juliana laughed. "It is a risk I shall take."

They found the stall and purchased tarts before a young woman stopped Isabel to discuss something about uniforms for the Townsend Park servants. Juliana wandered slowly, lingering in the stalls nearby as she waited for the conversation to finish, watching as the greensward grew dark, the only light at the center of the square coming from candles that people held as they chatted with their neighbors and waited, presumably, for the bonfire to be lit.

Everything in this little village had been distilled to this simple moment of conversation and celebration. The air was crisp with the smell of autumn, the leaves from the trees around the greensward were falling on the breeze, and there was no worry in this moment . . . no sadness. No loneliness.

Here she was in the country, where life was rumored to be simpler. She had come for this. For bonfire night and children's rhymes and apple tarts. And, for one evening, she would have it.

She would not let him stop her.

She paused outside a booth filled with dried herbs and flowers, and the large woman manning the stall looked up from the sachet she was tying. "What's your pleasure, milady?"

"My pleasure?"

The woman hefted herself from her stool and made her way to the high table where Juliana stood. "Children? Money? Happiness?"

Juliana smiled. "Plants can give me those things?"

"You doubt it?"

She gave a little laugh. "Yes."

The woman watched her for a long moment. "I see what you want."

"Oh?"

I want one evening of simplicity.

"Love," pronounced the shopkeeper.

Far too complicated. "What about it?"

"That's what you want." The woman's hands flew over the collection of herbs and flowers, faster than someone of her size should be able to move. She pinched a tip of lavender, a sprig of rosemary, thyme and coriander and several things that Juliana could not identify. She placed them all in a little burlap bag, tying it up with a length of twine in a knot Odysseus himself would not be able to undo. She handed the pouch to Juliana then. "Sleep with it under your pillow."

Juliana stared at the little sachet. "And then what?"

The woman smiled, a great, wide grin that revealed several missing teeth. "He will come."

"Who will come?" She was being deliberately obstinate.

The woman did not seem to mind. "Your love." She put out a wide hand, palm up. "A ha'penny for the magic, milady."

Juliana raised a brow. "I will admit, that does seem a bargain . . . for *magic*." She dropped the herbs into her reticule and fished out a coin.

"It will work."

"Oh, yes, I'm sure it will."

She turned away resolutely and froze.

There, propped against the post at the corner of the stall, arms crossed, was Simon, looking as little like a duke as the Duke of Leighton could look.

Which was still extraordinarily ducal.

He wore buckskin breeches and tall, brown riding boots, a white linen shirt, and a green topcoat, but there was nothing elaborate about the clothes—his cravat was uncomplicated, his coat simple and unassuming. A cap rather than a hat was pulled down over his brow and, while he was wearing gloves, he did not carry the cane that was required in town.

This was Simon with a nod to the country.

A Simon she could love.

Then she would give him up. To his reputation and his propriety and his responsibility and all the things she had come to love about him.

But tonight, they were in the country. And things were simpler.

Perhaps she could convince him of it.

The thought unstuck her. She began to move.

Toward him.

He straightened. "Are you buying magic potions?"

"Yes." She tossed a look over her shoulder at the woman, now standing just outside the stall.

She smiled her toothy grin. "You see how quickly it works, milady?"

Juliana could not help but smile. "Indeed. Thank you."

Simon looked uncomfortable. "What did she sell you?"

She met his gaze for a long moment.

It was now or never.

"What if I said she sold me one evening?"

His brow furrowed. "One evening of what?"

She gave a little shrug. "Simplicity. Ease. Peace."

One side of his mouth lifted in a half smile. "I would say, let's buy a lifetime of it."

Juliana thought about the conversation long ago, when they had discussed the perfect Leighton lineage—the reputation he protected, the honor he valued. She recalled the pride in his voice, the heavy responsibility that was understood.

What must it be like to bear such a burden?

Difficult enough to be tempted by a night of freedom.

Juliana shook her head. "We can't have a lifetime. Just one evening. Just this evening."

He watched her for a long moment, and she willed him to accept her offer. This night, in this simple town in the English countryside, without gossip or scandal. A bonfire and a fair and a few hours of ease.

Tomorrow, next week, next month might all be horrible. Would likely be horrible.

But she would have now.

With him.

All she had to do was reach out and take it.

"I've enough for both of us, Simon," she whispered. "Why not live for tonight?"

Please.

He hovered on the brink of answering, and she wondered if he would turn her away—knew he should turn her away. Her heart pounded in her chest as she watched the muscles in his jaw twitch, preparing for speech.

But before he could answer, the church bells on the far side of the square began to chime—an explosion of sound. Her eyes went wide as the people around them let up a powerful, raucous cheer. "What is happening?" she asked.

There was a beat, as though he had not heard the question right away. Before he offered her his arm. "The bonfire. It's about to begin."

Why not live for tonight?

The words echoed in Simon's mind as they stood in the heat of the blazing bonfire.

One evening.

One moment that would be theirs, together, here in the country. Without responsibility or worry . . . just this Bonfire Night, and nothing more.

But what if he wanted more?

He could not have it.

Just one evening. Just this evening.

Once again, Juliana was issuing a challenge.

This time, he was afraid that if he accepted, he would never survive.

He turned slightly, just enough to take her in. She was in profile, staring at the bonfire, a look of glee upon her face. Her black hair was gleaming in the firelight—a riot of reds and oranges, a magnificent, vibrant thing. And her skin glowed with the heat of the fire and her excitement.

She sensed his gaze, turning toward him. When she met his eyes, he caught his breath.

She was beautiful.

And he wanted this night. He wanted whatever he could get of her.

He leaned down, his lips close to her ear, and resisted the urge to kiss her there, where she smelled so wonderfully like Juliana. "I would like the potion."

She pulled back, her blue eyes navy in the darkness. "You are certain?"

He nodded.

Her lips curved in a wide, welcome smile, open and unfettered, and he felt that he had experienced a wicked blow to the head. "What now?"

An excellent question. People had begun to wander away from the fire; they were returning to the rest of the excitements on the square. He offered her an arm. "Would you take a turn about the green with me?"

She considered his arm for a long moment, and he understood her hesitation, saw the trepidation in her gaze when she met his gaze. "One evening."

Every bit of him screamed that it wouldn't be enough.

But it would have to be.

And he would not allow himself to think on what came tomorrow.

He dipped his head. Acquiesced. "One evening."

And then her hand was on his arm, warm and firm,

and they were moving away from the fire. The light faded, but the heat stayed, blazing hotter than before.

They walked in silence before she said, waving back at the pyre, "I confess, I am honored. All this, for Catholics."

A crisp wind ripped through the square, pressing her closer to him, and he resisted the urge to wrap one arm around her. "For a specific Catholic," he said. "Guy Fawkes nearly blew up Parliament and killed the king. Bonfire Night is a celebration of the foiling of the plot."

She turned toward him, interested. "The man at the top of the fire . . . that is your Guy?" He nodded, and she turned to finger a bolt of cloth in one of the stalls. "He does not look so dangerous."

He laughed.

She looked over her shoulder at the sound. "I like to hear you laugh, Your Grace."

He resisted the title. "Not Your Grace tonight. If I get an evening of freedom and ease, I don't want to be a duke." He did not know where the words came from, but their truth was undeniable.

She inclined her head in his direction. "A reasonable request. Then who are you tonight?"

He did not have to think. He gave a little bow in her direction and she laughed, the sound like music in the darkness. "Simon Pearson. No title. Just the man."

For one evening, he could imagine that the man was enough.

"You expect people to believe that you are a mere mister?"

If it was a game, why could he not make the rules? "Is this potion magic or not?"

She smiled softly, returning her hand to his arm. "It might be magic after all."

They moved on in silence, past a sweets cart and a booth where pork and chicken pasties were for sale.

"Are you hungry?" he asked. When she nodded, he purchased two of the savory treats and a skein of wine, and turned back to her with a smile. "Mr. Pearson would like to have an impromptu picnic."

The smile widened to a grin. "Well, I would not like to disappoint him. Not on Bonfire Night."

They moved to a more secluded part of the green, where they sat upon a low bench and ate, watching the revelers. A collection of children ran past—chasing or being chased—their laughter trailing behind them.

Juliana sighed, and the sound rippled through him, soft and lovely. "These evenings were my favorites as a little girl," she said, her voice lilting with her Italian accent. "Festivals meant an evening when things did not have to be so proper."

He imagined her as a little girl, too tall for her age, with dirty knees and a mass of wild curls tangling in the breeze, and he smiled at the picture. He leaned in, and said in Italian, "I would have liked to have known you then. To have seen young Juliana in her element."

She laughed, liking that he had switched to her native tongue, enjoying the privacy it afforded them. "You would have been shocked by young Juliana. I was always dirty, always coming home with a new discovery, getting in trouble for yelling in the courtyard, snatching *biscotti* from the kitchens—wreaking havoc."

He raised a brow. "And you think all that surprises me?"

She smiled and dipped her head. "I suppose not."

"And as you grew older? Did you break a string of hearts on these festival evenings?" He should not ask such a thing. It was not appropriate.

But this night, there were no rules. This night was easier. This night, questions were allowed.

She tilted her head up to the sky with a low, liquid laugh and the long column of her neck was illuminated

by the distant fire. He resisted the urge to press his lips
to the delicate skin there and turn the laugh into a sigh
of pleasure.

When she looked back at him, there was mischief in
her eyes.

"Ah," he said, stretching his legs out in front of him. "I
see I am not so far off."

"There was one boy," she said. "Vincenzo."

Simon was hit with a wave of emotion, curiosity and
jealousy and intrigue all at once. "Tell me the story."

"Every year in Verona, in April, there is the feast of *San
Zeno*. The city prepares for weeks and celebrates like it is
Christmas. One year . . ." She trailed off, as if she was
uncertain whether she should continue.

He had never wanted to hear the rest of a story so
much. "You cannot stop now. How old were you?"

"Seventeen."

Seventeen. As fresh-faced and beautiful as she was
now. "And Vincenzo?"

She shrugged. "Not much older. Eighteen, perhaps?"

Simon remembered himself at eighteen, remembered
the way he had thought of women . . . the things he had
wanted to do with them.

Still wanted to do with them. With her.

He had an intense desire to do this unknown Italian
boy harm.

"The young people in the town were enlisted to help
with preparations for the festival, and I had been car-
rying food to the churchyard for much of the morning,
Each time I arrived a new plate in hand, Vincenzo was
there, eager to help."

I imagine he was, Simon thought as she continued.

"This went on for an hour . . . four or five trips from the
house to the church . . . I had saved the largest tray for
last—an enormous platter of cakes for the celebration. I
left the house, my hands full, and cut through a narrow

alley leading to the church, and there, alone, leaning against one wall, was Vincenzo."

A vision flashed, a lanky, dark-haired young Italian—eyes bright with desire—and Simon's hands fisted.

"I thought he was there to take the plate from me."

"I don't imagine he was." His voice had gone to gravel.

She shook her head with a little laugh. "No. He wasn't. He reached for the plate, and when I made to give it to him, he stole a kiss."

He loathed this boy. Wanted him dead.

"I hope you hit him in the *inguine*."

Her eyes went wide. "Mr. Pearson!" she teased, switching back to English. "How very harsh of you!"

"It sounds like the pup deserved it."

"Suffice it to say, I handled the situation."

Pleasure shot through him. Good girl. He should have known she would take care of herself. Even if he wished he could have done it for her. "What did you do to him?"

"Sadly, Vincenzo now has a reputation for kissing with the enthusiasm of a slobbering dog."

Simon laughed, loud and unrestrained. "Well done."

She grinned. "We women are not so helpless as you think, you know."

"I never thought you helpless. Indeed, I have thought you a gladiator from the beginning," he said, offering her the skein of wine.

She smiled wide at the words. "*Un gladiatore?* I like that very much," she said before drinking.

"Yes, I imagine you would." He watched her drink, and when she lowered the flask, added, "I confess, I am very happy that he did not know how to kiss."

She smiled, and he was transfixed by the motion of her tongue as she reached out to lick a lingering droplet of wine from her lips. "You needn't worry. He is no competition for you."

The words came out casually before she realized their

implication. The air thickened between them almost immediately, and she dipped her head, color washing over her cheeks. "I didn't mean . . ."

"You have said it now," he teased, his voice low and filled with the need that was coursing through him—the need to take her in his arms and prove her correct. "I shan't allow you to withdraw."

She looked up, through her long, ebony lashes, and he was struck by her lush beauty. *A man could spend a lifetime looking at her.*

"I don't withdraw."

His pulse pounded at the words, and he wished they were anywhere but here, in this crowded square, with her brother and half of Yorkshire within shouting distance.

He stood, knowing that if he did not, he would not be responsible for his actions. Reaching down, he offered her a hand and pulled her to her full height. He was awash in the smell of her—that strange, exotic blend of red currants and basil. She lifted her face to his, the orange glow of the bonfire flickering across her skin, and he saw the emotion in her gaze, knew that if he took her lips here—in this public place—in front of everyone, she would not push him away.

The temptation was acute.

For a fleeting moment, he wondered what would happen if he did it—if he branded her as his here, in the middle of this country square. It would change everything in an instant. Honor would demand that they marry, and Georgiana's scandal would take second place to the Duke of Leighton's throwing over the daughter of a double marquess to wed an Italian merchant's daughter of questionable legitimacy.

But he would have Juliana.

And in that instant, it almost felt that it would be enough.

He could do it; her mouth was mere inches from his, all softness and temptation, and all he had to do was close the distance between them. And she would be his.

He watched as the tip of her pink tongue stroked along her lower lip, and desire lanced through him. When she spoke, her voice was light and casual. "Shall we walk some more?"

She didn't feel it, the twisting, unbearable need that roiled inside him.

He cleared his throat, taking a moment to draw out the sound in the hopes that his head would clear as well.

"Of course," he said, and she was off, leaving him to trail behind her like the tragic pup that he had become. He was never more grateful than when she led him back to the line of stalls; he was more stable when near other people, when moving, when he did not feel her heat along the length of him.

She lifted her chin to the night air as they walked, taking a deep breath and letting it out on a long sigh. "I think I could like the country."

He was surprised by the statement; she had such energy about her that this quiet, country village did not seem to suit. "You prefer it to London?"

She smiled and he saw the self-deprecation in the gesture. "I think it prefers me."

"I think you belong in London."

She shook her head. "Not anymore. At least, not for the rest of the year. I think I shall stay here in Yorkshire. I like the ladies of Minerva House, Lucrezia likes to run on the heath, and I am ready to be done with the season."

He hated the idea of leaving her in the country. Of returning to London—to his staid, boring life there—without her added excitement. Her vibrancy was lost here amid the fields and the sheep. She should be riding through the morning mist in Hyde Park, waltzing through society ballrooms, draped in silks and satins.

With him.

He caught his breath at the vision that flashed, Juliana on his arm, holding court over society. *Impossible.*

She stopped at the opening to one booth, trailing her fingers along the green lace edge of a simple bonnet. He watched her smooth, delicate nail scrape along the brim, wondered how that finger would feel scraping along his neck . . . his shoulders . . . down his torso . . .

He grew instantly hard and shifted, thankful for the darkness, but did not look away, fascinated by the way she stroked the hat. Finally, when he could not bear watching her fondle the headpiece a moment longer, he drew a pouch of coins from his pocket and said to the shopkeeper, "I should like to buy the bonnet for the lady."

Her eyes grew wide. "You cannot."

But the man in the stall had already taken the coin. "Would you like to wear it, milady?"

She ignored him, looking up into Simon's gaze. "It's not done. You cannot buy me clothing."

He lifted the bonnet from where it lay and tossed an extra coin to the salesman. Holding it out to Juliana, he said, "I thought we drank the potion?"

She looked at the hat for a long moment, and he thought she might not take it. When she did, he let out a long breath that he had not known he was holding.

"And besides," he teased, "I promised to buy you a bonnet to replace the one you lost."

He watched as the memory played over in her mind. Remembered the feel of her, cold and shivering in his arms. Wished he had not brought it up.

"If memory serves, Mr. Pearson—" She hesitated, turning the bonnet in her hands, and he warmed at her use of the evening's pseudonym. "You offered to buy me a dozen."

He nodded once in mock seriousness and turned back

to the keeper of the stall. "Do you have eleven more of these? Perhaps in other colors?"

The man's eyes grew wide, and Juliana laughed, grasping his arm and tugging him away from the booth. She smiled wide at the salesman. "He does not mean it. Apologies."

The man's eyes lit up. "'Tis Bonfire Night, milady, something about burning the Guy makes us all a mite mad."

As they walked away, Simon said, "I would have said a mite more amusing."

"Six of one, a half a dozen of the other when it comes to your sex," she said drily, and it was his turn to laugh.

They had gone several yards when she slowed down once more, casting him a sideways look before returning her attention to the bonnet in her hands. "Thank you."

"It was my pleasure."

And it had been. He wanted to buy her a hundred hats. And cloaks and gowns and horses and saddles and pianofortes and whatever else she wanted. Whatever made her happy, he wanted her to have it in abundance.

So when she said, "I'm sorry," and he heard the sadness in her tone, he did not like it at all.

He stopped, until she turned back to face him once more. "For what?"

One shoulder lifted in a tiny shrug. *Lord, he was coming to adore those shrugs.* "For all of it. For being so difficult. For challenging you, and provoking you, and sending you inappropriate, unwanted notes, and for angering you and frustrating you and making this all so . . . difficult." She met his gaze, and he saw the honesty and contrition in her enormous blue eyes.

She shook her head once, before continuing. "I did not know, Simon . . . I did not know that you had such reason to be so concerned for propriety and reputation. Had I known . . ." She trailed off, looking over his shoulder at the bonfire, as though looking at him might be too painful. And then she whispered, "Had I known, I never would have made the silly challenge. I never would have pushed you so far."

The words were so soft, if the breeze had been blowing in another direction, he would not have heard them. Would not have heard the sadness in them.

"I am sorry."

They were at the far end of the green now, where the line of stalls ended, and Simon did not think twice about pulling her farther into the darkness, around the last booth and into a cluster of trees in the corner of the square.

"I thought we agreed that tonight was for simplicity," he said, the words soft in the privacy of the space—the trees giving them cover of darkness, the flickering light and sounds of the bonfire far enough away that everything seemed like a dream.

As though they really had taken a magic potion.

As though tonight was different.

He felt rather than saw her shake her head. "But it's not, really, is it? You are still a duke, and I . . . well, I am who I am."

"No, Juliana," he whispered, stepping closer, lifting a hand to cup her chin and tilt her face toward him. "Not tonight."

He wished he could see her face.

"Yes, even tonight. Not even magic can unmake us, Simon. We are too well formed." Her voice wrapped around him, filled with emotion, making him ache. "I just want you to know . . . I want you to know that I understand. And that if I could return to that night when I issued my challenge, I would take it all back."

He didn't want her to take it back.

"I wish I could go back and choose a different carriage."

Irrational jealousy flared at the idea of this alternate reality, where another man had found her on the floor of his carriage.

She was his.

The wave of possessiveness was unsettling, and he released her as he attempted to control it.

She misunderstood his movement and stepped back, putting distance between them. He felt the loss of her keenly. "It is two weeks today, did you know that?"

He had not thought of the bargain in days. Not since he'd left for Yorkshire. He did a quick calculation of time. "Two weeks tonight. Yes."

And you have kept your promise to show me passion.

He did not say the words. Did not have a chance to.

"I have not brought you to your knees."

She'd done worse. It felt like she'd ripped his heart from his chest.

"Somewhere, my plan went wrong," she said, her voice so soft he could barely hear it in the darkness. "Because instead of your discovering that passion is everything, I discovered that passion is nothing without love."

What was she saying?

Was it possible she . . .

He reached for her, his fingers brushing her arms as she pulled away, retreating farther into the darkness. "What does that mean?"

A little, humorless laugh sounded, and he wanted desperately to see her face.

"Juliana?" He could barely make out her silhouette in the darkness.

"Don't you see, Simon?" There was a tremor in her voice, and he hated it. "I love you."

It was not until he heard the words on her tongue, in her beautiful, lyric accent, that he realized how very much he had wanted her to say them. *She loved him.* The thought washed over him, pleasure and pain, and all he could think was that he would die if she wasn't in his arms.

He wanted nothing more than to hold her.

He did not know what would come after that, but it was a beginning.

She loved him.

Her name on his lips, he moved toward her, certain that for this moment—this evening—she was his.

He pulled her into his arms, and she struggled against his grip. "No. Let me go."

"Say it again," he said; he'd never wanted anything so much. He had no right to it. But he wanted it anyway.

"No." He heard the regret in her tone. "I should not have said it to begin with."

He smiled. He couldn't help it. "Obstinate female." He pulled her closer, one hand following the delicate curve of her throat, tilting her face toward his. "Say it again."

"No."

He kissed her, taking her lips with strength and purpose, and she yielded instantly to him. He groaned at her sweetness—the taste of wine and spice on her lips—but pulled back before he lost himself in her. "Say it again."

She gave a little huff of displeasure. "I love you."

He did not care that she sounded tortured. The words sent fire blazing through him. "With feeling, Siren."

She hesitated, and he thought she might pull away before she seemed to give herself up to the moment, her hands on his arms, stroking up to the nape of his neck, fingers in his curls, stroking in that way that set him aflame. Her mouth was a hairsbreadth from his, and when she spoke, her voice was low and soft and perfect.

"*Ti amo.*"

And as she said the words in her native tongue, he heard the truth. And it slew him. In that moment, he would have given her anything she asked for . . . as long as she never stopped loving him.

"Kiss me again," she whispered.

The request was unnecessary; his lips were already on hers.

Again and again he took her mouth, searching for the perfect angle, molding her against him and stroking deep in long, slow kisses that threatened his strength and his sanity. They kissed as though they had an eternity, long and languid, and she matched him move for move, rough when he was rough, gentle when he gentled.

She was perfect.

They were perfectly matched.

"Juliana," he said, barely recognizing his own voice as he paused between kisses. "God, you are beautiful."

She laughed, and the sound went straight to his core. "It is dark. You cannot see."

His hands stroked down her body, beautifully rounded in all the proper places, cupping her tightly to him until they both gasped at the sensation. "But I can feel," he whispered against her lips, and they kissed again, all soft lips and tangled tongues.

When she pulled back, and stroked along his bottom lip with her silken tongue, sending a lance of desire straight through him, he groaned and cupped one of her full, high breasts, pinching its pebbled tip through the layers of her clothing. She gasped, and the sound was a siren's call, begging him to strip her bare and cover her with his mouth and body.

He wanted to lay her down upon the grassy floor of this little heaven and make love to her until neither of them remembered their names.

No.

They were in a public square.

He had to stop.

She deserved better.

They had to stop.

Before he ruined her.

He pulled away, ending the kiss. "Wait." They were both breathing heavily, the little gasping rhythm of her breath making him ache with need. He released her and stepped back, his entire body protesting. "We must stop."

"Why?" The simple, pleading question nearly did him in. He deserved a medal for exercising such restraint.

God, he wanted her.

And it was becoming impossible to be near her without seriously threatening her reputation.

Threatening her reputation?

Her reputation would be shredded if anyone found them.

"Simon . . ." she said, and he hated the calm in her tone. "This is all we have. One evening."

One evening.

It had sounded so simple an hour ago, when they were laughing and teasing and pretending to be other than who they were.

But now, as he stood in the darkness with her, he didn't want to be someone else. He wanted to be him. And he wanted her to be her. And he wanted it to be enough.

But it wasn't.

Neither was one evening.

He could not be near her any longer. Not without taking what he wanted. Not without ruining her.

And he would not ruin her.

So he said the only thing he could think to say, grateful for the darkness that kept her from seeing the truth in his eyes. That with a single word, she could have him on his knees, begging for her.

"The evening is over."

She froze, and he hated himself.

Hated himself even more when she turned and fled.

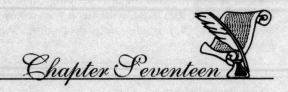

Chapter Seventeen

House parties are rife with temptation.
The exquisite lady locks her door.

—*A Treatise on the Most Exquisite of Ladies*

We blame an epidemic of love matches for the shocking
lack of broken engagements this season . . .

—*The Scandal Sheet, November 1823*

Several hours later, all of Townsend Park was
asleep, but Juliana paced the perimeter of her bedchamber, furious.

Furious with herself for confessing her feelings to
Simon.

Furious with him for refusing her, for pushing her
away.

One moment they had been jesting about magic potions and an evening of simplicity, and the next, she had
confessed her love and was in his arms. And it was wonderful, right up until the moment when he had turned
her away.

What a fool she had been, telling him that she loved him.

It did not matter that it was true.

She stopped at the foot of the bed, eyes closed in abject mortification.

What had she been thinking?

She clearly hadn't been thinking.

Or perhaps she had been thinking that it might change something.

She sat on the end of the bed with a sigh, then covered her face in both hands, letting the humiliation course through her until it gave way to sadness.

She loved him.

She knew she could not have him. She knew that he could not turn his back on his family and his title and his fiancée, but perhaps, in some quiet, dark corner of her mind, she'd hoped that saying the words would unlock some secret world where her love was enough.

Enough to overcome the need for propriety and reputation.

Enough for him.

And then she'd said it. Aloud. And as the words echoed around the little collection of trees, she'd wished, instantly, that she could take them back. That she could make them unsaid. Because now that she had confessed her love, it made everything worse.

Because speaking them aloud had made them so much more real.

She loved him.

Before tonight, she had loved the proper, arrogant, unmoving Simon, with his penchant for right and his calm, cool façade. And she had loved to move him, to crack that façade and unleash the heated, passionate Simon who could not stop himself from kissing her, from touching her, from speaking to her in his dark, wicked way.

But tonight, she had fallen in love with the rest of him—the secret, smiling, teasing Simon who lurked inside the Duke of Leighton.

And she wanted him for herself.

Except, he would never be hers. She was a collection of flaws that this culture would never accept in his wife—that *he* would never accept—the Italian, Catholic daughter of a fallen marchioness who continued to stir up scandal. And as long as he was the Duke of Leighton, their match was never to be made. They were destined for others.

Well, *he* was destined for another.

She stilled at the thought, and suddenly, with stunning clarity, she knew what came next. She stood, moving to the dressing screen in the corner.

She would give him up for one night.

Tomorrow she would think about what came next— London, Italy, a life without Simon.

But tonight, she would allow herself this. One night, with him.

She pulled on a silk dressing gown, tying the sash around her waist and heading for the door to her chamber before she could rethink her actions.

Slipping out of the room, she crept down the edge of the dark hallway, one hand trailing along the wall, counting doors as she went. Two. Three. At the fourth, she paused, hand splayed flat on the mahogany, heart beating heavily in her chest.

If she proceeded, at long last, her actions would be as scandalous as society had always expected them to be. And she would likely pay.

But she would not regret.

Indeed, if she did not take her one night . . . she would regret it forever.

She took a deep breath and opened the door.

The only light in the room was from the fireplace, and

it took Juliana a moment to see Simon, standing by the fire, tumbler of scotch in hand, dressed only in his boots and breeches and pristine white shirtsleeves.

He spun toward the door as she closed it firmly behind her, the shock on his face quickly replaced with something more dangerous. "What are you doing here?" he asked, stepping toward her before stopping midstride, as though he had hit an invisible wall.

She took a deep breath. "The night is not over, Simon. You owe me the rest."

He closed his eyes, and she thought he might be asking for patience. "Tell me you are not in this room with me. Tell me you are not here wearing nothing but your nightclothes."

He opened his eyes, and his gaze found her, warm and liquid, like honey. It seared through her, reminding her of how much she loved his heat, his touch, his kiss . . . him.

She could not live the rest of her life without this moment . . . this night . . . without knowing what it was like to be his.

It was now or never. And there was no time for hesitation.

She put her hands to the sash of her silk robe and undid it in quick, economical movements, before he could stop her. Before she could stop herself.

One night.

Calling the siren in her, she said, "I am not wearing nightclothes, Simon."

She let the silk drop to her feet in a lush sapphire pool.

As Simon took in her stunning, bare body, all long and lush and perfectly beautiful, he was not thinking that she was a staggering beauty, although she absolutely was.

He was also not thinking that he should resist her—

that he should pack her back into the silk bit of nothing that she had discarded and return her to her bedchamber—although he absolutely should have done so.

Nor was he thinking that he should forget this had ever happened, because in all honesty, he knew an exercise in futility when faced with one. And he would never, ever forget this moment.

The moment when he realized that she was going to be his.

The truth of the words was almost unbearable as he watched her facing him—bold and brave and perfect, and willing him to take what she offered.

She was here. And she was naked.

And she loved him.

He had neither the will nor the strength to turn her away—not when he wanted her so much.

There wasn't a man on earth who could resist her.

And he was through trying.

Everything would change.

The words whispered through his mind, and he was not sure if they were a warning or a promise. But he no longer cared.

She stood proud and still, facing him, her beautiful skin gleaming in the flickering golden light, casting wicked, enticing shadows across her. She had taken down her hair, and it cocooned her, all ebony curls wrapping about her shoulders and high, firm breasts as though she were a classical painting and not real at all.

Her hands were by her side, fingers clenched as if she were consciously trying not to cover the perfect, dark triangle that hid her most tempting secrets. He nearly groaned at the perfection of her.

She was a sacrificial offering at the temple of his sanity.

She took a deep breath, letting it out on a long, shaky sigh, and he noticed her trembling—the soft skin of her lush, curving belly, the hesitant rise and fall of her breasts, the tremor in her throat.

She was nervous.

He dropped the glass in his hand to the floor, not caring where it landed or what it ruined—caring only about reaching her.

And then he was holding her, lifting her against him, and she had wrapped her arms around his neck and her legs around his waist, and plunged her fingers into his hair, and his mouth was on hers.

The kiss was rough and searing, and she matched his need; where he went, she followed, opening for him, giving him everything for which he asked with a series of little, wanton sighs that set him aflame.

She was his.

He tore his lips from her, giving her scant space to breathe. "If you stay . . . you give yourself to me."

She had to understand that. Had to make her own decision.

She nodded, eyes heavy with desire. "Yes. I am yours."

He shook his head, knowing he had seconds before his passion took over, and they were both lost. "Leave now if you have any doubts."

There was a pause, and the need to possess her coursed through him, thick and unforgiving and earth-shattering. Her gaze cleared, blue and beautiful. "I have no doubts, Simon." She leaned close, her lips barely touching his, threatening to drive him mad. "Show me everything."

His control snapped, and he no longer cared. He was overwhelmed with a primitive desire as he kissed her again and again, his hands running over her warm, endlessly smooth skin, pressing her to him, clasping her full, round bottom in his hands.

He pulled away enough to speak. "You are mine," he said, and he heard the lack of control in the words.

Didn't care. What he felt for her in that moment was utterly unrefined. "Mine," he repeated, refusing to let her have the kiss she was reaching for until she looked into his eyes. "*Mine.*"

"Yes," she said, rocking into him, her heat against the length of him making him wild. "I am yours."

He rewarded her with another kiss.

God, he loved kissing her. Loved her taste, her enthusiasm, the way she set him on fire with the stroke of her tongue. When he pulled back just briefly to meet her eyes again—stunningly blue with her desire—she shook her head almost instantly. "I am yours," she repeated, taking his bottom lip between her teeth and pulling him back into the kiss. He groaned at the roughness, punctuated by the soft, unbearably wanton stroke of her tongue over the spot where her teeth had been.

She was his siren. Had been from the beginning.

Gone was the refined duke who had turned her away in the town square—who had sent her back to her family with all the gentlemanly restraint befitting his position. In his place was a mere man—flesh and blood and starving.

And she was his banquet.

He carried her to the bed, knowing that everything was about to change and failing to care. He followed her down to the crisp linen sheets, pressing between her long, warm thighs and taking her mouth again and again, whispering to her between kisses in both English and Italian.

"My siren . . . *carina* . . . so soft . . . so beautiful . . . *che bella . . . che bellissima.*"

She writhed beneath him, pressing and rocking against him as her hands yanked on the linen of his shirt, pulling the garment up until she had access to bare skin. And then her fingers were on him, leaving trails of fire along his back, and he thought he might die if he could not get closer to her. He lifted off her, hissing his pleasure as the movement pressed him—hard and thick—against the softest, warmest part of her.

Looking down at her, he took in her wide, kiss-stung lips, her flushed cheeks, and her enormous blue eyes, filled with desire. Her hands traced around to his stomach and pushed up under the shirt, running over his chest until one wayward thumb found a nipple and he gasped.

Wicked knowledge flashed in her gaze, and she did it again once, twice, before he whispered, "You are killing me," and leaned down to take her mouth once more.

When he lifted his head again, she said, "Take it off. I want to be closer. As close as possible." And he thought he would drown in the heat of the words.

The shirt was gone instantly, and he took her mouth again, stroking deep before he rolled off her to give himself access to her lush body. She cried out at the loss of him, reaching for him before he captured her hands and pulled them over her head, holding them easily in one of his. "No. You are mine," he said, his free hand trailing down to stroke the tip of one beautiful breast, teasing until it was hard and begging for his mouth. "You came to me," he whispered at her ear, tonguing the soft lobe there. "Why, Siren?"

"I—" she began, stopping when he rolled the tip of one breast between his fingers.

"Why?" he repeated, desperate to hear her answer.

"I wanted the night . . ." she gasped.

"Why?" He trailed his lips down her throat, dipped his tongue into the hollow at its base.

"I—" She stopped as he pressed soft kisses to the skin of her breast, leaving a trail as he headed toward the aching tip. "Simon . . ." the whisper was a plea. *God, he loved the sound of his name on her lips.* He blew one long stream of air over the nipple, reveling in the tightening of the skin and her gasp. "Please . . ."

"Why did you come to me?"

Say it, he willed, knowing it was not his place. Knowing he did not deserve it.

"I love you."

A thrill coursed through him at the words, so simple. So honest. He took the straining tip between his lips, rewarding her with long pulls at the sweet flesh there. Loving the way she writhed against him, the way she cried out when he ran his tongue and teeth over her sensitive flesh, the way her hands twisted so that her fingers could thread through his.

When he lifted his head, they were both breathing heavily, and he was desperate to touch her everywhere.

To taste her everywhere.

"Again."

"I love you."

He released her hands, sliding down her body, placing warm kisses along her breasts and stomach and the soft crease where her thigh and hip met and the scent of her was unbearably perfect.

He was addicted to her softness, to the feel of her, to the way she pressed against the sheets and rocked her hips against him. He had never wanted anything in his life the way he wanted her. Now.

And she was here.

And she was his.

Simon slid off the bed, kneeling beside it. She sat up, instantly. "Where are you—?" The question gave way to a little squeak when he pulled her closer to the edge of the bed, letting her legs hang over the side, and stroked up her smooth soft skin from ankle to knee. He watched his hands, large and brown, follow the curve of her legs, and could not resist palming her strong, lean calves and easing her legs apart.

"What are you—? Simon!" she gasped, and he leaned forward, insinuating his body between her thighs. Her hands flew to cover the place he was desperate to touch, and he nipped the edge of her jaw lightly with his teeth.

"Lie back, Siren."

She shook her head. "I can't. You can't."

"You can. And I shall." He heard the gravel in his tone. Felt the desperate desire coursing through him. If she did not let him touch her soon . . . "You asked for everything," he said, the words thick at her ear. "This is part of it."

She pulled back, and if he had not been as hard and aching as he was, he would have laughed at the skepticism in his gaze. "I've never heard of this."

"You gave yourself to me," he said, pressing her thighs wider, sliding his hands higher, touching his tongue to the perfect arch of one of her cheeks. "This is what I want." She caught her breath as his fingers reached her hands, shielding her from view. He stroked his fingertips down the skin of her hands, a light, barely there touch that they both felt acutely. He stroked again, up to one delicate wrist, then back down. "I think you want it, too."

He moved back to her ear, loving her shyness, her uncertainty. Wanting to teach her to share her secrets. "You ache here, don't you?" She nodded, barely, and a surge of masculine pleasure coursed through him. "I can take it away."

She exhaled on a long, shaky breath, and the sound went straight to the hard, straining length of him. He gritted his teeth. *No.* This was for her. She would find her pleasure. He would give it to her, and take his from that.

"Simon," she said, her accent thick, wrapping around the syllables of his name like a fist. "Please."

"Lie back," he whispered, pressing her to the bed

with his kiss before trailing down to where he desperately wanted to be. He pressed a soft kiss on one of her knuckles. "Let me in." When she did, revealing the folds of her sex, he groaned his pleasure. He spread her soft lips gently, and she lifted her hips toward him. She was so tender, so ready for him. Slick and wet and perfect.

He ran one finger down the center of her, listening to her breathing, to the little cries she made as he explored. He discovered her, pressing and stroking to the sound of her pleasure, then sliding one finger into the hot, wet core of her. She was so tight, she came off the edge of the bed at the sensation.

He looked up her body as she lifted herself off the bed and drank in the vision of her, her gorgeous black hair, eyes like sapphires gleaming with pleasure, full, pink lips barely open as she gasped for breath.

He had never wanted anything like he wanted her.

He moved his hand, loving the way her eyes closed, then opened in time to the movement. He leaned forward, blew a long stream of air directly on the center of her pleasure, and gloried in the little cry of passion that she could not keep from escaping.

He was going to die if he didn't have his mouth on her soon.

He rubbed his thumb across the swollen, pulsing heart of her, and she gasped her answer, her shyness gone. "Kiss me."

"As you wish," he said, and settled his lips to her, holding her wide as he pressed his tongue to the place where his thumb had been, making love to her with slow, savoring strokes. She arched off the bed, plunging her fingers into his hair and holding him to her as she moved against his mouth. She was wine, and he was instantly obsessed with her taste, with learning the things that she loved, wanting only to give her pleasure. To drive her wild.

He did. Slow circles became gradually faster, tongue

working in time to the flexing of her fingers in his hair, and then she lifted herself from the bed offering herself to him. He took her, holding her to him while she found her pleasure, masculine satisfaction rippling through him.

And when she shattered in his arms, he was there, holding her, stroking her, bringing her back to earth.

He lifted his head after the last ripple of pleasure coursed through her, and he moved to lie beside her, wanting to hold her, to keep her safe.

He kissed her neck, sucking gently at the delicate skin there until she sighed. He could pleasure her forever. He could lie abed and worship her for an eternity. He took a nipple into his mouth, worrying it until she whispered his name, then kissed her, sliding his hand between her thighs in an undeniable urge to brand her as his.

Her legs parted against the weight of his hand, and her fingers slid down his torso to the waistband of his breeches. "Simon," she said, and the low, sated pleasure in her voice made him agonizingly hard. "Remove your pants."

God, yes.

He closed his eyes against the thought. "Are you certain?" If he was naked with her, there would be no going back.

She nodded, her sapphire eyes dark with passion. "Very."

She would have him. Again and again, for the rest of their days.

He kissed her again, slow and deep. "I could not deny you anything."

And as the words echoed between them, he knew they were true. She was everything he had ever wanted. And he would do everything in his power to keep her in his world. Nothing else mattered.

Her hands worked inexpertly at the buttons of his

breeches until he could not bear the fumbling pressure anymore, and he lifted himself off the bed to divest himself of pants and boots as quickly as possible. Returning to her, he groaned his pleasure as he settled between her silken thighs, desperate to be inside her.

"Wait," she whispered, scooting backward, away from him. "I want to see."

He narrowed his gaze on her and followed her across the bed. "Not now. Next time."

He took hold of her legs and pulled her to him, rubbing himself against her until she sighed at the friction. "But . . . we only have one night. This is my only opportunity to see you."

He froze at the words, his hands coming to her face, holding her firmly so he could look into her eyes. He saw the sadness there, the desperation, overwhelmed by passion.

This would not be one night. She had to know that.

He would never let her go.

Everything had changed.

"Juliana," he whispered, low and dark, thrusting through her wetness so that the tip of him rubbed her most sensitive spot. He watched her eyes widen, then cloud with pleasure. "Don't make me stop."

He repeated the motion, and her lids lowered. "No. Don't stop."

He pressed himself to the entrance of her, easing just inside her tight, blazing sheath before he paused—the hardest thing he had ever done—and looked down at her. "Is this all right?"

She nodded once, taking her bottom lip between her teeth, and the movement sent a shiver of desire straight to the core of him. But he would not ruin her first taste of passion. He held himself there, still, reveling in her heat, wanting nothing more than to thrust to the hilt and bury himself within her.

"I don't want to hurt you."

She shook her head. "You won't."

He reached between them, stroking the tender, sensitive core of her until she gasped her pleasure. "I will. But then I will do my best never to hurt you again." He met her gaze before running his tongue across her bottom lip, and saying, "Look at me. I want to watch you."

She nodded, and he rocked against her, easing farther and farther into her tight passage, trying to be gentle, watching pain and pleasure war within her as she adjusted to his smooth thrusts, each deeper than the last. He was soon buried to the hilt, and they were both breathing heavily.

She whispered, "You have the most beautiful eyes."

Pleasure coursed through him at the unexpected compliment, and he kissed her long and slow. Pulling back, he smiled, rocking gently against her. "Impossible. They are nothing compared to yours."

He was desperate to move. Desperate to take the release for which his body had been begging all night. Instead, he pressed a kiss to her jaw, and said, "Does it hurt, Siren?"

She shook her head, and when she spoke, he heard something wonderful in her tone. "No . . . it feels . . . Simon, I can feel you . . . everywhere." She relaxed and pressed up to meet his movements. He hissed his pleasure. She ran her hands down his back to the curve of his buttocks and clasped him tightly to her. "Do that again. Harder."

He groaned. She was going to kill him.

He began to move, deeper, faster, with more power, and she cried her pleasure in his ear, threatening his sanity. In moments, she was whispering his name, her hands tangled in his hair, moving in time to his deep, smooth thrusts. He had never been so ready to take his pleasure, but he would not let go without her. He wanted her with him when he threw himself over the edge.

They rocked together, sensation building, until they were both gasping for breath.

"Simon . . . it's . . . I can't stop it."

"Neither can I," he pulled out until he was almost gone from her, then returned, sinking into her heat. *How had he ever thought he could resist her?* "Look at me, love. I want to watch."

She did, and her tumble into pleasure was his undoing. He followed her over the precipice with a force he had never before experienced; she was the center of his world—he wanted to stay in her arms, in this moment, in this night forever.

He collapsed into her arms and lay there for a long moment, breath coming in harsh bursts, before he realized that his weight must be crushing her. Turning, he pulled her to sprawl across him, all soft, glowing skin and silken hair. He could feel her breasts rising and falling against his chest, and he gritted his teeth against the instant awareness that coursed through him.

He wanted her again. Now.

He ignored the desire, instead running his fingers across her smooth, bare shoulders, reveling in the little tremor that pushed her closer to him, loving the feel of her naked against him.

As he held her, soft and warm in his arms, he did not want to think of the future. He wanted to savor her.

He wanted to savor the now.

It had been a mistake.

Even as she reveled in the feel of him beneath her, all firm muscles and warm skin, she knew that she had just made everything worse.

He had given her everything she had ever imagined— she had never felt so close, so connected, so desired.

She had never dreamed she would love him with such intensity.

Tomorrow she would leave him. And he would marry another.

And Juliana would live knowing that the man she loved would never be hers.

She shivered at the thought, pressing closer to him, as though she could fuse herself to him, as though she could stay the movement of time.

He stroked one warm hand down her spine, leaving a trail of fire, and pressed his lips to her forehead. "Are you cold?"

No.

It was easier to say yes than to tell the truth.

She nodded, not trusting herself to speak.

He slid out from beneath her, pulling her up off the bed with him so he could turn down the sheets. He kissed her, full and lush, the caress blazing through her before he turned away to stoke the fire.

Feeling too vulnerable, she fetched her robe, pulling it on and knotting the sash before she turned back to watch his movements as he crouched before the fire, the muscles of his back rippling with the motion, his massive thighs gleaming in the orange glow—a god of fire.

When he stood, he looked to the bed. His brow furrowed when he discovered that she was gone, and he immediately sought her out, finding her in the shadows. He raised a hand, beckoning her to him, and she could not resist.

When she came to him, he lifted her into his arms, settling them both in a chair by the fire. He slipped one hand into the opening of her robe running it along her thigh as he pressed a kiss to the column of her neck. "I prefer you naked," he said, and she wondered at this new, teasing Simon.

She ran her hand up his forearm to his wide, muscled

shoulder. "I feel the same," she confessed. "I thought you could not grow more handsome, but watching you in the firelight . . . you are Hephaestus, all muscle and flame."

His eyes darkened at the comparison, and he pulled her to him, kissing her soundly before he tucked her to his chest, and said, "That makes you Aphrodite—an apt comparison."

But Aphrodite and Hephaestus were married. The thought whispered through her mind. *We have only one night.*

No. She would not think on it.

"You are promoting me from siren to goddess, then?"

He chuckled, and she loved the feeling of the sound rumbling beneath her. He captured one of her hands, threading his fingers through hers and bringing it to his lips. "It would seem so, clever girl."

"You see? I am more than just a walking scandal," she teased, and immediately regretted the words. She had just affected the most serious scandal of her life. And he knew it. Perhaps he even thought she had done it on purpose—to cause scandal.

She hated the thought.

Hated that she had put it in his head.

She sat up on his lap, desperate to make sure that he did not think ill of her. "Simon . . . you know that I did not . . . this was not . . . I would never tell anyone that this . . . that tonight happened." She winced at the words, utterly inarticulate. "You shan't have to worry about another . . ."

He watched her, his amber eyes serious, and she wished she could take it all back—the words, the actions, the night. His arms tightened around her, and he kissed her hand once more. "No more talk of it."

She hated that she had just become another thing for him to worry about. "I just . . . What I am attempting to say is that no one will ever know."

He reached out and brushed a lock of her hair back from her cheek. "Juliana, *I* will know."

Frustration flared. "Well, yes. Of course *we* will know. But I want you to also know that I will never ask anything of you. That I meant it when I proposed one night. One night only."

Something flashed in his honeyed gaze, something that she could not identify. "We both should have known that one night would not be nearly enough."

She stilled, the words coursing through her. He wanted more.

So did she.

But he was to be married.

Was he offering what she thought he was offering?

Could she take it?

If it was the only way she could have him . . . would it be enough?

It had to be.

She took a deep breath. "I could be your paramour."

He went utterly still beneath her. "What did you say?"

"Your mistress."

His hand clamped onto her thigh with immeasurable force. "Don't say another word."

She set her hands to his shoulders, leveraging herself up to face him. "Why? You once suggested I would make a fine mistress."

He closed his eyes. "Juliana. Stop."

She ignored him. "Would I not still make a worthy companion?"

"No."

Pain flared. She was too much of a scandal even to rate as his mistress? "Why not?" She heard the begging in her tone. Hated herself for it.

"Because you deserve better!" he exploded, coming to his feet in a rush and sending her toppling from his lap. He grabbed her to him before she could fall to the floor, lifting her to face him. His hands were on her arms, as though he could shake her into understanding. "I won't have you as my mistress. I wish I could go back and scrub you clean of the words. I wish I could go back and take a fist to myself for ever even suggesting it."

The words coursed through her, and she ached for the promise that should come next. Love. Marriage. Family.

The things he had promised to another.

Things he had promised to another because he could not see a future with her.

And suddenly the words were not enough.

"Come to bed with me," he whispered. "Let me sleep with you in my arms. We shall return you to your own chamber before the house awakes."

The temptation was nearly undeniable. There was nothing in the world she wanted more than to sleep with him, the sound of his heart beneath her ear.

"I must leave, Simon."

He reached for her, a smile playing across his lips. "Not yet. Stay a little while longer."

She shook her head, taking a step back. "I cannot risk—"

I cannot risk any more of my heart.

She took a breath. Tried again. "I cannot risk being caught."

He watched her carefully, his gaze boring into hers, and she willed him not to see the truth—that she was leaving him. *For good*, as the English liked to say.

But it did not feel good. It felt like torture.

He was still for a long time, as though considering his options, then he nodded once, firmly. "You are right. To-morrow, I shall speak to Nick."

"About what?"

"About our marriage."

Her heart leapt into her throat. "Our marriage?"

He could not marry her. There was a litany of reasons why.

She was an Italian. A Catholic. Her parentage was questionable at best. Her mother was a disaster. Her father had been a simple merchant. The *ton* barely tolerated her.

He was already engaged to a darling of the Beau Monde.

But even as she thought the words, a thread of hope coiled within, unbidden. Was it possible? Could he choose her, after all? Could they marry? Could she have him, this man she loved until she ached? Could she have what she had come to envy in the couples around her, paired off like doves?

"Don't look so sad," he teased. "You're finally getting your scandal."

She froze, stepping back from his embrace.

Scandal.

That was what she was to him—the common, scandalous Italian who he married after one night in the country. And someday, when the news about Georgiana was out and he did not have a wife with a pristine reputation by his side, when his children were mocked for having a common mother, when he saw Lady Penelope dancing across some ballroom with a perfect husband, the belle of the ball, he would regret it.

She'd never been more. Never worthy of his companionship. Never a possibility for his wife. She'd never once been anything other than a scandalous distraction from his duty and responsibility. He was a duke, and she was a scandal.

Never his equal.

Never good enough.

And she'd believed it, too. How many times had she compared herself to her mother? How many times had she played into their expectations? Lived up to them? How often had she vied for his irritation and his passion instead of his admiration and respect because she had not believed the latter to be within her reach?

It was more than she could bear.

She loved him.

Sometimes, love was not enough.

His sister's words echoed in her ears. "I cannot marry you, Simon."

He smiled at first, before the meaning of her words registered. "What did you say?"

She took a deep breath and met his gaze, that rich, amber gaze that she had come to love so much. "I cannot marry you."

"Why not?" There was confusion and disbelief in the words, then something close to anger.

"If tonight had not happened, would we even be discussing it?"

"I—" He stopped. Started again. "Tonight did happen, Juliana."

"You're engaged to another."

"I shall end it," he said simply, as if it were a perfectly reasonable thing to do.

"What of Lady Penelope? What of her reputation? And what of yours? And your plans to secure your family, your sister, your niece? What of your duty?"

He reached for her as she backed away. "Juliana, I compromised you. We shall marry."

Not out of love. Not out of respect. Not out of admiration.

"Because this is the way things are done," she whispered.

"Among other reasons, yes," he said simply, as though it were obvious.

"I am not what you envisioned in a wife." He stilled at the words, and she pressed on. "You've said it yourself. I am too reckless. Too impulsive. Too much of a scandal.

Before tonight, you'd never even considered marrying me."

"I proposed to you a week ago!" She heard the frustration in his tone as he spun away to fetch his dressing gown.

"Only after Gabriel discovered us in the stables. You proposed out of duty. Just as you do everything. You would have married me, but it would have been beneath you. Just as it would be now."

He shoved his arms into the silk brocade and turned back to her, eyes dark. When he spoke, his voice was hard as steel. "Don't say that."

"Why?" she asked, gently. "It's true, isn't it?"

He did not reply.

"I'll never be enough for you. Never good enough, never respectable enough, never proper enough—even if I tried, my past, my family, my blood would all make it impossible for us to be equal. What would they say? What would your mother say?"

"Hang them. Especially my mother."

She stepped toward him, lifting her hand and touching his square jaw for a fleeting moment before he pulled away from her touch and stepped back, refusing to meet her gaze.

Tears welled as she considered his beautiful, stony countenance, knowing that this was the last time they would be together like this, alone and honest.

One of them, at least, was honest.

"You once accused me of never considering the consequences," she said, willing him to understand. To see. "Of never thinking of what comes next."

"What comes next is, we marry."

She shook her head. "Now you are not considering the consequences. I shall always be your scandal, Simon. Never entirely worthy."

"That is ridiculous. Of course you would be." She was struck by how imperious he could sound in that moment as he stood before her clad in nothing but a dressing gown. So ducal, even now.

"No, I wouldn't be. Not in your eyes. And there would come a day when I was not worthy in my own." As she spoke the words, she was struck by the realization that she finally understood what it was she wanted from her life. From her future. "I deserve better. I deserve more."

"You cannot do much better than me. I am a duke." There was a slight tremor in his voice. Anger.

She brushed away a tear before it could spill over. "That may well be true, Simon. But if it is, it has nothing to do with your being a duke."

He ignored the words, and they stood there for long moments before she started to leave the room, and he finally spoke. "This is not over, Juliana."

"Yes, it is."

She was proud of the strength in the words.

A strength she was not sure she had.

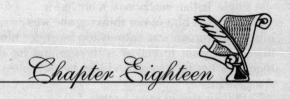

Chapter Eighteen

Matters of the heart are a challenge indeed.
The elegant lady follows the gentleman's lead.

—*A Treatise on the Most Exquisite of Ladies*

By day, late night visits are made more exciting . . .

—*The Scandal Sheet, November 1823*

She'd left him.
It wasn't possible.

Simon had woken and gone to saddle their horses, wanting to take Juliana riding, wanting to get her away from this house so that he could talk some sense into her, and he'd instead discovered that Lucrezia was missing. A few questions in the stables had revealed that she'd left Townsend Park that morning, under cover of darkness.

Like a coward.

How dare she leave him?

He was not some pup who sought her approval. He was the damned Duke of Leighton! He had half of

London falling over itself to do his bidding, and he could not secure the obedience of a single, Italian female.

A single, Italian *madwoman*, more like it.

She accused him of not thinking she was *enough* for him? The woman was entirely too much for him! She made him want to bellow with rage and hit things, then lock her in a room and kiss her senseless, until she gave in.

Until they gave in to each other.

Except, she had refused him.

Twice.

She'd left him!

And damned if it didn't make him desire her all the more.

So much that his hands itched with it. He wanted to touch her, to tame her, to take her in his arms and make love to her until they were both exhausted and unable to think of anything beyond their embrace. He wanted to sink into her rich ebony curls, her beautiful eyes, her infinite softness and never return.

He threw open the door to the Townsend Park breakfast room, sending the thick oak crashing into the wall behind and surprising a tableful of ladies during their morning meal as he bore down on St. John, who was calmly buttering his toast. "Where is she?"

Nick took a long sip of tea. "Where is who?"

Simon fought off the urge to pour the contents of the tea service over his head. "Juliana."

"She's gone. Left at first light," St. John said casually. "Have a seat. We'll bring you some bacon."

"I don't want any damned bacon. Why don't you bring me your sister?"

The statement, inappropriate in a staggering number of ways, was apparently what it took to secure St. John's attention—and the attention of the half dozen women in the room, who all stopped eating at once. Nick cut a look at Simon and stood, pushing back his chair and coming to his full height. "Perhaps you'd like to apologize to the ladies and join me in the study?"

Finally.

He bowed stiffly to the table of women. "My apologies," he intoned, before turning on his heel and following Nick from the room.

They did not speak until they were safely inside the earl's study, but when the door closed behind them, they both started in.

"First, it's excellent bacon, and I'm not thrilled I had to stop eating it."

"I don't have time to play games—"

Nick ignored him and pressed on. "And second, what in the hell were you thinking, speaking in such a manner about my sister?"

"I am going to marry her."

Nick blinked. "Really? Because I'm fairly certain that neither Ralston nor I have given our permission for you to even court her . . . let alone marry her."

Fury blazed at the words. "I don't need your permission. She's mine."

Nick's gaze narrowed. "May I suggest you rephrase that last bit, Duke?"

Simon took a deep breath, willing himself to remain calm even as every inch of him wanted to pummel Nick. "I should like to court your sister."

Nick nodded once. "Much better."

"Excellent. Where is she?"

"I have not given my permission."

Simon heard the low growl rising in his throat. He'd never been a violent man, but Juliana's brothers appeared to be the exception to the rule. "Are you going to give it?"

"I don't think so, no."

Simon was through with this family and their insanity. "Why the hell not?" he thundered.

"Any number of reasons. Shall I list them?"

"I don't imagine I could stop you. I've had enough. If she's headed for London, I can still catch her. I can ride faster than her coach."

He headed for the door. "You aren't leaving this house, Leighton. Not in your mood."

Simon turned back, shocked. "You think I would hurt her?"

"No, but I think you would upset her, and right now, she doesn't deserve it."

"You think you can stop me?"

"I know I can. I do not have to remind you of the caliber of security employed by the Park."

Simon began to pace the room. "I'm a duke! How is it possible that the title opens doors the world over, but in this family, it seems only to count against me?"

Nick grinned. "Our perverse nature. It's first on my list of reasons why I don't like the idea of your marrying Juliana."

"Yes. Being a duchess is a difficult thing indeed."

Nick ignored the dripping sarcasm. "It would be for her. She would hate it. The Beau Monde would never forgive her for flouting their rules. And your precious reputation would suffer for it."

He didn't care. He would slay the dragons of the *ton* for her.

In the mood he was in, he would do it with his bare hands.

Nick pressed on. "And even if she were well behaved—although I've never known Juliana to take the meek path—she will never escape the specter of our mother. The *ton* will forever judge her for her parentage. And you will come to resent her for it."

"It's not true." But even as he said the words, he understood why they all would think it. They were true, until recently. Until her. Until she'd taught him that there were things that were infinitely more important than reputation.

"No?" He heard the disbelief in Nick's voice. Did not like it. "Leighton, for as long as I've known you, you've made it a mission to stay clear of scandal. You have been raised to avoid excitement. You are cold and unmoving and utterly proper in every way."

The words rippled through Simon. *Cold. Unmoving.*

He did not feel cold or unmoved right now.

She had rocked him to his core.

And then she had left him.

Nick pressed on. "You have lived your whole life keeping your reputation untarnished. For God's sake, man. You left your *sister* in the country with us rather than face the fact that she had not lived up to your expectations. And you want me to give *my* sister over to you?"

The question hung in the air between them, and Simon knew that Nick was right. He'd spent his entire life judging those with less-than-perfect reputations, less-than-perfect families, less-than-perfect pasts. He had been the Duke of Disdain—swearing that he was above such base and common things as scandal . . . and love.

Until she'd taught him he wanted her bold ideas and her brash laugh and her too-wide smiles and her scandalous nature that was not so scandalous, after all.

He wanted her in his life.

Beside him.

As his duchess.

And it would not be a sacrifice to call her such. It would be an honor.

He loved her.

Juliana changed everything. She made him want all

of it. She made him want to face the messy challenge of love. To embrace it. To revel in it. To celebrate it.

He would be proud to have her on his arm.

Would have been long before this morning if he were honest with himself.

He cared only about having her. About marrying her and giving her children and living with her forever . . . and hang the gossips. He didn't care how big or brutal her brothers could be. They would not stand in his way.

"Juliana's suffered enough . . ." Nick said, his voice quiet alongside Simon's raging thoughts. "She doesn't deserve your charity."

The words sent him flying across the room, grabbing Nick's coat and pushing him up against the wall with mighty force, shaking the pictures in their frames. "Don't you . . . ever . . ." He pulled Nick from the wall and slammed him back again. "Ever . . . refer to what I feel for your sister as *charity*. She is bold and beautiful and brilliant, and you are lucky to breathe the same air she breathes." His anger was so acute, he could barely get the words out. "She thinks herself unworthy? It is *we* who are unworthy of *her*, and if you call her a scandal one more time, I'll destroy you. With visceral pleasure."

They stood there like that for long minutes, Simon breathing heavily, before Nick said, calmly, "Well. That was unexpected."

Simon took a deep breath, attempted to regain his calm.

Failed.

He loved her.

With stunning, undeniable force.

Simon let Nick go and stepped back.

She was all he wanted. He would give everything for her. Without thought. Without regret.

Because without her, he had nothing.

"I'm going after her. Try to stop me."

"But Leighton . . ." Nick's voice cut through his thoughts. "You're betrothed. To another."

Betrothed to another.

He cursed, the word harsh and wicked.

He'd forgotten about Penelope.

"I've made a mistake."

Georgiana lifted Caroline from her cradle and met Simon's gaze with a feigned look of shock. "Certainly not. Pearsons do not make mistakes. Consider me, if you will. Perfect in every way. A shining example of good behavior."

"Juliana is gone."

Georgiana did not appear surprised. "I heard that."

"I was an idiot."

She sat in the rocking chair next to Caroline's cradle. "Go on."

He did not know where to begin. Did not entirely understand how everything in his life had gotten so completely away from him. "I—" He stopped, dropped into the chair across from his sister, leaned forward, elbows on his knees, and said the only thing he could think to say. "I love her."

"Juliana?"

He nodded, thrusting one hand through his hair.

"Then why are you marrying the wrong woman?"

An ache started deep in his chest at the question—the only question that mattered, to which he did not have an answer. There had been so many excellent reasons when he'd devised the plan, and now it seemed that none of them carried much weight.

"I don't know."

Georgiana rocked back and forth in her chair, back and forth, her soft words belying their importance. "You do not love her."

"I did not *need* to love her. And yet . . ." *And yet he*

found he could not help but love another. He put his head in his hands. "I've made a mistake," he repeated.

He could not back out without ruining Penelope, and she did not deserve such treatment.

"Simon . . ." There was a softness in his sister's voice. Care that he did not deserve.

He loved Juliana.

Juliana, who haunted him with her flashing eyes and her quick wit and her brilliant mind and her fiery temper and those smiles and promises and kisses that made him want to worship her for as long as he drew breath.

"You can have her, Simon. Neither of you is married. Betrothals can be broken."

He shook his head. "Not without ruining Penelope."

Georgiana shook her head. "Lady Penelope is daughter to a double marquess with an estate the size of Windsor. You think she cannot find someone else? Someone who might someday care for her with more than passing interest? Someone who is not in love with another?"

Of course someone would marry her. But Simon would not be the one to throw her to the wolves. "I cannot."

"You are far too gentlemanly for your own good!" Irritation flooded her tone, and Caroline stirred in her arms. Georgiana quieted immediately. "You have it in your power to make both you and Juliana happy. Forever. And, I assure you, Simon, there is no prize in marrying a man who loves another."

The words, so tempting, shook something free in him. "I don't care about the scandal. I don't care about the lady! All I care about is having Juliana in my life! But if I do this, if I ruin Penelope, what will Juliana think of me? How can I ever ask her to trust me with her name if I am so callous with another's?"

His words hung between them in the quiet nursery for long minutes before he said, "I cannot do it. Not without being less of a man for Juliana. Not without being less than she deserves."

Even as the words were out of his mouth, he knew he would never be what Juliana deserved—someone who would see her brilliance and beauty and worth from the very first moment—someone who would place her well above himself from the very beginning. Someone without his faults, without his arrogance, without his failings.

But he would be damned if he would give her up.

He'd found her.

And he wanted a lifetime with her.

"At least give Penelope the opportunity to choose, Simon." She watched him carefully, taking in his anguish. His conflict. "She deserves a chance to choose. And God knows you and Juliana deserve the chance at happiness."

That part, at least, was true. Hope flared. "Do you think there is a chance that Penelope will release me?"

Georgiana smiled, and there was something in her eyes—a knowledge that he did not entirely understand. "I do."

They fell silent, and he watched Caroline, asleep on his sister's shoulder, her little mouth making soft, sweet motions while she dreamed. And he imagined another child, with dark hair and sapphire eyes, asleep on her mother's shoulder.

He closed his eyes at the image, longing spiraling sharp and deep.

He wanted that child. He wanted that family.

Wanted their life to begin.

Immediately.

But first, he owed his sister an apology. "I made a mistake with you as well."

"Only one?" He scowled, and she grinned. "To which mistake do you refer?"

"I should not have left you here. In Yorkshire."

Georgiana considered the words for a long while. "I wanted to be here."

"Yes. And you could have stayed here. But I should not have left when I did. The way I did. I should have been more concerned for you. And less for the scandal." He went to the window and looked out over the heath. "I cannot change it. But I am sorry."

"Thank you," she said, simply, and he was struck by how she had grown, by the young woman she had become.

"I wish I could have fixed it. I wish you would tell me who—"

She stopped him. "He is gone."

"I could find him. We could still repair this damage."

"You could not find him," she said. "Simon, I am beyond repair. Surely you must see that."

Frustration flared in him, the urge to protect her undeniable. "It's not true. So we are too late to find a man to claim the child . . . but you are the daughter of a duke. We could surely find a man to wed you. To be a good husband to you. A good father to Caroline."

"Stop." He watched as she stroked one hand down the baby's back, an instinctive, soothing touch.

"You think you can stay here in this little corner of England for the rest of your lives? What will happen when Caroline is old enough to understand? How will you answer her questions about who she is? Where she came from? What will happen when this is discovered? I cannot hide you forever, Georgiana."

Georgiana met his gaze, firm and unwavering. "I never asked you to hide us. Indeed, I would prefer not to be hidden. My reputation is ruined, Simon. You can try all you like to change such a thing, but the die has been cast."

The words were so simple, as he imagined the truth often was.

"You deserve—"

"I deserve to be a mother. I deserve to raise a child who is healthy and strong and who knows that she is loved. God knows we did not have such a thing."

"I want you to be happy," he said.

Funny, how he had never given happiness much thought until recently. Until Juliana.

Georgiana smiled. "And I will be, in time. But not in the way you had planned."

The irony of the situation was not lost on him. She was sister to one of the most powerful men in England. And still, with all his concern for reputation and honor, he could not change the course of her life. He could not restore her reputation or stop the gossip that would eventually find her—find them all—but he could give her his support. And he could give her his love.

"Georgiana," he said, his words thick with promise. "Whatever you want. Whatever you decide. It is yours. You and Caroline—I shall stand beside you."

"Are you certain you wish to tempt fate in such a manner?"

One side of his mouth lifted in a half smile. "I am."

"I ask because the sentiment may be tested sooner rather than later."

He narrowed his gaze on her. "What does that mean?"

"Only that I wish for one of us to have our happy ever after, Simon. And since it cannot be me, it shall have to be you."

Juliana.

She was his happiness. She was his passion.

And he could no longer live this passionless life.

He had to go after her. Now.

He stood and moved toward his sister and niece. Bending low, he placed a kiss on the top of Caroline's head and another on Georgiana's cheek. "I must go. I must get her back."

Georgiana smiled. "Mother will be furious."

Simon lifted a brow. "Mother will make an excellent dowager."

She laughed. "Tell me you plan to put her out to pasture."

"It is not an impossibility," he tossed over one shoulder, heading for the door, thinking only of Juliana.

"Simon?" his sister called.

He turned back, eager to follow his love.

Eager to begin his life.

"Your betrothal gift is already on its way to London." Her face split in a wide grin. "Give Mother my regards."

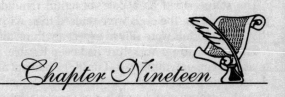

Chapter Nineteen

Reputation is all any woman can claim.
The refined lady protects hers at all cost.

—*A Treatise on the Most Exquisite of Ladies*

There are times when the source of the scandal surprises even us . . .

—*The Scandal Sheet, November 1823*

*J*uliana went straight to see her mother.

It was late in the evening, long past an appropriate time to make or receive calls, as she stood in the
beautiful receiving room of Nick and Isabel's London
town house, filled with Greek and Roman marbles collected during Nick's time abroad, and waited for her
mother to join her.

There was a statue of Aphrodite and Eros at the center
of the room, a stunning depiction of the goddess of love,
holding her son in her arms as he reached for something beyond her shoulder. The child god's every muscle
seemed to strain, his arms and fingers extended, his

chubby legs kicking out from his mother's chest, pushing in desire for something he would never reach.

The statue stood as a pale, beautiful reminder that sometimes even the gods were refused their wishes and that mere mortals were silly to expect anything different.

The journey from Yorkshire had been terrible, Juliana unable to eat, unwilling to rest until she had put as much distance as possible between herself and Simon . . . as though distance could cure her of the devastating ache in her heart that came whenever she thought of him.

Which was constantly.

She had known that running was not the most respectable of actions, but she could not stay in Yorkshire—in that house—not while he tempted her into his arms and his bed and his life. Not when she knew that she would never be enough for him.

Not when she could not give him that which he held in such high regard—a fine pedigree, an untarnished reputation, propriety.

All she had for him was a messy past and her love.

And sometimes, sadly, love was not enough.

How I wish it could be.

She sighed, running a finger along the perfectly wrought foot of Eros. She should not be here. Not at this hour, likely not at all. But four days trapped in a carriage with nothing but her thoughts had made her desperate to prove herself.

She had nearly driven herself mad playing over the last weeks in her head—all the time with Simon, all the conversations, all the moments when he had questioned her actions, when he had saved her from scandal.

When he had held her in his arms and made her believe that she might be enough for him.

Her breath caught in her throat.

She knew better . . . knew that the faster she left, the better off they would all be. She would never have him—she could never be a true partner to him. He would always be a duke, she always a commoner with a questionable history. But it did not make her love him any less, even as she wished it did.

She could not prove to him that she was more.

But she could prove it to herself.

And so she waited for her mother.

She was here because of the scandal. Because her mother's actions had colored the world's view of her . . . for her entire life. Because her mother's actions had made her question her own actions, her own motivations, her own desires.

Because she had to know, once and for all, that blood did not out.

She had to know she could be more. Better. Different.

She had lived for too many years in her mother's shadow; it was time for her to come out into the sun.

"An odd time for a call," Louisa said as she entered the room, swathed in a dressing gown that floated around her as though she were wrapped in wind. She looked beautiful. As usual.

She sat, casting a critical eye over Juliana, taking in her gown, wrinkled and dusty from the journey, her mud-covered boots, and her hair, coming loose from the simple coif that Carla had arranged at the last staging post. "You look awful."

Juliana resisted the temptation to smooth or settle. She had nothing to prove to her mother. Instead, she sat and watched as Louisa poured a glass of sherry without offering Juliana anything.

"So you have come to visit me in prison."

"Hardly a prison," Juliana said drily.

Louisa waved a hand dismissively. "All these statues make me feel like I live in a museum."

"No one is forcing you to remain in London," Juliana pointed out.

"That much is true . . . but I don't have anywhere else to go, darling." Juliana did not care for the endearment, so cold and casual. "I don't suppose that Gabriel has decided what to do with me?"

"I don't think so."

"Well, I hope he does it sooner rather than later. I should like to be gone from here before I am made a grandmother. I do not need the reminder that I grow old."

One side of Juliana's mouth rose at the complete and unbelievable self-absorption. "I do not think that Gabriel has much interest in your schedule."

Louisa rolled her eyes. "It is not that I am not happy for him. He and his wife seem comfortable. But that life . . . the clinging children . . . the crying . . . the incessant requests . . ." She sat back in her chair. "It was not for me."

"I had not noticed."

Louisa's gaze narrowed on her. "You have grown up to have your father's bold tongue."

Juliana shrugged, knowing the movement would grate on her mother. "I was lacking additional examples."

Louisa sighed. "Well, if you are not here to bring news of my future, what brings you here in the middle of the night?"

So typical. Such concern for herself and no one else.

Juliana did not hesitate. "Do you regret it?"

Louisa was not a fool. She did not pretend to misunderstand. "Which part?"

"All of it."

She did not have to think about the answer. "I do not regret it on the whole, no. I do not regret being a marchioness, or even a merchant's wife—though your father was less wealthy than he initially let on, and things were not always easy . . ."

"I assure you, things did not become easier after you deserted us."

"*Deserted*," Louisa scoffed. "What a dramatic word."

"Would you refer to it in another way?"

"Juliana . . . it was my life. And I wanted it to be lived. Surely you can understand that, darling. You are so obviously that way."

The casual observation sent a chill through her. "What does that mean?"

"Only that one learns plenty of things when one is trapped in a town house with nothing to read but the gossip rags from the past six months. You have been as scandalous as I was. All garden trysts and toppling vegetables and falling in the Serpentine!" Louisa laughed, a high, tinkling sound that Juliana loathed. "My! What fun that must have been!"

"It was terrifying. I nearly drowned."

He saved me.

"Oh, I'm sure you're exaggerating. And you were rescued by a dashing duke! It sounds precisely like something I would have done if I hadn't been married at a foolishly young age and become the mother of twins. I will tell you, if I had it to do again, I would have been more of a scandal and less of a marchioness, that is certain."

"You were plenty of scandal, Mother, I assure you."

"Yes, but I wasn't here to see it, darling, so it's almost as though it didn't happen," she said as if she were speaking to a child. "You, however . . . you are living your scandal."

It wasn't true. She was living the reputation that she had inherited from this woman, who seemed not to care at all for the burdens with which she had saddled her children.

She was more than that.

Wasn't she?

Her mother pressed on, her tone airy, as though she had never given much thought to her actions. To the way they might have affected others. "You did well without me, darling. To think . . . you've found your brothers . . . and they care for you. Yes . . . I've done my job."

Louisa's self-satisfaction was undeniable. Juliana could not help her laugh. It was rather impossible to hate someone who seemed so utterly disconnected from her own actions.

"I know you want a better reason, Juliana. I know you wish there were some answer that would make everything cleaner. That would make you forgive me. But there isn't. I made some difficult choices. And if I had it to do over again, I'm not sure I would make them again."

"You mean, choosing to have us? Or choosing to leave us?"

Louisa did not speak.

She did not have to. The answer was in her eyes.

And everything became clear.

She was nothing like her mother.

Juliana let out a long breath, a breath she felt she had been holding for a decade, and stood, taking in her mother, who looked so much like her—as though she were looking into the future.

A different future than before.

A better one.

Because of a mother who had never once shown caring or attention, and who, once she had left, had never looked back, Juliana at last had a family. And perhaps it was enough.

Perhaps she could convince herself of it.

Soon her brother's house would be filled with laughing children and loving parents, and perhaps the noise would block out the time when she had been close to finding love of her own.

Perhaps there would be a time when he was not constantly in her thoughts.

When she did not love him so much.

It seemed impossible.

She looked to the statue again, watching as Eros stretched for that elusive thing beyond his reach.

It was all she could hope for.

Simon stood just inside his study, exhausted and covered in mud from his journey across England. He'd arrived at his town house in the dead of night, only to discover that all hell had broken loose while he was gone.

Boggs had taken his cloak and hat, handed Simon the *Gazette* with an even-more-somber expression than usual on his usually-quite-somber face, and gone to find food, as Simon had done nothing but change horses in the last eighteen hours, so desperate had he been to get back to London.

And to Juliana.

Simon stared down at the newspaper, reading the words again and again, as though repeat viewings could somehow change them. Take them away. But no, every time he read the article, it was precisely the same. Precisely as damning.

First person account . . . Duke of Leighton . . . his sister, not even out . . . in a family way . . . a daughter, born just days ago.

He was going to murder his sister.

She'd known he would never reveal the scandal himself. She'd known he'd never risk her reputation, or Caroline's, in such a way.

And so she'd taken matters into her own hands.

Why?

The answer flashed, quick and so obvious, he couldn't believe he had missed it. He moved to his desk and lifted the pile of correspondence there, sifting through until he found the square of paper that he was looking for.

Slipping his finger beneath the wax seal, he allowed himself to hope. Not much. Just until he read the single line of text there, underlined. Twice.

The engagement is off. —Needham

Georgiana had made certain that his betrothal to Penelope could not stand.

Your betrothal gift has already been sent to London.

She'd ruined herself. Ruined them all.

To ensure his happiness.

Now he had only to reach out and take it.

The Northumberland autumn ball was planned as the last official event of the season, before Parliament's special session finished and society packed up and headed for the country for the close of the year.

The stairs leading up to the house and the foyer were packed with throngs of revelers, passing their heavy cloaks to footmen and moving up the grand staircase to the ballroom, where the main festivities were already under way.

All of London society had braved a particularly nasty rain to be there, a fitting end to this altogether-too-long of a season.

And if Simon's evening went according to plan, this ball was going to be the talk of not only that season but several more to come.

Unfortunately, he appeared to have been uninvited to the festivities.

"I am sorry, Your Grace, but the duke and duchess are not receiving." The head footman of Northumberland House, who'd been assigned the unfortunate task of asking Simon to step out of the crowd, delivered the unfortunate news with a slight tremor.

"I beg your pardon?"

The servant backed up a step. "They are not . . ." He cleared his throat. "Receiving."

Simon turned to look at the stream of people dressed in their very finest, moving up the center staircase of the house, headed for the ballroom. "And so I suppose all these people are . . ." He trailed off, waiting for the footman to complete the sentence.

". . . Family?" The footman finished, uncertain.

Simon supposed he should sympathize for the poor man, who had likely never turned away a duke before, but he could not muster the emotion. He was too irritated. "And the music from above. It is part of a . . . family gathering?"

The servant cleared his throat. "Erm. Yes?"

He was being turned away from Northumberland House because his sister had borne a child. Out of wedlock. The Leighton name was now synonymous with scandal. It had taken less than a day, and all invitations he had received for events to be held in the coming weeks had been politely revoked—it seemed a rash of cancellations had taken place across London.

Perhaps, had it been another day—another ball—he would have done what was expected and left, but Juliana was inside that ballroom. And he had a plan to win her. One that relied heavily on this, the last ball of the season.

Simon had had enough. "Well, I suppose we're lucky that Northumberland is a distant cousin." He pushed past the servant and started up the staircase, taking the steps two at a time as the servant followed along behind.

"Your Grace, you cannot!"

On the landing, he turned and faced the footman. "And how do you plan to stop me?"

"Your Grace . . ." The servant apparently planned to appeal to Simon's better judgment.

Little did he know that Simon's better judgment was already engaged in an alternate purpose that evening—to find Juliana and make her his.

He ducked around a cluster of revelers and pushed into the ballroom, finding her in the crowd the moment he entered; he was drawn to her like a moth to a flame.

He had missed her with a powerful intensity, and seeing her filled him with acute pleasure. She was his drug. He craved her nearness, her laugh, her courage, the way she moved her hands when she spoke, that little shrug that had driven him mad when he had first met her and that he ached for now.

She waltzed across the room on Allendale's arm, dressed in a lovely gown of the palest pink, and for a fleeting moment, Simon was distracted by the fact that she wore such an uninteresting color—a color that made her blend in with the rest of the young, unmarried women in the room—until a turn in the dance gave him a view of her beautiful face, and it no longer mattered what she was wearing.

The only thing that mattered was the sadness in her eyes. The longing in them. For him.

Thank God.

For he could not bear it if she belonged to someone else.

The thought came on a wicked wave of desire—desire to march up to her, pull her from the earl's arms, and steal her away.

Which, as luck would have it, was precisely the plan.

He had not removed his cloak when he had entered, and as he moved through the crowd, clusters of revelers stopped, first to stare, then deliberately to turn away from him. He knew what they were doing—had done it himself dozens of times before—and he would be lying if he said that the cuts were not painful.

But the embarrassment and shame that he should be feeling as each of these people who, mere days ago, were desperate for his approval, turned their backs to show him their disapproval paled in comparison to the pleasure he felt at the way they eased his passage to his single, undeniable goal: Juliana.

His Juliana.

He took a deep breath and, defying all convention and everything he had ever been trained to do or be, crossed directly into the center of the room, stopping dancers in their tracks.

Proving, once and for all, that she had been right all along—and that reputation was nothing when compared to love.

Allendale saw him coming. The earl's friendly smile faded into a look of shock, and he slowed Juliana to a stop. The orchestra played on as Simon drew nearer to them, and he heard the confusion in Juliana's voice when she said, "What has happened?"

Her voice was a benediction—that lilting Italian accent that he craved, the way she drew out her syllables and let them linger on her tongue. She turned to him, and her eyes widened—at his nearness or his attire or both—her lush mouth fell open, and the entire room disappeared. It was only her. Only them. Only now.

"Your Grace?"

He did not trust himself to speak to her. Not when he wanted to say a hundred things that were for her and her alone. So he turned to the earl instead, saying with a lifetime of ducal imperiousness, "Allendale, I am taking your partner."

Benedick's mouth opened, then closed, as if he were trying to recall the exact protocol for this situation.

Finally, the earl turned to Juliana, allowing her the choice.

Simon did the same, holding out one gloved hand, palm up. "Juliana?" he asked, adoring the way her sapphire eyes darkened and her lips parted at the word. "I should very much like to cause a scandal."

She stared at the hand for a long moment, then met his gaze.

And there was an unbearable sadness in her eyes.

Suddenly, he knew what she was going to do.

And he could not stop her.

She shook her head. "No."

He stood there like a fool, arm extended, not understanding.

She shook her head again and whispered, "I won't be your scandal. Not this time." The words crashed around him, and he watched as her eyes went liquid with unshed tears. "No," she repeated, and she hurried past, heading for the exit.

It took him a moment to realize what had happened— that she was leaving him. That she had rejected him. He met Allendale's gaze, blood roaring in his ears, shame and confusion and something else flooding through him, hot and furious.

"How could you do such a thing to her?"

The words barely registered before Allendale was pushing past him as well, following Juliana through the crowd.

He turned to watch them, to watch her rush through the room, their massive audience moving aside to let her pass, and he did the only thing he could think to do; he called after her. "Juliana!"

A collective gasp rippled through the room at the sound, a booming shout that was entirely out of place in a ballroom, or anywhere a cultured gentleman happened to be. But he did not care. He took a step toward her, following, and an arm came across his chest.

Ralston held him back.

He fought against the grip, calling out again, her name tearing through the room, echoing up into the rafters, silencing everyone in the room, including the orchestra. "Juliana!"

She turned back. He met her gaze—the color of Ceylon sapphires—and said the only thing he could think to say. The only thing he could imagine would keep her there. With him. The only thing that mattered. "I love you."

Her face—her beautiful, perfect face—crumbled at the words, and the tears that she had held at bay spilled over.

She ran from the room, Allendale on her heels.

Simon tore himself from Ralston's grip, followed, determined to reach her. Determined to fix it.

And damned if the *ton* didn't protect her from him.

The orchestra resumed its playing, and there were suddenly throngs of people in his way. Everywhere he turned, there was a waltzing couple trapping him on the dance floor, and when he reached the edge of the ballroom, a constant stream of guests simply happened into his path.

Not one of them met his eyes; not one spoke to him. But they made it impossible for him to catch her.

When he had fought his way through the crowd, down the stairs, and out the door, she was gone, and there was nothing but a drenching London rain to greet him.

And at that moment, as he stared into the fog, replaying the events of the last few minutes over and over, he recognized the emotion coursing through him.

It was fear.

Fear that he had lost the only thing he had ever really wanted.

Chapter Twenty

Society does not forgive scandalous behavior.
Such is the delicate lady's maxim.

—*A Treatise on the Most Exquisite of Ladies*

With the spectacle playing out in the Beau Monde this
year, the theatre seems unnecessary . . .

—*The Scandal Sheet, November 1823*

The entire family was back at Ralston House within
the hour.

They congregated in the library, Benedick and Rivington sitting in the high-backed chairs near the enormous
fireplace, in front of which Ralston paced. Juliana sat on
a low chaise, flanked by Mariana and Callie.

Amo, amas, amat.

I love, you love, he loves.

He loves.

He loves me.

She took a deep breath, a hitch catching in her throat.

Callie stood and headed for the door. "I think I shall call for tea."

"I think we need something slightly stronger than that," Ralston said, heading for a decanter of whiskey on the sideboard. He poured three glasses for the men, then, after a long moment, a fourth. He walked it over to Juliana. "Drink this. It will settle you."

"Gabriel!" Callie reprimanded.

"Well, it will."

Juliana took a sip of the fiery liquid, enjoying the burn it sent down her throat. At least when she was feeling that, she was not feeling the devastating ache that Simon had left with his profession of love.

"Perhaps you could explain to me how it is that Leighton came to profess his love to you in the middle of a crowded ballroom?"

The ache returned.

"He was in Yorkshire," she whispered, hating the sound of the words. Hating the weakness.

Ralston nodded. "And tell me, did he lose his mind there?"

"Gabriel," Callie said, warning in her tone. "Have a care."

"Did he touch you?" Everyone stiffened. "Don't answer. There's no need. No man behaves in such a way without . . ."

"Ralston." Benedick interrupted. "Enough."

"He wants to marry me."

Mariana squeezed her hand. "But, Juliana, that is good, is it not?"

"Well, after tonight, I am not certain that he would make a very good match," Ralston said wryly.

Tears welled in Juliana's eyes, and she took a sip of scotch to force them away.

She'd been trying so hard—so hard to be something

more than a scandal. She'd worn a dress that was the required color, she'd danced appropriately with only the most gentlemanly of men, she'd convinced herself that she could be the kind of woman who was known for propriety. Who was known for reputation.

The kind of woman he would want by his side.

And still, she'd been nothing more to him than a scandal. Nothing more than what he'd seen in her since the beginning. And when he had professed his love there, in front of the entire *ton,* that dark, scandalous part of her had sung with happiness. And she ached for wanting him. For loving him.

And still she wanted more.

He made her a perfect match.

"If he seduced you, I have the right to tear him limb from limb."

"That's enough," Callie said, standing. "Out."

"You cannot exile me from my own library, Calpurnia."

"I can and will. In fact, I have. Out!"

He gave a harsh laugh that did not hold much humor. "I am not going anywhere." He turned to Juliana. "Do you want to marry him?"

Yes.

But it was not so simple.

The room was suddenly too small. She stood, heading for the exit. "I need . . . *un momento,*" she paused. "*Per favore.*"

As she reached the door, her brother called out to her, "Juliana." When she turned back, he added, "Think about what you want. Whatever it is, you can have it."

She left, closing the door behind her, allowing the hallway to cloak her in darkness.

She wanted Simon.

She wanted his love, yes. But she also wanted his respect and admiration. She wanted him to consider her his equal. She deserved as much, did she not? Deserved what she saw in Callie and Ralston, in Isabel and Nick, in Mariana and Rivington.

She wanted that.

And she did not have it.

Did she?

She took a deep breath, and another, replaying the events of the evening over and over in her mind.

He'd broken every rule he had—he'd ignored protocol and attended an event from which he had been uninvited, he'd allowed all of London to turn their backs on him, he'd *stopped a ball.*

He'd stopped a ball—bringing even more scandal down upon him—even as all of London turned their backs on him.

And he'd done it for her.

Because he cared for her.

Because he wanted to show her that she was more important than anything else. Than everything else.

And she'd refused him.

She'd refused his love.

She wrapped her arms around her middle, the realization coming like a blow to the stomach, and the door to the library opened.

Benedick stepped out into the hallway, a kind smile on his face. He closed the door behind him, shutting Callie and Ralston's argument inside, and coming toward her.

She forced a smile. "Are they still arguing about me?"

He grinned. "No. Now they are discussing whether Callie should be riding still now that she is with child."

She gave a little huff of laughter. "I imagine she will win."

"I would not be so certain." They were silent for a

moment. "There is something I should like to discuss with you."

"Is it about the duke? Because I would prefer not to discuss him, honestly."

"Not exactly."

"What, then?"

He hesitated, then took a deep breath. "Juliana, if you would like, I would have you. To wife."

As proposals went, it was not the most eloquent, but it was honest, and her eyes went wide at the words. She shook her head. "Benedick—"

"Just hear me. We enjoy each other's company, we are friends. And I think we would have a good time of it. You do not have to answer me now, but should you . . . have need of a husband . . ."

"No," she said, leaning up to kiss him on the cheek. "Thank you very much, Benedick, but you deserve more than a wife in need of a husband." She smiled. "And I deserve more than a husband who will simply have me to wife."

He nodded once. "That much, at least, is true." He paused. "For what it is worth, I think Leighton loves you very much."

The words sent a sad little thrill through her. "I think so, too."

"Then why not marry me?"

She snapped to attention at the words. Simon stood at the top of the stairs, soaked to the skin, face etched with lines of exhaustion. He had removed his hat, but his hair was plastered to his head and his coat hung wet and ragged from his shoulders. He looked terrible.

He looked wonderful.

"How did you . . . how did you get in here?" she asked.

"This is not the first house into which I have stormed this evening. I'm making quite a career of it."

She smiled. She could not help it.

He let out a long sigh. "I had hoped to make you smile, Siren. I hated making you cry."

She heard the truth in the words, and tears returned, unbidden.

He cursed in the darkness, "Allendale, I'm going to forgive your proposing to the woman I love. In return, do you think you could give us a moment?"

"I'm not certain I should."

"I'm not going to ravish her on the landing."

Benedick turned to Juliana for approval. After a long moment, she nodded. "Five minutes." The earl met Simon's gaze. "And I'm coming back."

He returned to the library, and the second the door closed, Simon took a step toward her, reaching for her even as he stopped several feet away. He dropped his arms, raked one hand through his drenched hair, and shook his head. "I don't know what to do. I don't know how to win you."

You've already won me, she wanted to say. *You've already ruined me for all others.*

He continued. "So I shall simply tell you the truth. I have spent my entire life preparing for a cold, unfeeling, unimpassioned life—a life filled with pleasantries and simplicity. And then you came into it . . . you . . . the opposite of all that. You are beautiful and brilliant and bold and so very passionate about life and love and those things that you believe in. And you taught me that everything I believed, everything I thought I wanted, everything I had spent my life espousing—all of it . . . it is wrong. I want your version of life . . . vivid and emotional and messy and wonderful and filled with happiness. But I cannot have it without you.

"I love you, Juliana. I love the way you have turned my entire life upside down, and I am not certain I could live without you now that I have lived with you."

He moved again, and she caught her breath as her

great, proud duke lowered himself to his knees before her. "You once told me that you would bring me to my knees in the name of passion."

"Simon . . ." She was crying freely now, and she stepped forward, placing her hands on his head, running her fingers through his hair. "*Amore*, no, please."

"I am here. On my knees. But not in the name of passion," He took her hands in both of his and brought them to his lips, kissing her, worshipping her. "I am here in the name of love."

He looked up at her, his countenance so very stark and serious in the dimly lit hallway. "Juliana . . . please, be my wife. I swear I will spend the rest of my days proving that I am worthy of you. Of your love."

He kissed her hands again, and whispered, "Please."

And then she was on her knees as well, her arms wrapped around his neck. "Yes." She pressed her lips to his. "Yes, Simon, yes."

He returned the kiss, his tongue sliding into her hot, silken heat, stroking until they both required air. "I'm so sorry, my love," he whispered against her lips, pulling her to him, as though he could bring her close enough that they would never be apart again.

"No, I am sorry. I should not . . . I left you there . . . at the ball. I didn't see until now . . . how much it meant."

He kissed her again. "I deserved it."

"No . . . Simon, I love you."

They stayed there for long minutes, wrapped in each other, whispering their love, making promises for the future, touching, reveling, celebrating in one another.

And that was how Ralston found them.

He opened the door to the library, the lush golden glow from the candles beyond flooding the hallway and illuminating the lovers.

"You had better get a special license, Leighton."

Simon smiled, bold and brash, and Juliana caught

her breath at him—her angel—the handsomest man in England. In all of Europe. "I already have one."

Ralston raised a black brow. "Excellent. You have two minutes to compose yourself before we go downstairs and discuss this." Juliana smiled at the words, and Ralston caught her gaze. "You, sister, are not invited."

He closed the door to Simon and Juliana's laughter.

An hour later, Simon exited Ralston House, having made all the appropriate arrangements with his—he winced—future brother-in-law. He supposed it was only right that he was finally tied to this raucous family, the only people in England who did not care that he was a duke. Rather, the only people who had never cared. Now most of London would happily turn their backs on the House of Leighton for fear of being touched by its scandal.

And he found he did not care much about it.

He had a healthy niece and a woman who loved him, and suddenly those things seemed like more than enough.

He had wanted desperately to say good night to Juliana, but she had been nowhere to be found as he was leaving, and Ralston seemed disinclined to allow Simon abovestairs to seek her out. He supposed he could not blame the marquess; after all, he was not exactly good at keeping his hands off of his soon-to-be wife.

But they were to be married in less than a week, and he would bear the loss of her tonight, even if it brought with it an all-too-familiar and utterly unpleasant ache.

He waved the coachman off his duty and opened the door to his carriage—the one where it had all begun weeks ago. Lifting himself up and in, he took his seat and swung the door closed, rapping the roof quickly to set the coach in motion.

It was only then that he noticed that he was not alone.

Juliana smiled from the other end of the seat. "You did not think I would let you leave without saying good night, did you?"

He quashed a flash of intense pleasure and affected his most ducal tone. "We are going to have to discuss your penchant for stowing away in carriages."

She moved toward him slowly, and a wave of awareness shot through him. "Only one carriage, Your Grace. Only yours. This time, I checked the seal before entering. Tell me, what do you plan to do with me now that I am here?"

He watched her intently for a long moment before leaning in, stopping a hairsbreadth from kissing her. "I plan to love you, Siren." He wrapped one hand around her waist, hauling her onto his lap so that she was above him.

She looked down at him with wicked intensity. "Say it again."

He grinned. "I love you, Juliana."

His hands were stroking up her sides, tracking over her shoulders, tilting her head to bare her neck. He pressed a soft kiss to the skin at the base of her throat, where her pulse was pounding.

"Again." She sighed.

He whispered the words against her lips—a promise—and claimed her mouth, his hands stroking, pressing everywhere.

She opened for him, matching his long, slow kisses stroke for stroke. For the first time, there was no urgency in the caresses—no sense of their being stolen from another time. *From another woman.*

She pulled back at the thought, lifting her head. "Penelope," she said.

"We must discuss this now?" One of his hands was headed for the full swell of her breast, and she bit back a sigh of pleasure as it reached its destination.

"No." She scrambled off his lap and onto the seat across from him.

He followed her, coming to his knees in front of her, the carriage rocking them together. "Yes."

"Lady Penelope's father has dissolved the agreement." His hands grasped her ankles, and Juliana was not sure if it was the feel of his warm hands stroking up her legs beneath her skirts or the fact that he was no longer engaged that made her light-headed. He met her gaze, serious. "I would have ended it if he hadn't, Juliana. I couldn't have gone through with it. I love you too much."

A thread of pleasure coiled through her at the words. "He called it off because of Georgiana's scandal?"

"Yes," he said, and the way the word rolled from his tongue gave her the distinct impression that he was not replying to her question. He folded back her skirts with reverence and cursed, dark and wicked in the carriage, and pressed a kiss to the inside of one knee.

She clamped her legs together, resisting his movements. "Simon . . ."

He stilled, meeting her eyes in the flickering light from outside before he kissed her again, long and thorough before he pulled back abruptly. "My sister announced her own scandal. Actually sent a letter to the *Gazette*! It was her wedding present. To us."

Juliana smiled. "A broken engagement?"

"In exchange for a quick one," he replied, taking her lips again, his urgency sending a wave of fire through her.

She reveled in the caress, in the feel of him, for a long minute before pushing him away once more. "Simon, your mother!"

"She is not at all a topic I care to discuss right now, love."

"But . . . she will be furious!"

"I don't care." He returned his attention to the inside

of her knee, swirling his tongue there until the silk was wet. "And if she is, it shan't be because of you. You are her best hope for a respectable grandchild. *I'm* the one with the terrible reputation."

She laughed. "An abductor of innocents. A seducer of virgins."

He parted her legs slowly, pressing lovely, languorous kisses up the inside of her thigh. "Only one innocent. One virgin." She sighed and let her eyes close against the pleasure as he licked at the place where garter held stocking, a promise of what was to come.

"Lucky me." She leaned forward, taking his unbearably handsome face between her hands. "Simon . . ." she whispered, "I have loved you from the beginning. And I will love you . . . I will love you for as long as you'll have me."

His gaze darkened, and he grew very serious. "I hope you plan to love me for a very long time."

She kissed him again, pouring herself and her love into the caress, because words suddenly seemed lacking. When they stopped, both gasping for breath and desperate for more of each other, Juliana smiled. "So how does it feel to have thoroughly ruined your reputation?"

He laughed. "I shall never live it down."

"Do you regret it?"

"Never." He pulled her to him for another kiss.

Simon's scandal was one for the ages. It would be fodder for whispers in ballrooms, and chatter on Bond Street and in the halls of Parliament, and years from now, he and Juliana would tell their grandchildren the story of how the Duke of Leighton had been laid low by love.

Epilogue

May 1824

$\mathcal{H}$er Grace, the Duchess of Leighton, was high on a ladder in the library—too high to hide—when her husband entered the room, calling her name, distracted by a letter he held.

"Yes?"

"We've news from—" He trailed off, and she knew that she had been discovered. When he spoke again, the words were low and far—too calm for her husband, who had found that he rather enjoyed the full spectrum of emotion now that he had experienced it. "Juliana?"

"Yes?"

"What are you doing twenty feet in the air?"

She brazened on, pretending not to notice that he had positioned himself beneath her, as though she would not crush him like a beetle should she go hurtling to the ground. "Looking for a book."

"Would you mind very much returning to the earth?"

Luckily, the book for which she had been searching revealed itself. She pulled it off the shelf and made her way back down the ladder. When she had both feet firmly on the ground, he let loose. "What are you thinking, climbing to the rafters in your condition?"

"I am not an invalid, Simon, I still have use of all my extremes."

"You do indeed—particularly your extreme ability to try my patience—I believe, however, that you mean extremities." He paused, remembering why he was irritated. "You could have fallen!"

"But I did not," she said, simply, turning her face up to his for a kiss.

He gave it to her, his hands coming to caress the place where his child grew. "You must take better care," he whispered, and a thrill coursed through her at the wonder in his tone.

She lifted her arms, wrapping them around his neck, reveling in the heat and strength of him. "We are well, husband." She grinned. "Twelve lives, remember?"

He groaned at the words. "I think you've used them up, you know. Certainly you've used your twelve scandals."

She wrinkled her nose at that, thinking. "No. I couldn't have."

He lifted her in his arms and moved to their favorite chair, evicting Leopold. As the dog resumed his nap on the floor, Simon settled into the chair, arranging his wife on his lap. "The tumble into the Serpentine . . . the time you led me on a not-so-merry chase through Hyde Park . . . lurking outside my club . . ."

"That wasn't a real scandal," she protested, cuddling closer to him as his hand stroked across her rounded belly.

"Scandal enough."

"My mother's arrival," Juliana said.

He shook his head. "Not your scandal."

She smiled. "Nonsense. She's the scandal that started it all."

"So she is." He pressed a kiss to her temple. "I shall have to thank her someday." He pressed on. "Toppling Lady Needham's harvest bounty . . ."

"Well, really, who decorates a staircase in vegetables? And if we're going to count all my scandals, how about the ones in which you were scandalous as well?" She ticked them off as she listed them. "Kissing me in my brother's stables . . . ravishing me at your own betrothal ball . . . and let's not forget—"

He kissed the side of her neck. "Mmm. By all means, let's not forget."

She laughed and pushed him away. "Bonfire Night."

The amber in his eyes darkened. "I assure you, Siren, I would never forget Bonfire Night."

"How many is that?"

"Eight."

"There, you see? I told you! I am the very model of propriety!" He barked his laughter and a worried look crossed her face. "Nine," she said.

"Nine?"

"I insulted your mother at the dressmaker's." She lowered her voice. "In front of people."

His brows shot up. "When?"

"During our wager."

He grinned. "I would have liked to see that."

She covered her eyes. "It was awful. I still cannot look her in the eye."

"That has absolutely nothing to do with cutting her in a modiste's shop and everything to do with the fact that my mother is terrifying." She giggled. "There were at least two that first night—at the Ralston ball."

She thought back. "So there were. Grabeham in the gardens and your carriage."

He stiffened. "Grabeham, was it?"

Her fingers wandered into the curls at the nape of his neck. "He does not require additional handling, Simon."

Simon raised a brow. "You may not think so . . . but I shall enjoy paying him a visit."

"If you are allowed into his home, considering what a scandal *you* are," she teased.

"There! That is your twelfth. The Northumberland Ball," he announced, wrapping her tightly in his arms. "No more climbing of ladders while *incinta*."

"Oh, no," she protested. "Your storming of Northumberland House is entirely *your* scandal. I had nothing to do with it! Take it back."

He chuckled against the side of her neck, and she shivered at the sensation. "Fair enough. I claim that one in its entirety."

She smiled. "That's the best one of them all."

He raised a brow in ducal imperiousness. "Haven't I told you that I find it is not worth doing anything if one does not do it well?"

Her peal of laughter was lost in his kiss, long and expert, until they pulled apart, gasping for air. He pressed his forehead to hers and whispered, "My magnificent wife."

She dipped her head at the worshipful tone, then remembered. "You had news. When you entered."

He settled back in the chair, removing a letter from his jacket pocket. "I did. We have a nephew. The future Marquess of Ralston."

Juliana's eyes went wide with pleasure, snatching the paper from his hand, reading eagerly. "A boy! Henry." She met Simon's gaze. "And two becomes three." Nick's daughter, Elizabeth, had been born two weeks earlier, and now shared the nursery at Townsend Park with a growing, happy Caroline.

Simon pulled Juliana to him, placing a kiss at the tip

of her eyebrow and tucking her against his chest. "Come autumn, we shall do our part and add a fourth to their merry band."

Pleasure coiled as she thought of their blossoming family—a wild, wonderful family she'd never dared imagine. "You realize that they shall be the worst kind of trouble," she teased.

He was silent for a long time—long enough for Juliana to lift her head and meet his serious, golden gaze.

When she did, he smiled, broad and beautiful. "They shall be the very best kind of trouble."

And they were.

Acknowledgments

As the third book in this series comes to a close, I must make a confession. Gabriel, Nick, and Juliana would never have found their way to the page without the help of some amazing people.

Carrie Feron, my editor, has flawless insight and infinite patience, and she made these books what they are. Carrie comes handsomely packaged with the fabulous Tessa Woodward and the rest of the incomparable Avon Books team—Pam Spengler-Jaffee, Christine Maddalena, Jessie Edwards, Adrienne DiPietro, Tom Enger, Gail Dubov, Ricky Mujica, and Sara Schwager—who have worked tirelessly to bring this series to life.

My agent, Alyssa Eisner-Henkin, had the surprise of her life when I told her that I was writing an adult romance. Alyssa, thank you for taking this leap with me.

Then there are my friends—geniuses all—without whom these books would have either never been written or simply been awful. Thanks to Sabrina Darby, Cate Dossetti, Saundra Mitchell, Aprilynne Pike, Carrie Ryan, Lisa Sandell, and Meghan Tierney for helping me find paths out of the weeds. Sophie Jordan, I still can't believe you take my calls; thank you for showing me the ropes. And thanks to all my Facebook and Twitter friends for endless encouragement!

To my family, thank you for always letting me come back home. Special thanks go to my parents for checking my Italian (all errors are entirely my own), and equally to my father for proverbial brilliance and Juliana's lovable quirks.

And to Eric, thank you will never be enough. Ever. I am yours.

Four scandals, whispered about in
ballrooms across Britain.

Four aristocrats, exiled from society,
now royalty in the London underworld.

Four loves, powerful enough to tame the darkness
and return these fallen angels to the light.

A ROGUE BY ANY OTHER NAME

The first book of The Fallen Angel
A new quartet from Sarah MacLean
Coming Winter

NEW YORK TIMES BESTSELLING AUTHOR

SARAH MACLEAN

Nine Rules to Break When Seducing a Rake

978-0-06-185205-3

Lady Calpurnia Hartwell has always followed the rules of being a lady. But now she's vowed to live the life of pleasure she's been missing. Charming and devastatingly handsome, Gabriel St. John, the Marquess of Ralston, is a more than willing partner.

Ten Ways to Be Adored When Landing a Lord

978-0-06-185206-0

Nicholas St. John has been relentlessly pursued by every matrimony-minded female in the *ton*. So when an opportunity to escape presents itself, he eagerly jumps—only to land in the path of the most determined, damnably delicious woman he's ever met!

Eleven Scandals to Start to Win a Duke's Heart

978-0-06-185207-7

Bold, impulsive, and a magnet for trouble, Juliana Fiori is no simpering English miss. Her scandalous nature makes her a favorite subject of London's most practiced gossips . . . and precisely the kind of woman the Duke of Leighton wants far *far* away from him.

At Avon Books, we know your passion for romance—once you finish one of our novels, you find yourself wanting more.

May we tempt you with . . .

- **Excerpts** from our upcoming releases.

- Entertaining **extras**, including authors' personal photo albums and book lists.

- Behind-the-scenes **scoop** on your favorite characters and series.

- **Sweepstakes** for the chance to win free books, romantic getaways, and other fun prizes.

- Writing **tips** from our authors and editors.

- **Blog** with our authors and find out why they love to write romance.

- **Exclusive content** that's not contained within the pages of our novels.

Join us at
www.avonbooks.com